TENNESSEE TAKEDOWN

BY
LENA DIAZ

MILLS & BOON

Published in Great Britain 2014
by Mills & Boon, an imprint of Harlequin (UK) Limited,
Eton House, 18-24 Paradise Road, Richmond, Surrey, TW9 1SR

© 2014 Lena Diaz

ISBN: 978 0 263 91350 7

46-0214

Harlequin (UK) Limited's policy is to use papers that are natural, renewable and recyclable products and made from wood grown in sustainable forests. The logging and manufacturing processes conform to the legal environmental regulations of the country of origin.

Printed and bound in Spain
by Blackprint CPI, Barcelona

"You're cold." He shoved his gun in the holster and started to unstrap his Kevlar vest as if to wrap it around her.

She placed her hand on his, stopping him. "No. That's all you have to keep yourself warm. You already gave up your shirt for me. I'll not have you freeze to death by giving me your vest."

He nodded. "At least this cave is dry. I'd start a fire but it would be a beacon to the gunmen. Come on. Sit and we'll huddle together to get warm."

The images *that* conjured in her mind had her feeling warm all over.

"I promise I'll behave," he added, as if he thought she might be worried about his intentions.

Ashley snorted. "Don't expect me to make the same promise."

He chuckled and pulled her closer. "Are you always this shy, or am I special for some reason?"

Oh, he was definitely special, but no way was she saying *that*.

Lena Diaz was born in Kentucky and has also lived in California, Louisiana and Florida, where she now resides with her husband and two children. Before becoming a romantic suspense author, she was a computer programmer. A former Romance Writers of America Golden Heart® finalist, she has won a prestigious Daphne du Maurier award for excellence in mystery and suspense. She loves to watch action movies, garden and hike in the beautiful Tennessee Smoky Mountains. To get the latest news about Lena, please visit her website, www.lenadiaz.com.

Thank you, Allison Lyons and Nalini Akolekar.

This one is for Sean and Jennifer, and the fun memories of horseback riding and white-water rafting in Tennessee. Exploring the Smoky Mountains with you was a true joy. Looking forward to many more years of happy memories to look back on.
Am so *very* proud of both of you. Love you.

Chapter One

Ashley edged farther under the desktop in the cubicle, her fingers clutching the phone to her ear, her knees scraping against the coarse commercial carpet. *Breathe...in, out, in, out. Focus, listen. Where is he?*

Her breaths wheezed between her teeth, making a sharp whistling sound.

Calm down. He'll hear you if you don't calm down.

"Why don't I hear any sirens yet?" she whispered to the nine-one-one operator.

"They're on the way, ma'am. Is the shooter still in the building?"

"I'm not sure. I think so."

"Stay where you are. Stay on the line. The police will be there soon."

Her fingers tightened around the phone. That's the same thing the operator had told her *ten minutes ago*— after the shooter killed Stanley Gibson.

They'd both been standing by the copier, chatting about nothing in particular while the machine spit out reports for their next meeting. A soft *pfft* sound whooshed through the air. A bright red circle bloomed on Stanley's forehead. His eyes rolled up and he crumpled to the floor.

Ashley had stood frozen, too horrified to acknowledge what her subconscious already knew—someone had just shot one of her coworkers.

That's when the screams began.

She'd whirled around. The shooter stood in the main aisle, his silver hair forming spikes across his head like porcupine quills. His dark gaze locked on her.

And then he smiled.

Ashley's fight-or-flight instincts had kicked in. She ran. Around the corner, past the glass-enclosed offices the managers used. *Empty. Thank God.* At least half the company was out to lunch. But the rest were here, like her, trapped between the shooter and the only exit.

She kept running, to the other side of the building, to another maze of cubicles. She dove into the nearest one and grabbed the phone from the top of the desk. That was when she'd called nine-one-one.

A terrified scream echoed through the room.

Ashley's pulse sputtered. "He's still here," she whispered.

"Help is on the way."

The operator's calm, matter-of-fact tone had Ashley clenching her teeth so hard her jaw ached. Didn't the operator realize people were dying? Had the woman even *called* the police?

Leaning as far out of the cubicle as she dared, she risked a glance down the main aisle. The shooter's progress through the offices of Gibson and Gibson Financial Services was marked by screams and shouts coming from the other side of the building.

The mournful wail of police sirens erupted outside the windows.

Thank you, thank you, thank you!

"I hear sirens," she whispered. "They're close."

"Yes, ma'am. Are you still in the same location?"

"I haven't moved."

"I've notified the police where you are. They'll be there soon."

Ashley was really starting to hate the word *soon*. And she also sorely regretted taking the auditing contract in Destiny, Tennessee. If she were in her home office in Nashville right now, she wouldn't be cowering in a cubicle with a crazed shooter on the loose.

One of the young temps stuck her head out of another cubicle several aisles away. What was her name? Karen? Kristen? Ashley had only met her once and couldn't remember. The girl's face was ghostly pale, her eyes wide with terror as she silently begged Ashley for help.

Ashley's stomach jumped as if she'd plunged down a steep drop on a roller coaster. The girl couldn't be more than nineteen. Ashley *had* to help her. But how? Which cubicle was safer? Should she run to the girl, or have the girl run to her?

She sucked in a breath. *Oh, no.* Spiky gray hair showed above a row of cubicles down a side aisle. *The shooter.* And he was heading straight toward the temp.

Ashley frantically motioned for the girl to hide.

The girl's brow furrowed and she raised her hands in the air, not understanding what Ashley was trying to tell her.

In a few more steps, the gunman would be able to see them both.

"Go back," Ashley mouthed, desperately pointing at the approaching shooter.

He rounded the corner. Ashley ducked back behind the partitioned wall.

A high-pitched scream echoed through the room, then abruptly stopped.

She clamped her hand over her mouth. *No, no, no.*

A shoe scraped across the carpet. Ashley froze. A swishing sound whispered through the air, as if someone had brushed up against one of the fabric-covered cubicle walls. Close.

Too close.

"Ma'am, the police are evaluating the situation," the operator said through the phone in her monotone voice.

Ashley quickly covered the receiver. Her pulse slammed in her ears as she waited, listened. Was the shooter the one who'd made that swishing noise? Had he heard the operator? Her hand shook as she gingerly hung up the phone. She couldn't wait for the police anymore. If she didn't do something, right now, she'd be as dead as Stanley Gibson.

DILLON GRAY CROUCHED beneath the window, cradling his assault rifle. He and the rest of his six-man SWAT team waited for the green light to begin the rescue operation in the one-story office building of Gibson and Gibson Financial Services.

Beside him, his friend since childhood, Chris Downing, watched the screen on his wristband, showing surveillance from the tiny scope he'd raised up to the window. "Casualties at three and five o'clock," he whispered into the tiny mic attached to his helmet. "One more at eleven o'clock. No sign of a shooter."

Dillon's earpiece crackled and his boss's voice came on the line. "Witnesses indicate there could be two shooters. Descriptions inconsistent. Shooters are dressed in black body armor. Kill shot will be a headshot. They're using handguns. No long guns or explosives reported."

"Do we have the go ahead to move in?" Dillon asked, inching closer to the door.

"Negative. Still gathering intel. Hold your position."

His team looked to him for direction, their faces taut with frustration. They wanted to go in as badly as he did.

"Do we have a count yet on how many civilians are inside?" Dillon asked his boss.

"Negative," Thornton replied. "Workers are still pulling into the parking lot after lunch. Impossible to know how many escaped and how many remain."

Meaning there could be dozens or more inside. Defenseless. Hiding under desks, in conference rooms, in closets, waiting, praying someone would help them. What chance did an unarmed office worker have against men with guns, picking them off like targets at a gun range?

The stock of his rifle dug into Dillon's clenched fist. The Destiny, Tennessee, police department was small and more accustomed to patrolling acres of farmland and gravel roads than suiting up in flak jackets and storming buildings. His SWAT team consisted of beat cops, desk jockeys and other detectives like him, but they'd all been hunting and shooting since they could walk. And they trained regularly, and hard, for this type of situation. What was the point of that training if they cowered and did nothing? How many civilians had died in the few minutes his team had been crouching beneath the windows? How many of those civilians were their own friends and neighbors?

"The team is ready and willing to go. *Strongly* requesting permission to enter, sir."

"Negative," Thornton replied. "Stand down, Detective Gray. Await further instructions."

Dillon cursed.

Chris tapped his shoulder. "Movement on the east corner," he whispered. "Appears to be a civilian. Belly crawling toward the exit." His tortured gaze shot to Dillon. "Heavy blood trail."

Dillon closed his fist around the mic so his boss wouldn't hear him as he addressed his team.

"Chief Thornton ordered us to sit tight and wait. You've got nothing to be ashamed of if you follow orders. Some of you have families to support. I don't. If he fires me, so be it. But I'm not waiting one more minute while people die inside. I'm going in."

Every one of his teammates raised their thumbs, letting him know they were all in.

He glanced at the only woman on the team, Donna Waters.

"Don't even say it," she warned. "You've never been sexist before. Don't start now. I'm not waiting outside while the guys get all the fun."

Dillon ruefully shook his head and held his fingers in the air. "We go in five, four—"

"Gray, what are you doing?" Thornton demanded. "I told you to stand down. That's an *order.*"

"—one." Dillon waved his hand in a forward rolling motion.

Donna yanked the door open. Dillon ran inside, first as always, crouching down, swinging his rifle left to right, covering his team as they rushed in behind him.

"Clear," Dillon whispered, thankful his boss had shut up, leaving the airway free for communication among the team. When this was over, Thornton would give him hell, or fire him. But for now, the chief knew to butt out.

Dillon pointed to the injured civilian trying to crawl to the door. The two closest men grabbed the injured man and carried him outside. Dillon gave Donna a signal to wait for the two men to return before beginning her search on the west side of the building, while he and the two men with him headed to the east side.

The building formed a rectangle, with rows of six-foot-high cubicle walls divided in the middle by a line of glassed-in offices, bathrooms and conference rooms. Solid walls acted as firebreaks every twenty feet. The two teams would have to search and clear each section in a grid pattern before moving to the next.

When he reached the first body, Dillon sucked in a quick breath. The man was only a casual acquaintance, but Dillon had shared math classes with him in high school. The shooter, or shooters, had gone for a head shot. The vic never had a chance.

They continued on, finding two more casualties. A scratching sound whispered from the next aisle. Dillon crouched down and signaled his men to approach in a flanking maneuver from each end of the aisle. When they were in position, he held up five fingers, counting down. *Four. Three.* He rushed into the cubicle in front of him, silently continuing the countdown, as he knew his men would do. He climbed onto the countertop that formed a desk in the cubicle. When the count reached zero, he jumped to his feet and aimed his rifle over the top of the wall.

At the same time, his men rushed into the ends of the aisle to prevent escape. The scratching stopped. A young woman lay half in and half out of a cubicle, her face an ashen-gray color, with blood running down the side of her head. Her fingernails dug into the carpet, probably the scratching sound they'd heard.

Dillon stood guard over the top of the wall. Chris hoisted the young woman in his arms while the other man covered him. Together they retreated toward the exit, with Dillon watching over them until they were safely out the door.

Two civilians rescued. How many more were still hiding? And where the hell was the shooter?

A soft *pfft* sound had Dillon diving to the floor and rolling into the aisle. The cubicle wall near where he'd been standing seconds ago now boasted a small round hole. A bullet hole.

"This is Gray," he whispered into his mic. "I've got gunfire on the east side, fifty feet in. Shooter's weapon is silenced." He jumped to his feet and hurried to the end of the aisle.

"Affirmative." Donna's voice came through his earpiece. "West side clear so far. Do you need backup?"

"Negative." He peeked around the wall. "Witnesses reported two shooters. Continue search and rescue on the west side. I've got this."

"You sure about that, country boy?" A gun muzzle pressed against Dillon's back.

Chapter Two

The shooter was playing a deadly game of hide-and-seek with Ashley, searching every aisle, every cubicle. So far she'd managed to stay one step ahead of him. Barely. She rounded the end of another aisle. Her breath caught in her throat. The shooter's profile was silhouetted against the wall of windows.

And his gun was pointing at a SWAT officer's back.

Ducking into the adjacent aisle, Ashley struggled to keep her breathing shallow, quiet, so the shooter wouldn't hear her. Gathering her courage, she risked another quick peek around the wall. The officer said something to the shooter. The shooter shook his head and gave him a gruff command. The officer tossed his rifle to the floor.

Dang it.

The exit door was only thirty feet away now. If Ashley was quiet, she might make it. But what would happen to the SWAT guy? He'd risked his life to rescue her and the others. Could she abandon him and leave him here to die?

No, she couldn't.

Cursing her conscience, she ducked back and grabbed one of the heavy, old-fashioned phones from a cubicle desktop. After unplugging the cord, she crept down a parallel aisle, hoping to sneak up behind the shooter. She offered up a quick prayer that he hadn't moved or turned around as she rounded the end of the row. *Yes.* His back was still facing her. But the SWAT guy was now facing the shooter, and Ashley, his hands raised.

Ashley crept forward, biting her lip, holding the phone in the air. She was pretty sure SWAT guy had seen her. He hadn't looked directly at her, but his body tensed, and the lines around his eyes tightened.

"Too bad your buddies left you by yourself," the shooter said. "Looks like they'll be carting one of their own out the door next." He raised his gun toward the officer's face just as Ashley swung the phone with both hands at the shooter's head.

But instead of hitting him, she hit empty air, spinning in a circle then falling against the wall beside her.

It took her a moment to realize SWAT guy had lunged for the shooter right when she'd swung the phone. He'd grabbed the shooter's gun and swept his legs out from beneath him. Now both men were rolling on the floor, wrestling for control of the gun.

"Get out of here," SWAT guy yelled.

Ashley realized he was yelling at her.

The two men rolled into the side aisle, grappling for control.

Leaving SWAT guy's rifle lying on the floor.

"Go, go, go," the officer yelled again. "Get out of here, run!"

SWAT guy was heavily muscled and tall, but the shooter was on top of him and must have outweighed him by at least forty pounds. The pistol was slowly, inexorably moving up toward the officer's face, the only part of his body not covered in armor.

Ashley made her choice. She dropped the phone and grabbed for the rifle.

The shooter twisted toward her and slammed his foot against her calf. She screamed and fell to the floor. Before she could scramble away, he grabbed her long hair and yanked her in front of him like a human shield.

SWAT guy crouched in the aisle a few feet away, glaring at Ashley before focusing on the shooter. The wicked-looking hunting knife in the officer's hand, along with his glare, had Ashley groaning inside. Instead of helping, she'd gotten in the way and messed everything up. She hadn't realized the policeman had a knife, and that he'd apparently been about to use it when she'd interfered.

"Let her go," the officer ordered. "You're surrounded."

Ashley glanced around, stunned to see he wasn't bluffing. She hadn't heard or seen the other SWAT officers come in, but there were two on her left, another one on the far side of the shooter and, as she watched, a fourth officer entered the aisle behind SWAT guy, who was now crouched in front of the shooter, still holding his knife.

Surrounded was putting it mildly.

"Let her go," SWAT guy repeated.

The shooter scooted back, pulling Ashley with him, keeping his gun trained on SWAT guy. Ashley struggled against his hold, but he squeezed hard, crushing her in a painful grip against his chest. He scooted back until he was pressed against the wall and couldn't move any farther.

"I'll kill her." He yanked her hair.

Ashley sucked in a sharp breath at the fiery pain.

It felt as though he was yanking half her hair out by the roots.

"Back off or she's dead. You can't shoot me without hitting her. Back. Off."

Ashley struggled to draw air into her lungs. She could barely breathe with her head twisted back so hard and tight.

Swat guy clutched his knife and motioned to the two SWAT officers on Ashley's left side. "He's right. Lower your weapons and back away. Give him room."

The shooter turned his head to the side, watching the officers lower their rifles.

He suddenly jerked against Ashley, a guttural moan wheezing out of his throat.

SWAT guy lunged forward, grabbing the shooter's gun and tossing it away. He chopped his hand down on the shooter's arm, breaking his hold on Ashley before yanking her away from him.

She twisted in the officer's arms, looking back toward the shooter. The gunman lay on the floor, convulsing, the haft of a knife sticking out of his neck. Blood bubbled out of the wound.

She clutched the officer's arm where it circled her waist.

"You—you threw your knife, while he was *holding* me?" she squeaked.

He gently grasped her chin, forcing her to turn away from the shooter.

"Look at me," he ordered, his voice gruff but laced with concern.

She dragged her gaze up his armor-covered chest to stare into a pair of stormy blue-gray eyes.

"Are you injured? Did he hurt you?" he demanded.

She swallowed and shook her head. "No. No, he

didn't… I don't think…" She shuddered. "I'm fine. He didn't hurt me."

"How many are there? Did you see any other gunmen?"

"He's the only one I saw."

He lifted her away from him. "Get her out of here."

A pair of strong arms grasped her waist and pulled her away.

Another officer hauled SWAT guy to his feet.

"Sit rep on the shooter?" he asked one of the others.

"Deceased."

SWAT guy, obviously the leader, motioned to the man holding Ashley's arm and another officer standing by the window. "Stay alert. Assume a second shooter is still in here. Get her out while we clear the rest of the building."

YELLOW CRIME-SCENE tape fluttered in the early-summer breeze, bringing with it the smell of impending rain. Ashley sat on one of the folding chairs the police had set up in the parking lot. Most of her coworkers had already been interviewed and had been allowed to leave. Ashley had been interviewed, too, but the detective who'd spoken to her had asked her to wait. She wasn't sure why.

The dead—eight in all—were still inside the building as crime scene technicians took pictures of the carnage and documented what had happened. The wounded— only three had been shot and survived—had been taken to the hospital.

The company's owner, Ron Gibson, stood talking with a couple of detectives about twenty feet away. The grief on his face reminded Ashley that he'd lost his only son today—Stanley. But Gibson was apparently a hero. He'd dragged one of the wounded out the exit before the police arrived, and he was going to be okay. The temp, whose name Ashley still couldn't remember, was also going to recover. The bullet had only grazed her head.

Another gust of wind blew through, swirling Ashley's hair. She pushed it out of her face and wished she had a ponytail holder with her. A shadow fell over her and she glanced up to see the SWAT officer who'd rescued her by throwing his knife at the shooter.

He'd shed the heavy body armor and vest with the big white letters on it marking him as SWAT. In dark blue dress pants and a white dress shirt, he could have been one of her coworkers, except that none of her coworkers were quite as muscular and fit-looking as this man. Then again, if he made his living wearing all that heavy equipment, she supposed the muscles were honestly earned.

He smiled and shook his head. "You didn't hear anything I said, did you, Miss Parrish?"

"I'm sorry, no. I was…thinking. What did you say?"

He pulled another folding chair over and sat across from her. He held out his hand and she automatically took it.

"I'm Detective Dillon Gray. I know you've already been interviewed, but I wanted to ask you a few more questions. Are you up to it?"

She shook his hand, but when he mentioned asking questions, all she could think about was the knife sticking out of the shooter's throat. She clutched his hand instead of letting go.

He didn't seem to mind. He held her hand and simply scooted his chair closer, resting his forearm across his knees.

"How long have you worked at Gibson and Gibson?"

She shook her head. "I don't work here. I mean, not for the company. I'm an independent consultant, an auditor. I work short-term contracts. I came here three weeks ago—no, four. Tomorrow…tomorrow would have been my last day." She shivered.

A look of interest lit his blue-gray eyes. "Were you brought in because of a problem? Did you find anything that concerned you when you performed the audit?"

"No, on both counts. Mr. Gibson—" she nodded toward the owner, who was being escorted to his car by one of the policemen "—he applied for a substantial loan to expand the business. The bank hired me to perform a routine audit before granting the loan. Everything checked out. I was going to recommend the loan move forward. I was supposed to finish the formal report today."

A coroner's van pulled up to the front of the building. Bile rose in Ashley's throat.

"Ignore them. Focus on me." Gray's deep voice was low and soothing, but it had the bite of authority.

She looked away from the van and met his gaze.

"I'm almost done," he said, his voice gentle. "Then you can go."

She nodded. When she heard the squeaky wheels of the coroner's gurney rolling toward the front door, she clutched his hand harder, using him as her anchor.

Another gust of wind, stronger than the rest, slapped the detective's pants against his legs. He looked up at the sky, which was casting a dark pall over the parking lot. "Looks like the weatherman was right. We're in for a heck of a storm."

He smiled at her again, and somehow the tension squeezing her chest eased, if only a little.

"I'll make this quick," he said. "You said your time here was temporary. Where's home?"

"Nashville. I've got an apartment there."

"Made any enemies in Nashville that might have come here looking for you?"

She blinked in surprise. "Me? You think the shooter was after *me,* specifically?"

"Routine questions. Just exploring all the possibilities."

The panic that had started inside her faded beneath his matter-of-fact tone. "The answer is no. I don't have any enemies. Not that I know of."

"You didn't recognize the shooter, correct?" he asked.

"I've never seen him before."

"Did he speak to you, call you by name?"

"No. He just…smiled, this really creepy, spooky smile."

His brows lowered. "What do you mean?"

"I was at the copier, with Stanley Gibson. The shooter shot Stanley, and when I turned around, he looked directly at me and…smiled. That's when I ran. I hid and kept going from aisle to aisle as he went through the room. I tried to stay a step ahead, but he caught up to me. He was on my aisle, but he was crouching down. I climbed over the wall to the next aisle before he reached my cubicle." She shivered and tugged her hand out of his grasp. The wind was colder now, making her shiver. She wrapped her arms around her middle.

Detective Gray motioned to one of the uniformed policemen nearby. "Get Miss Parrish a jacket, please."

"That's not necessary," she said. "If someone could please…get my purse…out of my cubicle inside, so I can get my car keys, I'll just go home. If you're finished with your questions?"

"By the time the officer retrieves your purse, I will be."

Ashley told the policeman where her purse was. He headed back toward the building.

"Does the name Todd Dunlop mean anything to you?" he asked.

"No. Was that the shooter's name?"

"I can't officially confirm that at this time."

"I understand. No, I've never heard that name before."

He asked her several more questions about her routine and whether she'd seen anything out of the ordinary when she got to work this morning. He asked her about any recent firings, but she wasn't aware of any.

"I'm sorry, Detective. But other than the officers of the company, I haven't even spoken to most of the people who work here. I've been stuck in a conference room most of the time, poring over years of financial reports. I wish I had better answers for you."

"You're doing fine, Miss Parrish." His white teeth flashed in a reassuring smile.

The policeman returned with her purse. She thanked him and he hurried away.

"May I go home now?" she asked the detective.

"Of course. I've got your address and your phone number. If I think of more questions, I'll stop by or give you a call. When are you leaving town?"

"The end of the week."

He walked her to her car.

She tried to unlock the car three times, but her hands were shaking so hard she couldn't get the key in the lock.

He gently took the keys from her and unlocked the door. "The clicker's broken, I assume?" He held up the electronic key fob attached to her key chain before handing back her keys.

"I think it's the battery. I keep forgetting to replace it." She slid into the driver's seat.

"You should get that fixed as soon as possible, as a security precaution," he said.

She nodded, in full agreement. After today, she was suddenly hyperaware of how dangerous the world could be. Fumbling for her keys when a simple click of a button could unlock her door didn't strike her as smart.

"Detective Gray?"

He crouched down beside her door, giving her that same kind smile he'd given her earlier. "Yes?"

"I'm sorry that I interfered, back inside. I thought I was helping, but I realize now that I could have gotten you hurt—" she swallowed hard "—or killed."

"You were very brave. You have nothing to apologize for. Everything worked out."

She offered him a shaky smile. "You saved my life. I don't know how to pay someone back for something like that."

"Fix that clicker. That's payback enough. Then I won't have to worry about you fumbling with your keys." He fished a business card out of his pocket and handed it to her. "If you think of anything else you want to tell me about what happened, anything that can help us sort through this mess and figure out why this guy picked Gibson and Gibson, give me a call."

DILLON WATCHED THE surprisingly brave, pretty little auditor drive away in her aging dark blue Chevy Lumina. He couldn't remember the last time he'd seen one of those cars on the road. Obviously Ashley Parrish wasn't making a fortune in her chosen occupation, which made any obvious financial motive for the shooter to target *her* seem unlikely.

"Did she tell you anything useful about the shooter?"

Dillon turned at the sound of Chris Downing's voice behind him.

"No. But she's pretty shaken. She might think of

something later." He glanced past his friend. His boss was standing with the rest of the SWAT team, his face animated—not in a good way—as he spoke to them. "Let me guess. Thornton sent you to get me."

"Yep. He's riled up like a preacher on Easter Sunday, all fire and brimstone raining down on our heads for going in against orders."

Dillon let out a deep sigh and started toward his boss, with Chris at his side. He wasn't in the mood to take a tongue-lashing right now, but he'd have to endure it to try to keep his job, and to keep his men from being blamed for what had essentially been a mutiny.

Regardless of the consequences, he had no regrets. The three wounded survivors they'd pulled out had lost a lot of blood and wouldn't have lasted much longer if they'd waited. And he didn't know what would have happened to Ashley Parrish. She wasn't the only survivor they'd rescued, but she was the only one the shooter had essentially stalked through the building.

Maybe he'd stop by her house on the way home tonight, to make sure she was okay and see if she'd thought of anything else that might help with the investigation. Their initial inquiries hadn't yielded any connections between the shooter and Gibson and Gibson. If the shooter had never worked there, and had never conducted any business with the company, why would he choose this particular office complex?

It was isolated, a few miles out of town, which might have made the shooter think he could shoot the place up and escape before the cops got there. But if he'd wanted to kill a lot of random people, there was a mall five minutes away that would have yielded plenty more potential victims. So why had he chosen Gibson and Gibson?

Dillon would lay odds it was something personal, and

he'd bet his ten years as a detective that the personal part was somehow related to the woman who'd just driven off in a beat-up old Chevy with a key fob that didn't work.

ASHLEY CLUTCHED HER cell phone to her ear and peered out the front window. Lightning flashed, illuminating the acres of green grass and long gravel driveway that formed the front yard of her rental house. In the distance, the Smoky Mountains loomed dark and menacing.

She'd never wanted to live this far from the conveniences in town, but her options were limited, since most people insisted on a long lease. Still, she hadn't minded living here temporarily. But with this morning's shooting fresh in her memory, the isolation was making her feel uneasy, and vulnerable.

Thunder boomed overhead.

"What was that?" Lauren asked over the phone.

"Thunder. The weathermen have been predicting a big storm all week. Looks like it's finally here. It's pitch-black outside even though it's only six o'clock. And the rain's been coming down like a monsoon for the past couple of hours. After all the rain we had last week, we sure don't need this. The river's already near flood stage."

"Should you get out of there?"

"I'll be fine. The house is on high ground and the river's several miles from here. Plus, I've stocked up on essentials in case the road gets washed out again."

Lauren droned on about poor road maintenance and the crumbling infrastructure in the country while Ashley looked through the curtains again. She would have loved to leave Destiny far behind after the horrific shooting this morning, but she'd promised Detective Gray she'd stay through the end of the week. Even if she hadn't made that promise, it would be a real pain to try to change her schedule at the last minute. She'd already planned the walk-through with her landlord so she could get her deposit back and turn in her keys.

When Lauren had called, Ashley confessed some of the general information about the shooting, but she'd kept most of the details to herself. Lauren was on a week-long cruise she'd planned for well over a year. Ashley didn't want to upset her friend and ruin her fun. She also didn't want Lauren to call Ashley's family about the shooting and get *them* upset. There'd be plenty of time to tell them what happened *after* she got back home to Nashville.

"Are you sure you're okay?" Lauren asked. "You're even quieter than usual. Maybe I should cut my vacation short and go there to be with you."

"Don't you dare. You've had this trip planned forever and I doubt they'd refund your money. Besides, by the time you got off the ship, hopped a plane, then drove forever through the boonies to get way out here, I'll be back home." She forced a note of cheerfulness she didn't feel into her voice. "Now tell me, which tropical island are you touring right now?"

Lauren hesitated, as if she was going to argue, but she finally let out a long breath. "All right, you win. I'll quit bugging you, for now. Today the cruise ship took us to a little place right outside Jamaica."

"Nice."

Lightning flashed again, much closer this time. Ashley jumped and let out a little squeak.

"Oh, yeah, you sound fine to me," Lauren accused. "Don't you want to talk about what happened?"

"Sure. Let's talk about the SWAT detective guy who rescued me. He was really hot."

"Not-so-subtle way of avoiding the topic, but I'll bite. How hot was he? Scale of one to ten."

Ashley plopped down on the couch and tucked her legs beneath her. Lauren would probably drool over Detective Dillon Gray's broad shoulders and trim waist. She'd love his dark, wavy hair that seemed a bit too long and untamed for a cop. And she'd probably squeal over what Ashley thought of as sexy stubble that formed a barely there goatee, mustache and dark shadow that ran up his jawline. He looked the way she imagined a man might look after lounging in bed with his lover for days without taking time to shave.

As enticing as all that was, Ashley knew her friend wouldn't appreciate what Ashley thought of as Dillon's best feature—his kind smile—and the gentle way he'd held her hand when she'd desperately needed the warmth and contact of another human being who wasn't trying to kill her.

He'd given her the strength to hold herself together. Without the kindness and patience he'd showed to a stranger, she probably would have lost it and imploded into a mass of nerves. Somehow, with him there, focusing those thickly lashed blue-gray eyes on her, she'd managed to keep her composure.

"Ash, come on. Scale of one to ten. Rank him."

She idly traced little circles on the arm of the couch with her fingertips as she debated her answer. If she ranked Dillon too high, Lauren would probably pester her to call him and try to wheedle a date out of him. So instead of saying "ten," which was spot-on, she lowered the number.

"A six, I suppose. It was kind of hard to tell with all that body armor on." She didn't bother to mention she'd seen him later without the armor. "Maybe a seven. Yeah, I could stretch it to a seven."

"Seven? That's not hot. That's lukewarm," Lauren scoffed. "What's his name?"

"Dillon Gray."

"Hmm. Dillon's good. Not too keen on Gray, though. Sounds kind of morose, depressing. Maybe I'll change his name when I embellish the story to my cruise ship friends at dinner."

Ashley laughed. "You do that. Oh, darn it." She jumped up from the couch and headed into the kitchen.

"What's wrong?"

She dug into the cabinet under the sink until she found a large metal mixing bowl. "Looks like that roof repair last week didn't hold. There's a healthy drip coming through the living room ceiling again."

"Dang, girl. I told you to argue with the landlord about using cheap roofers."

"I know, but I'm leaving in a few days, so what does it matter?"

"It doesn't, as long as the roof doesn't come down on you."

"Maybe it's not the roofer's fault." She placed the bowl under the leak and peered up at the plaster ceiling. "As hard as it's been raining, even a good roof might leak right now."

"You are way too nice, as always. If it were up to me, I'd call the landlord and…"

"And what?" Ashley repositioned the bowl. The drips were coming faster now. Getting some sleep tonight wasn't looking like a good prospect, not if she had to keep emptying out the water and listening to the ping-ing sound of the constant drips. She crossed back to the couch but paused when she realized her friend still hadn't answered.

"Lauren, are you still there?"

Silence.

She pulled the phone away and looked at the screen. Great. The call had been dropped. She plopped down on the couch and dialed Lauren's number. No ringing. Nothing. Maybe Lauren's phone wasn't the problem. She tried to get a dial tone, but it was like the phone was...dead.

Weird, that had never happened here before. The storm must have shorted something out, or maybe knocked down the nearest cell tower.

She tossed the phone down and grabbed the TV remote off the coffee table. Casting a disparaging glance at the drips rapidly filling the bowl across the room, she yanked the blanket from the back of the couch and wrapped it around her.

Thunder boomed again, this time sounding more as if it was from the back of the house than from overhead.

She paused with her finger on the remote's power button. Wait. There hadn't been any lightning that time. She slowly lowered her hand. Another sound came from behind her, down the hall.

Someone was inside the house.

Chapter Three

Dillon wrestled the steering wheel to keep his Jeep on the road. The last time he'd seen a storm this bad, the bridge over Little River washed out, stranding an entire Cub Scout troop on Cooper's Bluff, the mile-long, uninhabited island smack-dab in the middle of the river. Thankfully the mayor had learned his lesson from that fiasco. This time he'd paid attention to the weather reports and Cooper's Bluff had been evacuated earlier this afternoon, the bridge closed until the weather broke. Since the storm wasn't expected to ease until tomorrow morning, the entire police department was on standby for storm-related emergencies.

Which was why Dillon was out in the middle of the blasted thing.

This was a hell of a way to spend his evening after facing off with a crazed shooter earlier today and spending the next hour listening to his boss's tirade about chain of command and following orders. Dillon had been on the verge of telling his boss to take a hike and walking out when Thornton received his first call from the weather station, warning him the storm was going to be worse than originally thought. Thornton had immediately called for all hands on deck. Everyone had to be ready to go if and when a call for help came in.

Dillon would have rather stayed at the station and worked on the workplace-shooting investigation. But he had a four-wheel drive with a winch, which meant he was in high demand to help stranded motorists escape rapidly rising water on some of the more isolated, two-lane roads. He'd spent the past six hours pulling half a dozen vehicles out of swollen ditches. Now his shoulders and back ached and all he wanted to do was pop the top on an ice-cold beer, lie down in his recliner and sleep.

The squawk of his cell phone had him clenching the steering wheel even harder. He ignored the first ring, irrationally hoping whoever was calling would call someone else instead, preferably someone who hadn't been working solid since sunup and was bone weary.

But when the phone rang again, his shoulders slumped and he answered, "Gray."

"Detective Gray, this is Nancy, nine-one-one operator. I have Lauren Wilkes on the line. She specifically asked to speak to you. Something about her friend possibly being in trouble. Should I patch her through?"

Dillon let out a long sigh. That cold beer would have to wait a little bit longer. "Go ahead, Nancy. Thanks."

"Pleasure."

The line clicked twice.

"Miss Wilkes, Detective Gray is on the line," the operator said. "Go ahead with your emergency."

"Emergency? Well, ah, yes. Thank you." The young woman's voice sounded nervous. "Detective Gray? Are you there?"

"I'm here. How can I help you?"

"I feel a little silly. I'm not sure anything is really wrong, but after what happened this morning I'm kind of nervous. I mean, there's the storm and all and maybe phones do that sometimes but I remember she told me your name and so when—"

"Miss Wilkes," Dillon interrupted. "Take a breath."

"What? Oh, yes. Okay."

"Tell me why you called." He pulled the Jeep to the side of the road. It was too dangerous trying to talk on the phone and fight the wheel in this wind and rain.

"It's my friend. I was talking to her and the phone went dead. I tried calling her back, over and over, but the call doesn't go through. I was wondering if you could check on her. I'm, ah, not close by, so it's not like I can hop in the car and go over there."

Dillon thumped his forehead on the steering wheel. "Ma'am, if the Smoky Mountains were by the ocean I'd call the storm we're in right now a hurricane. Storms this bad always knock landlines down."

"Oh, well, it's not a landline. It's her cell phone. Do storms knock those out, too?"

He straightened in his seat. "Not usually, no. I suppose something could have happened to a cell tower." Although he couldn't remember that ever happening around here before. He grabbed the notebook and pen lying in the console. "What's your friend's name and address? I'll do a wellness check for you."

"Oh, would you, please? That would be awesome. And if you'll call me back and let me know she's okay, I'd really appreciate it. I mean, we've been friends forever. I kind of get worried—"

"Ma'am, the name and address?"

"Oh, right. Sorry. She's renting a house at 1010 Little River Road. Her name is Ashley Parrish."

Dillon stiffened. Every cell in his body went on alert. Cell phone towers could go out, he supposed, but it was a hell of a coincidence for that to happen to the woman who'd survived a workplace shooting just this morning. He tossed the notebook and pen in the console and whipped the Jeep back onto the road.

"Tell me everything that happened," he said, fighting to keep the vehicle straight as he jostled the phone and headed back toward Little River Road. Ashley's house was only five minutes away. "Don't leave anything out."

In the rough weather, it took six minutes instead of the normal five to reach the right road, and another two minutes to reach the long, winding driveway that led to Ashley's house.

A few inches of water covered most of the gravel, but his four-wheel drive clung to the road like a billy goat. He parked next to the front porch steps, figuring he'd save himself some soggy boots by avoiding the puddles in the yard.

He shook the raindrops from the last outing into the storm off his ball cap, shoved it on his head and threw the car door open. He slammed it shut behind him and jogged up the steps. Lights were on inside. He rapped on the front door. A few seconds later he rapped again, and rang the doorbell.

Nothing.

"Miss Parrish?" he called out. "It's Detective Gray. We met this morning. I need to speak to you." Another knock, but again, no sound or movement from inside.

The mild alarm he'd felt after talking to Lauren Wilkes was giving way to genuine concern. The little hairs on his neck were standing up. He drew his gun and held it down by his side as he stepped to the front window. He could glimpse the room through a slit in the curtains, but not enough to really tell him anything.

His boots echoed hollowly on the wood as he strode

across the porch. At the corner of the house, he leaned around, looking toward the backyard. Pitch-dark. The landlord needed to get some lights out here, especially since the house was so isolated without any neighbors close by. He headed back to the steps to get a flashlight from his Jeep so he could walk the perimeter of the property.

The sound of a powerful engine had him jerking around.

Headlights flashed and a truck roared from the side yard. It raced past him, its tires throwing up huge sprays of water that splashed onto the porch.

There were two people in the truck. The passenger turned and looked right at him, her eyes wide, her face pale as her hands flailed ineffectually against the glass.

Ashley Parrish.

She definitely wasn't in that truck because she *wanted* to be.

Dillon crouched on the porch and fired off two quick shots at the truck's tires, hoping to disable it before it gained much speed.

The truck jerked to the side but kept going. Damn this rain and wind. He wouldn't normally miss a shot like that. Taking the stairs two at a time, he hopped into his car, wheeled it around and floored the accelerator.

The Jeep fishtailed on the wet gravel. Dillon cursed and let up on the gas, then took off at a slower speed. The headlights from the truck bounced crazily as it turned at the end of the drive. West, it was heading west.

He grabbed his phone and pressed the button for dispatch as he barreled down the driveway. Nothing. He held the phone up. The light was on and he'd pressed the right button, but the call hadn't gone through. Must be the bad cell tower, as he'd thought earlier.

After making the turn at the end of the drive onto the paved road, he floored the gas again. The truck's taillights were barely visible up ahead in the pouring rain. There weren't any streetlights out on this old rural two-lane. But he didn't need more than his headlights to tell him what he already knew. The road up ahead was full of dangerous, sharp S-curves. If the driver of that truck kept his current speed, on this slick, wet road, he'd likely end up in a ditch or plow headfirst into a tree.

ASHLEY CLUNG TO the armrest and braced her other hand against the dashboard. The rain was falling so hard the windshield wipers couldn't keep up. The truck's tires kept slipping on the wet road, making the bottom drop out of her stomach.

"Please slow down," she pleaded. "It's too dangerous to drive this fast in these conditions."

The driver raised his gun and pointed it at her without taking his gaze from the road.

She swallowed and held her hands up in a placating gesture.

He shoved the gun between his legs and put both hands back on the wheel, the veins in his forearms bulging from the effort it took to keep the truck on the road.

Ashley glanced in the side mirror. The lights from Dillon Gray's Jeep were barely visible in the distance, but he was steadily gaining on them. She didn't have a clue why he'd gone to her house, but he was the answer to her prayers. If he could catch up and somehow manage to get this eerily calm stranger to stop the truck…

She let out a yelp as the truck slid toward the ditch on their right.

Her captor let up on the gas. The wheels caught and spit the truck back toward the middle of the road.

DILLON'S HEART PLUMMETED as the black pickup carrying Ashley Parrish slid dangerously close to the edge of the road for the second time since he'd started pursuit. At the last second, the truck straightened out and shot back toward the centerline.

He let out a pent-up breath and pushed his Jeep even harder, the engine whining as it struggled to catch up. His four-wheel drive was built for power, not speed, which was why he didn't normally use it when on the job. And it wasn't aerodynamic enough to make the curves without greatly reducing his speed. Neither was the truck up ahead. The ditches along this road might as well be cliffs, as steep as they were. And with all this rain, they were full of water, a death trap if the truck slid into one of them.

He tried his phone again, but it was no use. He no longer believed a failed cell tower was to blame. He'd gone too far from Ashley's house for that to be the case. The driver of the truck had to have a powerful cell phone jammer. That would explain why Ashley's call dropped when she was talking to her friend, and why Dillon couldn't get a call through as he followed behind. His mouth tightened. Jammers weren't cheap, and they were hard to come by. The man who'd taken Ashley had gone to a lot of trouble, and expense, to do it. This wasn't a random abduction.

He debated pulling off the road to call dispatch for backup. But if he let enough distance pass between him and the truck to unblock his phone, he might lose their trail. He couldn't risk it.

The road curved ahead, but no matter how hard Dillon pressed his Jeep on the straightaway, he couldn't catch up before the pickup disappeared around the curve. When he rounded the bend, he slammed his fist against the steering wheel. The fool. The truck's lights were visible up ahead, but not on the two-lane it had been on. Instead, the driver had turned down the side road that led to Cooper's Bluff. And he was heading toward the low wooden bridge over Little River—the bridge the mayor had closed because the river was expected to top it.

Ignoring every sense of self-preservation he had, he pushed the accelerator all the way to the floor. The tires slipped. He cursed and let up on the gas, even though it nearly killed him to slow down.

The bridge was around the next curve, so he slowed the Jeep even more.

Taillights gleamed up ahead at a crazy angle.

Dillon's eyes widened and he slammed the brakes, bringing his car to a skidding halt at the edge of the roadway. The last twenty feet of asphalt had washed away. The bridge was completely underwater, its support beams sticking up out of the angry, roiling waves like the skeleton of some prehistoric water beast. The truck had slid off the collapsed roadway, narrowly missing the bridge's first support beam and sliding half into the river.

Dillon grabbed his flashlight and hopped out. He sprinted to what was now little more than a cliff, a fifteen-foot drop down to the strip of mud at the water's edge. The front of the truck was submerged beneath the water, all the way up to the doors. The bed of the truck stuck up in the air, and even as Dillon watched, the truck slipped a few more inches into the water.

He took off, racing parallel to the shore until he found a break where he could climb down. His boots slipped and slid in the muddy, rain-soaked ground.

In the beam of his flashlight he saw Ashley frantically tugging at her seat belt, her frightened eyes pleading with him for help as the water sucked and pulled at the truck. Dillon waded waist deep into the churning water to get to her door. The window was still rolled up, probably electric and stuck. He looked past her. The driver appeared to be passed out over the wheel. A rivulet of blood ran down the side of his face.

Ashley managed to get her seat belt off and yanked the door handle, but it wouldn't open against the current. She pounded the flats of her hands against the window.

"Turn away from the glass," Dillon yelled.

When Ashley moved back, Dillon used the hard case of his flashlight like a hammer against the window. It bounced and thudded against the glass. He tried again and again but the glass still held.

The truck slid deeper into the water.

Ashley screamed.

The driver stirred beside her.

Dillon shoved the flashlight under his arm and pulled out his gun.

"I have to shoot the window out," he yelled.

She nodded, letting him know she understood. She pulled her legs up onto the seat, squeezing back from the window.

Dillon aimed toward the corner, so his bullet would go into the dashboard, and squeezed the trigger.

The safety glass shattered but held. He slammed the butt of his gun against the window. This time it collapsed in a shower of tiny glass pieces. He started to shove his gun into his holster but Ashley dove at him in the window opening, knocking both the flashlight and the pistol into the boiling, raging water.

He grabbed her beneath her arms and pulled.

She screamed.

He froze, horrified that he might have cut her on the glass.

"Let me go. Let me go," she screamed again. But she wasn't talking to him.

Dillon looked past her into the steady, dark eyes of the driver. He had a hold of Ashley's waist and was playing a deadly game of tug-of-war.

"Let her go," Dillon yelled. "I'll pull her out, then come back for you. The truck's back wheels aren't going to hold much longer."

"We'll take our chances in the river." The man's voice was deadly calm, as if he wasn't the least bit concerned. He heaved backward, pulling Ashley farther into the truck, slamming Dillon against the door. His grip slipped.

Ashley frantically flailed her arms. He reached for her and grabbed her hands.

The wheels made a great big sucking noise as they popped free from the mud. Ashley's hands were yanked out of Dillon's wet grasp. The truck went twisting and floating down the rain-swollen river, with Ashley's terrified screams echoing back, tearing at Dillon's heart.

The normally calm river was now a dangerous cauldron of rapids and swirling currents. The truck wouldn't stay afloat for long. Even if Ashley made it out and into the water, she wouldn't survive. No one could swim in that current. Only a fool would go into the river now.

He cursed and tore off his jacket. Apparently, he was a fool.

He dove into the river.

Chapter Four

Another wave crashed over Dillon's head, shoving him back under like a waterlogged towel tossed in a giant washing machine. His lungs burned. His muscles ached from fighting against the current.

He kicked his legs and clawed his way toward the barely discernible sliver of moonlight that told him which direction was up. He burst to the surface, gulping air into his lungs. Lightning flashed in the sky, followed by a boom of thunder so loud it hurt his ears. The rain pummeled his skin like hundreds of tiny icy needles.

Another wave crashed down. Again he went under. Again he fought his way back up for another precious lungful of air. He'd lost sight of the truck. And he wasn't trying to swim in any particular direction anymore.

He was just trying to survive.

It was too dark to see more than a few feet in front of him. He didn't know where he was, or even if he was within reach of land. His muscles screamed for relief, cried out for rest. He couldn't keep fighting much longer.

Moonlight glinted off the whitecap of another wall of water rushing toward him. He inhaled deeply just as the wave slammed into him. Like a spear in his chest, the water pushed him down, down, down until he bumped against the muddy bottom of the river.

The pressure pinned him against a rock. He latched onto it, fire lancing through his lungs as he waited for the current to shift. His vision blurred. The irony that he might actually drown suddenly struck him as funny. A laugh erupted from him, sending a froth of bubbles up toward the surface. His lungs protested the loss of desperately needed oxygen.

He pictured the fireplace mantel in his parents' farmhouse, still filled with his decade-old swim trophies from high school, like open wounds that had never healed. What would his mother do when she heard her swim-champion son had drowned? Would she throw away the trophies that had made her so proud? Would she hate him for giving up?

He clenched the rock harder. Tired, so tired. All he had to do was open his mouth and take a deep gulp of water and it would be over. He wouldn't have to fight anymore. His eyes drifted closed. The last of his air bubbled out of his nose. He sank deeper against the rock.

The image of his mother's face drifted through his thoughts, surprising him with the anger in her faded blue eyes. She reached out, but instead of hugging him goodbye, she grabbed his shoulders and shook him.

She needs you. Help her.

His mother's face faded, replaced by Ashley Parrish's wide-eyed stare, her scream of terror as the truck went into the river.

Dillon's eyes flew open. He couldn't give up. Not yet. He had to try. One more time.

He let the rock go and pushed toward the moonlight again. Up, up, up. He broke the surface, inhaling deeply. The rush of air into his starved lungs was painful, like the rush of blood into a circulation-starved limb. He ducked beneath the next wave and came right back up this time. He was used to swimming in pools or the pond on his parents' farm, not this roiling nightmare that pounded at him and made his muscles shake with exhaustion.

Maybe that was the problem. He was fighting too hard. He thought back to the basics, something his first swim coach had taught him, something he'd never had use for. Until now. Dead man float. He dodged the next wave, gulped in a deep breath, another.

Then he stopped fighting.

Lying facedown in the water, he held his hands out in front of him to protect his head from any debris. He held his breath, no longer struggling against a monster he couldn't defeat, and let the current take him wherever it wanted as the freezing rain beat down on his back. He jerked his head out of the water, took another breath, relaxed again. Over and over he repeated the routine— breathe, relax, float, breathe, relax, float.

His arm banged against something hard and unyielding. The current shoved him against a solid object— the truck, tangled up in a downed tree at the edge of the river.

The powerful current tugged at him, trying to pull him back out. His wet hands flailed against the slippery metal. He kicked hard and slammed into the bumper. Latching on, he stubbornly refused to let go. Hand over hand, using the bumper like a towline, he carefully inched his way down the end of the truck.

His kicking feet struck bottom. He pushed, his calf muscles burning from exertion as he fought his way to the driver's door. Waves pummeled his back. He coughed up a lungful of water and kept pushing, one step at a time.

The rain wouldn't let up, and as more and more of Dillon's body rose up out of the water, he began to shiver. His teeth chattered so hard he wondered they didn't chip or break.

When he finally reached the door, he saw what he'd already suspected. The cab was empty. Had Ashley made it out alive? What about the man who'd abducted her?

That thought drove him harder, through the shallows toward land.

He wanted to curse and rail at the storm mercilessly pounding against him, and the sucking current trying to pull him away from shore. Every inch, every step, was a hard-fought victory. But he didn't say the foul words he wanted to say. He made as little noise as he could, because he didn't know if the man who'd taken Ashley was within earshot, perhaps waiting in the trees up ahead.

Hoping the dark, nearly moonless night would help conceal him, he struggled on. Past the truck now, clinging to the branches of the tree that had snared the vehicle. He pulled himself out of the water and collapsed on the muddy bank. If the kidnapper found him now, Dillon didn't think he could do anything to defend himself. He was limp and spent.

Shivering in the mud, he lay there, gasping in precious air, trying to gather his strength. It was the icy rain, painfully stabbing the skin on his exposed arms, that finally made him move. He crawled forward, forcing one knee in front of the other until he reached the cover of trees. Using the low-hanging branch of a pine tree for leverage, he pulled himself to his feet.

Where was he? He couldn't seem to get his bearings.

A flash of lightning lit the sky, making everything as bright as daylight for a split second, just long enough for him to see his Jeep parked at the drop-off where the bridge used to be.

On the other side of the river.

He was on Cooper's Bluff, with no weapons, no phone and no way off the island—presumably with an armed man holding a woman hostage.

Some days it didn't pay to even put his boots on in the morning.

He shoved off the tree and trudged deeper into the forest, his weary legs shaking beneath him. It was damned embarrassing how much the freezing water had taken out of him. Thankfully, none of his men were there to see his sorry state.

A muted yell sounded from somewhere deep in the woods.

Dillon stiffened and tried to pinpoint the direction the sound had come from. A scream jolted him into action. His misery and exhaustion forgotten, he plunged into the trees at a full-out run.

ASHLEY HELD HER hand to her aching jaw and warily eyed the man who'd knocked her to the ground. Biting his arm wasn't the smartest decision she'd ever made.

He towered over her, but it wasn't his height or his brawny build that held her attention. It was the gun in his hand, the business end pointing straight at her head. She'd wondered why he hadn't immediately chased her when the truck snagged in the tree and she dove out the window. Now she knew. He'd fished out the gun from the floorboard where it had fallen when the truck first went into the water.

Would it fire now that it was wet? The way her luck had gone today, she was betting it would.

He squatted down in front of her, the gun never wavering. Cold rain dripped through the thick foliage overhead, splashing onto his forearms. But he didn't seem to notice. If he had yelled at her, it would have been far less frightening than the emotionless, dead look in his eyes. She mentally dubbed him Iceman, because he was so cold, as if he had no soul.

"Miss Parrish, bite me again and the next time I hit you you'll be missing half your teeth." He motioned toward her feet. "Take off your shoes."

She frowned down at her sneakers. The idea of walking through the cold, soggy, rock-strewn forest without protection on her feet didn't appeal to her in the least. "My shoes?"

"I'm not in the habit of repeating myself."

"I don't understand. Why do you want—"

He backhanded her, sending her sprawling onto the ground.

A yelp of pain escaped between her clenched teeth. He grabbed one of her feet and yanked off her shoe. Before she could get away from him, he yanked off her other shoe. When he let her go, she scrambled back like a crab on all fours. She cast a furtive glance around, looking for some kind of weapon. All she saw were small, round river rocks. Pelting him with those would be like poking an angry bull with a toy spear.

Iceman jerked at the laces on her confiscated shoes, yanking them out of the eyelets.

A feeling of dread swept through Ashley. There was only one reason she could think of that he'd want those laces. To tie her up.

She scrambled to her feet to run into the trees behind her.

"I need you alive," his voice echoed, freezing her in place. "But you don't need kneecaps to live. Sit your butt back down."

She sucked in a sharp breath and plopped on the ground. "Who are you? Why are you doing this?"

"Hold out your hands." He squatted down in front of her again with one of the shoelaces.

It was so tempting to take advantage of his vulnerable position and turn him into a soprano, but without shoes she wasn't sure she could kick him hard enough to risk another swing of his fist. She was also rather fond of her kneecaps.

She grudgingly held out her hands.

The wet lace bit into her left wrist as he yanked it tight. He was just as rough with her right wrist, painfully tightening the shoelace against her skin, jerking it to ensure it wouldn't slip off. He knotted the two laces together, forcing her to lock her fingers in a two-handed fist to relieve the pressure.

"Police," a voice yelled behind him. "Put your hands above your head and lie facedown on the ground."

She sucked in a breath and stared past her captor. The silhouette of another man was visible about ten feet away. Lightning briefly lit the clearing, revealing his identity—Detective Dillon Gray.

His wet hair was plastered to his scalp and his Kevlar vest formed a dark shadow beneath his equally wet shirt. Her mouth dropped open. Did he actually *swim* across the swollen, raging river to rescue her? Shock and gratitude warred with disbelief. But any relief she felt turned to worry when she realized one thing—*he didn't have a weapon.*

Iceman wrapped his fingers around the gun shoved in his belt. Did he know the police officer behind him was bluffing?

Ashley stared into his dark eyes. They were no longer cold and dead. Instead, they shined with an unholy gleam and his mouth tilted in anticipation.

He knew. He knew Dillon didn't have a gun. He must have seen it fall into the river when Dillon was trying to pull Ashley out the truck window.

"Move away from her and lie on the ground. Now," the detective repeated, his deep voice authoritative and confident.

The cord of muscles in Iceman's thick neck pulsed, reminding her of a snake coiling to strike.

She whipped a glance at the detective, trying to warn him with her eyes. But it was so dark. He probably couldn't see her eyes any better than she could see his.

A vile curse flashed through her mind, the kind of curse that would have had her mama looking for the biggest, thickest switch she could find, if she ever actually heard Ashley say it—regardless of how old Ashley was.

The detective was a big man, tall and thick with muscles, but just like at the Gibson and Gibson office building, the thug he was facing was even bigger. Dillon had come out the winner in the earlier confrontation, but he'd had a weapon, and a team of officers to distract the bad guy.

The man crouching in front of Ashley had the only advantage that mattered right now. A gun. One little bullet was all it would take to end this standoff. Even if the vest protected Dillon, the force of the bullet would probably knock him flat on his back. Then all the gunman had to do was calmly stand over Dillon and shoot him in the head.

She needed to do something. But what? The last time she'd interfered with this same police officer she'd nearly gotten him killed.

Suddenly the gunman whirled around.

As if anticipating the move, Dillon lunged to the side. He rolled out of the way and scrambled to his feet.

Bam, bam— Iceman fired off two quick shots, flames shooting out of the muzzle like a warning flare.

Dillon grunted and fell to the ground. His body jerked, then lay still.

Ashley's nails bit into the backs of her tied fists. She silently urged Dillon to move, to run, but he lay facedown on the ground—stunned, or worse.

The gunman stalked toward him.

Ashley frantically looked around. There had to be *something* she could use as a weapon. But even though the icy rain was still dripping through the heavy canopy overhead, and the wind clacked the branches against each other, there wasn't even a large twig on the ground anywhere within reach.

Thunder sounded. Lightning lit up the clearing, illuminating Dillon. He still wasn't moving.

Oh, dear God, no.

Ashley jumped to her feet. If nothing else, she could swing her tied fists at the gunman and try to knock his gun out of his hand before he could shoot Dillon again. She charged forward.

The gunman stopped beside Dillon and raised his gun.

Ashley pulled her tied hands back like a bat to swing at him. Dillon suddenly jerked to the side and kicked Iceman's legs, knocking him to the ground. Ashley yelped and scrambled out of the way. The two men grappled with each other, locked in combat.

The storm was getting worse. Sheets of rain pelted them through the gaps in the trees. Ashley shoved her wet hair out of her face. Lightning cracked overhead in short bursts, a strobe light revealing the men's movements every few seconds, like a projector showing every other frame in a movie.

They rolled back and forth, grunting, twisting as they each strained for the advantage over the other. One of them got his arm free and swung his fist with massive force against the other man's jaw. A loud crack echoed in the clearing. His opponent screamed and fell to the side, clutching his face, shaking his head as if in a daze.

The victor climbed to his feet. Moonlight glinted off the gun in his hand.

Ashley pressed her hand to her throat. Who was lying on the ground? And who was holding the gun? Lightning flashed again, revealing the face of the man who was standing. Ashley's shoulders slumped with relief.

"I'm Detective Dillon Gray. You're under arrest," he gasped between deep breaths. His chest heaved from exertion, but the gun never wavered in his grip. "What's your name?"

The other man shook his head again, as if trying to get his bearings. He rubbed his jaw and glared up at Dillon while climbing to his feet. He staggered at first and then straightened to his full height, several inches taller than Dillon.

Thunder boomed, startling Ashley, but Dillon didn't even flinch.

"Your name," he demanded again, but the other man remained mute.

"Miss Parrish," Dillon said. "Get behind me. Make a wide berth around this gentleman, please."

Staying well away from her abductor, she hurried to

the other side of the clearing. Iceman's head swiveled, following her every move, like the sights on a rifle. She thanked God it was too dark for her to see the look in those creepy dead eyes. She stopped beside Dillon, but he shoved her behind him.

"Facedown, on the ground," he ordered the other man.

Ashley peeked around Dillon's broad shoulders. Her abductor wasn't cooperating. Instead of getting down, he braced his feet wide apart.

"Ah, hell," Dillon said.

Ashley clutched the back of his shirt. "Can't you just…shoot him?"

"I'd certainly like to, but my boss frowns on shooting unarmed civilians."

Iceman grinned, his teeth flashing in the moonlight like a wolf baring its fangs.

"That doesn't mean I won't," Dillon warned him. "If you take a single step, I'll shoot. I'm too exhausted for another boxing round and I'm freezing. Not to mention I have a civilian to protect. I *will* shoot if you force my hand. Get down on the ground. Now."

The man's grin faded. Ashley couldn't see well enough to identify the expression on his face, but judging by the way his shoulders stiffened, she'd bet he was considering charging the detective. If *she* had a gun, she wouldn't wait for the bad guy to make a decision. She'd shoot, right now. This man had already attacked both of them. If he got another chance, she had no doubt he'd do it again.

"Who are you?" Dillon repeated. "Why are you after Miss Parrish?"

"He said he needed me alive," Ashley said.

Dillon digested that for a moment. "Have you ever fired a gun?"

"Me?" she squeaked.

He sighed. "I guess that's a no. There's no safety. All you do is point and squeeze. I want you to point my gun directly at our guest while I handcuff him. If he moves, squeeze the trigger. Can you do that?"

"I'd have no trouble shooting this jerk. He stole my shoes," she said.

His mouth twitched, as if he was trying not to laugh. "If I didn't have to keep this gun trained on this fellow I'd cut those laces with my pocketknife. But I don't want to risk cutting you. Hold your hands up and I'll untie them."

She held her clasped hands on his left side while he kept his gun trained on the quiet, deadly stranger with his right hand.

He plucked at the laces, mostly by feel, and soon they were loose enough so she could unclasp her hands.

"I can get it the rest of the way." She worked the laces free and dropped them to the forest floor. Rubbing her aching wrists, she glared at the man responsible. Her glare was probably wasted since it was so dark, but it made her feel better.

"Okay, I'm ready," she said.

Dillon kept his gun trained on the other man while he pulled out a set of handcuffs from a holder on his belt.

"Mister, I strongly suggest you cooperate. If you lie still while I put the cuffs on, you won't get shot. But if you try anything, Miss Parrish seems quite anxious to repay you for her ill use tonight."

The man hesitated, then got down on his knees and lowered himself to the ground. He lay with his head to the side, watching both of them as he put his arms behind his back.

Dillon cursed softly beneath his breath.

"What's wrong?" Ashley whispered.

"That was way too easy."

"You think he's planning something?"

"I think he plans to fight me again. He's assuming you won't shoot."

"But I will. I promise."

His mouth twitched again. "Actually, I'd prefer you don't, since you've never fired a gun before," he whispered. "I don't want to get shot again. I'm already a walking bruise. We'll bluff, but don't shoot unless your own life is in danger. I repeat, do *not* shoot when I'm anywhere near him." He handed her the gun, keeping it pointed at the other man.

She tightened her fingers around the grip. It was heavier than she'd expected. Her hands dipped beneath the weight. He grabbed her wrists and steadied the gun.

"Like this." He adjusted her hold, making the gun more balanced. She nodded to let him know she had it this time.

"Only shoot as a last resort," he whispered again. "To save *yourself*."

"All right," she assured him. But she had no intention of doing *nothing* if Iceman tried something. If it came down to it, she *would* shoot, but she didn't tell Dillon that. He seemed too worried she'd shoot *him*. It was a bit insulting, really. How hard could it be to aim and pull a trigger from ten feet away?

He moved forward, keeping well clear of the other man's legs. He suddenly dropped down with his knee in

the small of the man's back. At the same time he twisted
the man's arms up between his shoulder blades.

Iceman let out a low roar of rage. Whatever he'd
planned to do was a moot point now. Dillon had im-
mobilized him before he could even move. Ashley was
thoroughly impressed.

Dillon snapped the cuff around one of the man's massive wrists.

A loud boom echoed through the trees. Dillon stiffened and fell to the side, landing hard on the ground
with a pained grunt.

A bald-headed man ran out of the woods holding a
gun. Iceman jumped up from the ground, the handcuffs
dangling from his left wrist.

Ashley aimed at Baldy and squeezed the trigger. The
gun boomed and jerked in her hands. She fell back on
her butt in the mud. *Dang it.* She twisted to the side
and scrambled to her feet, expecting to feel the bite of
Baldy's bullet any second.

But Baldy didn't have his gun anymore. Iceman had
it. Somehow her shot, instead of hitting the bald man,
had hit Iceman in the shoulder. Blood ran down his arm
and dripped from his limp fingers. He must have taken
the gun from his partner, because he glared at Ashley
and started to raise his other hand, the one now holding the gun.

She braced her legs so she wouldn't fall back this
time and squeezed the trigger again and again and again.
Both men shouted and dove to the ground. They took
off running into the woods.

An arm snaked around her waist and the gun was
plucked from her hands.

She jerked against her captor and tried to twist in his
arms to get the gun back.

"Stop fighting me." Dillon's harsh command sounded near her ear. She hadn't even seen him get up off the ground.

She blew out a relieved breath and stopped struggling. He let her go and she turned to face him. "I did really good! I scared them both away."

"You scared all of us the way your bullets were ricocheting around the clearing. I told you not to shoot."

"You're welcome," she grumbled. The least the man could do was be grateful since she'd probably saved his life. Her gaze dipped to his chest and she gasped at the sight of two bullet holes in his shirt. "That man shot you." She ran her hands over the fabric, feeling the vest beneath. "Did the vest stop the bullets? Did the other guy shoot you, too? Are you okay?" She trailed her fingers to his sides and then down his arms.

He sucked in a breath and plucked her hands off him. "I'm okay." His eyes widened and he stared past her across the dark clearing. "We can't catch a break, can we? I hear them. They're coming back. How much do you want to bet they probably *both* have guns this time?"

He grabbed her hand and tugged her toward the trees behind him.

One of her bare feet came down on a hard rock. She yelped and tugged her hand out of his grasp. "My shoes. I need my shoes. They're back over—"

The wood exploded on the tree by her right leg and a deafening boom echoed through the clearing.

Ashley took off running, leaving Dillon to chase after her.

Chapter Five

"Why are we stopping?" Ashley tried to say, but it came out more like "wwwwhy are wwweee stoppp-piiinng" between her chattering, clenched teeth. The cold wouldn't have bothered her so much if she wasn't cold *and* wet. And she had a stitch in her side from running so long and so hard over rough terrain. She clutched the nearest tree for support and drew deep, gasping breaths while trying to will away the painful ache in her side.

She certainly didn't mind stopping—that wasn't why she'd asked the question. She'd like nothing more than to curl into a tight ball on the forest floor and give her aching muscles a rest, in spite of the incessant rain still coming down. But she also didn't want to give their pursuers a chance to catch up to them.

Dillon didn't spare her more than a quick glance. He slid the clip out of the gun and checked it, then slid it back in until it clicked. He stood protectively in front of her, peering into the gloom surrounding them. The darkness would have been welcome under the circumstances, since it helped conceal them, but lightning kept flashing overhead like a spotlight.

"Why did we stop?" she repeated, proud she'd managed to speak coherently this time without her teeth chattering. She impatiently shoved her wet hair out of her eyes.

"We're almost at the end of the island." His voice was pitched low. "If we keep running, we'll end up in the river. We'll have to double back, find somewhere to shelter and take a stand." He glanced at her. "Besides, your feet are a bloody mess. The only reason you're still able to run is because the cold has made you numb."

She lifted one of her feet, gasping when she saw the blood. He was right. She hadn't even felt the pain. But of course, now that he'd mentioned it, her feet started throbbing.

"Okay, ouch. But it doesn't matter. We have to keep going. I'd really love *not* to get shot today."

Amusement lit his eyes and he raised a brow.

Her face flushed hot. "Yes, I know. *You've* been shot, what, two, three times? I'm really, *really* sorry about that."

He let out a puff of laughter. "You're not the only one." He absently rubbed his chest as if it pained him and scanned the trees again. Seemingly satisfied, he shoved his gun in his waistband, then pulled his shirt off over his head.

Ashley blinked in surprise, and her mouth suddenly watered in appreciation. The bulletproof vest hid much of his chest, but his bulging biceps were now displayed for her viewing pleasure. She'd always been a sucker for muscles and golden skin, and Dillon's arms were like a sculpted work of art. Her fingers itched with the desire to slide over that smooth skin, up his arms, over his broad shoulders to sink into his thick, dark hair. How good would it feel to have those strong arms close around her and cradle her to his chest? What would the rest of his body look like without the armor? Would it be as enticing as she imagined? Or even better?

A ripping sound had her blinking again. She'd zoned out, fixating on totally inappropriate thoughts given their circumstances. She blamed her lack of focus on blood loss from her injured feet. Dillon, thankfully, didn't seem to have noticed her distraction. He was too busy cutting strips off his shirt with a pocketknife.

"Detective Gray—"

"Dillon."

"Dillon, it's cold out here. And it's still raining. Or hadn't you noticed?"

"I did notice, actually. Especially since I swam in a freezing-cold river to get here."

She winced. "I never thanked you for that. Thanks."

He smiled. "We've both been a bit busy. And to answer your next question, the reason I took my shirt off and am currently destroying it is because I'm going to use these strips to wrap your feet." He put his knife away and waved at a fallen tree a few feet away, indicating for her to sit.

Normally, she'd decline the offer to sit on a half-rotted, probably bug-infested dead tree, but ever since he'd mentioned the cuts on her feet, they were stinging and throbbing. She gratefully plopped down.

Dillon crouched beside her with the cloth strips from his ruined shirt.

"Miss Parrish—"

"Detective Gray?"

He smiled. "Is that a hint to call you by your first name?"

"Nothing gets by you."

His grin widened before fading away all too quickly. "Ashley, other than your feet, are you okay? When I first reached the island, I heard you scream. Did he… Did that man…hurt you?"

Her face heated at his intent look, and the obvious meaning behind his question. He wanted to know if she'd been raped. She swallowed hard, only now realizing how *lucky* she'd been tonight. With all the awful things that had happened, it could have been so much worse.

"No," she quietly assured him, "he didn't hurt me. Not the way you mean, at least. He backhanded me across the face. Twice. But nothing else."

He frowned and studied her face. Lightning flashed, and he feathered his fingers across her cheek and jaw where the man had hit her. In spite of the gentleness of his touch, pain lanced through her jaw beneath his fingers. She drew in a sharp breath.

He dropped his hand. "Sorry. Nothing appears to be broken, but you're definitely going to have a couple of good bruises in the morning. Your cheek and jaw are already swelling. Unfortunately, there isn't much I can do about that. But I *can* wrap your feet."

"I'm not worried about my feet right now," she insisted, only half lying because it felt so good *not* to be standing on her aching feet. "Those men could be anywhere. We need to get moving again."

"You don't think I know that? You're leaving a blood trail that will be far too easy to follow when the sun comes up. We have to staunch the blood."

Her lips formed a silent "oh" and she dutifully lifted her left foot when he reached for it. She felt like a child who'd been reprimanded. Or a civilian who'd been reminded by a cop that he knew what he was doing.

Obviously, he *did* know, or she'd have been dead several times over today.

She sucked in a breath when he wrapped the strips of cloth around her foot. The pressure sent sharp, stinging pains zinging up her legs.

"Detective...Dillon, how did you find me? I mean, why did you come to my house tonight in the first place?"

"Your friend Lauren Wilkes was worried about you when she couldn't get a call through. I guess the shooting this morning had her spooked, so she called nine-one-one. It's a good thing she did." His movements were quick and economical, as if he'd done something like this many times before, and soon both feet were bandaged.

"Yes, it is. I'll have to thank her later. Assuming we make it off this island."

"Don't you worry. We'll make it." Straightening, he pulled the gun out again and held it down by his side. "I grew up around here. I know every inch of Cooper's Bluff. There are some caves where we can probably hole up for the night. It's a defensible position, probably the only one on the island. But it's a ten-minute hike from here." He looked down at her feet. "Maybe fifteen. Think you can make it?"

A thrashing sound echoed through the trees, faint, but definitely getting closer.

Defensible position sounded ominous to her, but those sounds of pursuit had her rising to her feet. The sudden fiery pain had her clenching her teeth to keep from crying out. Apparently the cloth had warmed some circulation back into her feet, making them throb far worse than before.

But that was nothing compared to what a bullet could do.

"I can make it," she announced, not entirely sure whether she could or not. But she had to try.

He gave her an approving look and took her hand, leading her through the dark, sure-footed as if he really did know the way by heart. Lightning still flashed, though less frequently now. But he didn't seem to need the bright light to guide him.

Careful to hold leaves and branches out of her way, he kept her close, guiding her footsteps. At first she thought he was being considerate, but as the sounds of pursuit faded, she realized everything he was doing was deliberate. He was helping her make as little noise as possible as they passed through the woods.

When her feet were throbbing so much she worried she couldn't take another step, he stopped.

"We're here," he whispered.

She wasn't sure where "here" was until lightning lit up the sky above them. They stood in front of a cluster of rocks that formed a small hill. But he led her around a large boulder and she saw what she hadn't seen before: the entrance to a cave.

He went in first, sweeping his gun out in front. What little light there was barely pierced the blackness of the cave. But the lightning filtered into the opening, showing it was empty.

She shivered at the thought of what could have been in there. Wild animals, she supposed. Probably nothing like a bear on a small island like this, but there could have been any number of smaller animals, all of them dangerous if cornered or if they carried rabies. She rubbed her hands up and down her arms. At least it wasn't raining here. That was something.

"You're cold." He shoved his gun in the holster on

his belt and started to unstrap his Kevlar vest as if to wrap it around her.

She placed her hand on his, stopping him. "No. That's all you have to keep yourself warm. You already gave up your shirt for me. I'll not have you freeze to death by giving me your vest."

He dropped his hands to his sides and nodded. "At least it's dry in here. I'd start a fire, but it would be a beacon to the gunmen. Come on. Sit and we'll huddle together to get warm."

The images *that* conjured in her mind had her feeling warm all over.

"I promise I'll behave," he added, as if he thought she might be worried about his intentions.

Ashley snorted. "Don't expect me to make the same promise."

He laughed. "I consider myself forewarned."

She gave him an answering grin, felt her way to the far wall and slid to the ground. Thankfully it was dirt, not rock, making it a *little* less hard than the solid wall at their backs.

He sank down next to her, keeping his gun on his far side, sitting close but not touching. She let out an exasperated breath. She was freezing. Now wasn't the time to worry that they were practically strangers. She scooted closer until his hard thigh pressed against hers. Not feeling nearly warm enough, she lifted his arm and pulled it around her shoulders.

He chuckled and pulled her closer. "Are you always this shy, or am I special for some reason?"

Oh, he was definitely special, but no way was she saying *that*.

"I wouldn't normally snuggle up to a stranger, but

I'm cold and you're like a furnace. Impossible to resist at the moment."

He laughed again and rubbed his hand up and down her arm, warming her even more.

Wouldn't he be surprised if he knew how tempted she was to crawl onto his lap and wrap her arms around him, to get as close as possible and *really* get warm? That thought almost had her giggling, and that's when she realized how exhausted she must be. She was not a giggling kind of girl. And she certainly wasn't a crawl-into-the-lap-of-a-stranger kind of girl, either.

"Miss Parrish—Ashley, what happened back at your house?" He asked the question in a quiet, hushed voice, as if to make sure no one outside could hear him.

She yawned, covering her mouth with her hand.

"I was on the phone with my friend Lauren, and the phone went dead. The next thing I knew, Iceman ran down the hall and pointed a gun at me."

"Iceman?"

"The first guy, the one who drove the truck. He pulled me out of the house and made me get into his pickup. Somehow he'd managed to park out back without me knowing."

"And you call him Iceman because?"

She shuddered. "Because his eyes are like ice. Cold and dead."

He lightly squeezed her arm. "You didn't recognize him? Or the other man?"

"Baldy? No, I didn't recognize either of them. Honestly, I have no idea why people are suddenly trying to kill me. I'm a CPA, for goodness' sake. I inspire fear in no one."

"I disagree. You perform audits, right? That's why

you were at Gibson and Gibson. Most people are intimidated by auditors."

"If I worked for the IRS, I'd agree with you. But when I audit a company, it's usually because that company hired me. They need my reports to convince banks to give them loans, or to prove their practices are pursuant to regulations and tax laws."

"So there *are* times when you're hired by an outside company? And the company you audit isn't happy that you're there?"

"Well, I suppose that's one way to look at it. Yes."

"What happens to a company if your audit reveals problems? Worst case."

"Well, worst case, someone goes to jail. But I don't think that's ever happened in any companies I've worked with. I really don't have any way of knowing that for sure. I just provide the information and leave. I'm not the enemy."

"Has anyone ever lost a loan because of your findings? Or been fired?"

She shifted her weight against the hard ground and stifled a yawn. Dillon's heat was starting to make her drowsy.

"Ashley?"

She blinked and realized she'd started to nod off. "Sorry. What did you ask?"

"Whether companies lose loans or employees get fired when you find discrepancies."

She nodded. "Of course. There's always something at stake in an audit. And there are always consequences."

"Then it sounds to me like you *are* the enemy, at least sometimes, to some people."

She thought back over the many contracts she'd had in the six years that she'd been an auditor. "Honestly,

I couldn't say. When I turn in audit results, that's the end of my assignment. I don't even know what happens once I'm gone. I move to the next contract, the next client." She yawned again.

He pressed her head down onto his shoulder. "We can talk more later. Try to get some sleep. Sorry you have to sleep in a cave, but we should be safe here. I'll keep watch for Iceman and Baldy."

She heard the laughter in his voice, but his teasing reminder about keeping watch had her blinking her eyes and looking toward the cave entrance again. How could she have forgotten about Iceman out there searching for her? Supposedly he needed her alive, for whatever purpose he had in mind, but she wasn't so sure he was going to stick to that dictate now that she'd shot him in the shoulder.

"I'll help you keep watch," she whispered. "There's no way I can sleep knowing those men are looking for us. As for the accommodations, no worries. This won't be the first time I've slept in a cave."

"YOU'VE SLEPT IN a cave before?" Dillon was both surprised and curious to know what circumstances would make her *want* to sleep in a cave. When he'd seen her in a conservative gray skirt and matching suit jacket this morning, she hadn't struck him as the outdoors, camping type. And he'd noticed the reluctance in her eyes when she contemplated sitting on the rotten hull of a tree earlier so he could bandage her cuts. Getting dirty or risking a bug or two crawling on her would probably go in her auditor column of negatives instead of positives.

Apparently he'd have to wait for the answer to his question. Her breaths had grown deep and even. She'd already fallen asleep. He couldn't help but smile. She'd probably be horrified to realize she'd fallen asleep after declaring she would help him keep watch. Not that he wanted her help. Her bravery in the face of danger had already scared the hell out of him today. Twice.

Most women he knew—heck, most *men* he knew—wouldn't approach an armed man unless they were armed, too. Ashley had done that twice in one day, both times to try to help him. He hadn't needed her help, but she hadn't realized that. She thought he was in trouble and had jumped right in, with no thought for her own safety.

That kind of bravery was rare, but it was also dangerous. Sometimes jumping in to help someone wasn't the best option, and it was more likely to get them hurt, or killed. Hopefully she'd never have to learn that lesson the hard way.

Like he had.

He shied away from those thoughts. Those memories were better left buried and taken out when his only company was a bottle of Jack Daniel's.

He settled more comfortably against the hard rock wall, wishing the storm would hurry and break. His men were probably out in the rain right now looking for him since he hadn't checked back in after his last callout. Once they found his Jeep and saw the deep ruts the truck had left beside the river, they'd figure out at least part of what had happened. He just prayed they'd figure it out before the gunmen realized he and Ashley were holed up in this cave.

If he'd been stranded on Cooper's Bluff by himself, he wouldn't hide. He'd go on the offensive, sneak up behind his pursuers. But with an innocent civilian to worry about, that wasn't an option. If something happened to him, Ashley would be left alone to fend for herself. That wasn't a risk he was willing to take.

She whimpered and jerked against him in her sleep, and mumbled something that sounded like "Iceman." He rubbed his hand up and down her arm, trying to soothe her, but she continued to toss and turn. Feeling helpless and rusty in the ways of comforting a woman, he whispered nonsensical words to her, much like he did to his horses back home when they were agitated. To his chagrin, she immediately calmed down and relaxed against his side. He had a feeling if she ever found out he'd treated her like a horse, she wouldn't be a bit pleased.

Several hours later, the storm finally relinquished its hold on Cooper's Bluff. Thunder rumbled only occasionally now in the distance, and the flashes of lightning were replaced with the first rays of sunlight filtering into the cave. He could pick out details now, like Ashley's curly brown hair falling across her face as she lay against his chest. However, the arrival of dawn was not something to celebrate.

Because the blood drops from Ashley's wounds were now visible to their pursuers.

This was the moment he'd dreaded. It had been too dark last night to be sure he'd wrapped her feet well enough to prevent the blood trail from giving their location away. And although he didn't think he'd broken any branches and he'd kept them walking on hard ground as much as he could, it was impossible not to leave some evidence of their passing in the damp earth. Staying in the cave was no longer a safe option. They'd have to take their chances on the run again.

He gently shook her. "Ashley, wake up."

She mumbled in her sleep and lightly punched his arm. Apparently she wasn't a morning person.

He shook her again. "Wake up. We have to—"

A loose rock shifted at the entrance.

Dillon dove in front of Ashley as a gunman stepped into the cave.

Chapter Six

"Whoa, whoa, whoa." Chris Downing raised his hands in the air, his pistol pointing up toward the roof of the cave. "You aren't still mad about Becky Abrams, are you? That was twelfth grade, man."

Dillon lowered his gun. "For the record, Becky slept with you because she knew I wasn't interested."

"Ouch." Chris grinned and holstered his weapon. "Looks like you're in one piece, but your lady friend could use a doctor. What happened to her feet?"

Ashley had slumped over but was still sound asleep with her head pillowed on her arm. Dillon winced when he saw the bright red splotches on her bandages.

"I didn't realize the cuts were that bad. We had to run halfway across the island and she didn't have any shoes." He looked past Chris to the cave opening. "Did you come alone?"

"Randy and Max came with me, but they're following a trail some clueless city slickers made. Two sets of footprints slogging through mud, broken branches all over the place. Whoever left that trail must have run through the woods like a herd of cattle in a stampede."

"I don't think they were worried about leaving a trail.

Make sure Randy and Max know the men they're following are armed and extremely dangerous."

"We all kind of figured that when we found the truck tangled up in the downed tree with the passenger window shot out."

"When are they supposed to report in?"

He checked his watch. "About six more minutes."

Dillon debated whether to wait for their call or retrieve his men right now so he could get Ashley off the island. She needed those feet tended to, might even need stitches. But if the men who were after her got away, she would still be in danger if they decided to come after her again. And next time, she might not be lucky enough to have a friend call the police.

She mumbled in her sleep and shifted position.

"You going to tell me what happened?" Chris asked. "We know you responded to a nine-one-one call to check on Miss Parrish, but never called to make a report."

"You found my Jeep?"

He nodded. "After a search up and down Little River Road, we started searching side roads until we found your car. We found tire tracks by the river, along with your jacket. Since the river had rapids last night an Olympic white-water rafter wouldn't dare try, I'm pretty sure I have to be wrong about what it looks like you did. Because no one with any brains in his head would have gone for a swim in that river, not in that storm. That would have been a suicide mission."

"Apparently not, since I'm still here."

Chris cursed. "You, of all people, know how dangerous a rain-swollen river can—"

"Don't," Dillon rasped, his fists clenching at his sides. "Don't you dare go there."

They stood nose to nose, each of them staring the

other one down. Finally, Chris backed up and held his hands out in a placating gesture.

"Sorry," he mumbled.

Dillon let out the breath he didn't even realize he was holding. He gave Chris a curt nod and forced his fists to relax.

Chris held his hand out. Dillon clasped it and Chris hauled him to his feet.

"Why didn't you call for backup?" Chris asked.

"I couldn't. My cell phone wouldn't work. I'm pretty sure the man who drove that truck had a cell phone jammer."

"A cell phone jammer? Fill in the gaps, boss man," Chris insisted.

"When I got to Miss Parrish's house, a man took off with her in a truck. I followed them and tried to call for backup, but the call wouldn't go through. I figured the signal was jammed but I couldn't risk falling back far enough to get a clear signal. I would have lost them. I followed them to the bridge, where the fool driver ended up in the water."

"Who shot the window out?"

"I did. I tried to pull Miss Parrish out the window before the truck slid the rest of the way into the river."

Chris crossed his arms. "And you thought it was a good idea to jump in? The river was too rough last night for us to risk taking the boat out, but you went for a frickin' swim."

"I told you. I didn't have a choice."

Chris's answering frown told Dillon what his friend thought of that statement.

"Regardless, when I got on the island the man who'd abducted her was tying her up. I managed to handcuff one of his wrists when another man came out of the woods and got the drop on me. You pretty much know the rest. We ran and hid in the cave."

"Tell me about these guys."

"I can't say much for the second guy, didn't get a good look at him. But the first one, the one who abducted Miss Parrish, he was hardcore, stone-cold dangerous, focused on his mission."

"He must not have been too focused, since you two are still alive."

Dillon shook his head. "He wasn't trying to kill us, or at least, he wasn't trying to kill her. He could have done that back at her house. His goal last night was to kidnap her."

"Any clue why?"

"Not yet."

"I don't suppose it occurred to you it's a heck of a coincidence that Miss Parrish was involved in two different shootings in one day?"

"I've thought of little else since last night. There's got to be a connection. Either that or she's the world's most unlucky accountant ever."

"I'm hoping for bad luck, personally," a feminine voice interjected. "Seems to be the lesser of two evils."

Dillon and Chris turned to see Ashley sitting up, shoving her hair out of her face.

Chris stepped over to her and offered his hand. "I'm Chris, in case you forgot. We met at Gibson and Gibson yesterday morning."

"I remember. I'd say nice to see you again, but I'd be lying. No offense." She shook his hand.

He laughed. "None taken."

A sound near the entrance had Dillon standing protectively in front of Ashley while Chris drew his gun.

"Police," a voice called out. Seconds later, Max and Randy stepped into view.

Chris holstered his weapon.

"You didn't find them," Dillon said, disappointment heavy in his voice.

"No. Looks like they had a boat on the east side of the island at the community dock. They must have left some time during the night, or maybe early this morning before we got here. We didn't hear a boat motor."

Dillon introduced Max and Randy to Ashley. "Destiny's a pretty small town, so our police officers fill many roles. Max, Randy and Chris—like me—are detectives and SWAT, when needed. They were at the office shooting yesterday, too."

Ashley waved and offered a small smile.

Dillon noted the light flush of embarrassment on her face and the way her eyes slid longingly toward the entrance. He had a pretty good idea he knew why. "Where'd you moor the boat?" he asked Max, meaning the police boat.

"Back side of the island, about a hundred yards due west, by the old Cub Scout campground."

"You guys go ahead. Miss Parrish and I will catch up in a few minutes. I need to ask her a question."

The men filed out and Dillon squatted down beside Ashley. "Can you walk?"

She nodded and started to push herself up. But the moment she put her weight on her feet, she gasped and fell back.

Dillon caught her and scooped her up in his arms, cradling her against his chest. "That's what I thought. We'll get you to a doctor first thing." He carried her out of the cave and set her down on a boulder near some bushes.

She glanced up, her eyes questioning. "I thought we were going to a boat."

"I figured your bladder might be suffering the same as mine after spending the night sleeping in a cave. And I didn't think you'd want to bump around in a boat without taking a quick break first. These bushes should offer you some privacy."

Her face turned a light shade of pink. "You're right. Thank you."

He bent down at eye level with her. "Do you need me to hold you up? I promise I won't look."

She shook her head back and forth, her face turning a darker shade of red. "No, thank you. I'll manage, somehow. Just give me a few minutes. Please."

"All right. I won't be far. Call out if you need me." He watched her hobble over behind the bushes, her face a mask of pain every time she took a step. When he was satisfied she wasn't going to fall on her face, he hurried off to give her the promised privacy, and to answer nature's call himself.

A few minutes later, he found Ashley sitting back on the boulder, her face still flushed a delightful shade of pink.

"Ready?" he asked.

She nodded, and he scooped her up in his arms again.

When they reached the boat, Chris gave them a curious glance but didn't say anything. Dillon set Ashley in the forward seat on the port side, a few feet from Chris's position at the wheel, while he and Randy took up positions on the benches that ran along the port and starboard sides. Max untied the mooring line from the back of the boat and Chris eased it out into the river.

Noting Ashley's curious glance at the fishing poles lying in the middle bottom of the boat, Dillon explained,

"Destiny's residents don't figure their tiny police force needs a fancy speedboat like some of the bigger cities have. This old fishing boat might not be fast or fancy, but it's sturdy, and generally suits our needs."

"Understandable, but why the fishing poles?"

Chris half turned and grinned. "Those are mine. I like to be prepared for emergencies."

"Is there such thing as a fishing emergency?"

"Of course. You never know when the fish will be biting." He turned the boat upriver, the glassy, smooth surface nothing like the roiling, raging death trap from last night.

"I can see that accountant's mind whirling now," Dillon teased. "You're wondering if Chris compensates the department for use of the boat, and the fuel."

"I was doing nothing of the sort."

"Sure you were."

She narrowed her eyes and turned to face the front as Chris steered the boat around a curve in the river.

Damage from the storm was far worse than Dillon had expected. White birch and oak trees had given up their fight and lay on their sides in several areas along the bank, broken branches trailing in the water, causing little eddies as the current swirled around them.

The guttural sound of a powerful engine roaring to life had Dillon whirling around.

"Look out," Ashley shouted. She lunged toward Chris and knocked him to the floor of the boat just as a shot rang out. The windshield in front of the pilot's chair exploded into a spiderweb, right where Chris's head had been seconds ago.

He blinked in shock at Ashley.

"Keep her down," Dillon ordered. Chris immediately covered Ashley with his body.

Dillon fired three quick shots at the gunman aiming at them from the speedboat on the other side of the river. It was coming up fast, directly toward them. Baldy was at the wheel. Iceman was beside him, taking potshots at the police boat.

"Grab the wheel, Randy," Dillon ordered as he and Max fired several more shots at the speedboat.

Randy ducked down and made his way around Chris and Ashley to steer the boat.

The speedboat accelerated.

Dillon cursed. "Make this thing move! Max, lay down cover fire. I'm going to try to pick off Baldy."

Max pulled the trigger, but the gun was empty. He tossed it to the floor. "Chris, gun!"

Chris tossed his pistol to Max, who caught it and whirled back around, shooting round after round.

Iceman dove to the floor of the speedboat, leaving the driver vulnerable.

"Who's Baldy?" Max yelled.

Dillon steadied his gun and took one very careful shot. *Boom!*

"He's history," Dillon gritted out.

Baldy slumped over the wheel and the speedboat turned hard to the port side, spinning out of control without someone to steer it. His body slid off the seat and the engine choked, then stopped. The boat bounced on its own wake and started drifting on the current.

"Cease fire," Dillon ordered. "Randy, bring the boat around. Max, stay alert."

Max stayed on his knees, aiming his gun toward the side of the speedboat, waiting for the other shooter to emerge again.

Dillon glanced at Chris, still covering Ashley. "Both of you okay?"

Ashley's wide-eyed gaze peeked out from beneath Chris's shoulder. She gave Dillon a tentative nod.

"Thanks to Miss Parrish, I didn't get my head blown off," Chris responded, his voice sounding raw.

Dillon tightened his hold on his gun and focused on the speedboat. Randy shut off the engine and let the fishing boat drift up to the side.

Max and Dillon aimed their guns into the floor of the boat.

Empty.

They glanced at each other in surprise, then both jumped into the boat.

"Where the heck did he go?" Max asked. He hurried over to the driver's body and felt his neck for a pulse, then shook his head.

Dillon stared out over the smooth, dark surface of the river. "My guess, he went into the water and swam to shore." He looked back at the police boat, a slow, lumbering beast. "Start making calls. Get the state police to put a chopper in the air and get another boat out here. Make sure they know a shooter might be in the woods. They'll need to stop short of this location and hike the rest of the way in. Have the Blount County coroner meet me at Cooper's Bluff Bridge, or what's left of it. And get a BOLO out on our missing shooter."

He gave Max a quick, detailed description for the be-on-the-lookout announcement that would go out to every law enforcement agency in the county, from Cades Cove to Rockford, as well as neighboring counties. "Max, put a personal call out to Chief Massey at Bitterwood P.D. over in Ridge County, too. Bitterwood's small enough and close enough to appeal to a gunman on foot trying to evade police."

Max nodded and grabbed his cell phone.

Dillon hopped back into the police boat. "I've got her now," he told Chris.

As soon as Chris moved out of the way, Dillon scooped Ashley up again and hurried with her to the speedboat. He set her on the floor. "Lie down. Don't sit up. Iceman's still out there."

She didn't answer. She was too busy staring at Baldy lying lifeless a few feet away.

"Don't look at him. Close your eyes."

She squeezed her eyes shut.

"Chris, get over here. You're coming with us," Dillon called out.

Chris was standing with Randy at the wheel of the police boat. He gave Randy a puzzled look then hurried to the speedboat and got in.

"What are you doing?" Chris asked.

"Getting the shooter's main target out of here. Once we get back to the bridge to Cooper's Bluff, you'll need to stay with the boat to wait for the coroner to pick up our dead friend here. I'll drive Miss Parrish back to town to get her medical attention."

Max put his cell phone away. "State police are on the way. And Chief Massey offered to send reinforcements if you need them."

"Good to know. Thanks, Max. Get back on the other boat. You guys get to shore and hunker down in the woods until the state police get here. If our guy's got some dry weapons stashed nearby, he'll start taking shots again. I don't want you in the middle of the river when he does."

Max frowned with obvious disappointment. "We don't need to wait. If the shooter's in those woods, Randy and I can find him."

"Wait for backup. That's an order."

Max gave him a curt nod and joined Randy.

Dillon restarted the engine, and turned the speedboat back toward the bridge.

WHEN DILLON CARRIED Ashley into the one-story offices of the Destiny Police Department, it only took a quick turn of her head to get the layout of the entire police station. One unisex bathroom to her left. Fifteen cheap laminate desks lined up in three rows in the middle of the rectangular room. A snack machine and tiny kitchenette on the right beside a door labeled Chief of Police, William Thornton. And along the back wall, two currently unoccupied cells with floor-to-ceiling iron bars.

Take away the computers and phones, sprinkle in a few cowboy hats, and the place could be the setting of an old TV Western.

"I'm sure I can walk," she whispered, feeling silly in his arms as he strode past the handful of police officers working at their desks.

"Doesn't mean you should." When he reached the first jail cell, he hooked one of the nearby desk chairs with his foot and dragged it over, then carefully set Ashley on the chair. "Give me a sec."

He crossed to a small cabinet built into the wall and unlocked it, then pulled out a big brass key.

Ashley watched in stunned amazement as he used the key to unlock the first cell and swung the door open.

He caught her watching him and raised a brow. "What?"

"You do realize what century we're in, right? You don't have electronic locks on the cells?"

He smiled and tossed the key in the air, easily catching it. "The city council wouldn't approve more than a cheap, used fishing boat for the police department. Do you really think they'd approve an expensive electronic locking system for our jail?"

She shrugged and eyed the cell. "Please tell me you're not thinking about locking me in there."

"You need to be protected. Makes sense to lock you up, don't you think?"

"I'm going home." She shot up out of her chair but immediately fell back to sitting when pain shot through her feet.

Dillon crouched down in front of her and took her hand in his. "That was a really bad joke. I promise I'm not going to lock you up. However, the cot in the cell is the most comfortable place with your feet the way they are. I figured you could lie down and elevate your feet while I call Doc Brookes. He still makes house calls and the nearest hospital is a long drive from here."

She bit her lip in indecision. "Promise you won't lock the door?"

He crossed his heart. "Scout's honor."

"All right then. Putting my feet up does sound good. I guess you get to carry me one more time."

He squeezed her hand and let go. "Trust me. Carrying you is not a burden."

He scooped her up before she could think too hard about that comment. She couldn't imagine he'd meant it the way it sounded, as if he was flirting with her. Because after being in a rainstorm, spending all night in a cave and wearing the same muddy, dirty clothes without being able to even wash her face, there was nothing about her that could be even remotely attractive.

He propped her feet up on a pillow and pulled a blanket over her. "I'll be right back."

"Wait, please. Do you have a phone I can use? You said Lauren called nine-one-one last night because she was worried about me. I need to let her know I'm okay. Preferably before she calls my family and gets them worried and they descend en masse on Destiny and get all in my business."

He grinned. "Big, nosy family, huh?"

"Like you wouldn't believe."

"My phone is at the bottom of the river somewhere, but I'll get you one. Give me a minute."

While he headed over to a young policewoman sitting at a desk by the window, Ashley self-consciously finger combed her hair. Dillon perched on the edge of the desk and several officers came over to talk to him. Even without a shirt, wearing nothing but his bullet-resistant vest, wrinkled dress pants and boots, he still looked amazing. Ashley was suddenly longing for a hot shower, some fresh clothes and her makeup bag.

If Lauren could see her now, she'd accuse Ashley of being in lust with Dillon, and she would probably be right. She had a lot of other things she should be worrying about instead of drooling over the tall, dark and handsome man who'd been a part of her life for less than twenty-four hours. In all likelihood, once her feet were finally taken care of, he'd probably take her statement and send her on her way. She'd likely never see him again, unless he caught a suspect and needed her to testify or something. One thing was for sure, as soon as she could she was leaving Destiny way behind in her rearview mirror, never to pass this way again.

No matter how sexy Detective Dillon Gray was.

Dillon brought a cell phone and let Ashley make a quick call, reassuring her friend everything was okay. As usual, Lauren's melodramatic streak made the call take much longer than Ashley wanted, particularly when Dillon was waiting. But at least Lauren hadn't called her family yet, and Ashley was again able to talk her out of cutting her cruise short. She hung up and gave the phone back to Dillon.

"Thank you."

"Disaster averted?" he teased.

"Just barely."

He motioned back toward the squad room. The policewoman he'd spoken to earlier headed over. At the same time, the main door opened on the far end of the room and Detective Chris Downing stepped inside.

"Ashley Parrish," Dillon said when the policewoman stepped into the cell, "this is Officer Donna Waters."

"Pleasure," Donna said, shaking Ashley's hand.

"Donna's going to go to your house and pack you a bag so you can change into fresh clothes. I'll leave you two here to discuss what you need. I'm still trying to locate Doc Brookes."

He headed back to one of the desks and grabbed the phone. Chris stopped beside him and spoke to him while Dillon dialed the number.

"So," Donna said, drawing Ashley's attention to her. "Looks like you're going to be our prisoner until we catch whoever's after you."

Ashley blinked in surprise. "Dillon... I mean, Detective Gray said he wasn't going to lock me up in here. Scout's honor."

Donna burst out laughing. "Dillon was never a scout. Trust me on that. Honestly, I assumed he was going to keep you here for your own protection. Maybe he's got other plans." She pulled a small notebook and pen from her front shirt pocket. "Now, tell me exactly what you want from your house and I'll be happy to get it. I've already got the address. Since I don't see a purse with you, I'm assuming you don't have your keys. Is there a spare somewhere?"

"My landlord has a key. He lives a few miles down from my house, Mr. Hartley."

"I know him. No problem. I'll stop there first. Now, worst case, assuming you may not be able to go home for a few days, what all do you need?"

DILLON HUNG UP the phone and shot Chris an irritated glance. "Doc Brookes isn't answering his cell. His assistant said he's probably out of range, up in the foothills seeing some patient. And from what Donna told me a few minutes ago, there are trees and power lines down all over Destiny. It'll take hours to get her to a hospital."

Chris grinned. "No reason she should wait." He clapped Dillon on the shoulder. "Not when we've got our own doctor." He headed toward the cell.

"Chris, get your butt back here," Dillon ordered, but Chris ignored him and hurried into the cell.

Dillon chased after him, hoping to head off a disaster.

"Miss Parrish, good to see you again," Chris said. "Looks like with the storm and all, we're down to only one doctor anywhere nearby who can take care of you."

Dillon strode into the cell and aimed a murderous glare at Chris.

"And here he is," Chris announced, waving toward Dillon.

Donna coughed as if she was trying not to laugh.

Ashley stared up at Dillon, her eyes wide with surprise. "You're a doctor?"

"No," Dillon said.

"Yes," Donna and Chris both said at the same time.

"Knock it off," Dillon ordered. "Miss Parrish, I did go to medical school, but not the kind of—"

"I'll get your bag," Chris announced. "I assume it's in the Jeep? You never go anywhere without it." He hurried out of the cell, steering well clear of Dillon's reach.

"Now everything makes sense," Ashley said. "You seemed to know what you were doing when you wrapped my cuts last night."

He closed his eyes and prayed for patience.

Donna laughed. "He's definitely good at doctoring. Did his schooling in Nashville."

He opened his eyes again and glared at her, not that it did any good.

"Really?" Ashley asked. "That's where I'm from. Did you go to TSU? I graduated from there."

"As a matter of fact, yes, I went to Tennessee State University. I'm trying to explain that I'm not—"

"He graduated with honors," Donna chimed in again.

"Here we go." Chris ran into the cell carrying a small black duffel bag. He set it beside the cot. "Go ahead, Dr. Gray. Fix her feet."

Dillon pointed to the cell door. "Out. Both of you. Now."

Donna patted Ashley's hand. "Don't you worry. I'll get what you need and be back in no time."

She and Chris hurried out of the cell, apparently deciding retreat was a good idea.

Dillon glared after them, then dragged the chair from outside the cell and settled it in front of the cot. He plopped down and tried to tamp down his anger before saying anything. Ashley looked completely confused, not that he could blame her.

"Detective—"

"Dillon."

"Right, sorry. What was all that about? What's going on? Are you really a doctor?"

He shook his head. "No, I'm not. That was Chris and Donna's idea of a joke. Unfortunately, Chris was right about one thing. There's no one around who can take care of you right now. I'm going to have to drive you to Blount Memorial in Maryville. Normally that would be a forty-minute drive, but with the storm damage, it's going to probably take closer to three hours. Do you want to leave now, or wait for Donna to get back with fresh clothes? There's a shower in the bathroom in the chief's office. I'm sure he wouldn't mind—"

She put her hand on his. Awareness shot through him, surprising him. He glanced up at her.

"Dillon," she said. "My feet hurt. A lot. If there's something you can do to help me, I'd really appreciate it. I don't relish the idea of driving for three hours with my feet throbbing if you can make me feel better right now. What were your friends teasing about, exactly? Did you not really graduate? Did you drop out early from TSU?"

He shook his head. "No. I graduated. But I did drop out of the University of Tennessee. I went there for my postgraduate studies."

A look of relief flashed across her face. "I don't care if you ended up with an official piece of paper or not. You had four years plus of training. Surely you can handle a few stitches and some fresh bandages. What's in the bag? I hope you have something stronger than Advil in there." She reached down and grabbed the bag.

Dillon rose out of his chair to stop her, but she'd already unzipped the bag before he could. Her eyes widened in horror.

"You're a veterinarian?"

Somewhere out in the squad room, Chris howled with laughter.

Dillon dropped his forehead in his hands and prayed

for patience. The sound of feminine laughter had him jerking his head back up.

Ashley's eyes danced with amusement. "Oh, come on. I figured out you studied veterinary medicine the minute Chris ran in here with that bag and made such a show out of calling you *doctor*. Plus, I went to TSU. I'm well aware they have a veterinary premed program there."

He shook his head. "You could have clued me in earlier."

"I was having too much fun. So what do you do, carry your bag around to take care of stray dogs and cats?"

"More like horses."

Her brows rose. "Horses. Cool." She looked in the bag. "Looks to me like you've got everything you could possibly need to sew a few stitches and bandage me up. I refuse to take any horse tranquilizers, so you're going to have to give me some of the strongest human medicine you can find in this office, or find a bottle of whiskey so I can get drunk first."

He dragged the bag toward him and pulled out a small jar. "If you don't mind the smell, I promise this numbing cream will work wonders. You won't feel a thing while I stitch you up."

"It can't smell worse than I probably already smell right now. Let's do this."

DAMN BLOODHOUNDS.

Luther would have been fine if it wasn't for the stupid dogs. He could have lain low in the woods until the local yokels gave up looking for him. Then he would have tracked down that detective to find out where he'd taken Parrish. But someone had called the state police to join the search, and sent in tracking dogs—probably the same nosy detective. Now he was forced to hightail it out of town in one of the cars he'd stashed for just such an emergency, which meant it would take that much longer to get the job done and put Hicktown, Tennessee, in his rearview mirror.

He checked the mirror again to make sure no one was following him before using the burn phone from the emergency bag he'd stowed in the car. Because of his hurt shoulder he had to keep the phone on the seat and use the speaker function. It was the only way he could drive and still punch the buttons, since he couldn't lift his right arm without it hurting like the dickens.

Ashley Parrish was going to pay for that, dearly.

"It's me," he said as soon as the phone clicked. "Johnson's dead, and the state police are looking for me. I've got to lie low for a few hours outside of town."

"Lie low? No, you can't. You have to do this *now.*"

He tightened his fingers on the phone. Very few people talked to him that way and lived to tell about it. If she were anyone else, he'd cut her tongue out for that. "If I go back right now, this whole thing is over. We both lose everything. Is that what you want?"

"No, no, of course not. I'm just anxious, worried. We don't have much time. I'm…sorry."

It probably killed her to say that. He couldn't help but grin.

"This is a minor blip in our plans. By this time tomorrow, I'll have Ashley Parrish exactly where we want her." He slowed and turned down the gravel road he'd been searching for. The bumpy ride sent a sharp pain shooting through his shoulder. He drew a sharp breath, then slowly let it out. "I've got to go."

"Call me as soon as you have her." She hung up without waiting for him to respond.

He squeezed the steering wheel so hard it bit into his palm. He'd had about all he could take of her orders and her lack of respect. Once he had his money, maybe he'd take the time to teach her a valuable lesson in how to deal with men like him.

He glanced in the rearview mirror again. But this time he didn't look at the road behind him. He looked at his guest sitting gagged and tied up in the backseat, staring at him with wide, fear-filled eyes—Dr. Brookes.

Chapter Seven

Showering in the police chief's executive bathroom had been an incredibly awkward experience. Dillon had wrapped Ashley's feet in plastic garbage bags to keep the bandages dry. Then he'd dragged in two chairs, one for her to sit on and one for her to prop her feet on, which made washing herself a difficult and time-consuming process. But all the trouble had been worth it to finally feel clean again.

Now, sitting with Dillon, Chris and Chief Thornton in the chief's office, which apparently doubled as a conference room, she felt awkward and sloppy dressed in loose sweats. The clothes were a present her mother had sent last week for her twenty-eighth birthday. She'd never worn them before, had never planned on wearing them, but she'd asked Donna to grab them in case she couldn't pull on any of her slacks over the bandages. Sure enough, they'd been the only clothes she could get on and she was grateful to have them. She'd have to remember to tell her mother later—much later, when it was too late to worry—that the sweats had turned out to be the best present she'd ever given her.

Now if only her mother had sent her some granola bars with those sweats, she'd be warm, comfy and her stomach wouldn't be eating a hole through her spine right now. It was getting close to noon and she'd yet to eat anything. That hadn't mattered until all her other aches and pains went away. Suddenly, it was almost all she could focus on—how hungry she was. If only she could be back home right now, cooking up one of her infamous breakfasts, the kind her brothers used to brag to all their friends about. Cooking was one of the few family traditions she'd actually appreciated.

"Miss Parrish?"

Ashley looked up at the police chief, chagrined to realize he must have been talking to her while she was fantasizing about eggs, bacon and waffles.

"Yes, sir?"

His eyes crinkled at the corners, reminding her of her father and how his smile always reached his eyes. She'd gotten the impression Dillon didn't care too much for his superior, but she'd found him nothing but charming.

"You must be tired and hungry," he said. "And we're obviously boring you with all this talk about the investigations. Detective Gray has volunteered to put you up at his house until we catch the man who abducted you and can ensure it's safe for you to go back home."

Ashley straightened in her chair. From the stony look on Dillon's face, she gathered *volunteered* might not have been the right description. What all had she missed while she'd daydreamed about comfy clothes and hot breakfast?

"Chief, I think there's been a misunderstanding," she said. "I don't live in Destiny. I'm only renting while on assignment here. My lease is up in two days— No, it's up tomorrow, actually. I don't need to impose on Detective Gray or anyone else. I'd appreciate an escort back to my house to get the rest of my things, but other than that, all I have to do is jump in my car and go back to my apartment in Nashville."

"How are you going to drive?" Dillon asked. "Or walk?"

Her face flushed hot remembering the house slippers she'd been forced to wear, since her feet were too swollen to fit in her shoes. Dillon had managed to wash up somewhere and was wearing one of his perfectly pressed suits again, looking ridiculously handsome and rested. And the other detectives—Chris, Max, Randy—had managed to bathe and change, as well. Looking at them reminded her how poor a condition she was in. Driving was the least of her worries. Dillon was right about that.

"I hadn't thought about the driving part. I'll get a cab to take me to the airport. I can come back for my car later."

"The nearest airport is in Knoxville," Chris piped in. "You're going to take a cab all the way from Destiny to Knoxville?"

She fisted her hands beneath the table. "I didn't say I had it all figured out yet. I'm saying, there's no reason for me to stay here. I don't *want* to stay here."

Dillon rested his forearms on his knees. "I know you're anxious to get out of this town, and I certainly can't blame you after everything that's happened. But I don't think you've really thought this through. Three different people have tried to kill or abduct you in the past twenty-four hours. They've gone to a lot of trouble, risk and expense to do so. What makes you think whoever's behind this isn't going to send their thugs to Nashville if you leave?"

She swallowed, hard. "Honestly, I hadn't really considered that possibility."

"You can go to Nashville if you choose," the chief

interjected. "We certainly can't stop you, and I'd have one of my officers escort you there to ensure you didn't encounter any problems—not to mention saving you an enormous cab fee. But I agree with Detective Gray. The odds point to one person, a powerful person, being behind all of this. I don't think they're going to stop just because you go home. Do you have family in Nashville that might be in danger if you go back?"

"Uh, no. Actually, my family is from…somewhere else."

"A boyfriend, coworkers, friends?" the chief continued.

Her gaze slid to Dillon. "No boyfriend, but of course I have people I care about back home. You don't really think they'd be in danger, do you? If I go back?"

"They might be, yes. One of the advantages of a small town like Destiny is that everyone knows everyone's business. I believe you're much safer here, with Detective Gray watching out for you, than you'd be at home. And having you here to answer questions and help with the ongoing investigations is quite helpful to us. We'd appreciate it if you'd at least consider staying for a couple of days."

She chewed her bottom lip. "Are the state police still searching for Iceman?"

His brow furrowed. "Iceman?"

"That's what she calls the shooter," Dillon said.

The chief smiled. "Okay, then no, they haven't found him. They're still looking, and two of my best trackers are with them. We will find him, eventually. But it's going to take some time. Meanwhile, I'd feel a lot better knowing you're safely tucked away with one of my best officers watching over you."

Dillon shot the chief a surprised look, as if he hadn't realized the chief considered him to be one of his best officers.

With the chief, Dillon and Chris watching her and waiting for her answer, all her arguments suddenly seemed foolish, and selfish. Stanley Gibson and seven others had died yesterday. If they'd died because someone was after her, then she owed it to them, to their families, to help find their killer in any way that she could.

"All right. I'll stay."

THE SUN WAS high in the sky announcing the noon hour by the time Dillon turned his Jeep down a long, dusty dirt road. Ashley was surprised that wherever he lived wasn't back in town. She'd expected him to want to live closer to the police station. Then again, as small as Destiny was, maybe close was all relative.

She heard the buzz of his cell phone and he reached down and pressed a button without even looking at it.

"Don't you need to see who's trying to call you?" she asked.

"It's the security system at my house. The motion sensors were triggered by my Jeep turning onto the access road. It automatically texts me to let me know I've got company coming. It even sends me a picture." He pulled the phone out and held it up.

The screen showed a strikingly clear picture of his Jeep with him at the wheel and her sitting beside him.

"Impressive," she said.

"Not half as impressive as all the pictures of stray cows I've been texted when they break out of my neighbor's fence and wander onto my property." He grinned. "But thankfully the sensor isn't set to trigger for anything much smaller than that. There are perimeter cameras on the property, too, overkill way out here. But security tends to be on my mind in my line of work. And I'd rather be too careful than careless."

She nodded, agreeing wholeheartedly.

When the Jeep topped the final hill and Dillon's home came into view, Ashley's mouth dropped open. On one side, acres and acres of rolling green grass spread out as far as she could see, dotted with small groups of horses grazing with the backdrop of the Smoky Mountains behind them. On the other side, eight-foot-tall stalks of bone-dry field corn, ready for harvest, marched in rows up and over a hill. All of it was bordered by pristine white wood fences. And smack-dab in the middle, at the end of the road, was a collection of whitewashed clapboard buildings set back behind a two-story, lovingly preserved farmhouse.

"Careful, you'll catch a fly," Dillon teased.

"That gorgeous house, this land, those *horses,* they're all yours?"

"Passed down from my father's grandfather's grandfather, through six generations of Grays. Dad didn't want to deal with the upkeep so he gave it to me. He and Mom moved to a smaller farm not too far from here." His pride and love for his legacy was evident in his tone and in the way his eyes lit up.

He parked the Jeep beside the house and hopped out. He rounded the car with her duffel bag hanging off his shoulder, opened the door and scooped her into his arms. Him picking her up was becoming a routine she could easily grow accustomed to. But now especially, without the vest and only a dress shirt separating the two of them, it was absolute heaven being cradled against him, feeling his warmth, being able to wrap her arms around his neck.

Since he was staring down at her, probably wondering why she was staring up at him, she rushed to fill the silence. "How many horses are there?"

"Thirty-two. I never planned to have that many. Started with Boomerang and three mares. Naturally, there've been some foals born out of that. But mostly, Harmony Haven is a rescue farm."

"Boomerang?"

"A stallion. He's whistle trained. He can be galloping away as fast as he can go and if I whistle he turns around and comes right back, like a boomerang."

She smiled. "You said this place is a rescue farm?"

"We take in horses that are abused or from people who can't afford them anymore. Our adoption rate is about sixty percent once we rehabilitate the animals. But some have been too traumatized or are too scarred up for anyone to want them. Those are our permanent residents." He jogged up the wide front steps to the wrap-around porch.

"You keep saying 'we' and 'our.' Does someone else live here, too? Someone else in your family?" She glanced at the large glass oval in the front door as he twisted the knob, and wondered who else she was about to meet.

"I live in the house alone, but my farm manager and half a dozen farmhands live in the bunkhouse out back. Don't worry. You'll have plenty of privacy. They don't come up to the house much. As I said, my mom and dad live up the road, about half an hour from here. But they're out of state right now, visiting my brother in Montana."

He carried her in, dropped the duffel bag on the floor

and set her on a soft sage-green couch. The floors were a rustic oak and the staircase in the back of the room was framed with a polished oak handrail and bright white wooden spindles. The main room was expansive, but the enormous burgundy throw rug in the middle of the room softened the space and helped make it homey.

"The master suite is on the bottom floor, that door behind you," he said, pointing over her shoulder. "I'll change the sheets and move some of my things to one of the rooms upstairs. It will be much easier for you to hobble around on the bottom floor. It's got its own bathroom, so that will make it easier, too."

"I hate for you to give up your room for me, but I really appreciate it. I'm not sure I could handle stairs right now."

"Are you—"

Her stomach chose that moment to rumble. Loudly. Her face flushed hot.

His lips curved up in a sensual smile that was like a punch in the gut. Good grief, the man was sexy.

"I was about to ask if you were hungry," he teased. "But I think I have my answer. I've been cooking for myself for over twelve years now, since the day I left for college. So I reckon I can rustle up something decent to eat. What are you in the mood for?"

"Anything that won't run away when I stick my fork in it."

He laughed. "That hungry, huh? You should have said something earlier. We could have grabbed food back in town. Soup and sandwiches are quick so you don't have to wait long. Sound okay?"

"Sounds wonderful. Thanks."

He grabbed the duffel and stood. "Chris mentioned he might stop by in a bit to brainstorm on the investigation.

I usually leave the door unlocked, but with everything that's happened, I'm keeping the house sealed up tight. If you see him at the front door, holler at him to use his key."

"Okay."

He grabbed a remote control off the thick oak coffee table and set it beside her. "If you want to watch TV, click that top button. The TV will pop up out of the table behind the other couch."

"Hmm. Sounds like a fancy luxury to have."

He gave her a droll look. "Electronic equipment isn't a luxury. It's a necessity. Especially during football season."

She rolled her eyes and he grinned again. Thankfully he headed to the bedroom to drop off her duffel bag before he could realize she was debating the merits of grabbing him and pulling him onto the couch with her. A girl could only take so many heart-melting smiles in twenty-four hours without suffering some kind of lust-crazed breakdown.

He headed back through the family room to what she supposed was the kitchen. But she carefully kept her gaze on his eyes this time instead of that devastating smile.

DILLON REACHED THE kitchen and sank into one of the chairs at the table in the middle of the room. He had to take a minute, just one, before making lunch. If Ashley smiled at him one more time he didn't know what was going to happen. Ever since she'd showered and came out in those sweatpants that molded to the contours of her perfect bottom, he'd been useless as a detective. All he could think about was pulling her onto his lap and kissing her until she begged him to take her to bed.

He drew a shaky breath, trying to focus on something else, anything else but the far-too-appealing woman in the other room. Thornton hadn't understood his reluctance to keep Ashley at his house. After all, any time some hotshot law-enforcement official or even a witness in a case needed somewhere to hole up, Dillon always offered his house. The only hotel in town was a disaster. And Dillon's farmhouse was huge, only twenty minutes outside of town, and his security cameras would pick up on any vehicles coming down the road long before they reached the house. But he'd known having Ashley here would kill his concentration. Unfortunately, he hadn't wanted to admit that to Thornton, so he'd grudgingly agreed to bring her home.

After another deep breath, he shoved out of the chair to fix the sexy little distraction something to eat. After that he'd call down to the office in the bunkhouse and make sure Griffin and his men knew to be on the lookout for anything suspicious. Iceman didn't strike Dillon as the kind of man to give up. And if he figured out Ashley was here, a few security cameras weren't going to stop him from going after his target again.

ASHLEY BLINKED AND opened her eyes. It took a moment to get her bearings. She was lying on the couch in Dillon's family room, a royal-blue quilt tucked around her and a soft pillow cushioning her head. The sun was fading from the large bank of windows out front and the glass oval in the door was turning black as the sun began to set. The last thing she remembered was thanking Dillon for the ham-and-cheese sandwich and vegetable soup. She must have fallen asleep and slept right through the dinner hour.

Deep voices carried to her from the back of the house

somewhere. She recognized Dillon's voice, and realized the other voice must be Chris. She must have been exhausted to sleep through his arrival.

She sat up and twisted around. The door to the bedroom wasn't that far away, and Dillon had mentioned there was a connected bathroom, a facility she was sorely in need of at the moment. Calling out to him to carry her to the bathroom was an embarrassment she didn't relish, especially if Chris was here, too. Surely she could hobble by herself without his help.

By using the arm of the couch, and then the back of the couch for support, she slowly, painfully made her way upright. Her feet were tender, bruised, but the fiery burn was gone. The salve Dillon had put on her cuts had already made a huge difference.

It took far longer than her bladder wanted, but she made it into the bathroom all by herself. She fist pumped the air, ridiculously happy to not be an invalid anymore, and quickly took care of her needs. She hobbled to the duffel bag on the bed and riffled through it. Sure enough, Donna had gotten everything on her list—clothes, makeup and even her laptop. Ashley grabbed a hairbrush and some makeup and made a mental note to find a way to express her appreciation to Donna and the men who'd risked their lives yesterday to save her, both at the office building and later on Cooper's Bluff.

A few minutes later, with her hair brushed and some makeup on her face, she felt like a brand-new woman. She slung the strap of her laptop case over her head, letting it hang across her shoulder. Then she cautiously made her way down the hallway she'd spotted underneath the staircase earlier.

Following the voices, she ended up in the doorway of a massive room in the back right corner of the house.

Floor-to-ceiling bookshelves lined two of the walls. The third wall had a bank of small TV screens, which she realized showed pictures of the road out front and various other angles of the farm—probably that fancy security system Dillon had told her about. The last wall was a bank of windows with an incredible view of the sun sinking over the mountains. Little puffs of white mist rose into the air all across those mountains. She remembered staring at that same mist as a little girl, asking her daddy if the mountains were on fire. He'd laughed and told her no, the mist was a natural phenomenon because of the climate, and the reason people called the mountains the Smokies.

"Well, hello," a male voice called out.

She tore her gaze from the picturesque view out the windows. Apparently Chris was the one who'd spoken, because he gave her a friendly wave. The two men sitting on either side of him around an enormous cherry-wood table in the middle of the room smiled at her, as well. They were the SWAT officers who'd been with Dillon and Chris yesterday, the same ones who'd rescued them on the island—Max and Randy.

She returned Chris's wave and hobbled into the room. "Where's Dillon?" she asked.

"Right behind you."

She whirled around in surprise at the deep voice that sounded so close. The movement sent a sharp, fiery spike of pain up her calves and she started to fall.

"Whoa, whoa, I've got you." He caught her in his arms and lifted her against his chest. "You okay? Did you need something?"

"I, uh, no. I don't need anything. And you certainly don't need to carry me again."

"I don't mind." He winked.

Her face flushed hot. "I woke up and thought I'd do a little work." She patted her laptop bag. "I heard voices and followed them back here."

His gaze traveled over her hair and her face in a soft caress. "Looks like you might have made it into the bedroom, too, and did a little primping," he teased, his voice a whisper only she could hear. "For the record, you were already beautiful. But you look even better now."

She blinked, not sure what to say.

"So what's the verdict? Now that you know all us guys are here, do you want to stay or go back to the family room? We're reviewing the case files and brainstorming."

"I'd rather stay, if you don't mind. I won't get in the way. And if you have any questions for me, I'll be right here."

"Works for me." He strode to the table and gently set her on one of the padded chairs, then sat next to her.

She set her laptop on the table and turned it on. But the silence had her glancing back up. Three pairs of eyes were watching her. The only one who wasn't watching her was Dillon, who was silently reading from one of many folders scattered across the tabletop.

"Um, hi," she said. "Don't mind me. I need to finish my report for Mr. Gibson's bank. I'll sit here quietly."

Chris slid a bowl of pretzels across the table to her. "Hungry?"

"I could eat. Thanks." She popped a pretzel in her mouth.

"You'll need a drink," Max said. He appeared to be the youngest of them, probably fresh out of school. His angular face and dark hair made her wonder if he might have some Cherokee in him. "Water? Sweet tea? Beer?" he asked.

"Seriously, no one needs to wait on me. I'm fine."

Dillon looked up and frowned as if just realizing his men were staring at her. "We have work to do, guys. Max, you can grab her a drink, then hurry and get back in here."

Max eagerly nodded and headed out of the room.

For the first time since she'd met him, Ashley realized Dillon seemed aggravated. He must be irritated that she'd interfered with their work. She gave him an uncertain smile and focused on her computer screen, determined not to interfere anymore.

When Max returned with a glass of water, she thanked him. He nodded and gave her a shy smile before returning to his seat. The conversation started up around her again and she tuned it out so she could concentrate on typing the final conclusions into her report. It didn't take long, since she'd been mostly finished with it.

Using the Wi-Fi hotspot feature on her computer to access the internet, she emailed the report to the bank, with a copy to Ron Gibson. The poor man was probably grieving over the loss of his son and didn't care about the report right now, but he would later. And when he did, he'd be pleased to know she'd concluded his company was sound with no obvious causes for concern. He'd be able to get that bank loan if he still wanted it. She sent another email to Lauren, letting her know she'd be delayed a few more days before going home, and reminding her of her promise not to worry Ashley's family.

After shutting off her computer, she stowed it back in her laptop bag and looked around the table. It shocked her to realize that Max and Randy had left and she hadn't even noticed. Chris had slid over into the chair Max had occupied earlier, the one next to Dillon. They were both speaking in low tones to each other as Dillon wrote notes on a legal pad.

Chris glanced at his watch and shoved his chair back. "I guess I'll see you bright and early tomorrow at the office. Or are you working from here?"

"That depends on Ashley," Dillon said.

"I don't mind going to the office with you, if that's what you're asking."

Both men looked at her in surprise.

Dillon smiled and stood. "I thought you were still buried in that laptop of yours. Did you finish your report?"

"Yes. Finally. What about you two? Any progress?"

"Some. I'll catch you up in a few minutes. I'm going to lock the door behind Chris."

"Actually, can you give me a minute alone with Miss Parrish?" Chris asked.

Dillon's brows rose but he nodded and headed to the door. "I'll meet you on the porch."

"Thanks." Chris waited until the sounds of Dillon's boots on the hardwood floor faded before turning back toward Ashley. He crossed to her chair and took the seat beside her.

When he didn't immediately say anything, she teased him, "Let me guess. You want some tax advice, right? Happens all the time. People hear I'm a CPA and they think I can save them some money on their taxes."

His look turned thoughtful.

"That was a joke," she said.

"Yeah, I know. But still. Maybe you can save me some money. We'll have to talk about that later."

She shrugged. "Sure, I don't mind. What did you want to talk to me about now?"

A light flush colored his cheeks and he stared down

at his hands. "I, ah, wanted to thank you, actually." His dark eyes shot up to hers. "You saved my life this morning, on the boat. You saw that guy, the one you call Iceman, before anyone else did. If you hadn't tackled me, I'd be dead. The bullet went right through the boat's windshield, right where I was standing. Thank you is hardly adequate but, well, thank you."

"Are you kidding? I'm the one who owes you and the entire SWAT team my thanks. If you hadn't risked your lives and gone into Gibson and Gibson yesterday, I'd be dead right now, or at the very least, a prisoner of Iceman. And I'm not kidding myself that he wants to keep me alive long-term, so either way you did save my life. Thank you."

He seemed to sit a little straighter in his chair. "Well, I guess we're equal, then. We saved each other. But I still owe you a debt of gratitude. If you ever need anything, I'm there. All right? Just say the word. I mean it."

She put her hand on his where it rested on the table. "The one thing I could use right now is a friend."

He grinned. "Now, that I can do. See you tomorrow, friend."

Ashley called out to him when he reached the door. "Hey, Chris?"

He turned. "Yeah?"

"Do you like chocolate?"

A look of confusion crossed his face. "Who doesn't? Why?"

"Just wondering. Good night. See you tomorrow."

He nodded and headed out the door.

Ashley yawned. The past twenty-four hours were catching up to her. Even with the long nap she'd had, she was suddenly exhausted.

"Let me guess. You're too sleepy to stay up for dinner and to hear an update on the case, right?" Dillon stood in the opening of the room Ashley thought of as the library, his tone teasing.

"Actually, yes. I'm bushed, and not at all hungry. Maybe you can catch me up on the case tomorrow at the office?"

"No problem."

She put her laptop bag over her neck and shoulder again and stood, wincing at the pressure on her sore feet. Suddenly she was in Dillon's arms and he was carrying her back through the house.

"I really can walk now, you know. You don't have to keep carrying everywhere."

"It gives me an excuse to hold you," he teased. "I really don't mind."

"I don't mind, either," she breathed.

He shot her a surprised look, then frowned and carried her into the master bedroom, depositing her gently on the bed.

What had that frown meant?

"I'd like to leave around seven, if that's not too early," he said.

"Not at all. I'm an early riser. I'll be ready."

He glanced at the windows and frowned again. He made a circuit around the room, checking the locks on the windows and closing the heavy curtains.

"Dillon, the name of your farm, was that handed down through the generations, too?"

He slowly shook his head no.

"Well, it's a pretty name, Harmony Haven. How did you come up with that name?"

He stood like a stone, his mouth drawing into a tight line. The silence stretched out between them, turning awkward, the air charged with some indefinable emotion. Pain? Regret? Anger? Then, without answering, he left and closed the door behind him with a firm click.

Chapter Eight

The sun was barely up the next morning by the time Dillon finished his rounds of the barns and checked in with Griffin, who assured Dillon that he and his men understood the danger and would be on their guard in case Iceman somehow ended up here.

Satisfied he'd done everything he could to keep his home and workers safe, Dillon left his filthy boots in the mudroom at the back of the house, washed up in the utility sink and headed into the kitchen. He froze at the smell of warm chocolate and stared right into the smiling eyes of Ashley Parrish.

His kitchen, in the two hours since he'd left the house, had been transformed into a bakery. And the person responsible was standing right in the middle of the chaos in a pair of jeans, fluffy pink bunny slippers and an adorable "Kiss the Cook" apron, watching him warily, as if she expected him to yell at her.

He sighed and locked the door behind him. He owed her an apology for last night, but Harmony was one subject he had no intention of discussing with her. Ever. She was here on a temporary basis. She'd made that abundantly clear. And he wasn't going to share the memory of Harmony with someone who'd be gone in a few days.

The unexpected sadness that shot through him at that reminder—that this beautiful, spunky, smart woman would be out of his life so soon—bothered him far more than he cared to admit.

She set the mixing bowl she'd been holding back on the counter and bit her bottom lip. "I'm sorry if you're upset that I made a mess of your kitchen, and used your supplies from the pantry. But I'd hoped you wouldn't mind. I love to bake, and I thought I'd make something special to thank everyone at the police department for everything they've done, and are still doing for me. I couldn't find you this morning and thought you wouldn't..." Her shoulders slumped. "You're angry. I should have waited and asked permission."

He reached her in three long strides and put his hand beneath her chin, gently forcing her to look at him. "I'm not angry."

Her whiskey-colored eyes searched his. "You're not?"

"Not even a little bit. I'm just...surprised." He glanced at the mounds of muffins and cupcakes and cookies piled on plates in the middle of the table. "Are we hosting a party for five-year-olds and I forgot?"

She lightly shoved him. "Don't be silly. Adults love cookies and cupcakes, too. And it's not all junk food." She hurried over to a plate of dark bread and held it up. "I made some bran bread. It's healthy and tastes good, if you want to try it."

He joined her at the table but passed up the bran bread in favor of one of the chocolate chip cookies. He took a bite and closed his eyes as the warm, gooey chocolate-and-cookie mixture did a dance across his taste buds.

"Do you like it?" She sounded worried.

He opened his eyes. "Best cookie ever. I mean it. The guys at the office are going to go crazy over this."

She grinned and clapped her hands together. "Thank goodness. For a moment there, I thought I'd lost my touch."

The sheer delight on her face because her hard work would make others happy tilted his world for a moment, long enough for him to consider doing something he knew he'd regret. But he couldn't help himself.

He leaned down and kissed her. Her soft lips tasted like chocolate and honey, a heady combination that had him lingering when he knew he should stop—especially since she'd frozen like a surprised rabbit as soon as his lips touched hers.

Frustration curled inside him, but he broke the kiss and pulled back.

She threw her arms around his neck. "Don't you dare stop now."

His shock at her boldness turned to laughter as she tugged at his hair to make him lean down. He put his arms around her waist and lifted her up until she was at eye level.

"Demanding little thing, aren't you?" he whispered before his mouth met hers. He turned with her in his arms, intending to brace her against the tabletop, but she surprised him again by lifting her legs and wrapping them around his hips.

White-hot heat whipped through him and he groaned low in his throat. Her soft lips opened beneath his in an invitation he couldn't have resisted if the entire town was under siege and he was their only hope to save them.

Neither of them seemed inclined to stop. The kiss grew wild and his pants grew uncomfortably tight. When he realized he was seriously considering shoving all her cookies and cakes off the table so he could make love to her right then and there, he finally pulled the strength together to break the kiss.

Ashley clung to him, her eyelids half-closed, panting through her swollen lips, every breath pushing her soft, full breasts against his chest, making him want her even more.

"We have to stop," he whispered, even as he leaned down to kiss the tip of her perky little nose. He moved to her cheek next and licked the small spot of chocolate smeared on her soft skin.

She whimpered in the back of her throat and closed her eyes, leaning back against his arm and turning her head for his wandering mouth. Her sheer joy in life and her trust in him to hold her and keep her safe stunned him. What would she do if he took her to the bedroom right now? Would she welcome him? Or would she come to her senses and stop him?

He took a step toward the kitchen archway. Then another.

No, stop it. What was he doing? He might not know Ashley Parrish very well, but he didn't believe she was a one-night-stand kind of woman. And that meant Ashley Parrish was off-limits.

It almost killed him to pull back and set her away from him.

She looked up at him questioningly, her eyes so full of trust, that it hurt to meet her gaze. Once again, he owed her an explanation. But once again, that was more than he could bear.

"I'll grab a couple of boxes to help us carry all those cakes and cookies into the office." With that incredibly thin excuse, he hurried out of the kitchen and tried to convince himself he hadn't seen the hurt in her eyes when he turned away.

DILLON WASN'T SURE exactly how he'd expected Ashley to act once he'd showered and changed for work. But surely after that earth-tilting kiss they'd shared she should have looked at him differently, or even been angry because he'd ended the kiss so abruptly without a decent explanation. He sure hadn't expected her to act as if nothing had even happened. But that's what she'd done, happily chattering all the way to the office.

Apparently baking made her a chatty Cathy. Maybe she should have been a baker instead of an accountant, because talking about recipes made her animated like nothing else. She looked so adorable waving her hands around, her eyes sparkling as she discussed the right temperature to bake the perfect banana-nut bread. And damn if he didn't want to kiss her all over again.

Well, he'd managed not to make a fool of himself by kissing her again, but three hours after arriving at the office, he wasn't so sure bringing her here had been any better of an idea. From the moment he'd set the boxes of baked goods in the kitchenette, everyone had shoved him out of the way to get at the cookies, cakes and breads. And once they'd tasted the heaven of Ashley's homemade concoctions, she'd become an instant celebrity.

They'd passed her from desk to desk, asking her secrets and talking recipes until he'd had to order some of the worst offenders to leave her alone and get back to work. The chief had come out of his office to see what the noise was about, and after a brief conversation with Ashley, he'd led her into his office. That was more than forty-five minutes ago and they were still in there. What was the chief talking to her about? How to bake the perfect brownie?

Chris rolled his chair over to Dillon's desk. "You look angry enough to kill someone. What's up?"

"Nothing." He forced his gaze away from the chief's closed door and tried to focus on the interview report in front of him, one of the many interviews from survivors of the Gibson and Gibson shooting. He'd already read the interviews several times, but he was rereading them to see if he could pick up on anything he'd missed.

"Nothing, huh?" Chris teased. "I don't suppose nothing has something to do with one very perky little brunette living at your house right now?"

"Did you complete that background report on Todd Dunlop I asked you to do?"

Chris chuckled and rolled his chair back to his desk. A moment later he wheeled back over and plopped a thick manila file folder on top of the interview Dillon had been reading. "I was going to review it again before I gave it to you, but hey, since you're so anxious for it, here you go."

Dillon flipped the folder open. "Give me the highlights."

Chris propped his feet on the edge of the desk and leaned back with his hands folded behind his head. "Todd Dunlop, fifty-five years of age. Married, father of three adult children—two sons and a daughter. Entrepreneur, started Dunlop Enterprises fresh out of college, which was basically a logistics company that provided transportation and storage for smaller businesses that couldn't afford to rent a warehouse. In less than five years the company was bringing in over fifty million a year in revenue. Dunlop expanded and diversified and five years after that he became America's newest billionaire. Then, for reasons unknown, two days ago he went freaking nuts and walked into Gibson and Gibson shooting anything that moved. Killed eight, injured three more. And as we both know, he followed Ashley Parrish around the office like a hunter after a trophy buck."

Dillon thumbed through the remaining pages in the folder. "Why does a man with everything throw it all away and go on a murderous rampage? The coroner's tox screen came back clean. He wasn't drunk or high. So what gives? There has to be more to it than what you've got in this report." He tossed the stack of pages back on his desk. "We have to dig deeper. What about the widow and his children? Are they back from their trip to Europe yet?"

"I've left five messages with the wife's attorney. He's supposed to call as soon as they get back, and he hasn't called."

"Doesn't sound like a close, loving family if they don't want to cut their vacation short to find out why their loved one went on a shooting spree. For that matter, you'd think they would have at least inquired about taking the body for burial."

Chris shrugged. "Rich people are different than other people."

"No, they're not. They may hide behind their wealth and possessions, but at their core they're like everyone else. They love and hate like the rest of us. Someone in that family had to know something about the father. There are always signs before someone snaps. We need to push the family harder, get them in here for an interview."

The door to the chief's office opened. The chief stepped out with Ashley. He kissed her on the cheek and wiped his eyes.

"What the… Is the chief…crying?" Dillon asked.

Chris shook his head. "I never thought I'd see the day. What's going on?"

"I have no idea."

The chief held Ashley's hand and spoke to her in low tones. Ashley nodded and smiled. Dillon didn't have a clue what they were talking about, but he was determined to find out. He shoved his chair back just as the front door opened.

A man wearing a dark suit that screamed federal agent stepped inside and held the door open for a woman in a shiny orange suit that screamed money. Her faded red hair was streaked with gray, and diamonds dripped from her ears, throat and fingers.

"You are not going to believe who the woman in the peach silk suit is," Chris said.

"Who is she?"

Chris grabbed the folder he'd pitched on Dillon's desk and flipped through to the back. He pulled out a picture and slapped it on top. "This is a picture of Todd Dunlop's wife. Look familiar?"

The picture was taken years ago but there was no mistaking the similarities. "Patricia Dunlop. The widow has finally arrived. What's she doing with a federal agent?"

"What makes you think he's a fed?" Chris asked.

"Cheap suit, white shirt, black tie. And he's way too pretty to make it as a regular cop. We'd eat him for breakfast."

"I think you're wrong. I think he's her lawyer," Chris said.

"Fifty bucks?"

"You're on."

Dillon and Chris started across the room. At the same time, the woman turned and pointed at Ashley.

"There she is," she said, in a voice dripping with

venom. She marched over to Ashley, leaving the suit to chase after her. She stopped directly in front of her. "That's the woman who ruined our company and killed my husband." She drew back her fist and punched Ashley across the face.

ASHLEY HELD THE ice pack to her throbbing cheek and warily eyed the woman who was arguing with the chief on the other side of the room.

"Are you sure you're okay?" Dillon asked, crouching in front of her chair.

"Okay is relative, I suppose. At least she didn't knock out any teeth."

Dillon's mouth tightened into a thin line. "Let me arrest her for assault. She deserves to be locked up for what she did to you."

She lowered the ice pack and placed it on top of the desk. "No. She doesn't. She just lost her husband. No matter what he did, it's as much a shock to her as everyone else. Her whole world has been destroyed."

"She's a billionaire. I hardly think her world has been destroyed, but I get the point." He sighed heavily. "All right. I won't arrest her. For now. But if you change your mind, let me know."

"I won't."

He smiled. "Yeah. I figured. By the way, before Cruella de Vil showed up, what were you doing in the chief's office so long?"

"Taxes."

"Taxes?"

She nodded and picked the ice pack up. "I told him about some deductions he's been missing. If he amends his past returns, he'll probably get about ten thousand dollars back." She held the ice against her cheek, hoping to numb the pain.

Dillon grinned. "I should have known it was about money. That's the only thing that would make the chief cry." He pressed a kiss against her forehead and stood. "I'll see if I can get to the bottom of this mess. Chris will watch over you until I get back."

Ashley blinked in surprise at the unexpected kiss as Dillon walked away and joined the chief on the other side of the room. She tore her gaze away from Dillon when Chris rolled his chair up beside her.

"Don't worry. We've all got your back. Cops are like stray cats—feed them once and they'll love you forever." He leaned in close, his expression turning serious for once. "But watch out for Dillon. He's more of a brother to me than my own brothers could ever be, which means I know him better than anyone else, except maybe his mother."

She lowered the ice pack again. "I don't understand. What do you mean, watch out for him?"

"He's a sucker for hard-luck cases, which makes you darn near irresistible. But don't expect him to ever be able to commit to anything. He suffered a terrible loss and blames himself. He's a wreck inside. I'm just saying, I saw the way he was looking at you earlier. And I can count on one hand the number of women he's ever kissed, no matter how innocent, in front of anyone else. If you encourage him, you'll only end up hurt. And so will he."

She was about to protest that she had no intention of pursuing a relationship with Dillon when a commotion had both of them looking toward the front of the room. Patricia Dunlop aimed a glare Ashley's way, then stalked out the front door. The man who'd come in with her looked noticeably relieved when she left.

Dillon left the small group huddled around the stranger and came back to Ashley. Tiny lines at the corners of his eyes broadcast the tension in him when he stopped in front of her.

"Ashley, you need to come to the chief's office."

She put the ice pack down again. "Okay, but why? What's going on?"

"Yeah, spill, buddy," Chris said from his seat beside her.

"That man in the suit, the one who came in with Mrs. Dunlop, is Special Agent Jason Kent. He's with the FBI and he's investigating a string of embezzlement cases. He's here to arrest you."

Chapter Nine

Ashley shook her head and looked around the room. She was sitting in Chief Thornton's office with the chief, Chris, Dillon and the FBI agent. But it felt more as though she was in the middle of a horrible nightmare that wouldn't end.

"I don't understand," she said. "You're accusing me of stealing millions of dollars from companies I never even worked for."

Special Agent Kent held up the briefcase he'd brought with him. "I have extensive reports in here that say you did. Your name is all over the audits that were performed on these companies."

"But that's not possible. Could there be another Ashley Parrish out there? That has to be it. You have me confused with someone else."

He rattled off a Social Security number. "That's the number the auditor gave to each company when they made checks out to her for services rendered. Sound familiar?"

She fisted her hands in her lap. "Well, yes, it's mine, but that doesn't mean anything. Someone must have stolen my identity."

"And performed audits, under your name, for over

a year? People generally steal identities to pilfer credit cards and get into people's bank accounts. Your typical identity thief wouldn't be able to fake an audit, and honestly, that sounds ridiculously farfetched."

Dillon leaned forward in his chair. "Maybe, maybe not. You did say the auditor was able to embezzle millions of dollars. That's a heck of a carrot for someone with auditing skills to put in the work to steal Miss Parrish's identity."

Kent's sharp gaze zeroed in on Dillon like a laser-guided missile. "Are we speaking about the same Miss Parrish that you kissed a few minutes ago? I hardly think you're an unbiased party in this matter."

Dillon's jaw went rigid. "A peck on the forehead is hardly a kiss. And I don't exactly think you can claim you're unbiased, since you walked in here with one of the alleged victims in the embezzlement case."

This time it was the FBI agent's turn to look angry. His brows drew down and he narrowed his eyes at Dillon. "Mrs. Dunlop is one of many witnesses I've questioned in the course of this investigation. When word of the shooting reached our office in Knoxville and I found out one of the survivors was listed as Ashley Parrish, I called Mrs. Dunlop. I asked if she'd accompany me down here so she could make a positive ID so I could arrest Miss Parrish. And of course, I offered condolences on her husband's death."

"Her husband the shooter, right? We're talking about the same man who killed eight people and tried to kill Miss Parrish?" Dillon gritted out.

"More to my point, Detective. Have you been able to find a motive behind the shooting?" He paused and watched Dillon. "From your expression, I'm guessing the answer is no. How does five million dollars, which also happened to destroy Dunlop's financial empire, sound as a motive? Mr. Dunlop might have been a billionaire on paper, but his company was going through tough economic times and was severely in debt. The five million dollars that disappeared from the company's accounts—after Miss Parrish's audit—wiped out the company's liquidity. They couldn't make payroll and had to file for bankruptcy last week. A couple of days before Mr. Dunlop's murderous rampage at Gibson and Gibson. It's no wonder his widow blames Miss Parrish for her husband's death."

The room went silent and all eyes seemed to focus on Ashley.

She threw her hands in the air in a helpless gesture. "But I never worked for Dunlop Enterprises. And I've never even seen Mrs. Dunlop before."

Kent reached into his suit jacket and pulled a picture from his pocket. "Is this your picture, Miss Parrish?"

She stared at the black-and-white photo of her in a business suit, smiling at the camera. "Yes," she whispered. "But I've never seen that picture before."

"Really?" He plopped it on the chief's desk. "I find that hard to believe, since it's on the home page of your company website."

She dragged her gaze from the photograph back to the agent. "What?"

"You did create an LLC under your name, correct?"

"Well, yes. I'm self-employed, so registering myself as a limited liability company makes sense. Of course I—"

"And you have a website?" He rattled off a URL.

She shook her head. "No, no. I don't have a website. I've never needed one. Most of my cases are referrals from other clients."

"I've got signed affidavits from six different companies you performed audits on in the past twelve months. Every one of them had hundreds of thousands of dollars stolen from their accounts right after you performed your audits. You're telling me that's a coincidence?"

She glanced around the room, but no one would look her in the eye anymore. She swallowed against the thick lump in her throat. "You have to believe me. I've never heard of any of the companies you mentioned at the start of this meeting. I don't have a website. I've never seen that picture before. I don't…I don't know what else to say, except that if you think an auditor has access to company accounts, you don't have a clue what an auditor does. I rarely even get a log-on ID when I audit a company. They provide me printouts, statements, company financial records, which I review. That's it. I couldn't embezzle from them even if I wanted to."

"I agree, which is why this case puzzled me for so long. I eventually came up with the theory that you must have found a weak link at the companies you embezzled from. An employee with access to the accounts, perhaps someone you blackmailed because you found evidence of mismanagement or wrongdoing. Rather than report it in your audit, you used the evidence against the employee to get them to give you company funds."

"I'm hearing a lot of conjecture," the chief said, rapping his fist on his desk. "But I've yet to see one iota of proof against Miss Parrish."

"My entire briefcase is loaded with proof, but I'll make this easy for all of you." He looked at each one of them until they were all focused on him. "You had another shooting, aside from the one at Gibson and Gibson. A shooting involving Miss Parrish, correct?"

The chief shot Dillon a surprised glance before looking back at Kent. "Yes, we did. We killed one of the shooters but haven't established an ID on him yet. The other one is still at large."

"Perhaps I can help you with that." Kent pulled another picture out of his pocket and held it up for them to see before placing it on the desk.

Ashley drew in a sharp breath as recognition slammed into her. "Baldy," she whispered.

"What's his name?" Dillon demanded.

"Keith Johnson. He worked for one of the companies Miss Parrish audited. He had direct access to the company's accounts. I'm guessing she cut him out of the profits and he went looking for revenge, or perhaps he wanted to force her to give him his share. Makes sense, since he didn't try to kill her. He only tried to abduct her."

The chief glanced at Ashley, then looked away.

"I swear, I never saw that man before that night on Cooper's Bluff," Ashley said, watching Dillon, hoping he would look at her.

But he didn't. Instead, he stared at the picture on the desk.

Kent held up another picture.

Ashley clasped her hand to her throat as she stared into the cold, dead eyes of Iceman.

"This man is Luther Kennedy. I'm willing to bet he's your second shooter." He looked at Dillon, who gave him a crisp nod.

"Luther is more or less a thug, with a history of charges that never stuck. But for some reason, Todd Dunlop trusted him. He was his right-hand man. He handled security and a host of other tasks for Mr. Dunlop, with full access to his accounts. He's one of only a handful of people who could have funneled money out of the accounts of Dunlop Enterprises. We believe he must have been Mr. Dunlop's go-between, personally carrying company papers to the woman who was auditing the company. Ashley Parrish."

"Obviously Luther's the hired hand," Dillon said, "but what makes you so sure he's the one who accessed the accounts and worked with…the auditor on the side? You mentioned a handful of people could have funneled the money out."

"Yes, but only one of them had motive. The handful of people includes Dunlop's wife, daughter and two sons, all of whom live a wealthy, pampered lifestyle with no motive to try to steal Todd Dunlop's money. But Luther, even though Dunlop relied heavily on him, was given only a moderate salary. He had financial problems and bad credit, and toward the end, before Todd Dunlop went on his rampage, witnesses said Luther and Todd argued a lot. One witness even said Luther asked Todd for a loan and was refused. After ten years of being his errand boy, that had to sting. Let's face it. The only one with access *and* motive is Luther Kennedy."

Special Agent Kent plopped the picture of Iceman down on the growing stack of pictures on the chief's desk. "Look, Destiny is a small town, with a few thousand residents. I understand you don't get complicated cases very often, not like we do in Knoxville. And it's perfectly understandable you wouldn't connect the dots like I did. You don't have the resources out here in the country, or the experience, but I do. And I've already done the legwork. I'm not here to convince you. I'm here to take Miss Parrish into custody."

This time all eyes focused on Agent Kent, and their gazes weren't friendly.

He cleared his throat, his face turning slightly red.

"That didn't come out the way I meant it to. I wasn't trying to criticize your abilities."

The chief straightened in his chair and smiled. "Of course not. Think nothing of it. This office has always had an exemplary relationship with the feds and I'm sure you wouldn't intentionally do anything to jeopardize our long-standing tradition of cooperation. How about we start all over? No one offered you coffee when you came in, did they? How do you like it? Black?"

Kent relaxed against his chair, looking relieved. "Actually, some cream and sugar would be great. Thank you, Chief Thornton. I appreciate your understanding in this matter."

"Of course, of course. It's not like we'd try to give you the runaround, or turn a blind eye. Chris, go get Agent Kent that coffee. Make it quick."

Chris almost knocked his chair down in his eagerness to leave the office. He hurried out and shut the door behind him.

"Agent Kent, why don't you set that briefcase up here on my desk? If you've got information that can help me clear the Gibson and Gibson shooting as well as the Cooper's Bluff fiasco out of my in-box, I'm all for it. Show me what you've got."

Kent glanced at Ashley. "I don't think the suspect should be privy to all of this information."

"Right, what was I thinking? You know us country folk. Not used to how you do things in the big city."

Ashley detected an edge to his voice and wondered if Kent had picked up on it, too.

"Detective Gray," the chief said, "get Miss Parrish out of here, please. And if I don't see you before you leave on vacation, give your mama my best."

Dillon shot to his feet and grabbed Ashley's arm, pulling her to her feet, as well. "Will do, Chief. Nice to meet you, Special Agent Kent."

"Nice to meet you, too."

Ashley's mouth fell open. She couldn't believe this was happening. She looked up at Dillon, but he was stone-faced and silent as he pulled her toward the door.

The door opened and Chris stood there with a cup of coffee in his hand. He gave a slight nod to Dillon before hurrying inside without looking at Ashley.

Dillon pulled the door shut behind them and leaned down next to her ear. "Hurry, we probably only have a few minutes."

"What? What do you mean?" She stumbled trying to keep up with his long strides. Her feet, though much better, were still sore.

He immediately slowed and let go of her forearm. His fingers instead entwined with hers as he pulled her toward the door.

Ashley glanced around in confusion. Everyone in the squad room had their backs to her, as if they were purposely avoiding looking her way. Her cheeks grew hot and her stomach clenched into a hard, cold knot.

"What happened while I was in the chief's office? Did Chris tell everyone I'm a thief? Now they all hate me."

Dillon stopped at the door and looked back at his fellow officers. For the first time since the nightmare in the chief's office had begun, he smiled. "No, they don't hate you. They're showing you their solidarity. They're turning a blind eye."

She frowned. "A blind eye?"

His grin widened. "Yep. And now I've got to start my formerly unplanned vacation."

"I don't understand. What are you talking about?"

"We're about to give Special Agent Kent the runaround."

Chapter Ten

Ashley sat on Dillon's bed while he shoved the folders he'd grabbed from his library into a duffel bag that was much like hers, except that his was camouflage-green.

"Are you absolutely sure Chief Thornton is okay with this?" Ashley asked. "I wouldn't want you to lose your job or anything."

He paused in front of her. "Do you remember the chief saying he had a long tradition of cooperating with the feds? Well, trust me, he's *never* cooperated with the feds. He's old-school, resents their interference. Me, I never had a problem with them, until now." He turned and opened another drawer in his dresser.

"So he was speaking some kind of code then? When he talked about turning a blind eye and giving someone the runaround and you going on vacation, he was telling you to take off with me and hide me?"

"Pretty much."

"But isn't that illegal?"

"It violates the spirit of the law but not the letter. Agent Kent never got around to arresting you. And he didn't serve you or anyone else with a subpoena or a warrant. So technically, all we did was have a conversation. I'm now on vacation, and I happened to take you with me. You're a witness in an investigation whose life is in danger until we catch Luther Kennedy. So the chief can argue later that you're just in protective custody."

"Sounds dicey to me. I'd red flag that like crazy in an audit."

He laughed. "Yeah, I probably would, too."

He shoved a thin blanket into the duffel bag and zipped it closed.

"Dillon? Why are you helping me? All those things that man said about me... If it wasn't happening to me, if he'd said that about someone else, I'd believe him. Why are you helping me, and why is the chief helping me?"

He plopped down on the bed beside her, making the mattress bounce.

"Honestly, the chief is probably responding more to Kent's denigration of us country folk than to anything else. He doesn't appreciate city slickers coming in here and acting like we're a bunch of idiots because we talk slow and there's only one red light in town. He's protecting his investigation more than anything else. He'll be pushing Chris and the others to figure out exactly what's going on, hoping to show up the FBI and prove the local yokels can out-investigate the feds."

"I guess that makes a little more sense than blind faith in me, since we basically just met. What about you? Are you helping me because you want to prove Destiny cops are as good investigators as federal ones? I'd appreciate your honesty."

"My honesty?" His gaze slid away from hers and he stared toward the front window, but Ashley didn't think he was seeing anything outside. His gaze was turned more inward, as if he was remembering something. Or someone.

"Honestly, I don't know what's going on, what you're

in the middle of," he finally said, his voice low, halting. "My instincts tell me to trust you, that you're innocent. But the evidence says otherwise. The only thing I'm sure of right now is that you need protection. I'm not going to turn you over to anyone until I'm sure you'll be safe. We're going to get out of here and lie low until everything is sorted out. Once Luther is in custody and the investigation is over, if the evidence shows you're guilty, I'll put you in a cell myself." His gaze slid back to hers. "How's that for honesty?"

She swallowed against the lump in her throat. "I guess I asked for that, didn't I?"

He put his hand beneath her chin and tilted her head up.

"If you're innocent, you've got nothing to fear, not from me or the law, anyway. Okay?"

She pushed his hand away. "Okay."

He frowned and looked as though he was going to add something else, but the squawk of a radio filled the room.

"John Wayne and Daisy Duke, this is Billy the Kid. Come in. Over."

He rolled his eyes and grabbed a small black phone-looking device with an antenna off the top of his dresser. It reminded Ashley of the walkie-talkies she and her siblings played with as children, but the device Dillon was holding looked a lot more sophisticated.

"This is John Wayne," Dillon said. "Over."

"Rosco P. Coltrane is ticked off like you wouldn't believe. And he's smarter than he looks. Boss Hogg advises you to get out of Dodge ASAP."

"Ten four, *Billy Bob.*"

"Ah, negative. This is Billy the Kid. No Billy Bob

here. Estimate you have fifteen minutes, tops, to make your getaway."

Dillon cursed. "Got it. Thanks. Over."

He shoved the walkie-talkie into the side zipper pouch on his duffel bag.

"Was that Chris?" Ashley asked.

"Yep."

"And you understood that?"

"Yep. He said Special Agent Kent figured out I was hiding you and he's ticked about it. He's on his way. He'll be here in fifteen minutes. Chief Thornton told us to get out of here before Kent gets here." He tossed the duffel over his shoulder and grabbed her duffel off the foot of the bed.

"So I'm Daisy Duke?"

He cocked a brow. "Only if you want to be."

She grinned. "Abso-freakin-lutely."

"Horses? We're making our getaway on horses?" She was wearing a pair of borrowed boots, while Dillon and his farm manager, Griffin, saddled Dillon's stallion and a mare. Apparently with the expectation that she and Dillon were actually going to ride the darn things.

Dillon pressed his knee into the mare's side, forcing her to blow out a breath so he could cinch the saddle more tightly. "You have a better idea?"

"Well, yeah. When you moved your car out behind the shed, I figured we were going to head down some private road at the back of your property that no one else knows about."

"Nope, there's no secret road out here. And everyone in Blount County knows my bright red Jeep. We can't risk Kent seeing it since it was parked in front of the police station when he got there. Too obvious."

"And riding a horse isn't?"

"Not where we're going." He narrowed his eyes at her. "You *have* ridden a horse before, haven't you?"

"Sure. When I was fifteen."

"It's like riding a bike, ma'am," Griffin called out. "You'll remember how."

Dillon nodded, as if Griffin had quoted some sage advice. "Plus, Gracie here is an old trail mare. As long as she has a horse in front of her to follow, she won't give you any trouble."

He finished securing Ashley's duffel bag behind the saddle and turned around. "Need a leg up?" He bent down and cupped his hands. "Or are your feet too sore? I could lift you up."

Ashley stiffened. "I can mount all by myself, thank you very much." She put her boot in the stirrup, grabbed the saddle horn and hoisted herself up. She swung her right leg over the mare's back and gently settled into the saddle, all in one quick, smooth motion.

Dillon's brows rose. "I thought you said you hadn't ridden since you were fifteen."

"I haven't. But I might have neglected to mention that I was in a saddle since before I could walk and have so many riding trophies on my mom's mantel the fake-gold paint practically blinds you when you walk into the house."

She expected him to laugh, or accuse her of being a ringer. But instead his expression turned serious.

"Your mom's mantel, huh? Imagine that." He strode to the bay-colored stallion Griffin had finished saddling, the one Dillon had told her he'd named Boomerang. He gracefully and expertly mounted the horse, making Ashley feel like an amateur.

"Nice form," she grudgingly complimented.

He gave her a curt nod.

The two-way radio crackled again. "Billy the Kid calling John Wayne. Over."

Griffin's old, wrinkled face split into a wide grin. "Is that Chris?"

"I'm humoring him," Dillon muttered. He held up the walkie. "Go ahead, Billy. Over."

"Annie Oakley spotted Rosco P. Coltrane headed your way, two minutes out."

A pained look crossed Dillon's face. "Is Annie Oakley someone I know?"

"You see her every day, Mr. Wayne."

"Got it. Tell Annie thanks for the warning. Over." Dillon shoved the radio into a holder he'd strung around the saddle horn in front of him.

"Who's Annie?" Ashley asked.

"I'm guessing Officer Donna Waters. She's the only woman I see every day. Griffin?"

"Yeah, I know, Boss. I never saw either of you."

"That would make it hard to explain my Jeep if anyone looks around. Just tell the truth, that you don't know where we're going. Because you don't."

Griffin nodded and ran to the sliding doors at the back of the barn facing away from the house. He slid one of the tall, heavy doors open, revealing a breathtaking view of the mountains. But separating the barn from those mountains was a deep green, open field.

"Come on," Dillon urged. "Let's go."

Ashley nudged her mount over beside Dillon's. "But there's no cover. Agent Kent will see us if we go that way."

"That's why we're not going that way." He pointed out the door to the right. Acres and acres of tall cornstalks waved in the afternoon breeze. His mouth quirked up in a grin. "Let's see if you earned those riding trophies honestly or not. Try to keep up."

He kicked his heels into Boomerang's side and the stallion took off in a gallop. Before Ashley could do more than blink, he disappeared into the cornfield.

"Keep up. Keep up? I'll show you keep up." She kicked her mount and took off in pursuit.

LUTHER ADJUSTED HIS position on the rocky outcrop in the mountains high above Harmony Haven and trained his binoculars on the FBI agent far below. Special Agent Jason Kent had been a burr in Luther's side for months now. It was kind of nice seeing the agent have so much difficulty for a change.

Kent raised his hands in the air, obviously angry and frustrated as he talked to another man in front of the barn behind the house where Detective Gray and Ashley Parrish had been a few minutes ago. He whirled around and marched to his car parked on the side of the house. A cloud of dust spit up from his wheels as he punched the accelerator and drove back the way he'd come. The FBI agent was too dumb to take a harder look around. If he had, he would have discovered Gray's red Jeep parked behind one of the outbuildings, not visible from the road. Kent hadn't even considered that Gray and Parrish might have gotten away on horseback.

But Luther had no such affliction.

He'd seen them race out of the back of the barn and hightail it into the cornfield. And from his vantage point, he could see all four corners of that same field. All he had to do now was wait.

Sure enough, a few minutes later at the northeast corner, two horses and riders emerged from the waving dried-up stalks, moving at a fast clip toward a cluster of pine trees. Luther fondled the rifle in his hand. Tough shot from here, lots of variables—long distance, wind, heat, the unpredictability of horses who might shy or move sideways at any time. If he missed, he'd alert his prey he was following them. And while killing Gray wouldn't bother him one bit, Gray was riding too close to Parrish to take the shot. He decided the risk wasn't worth it. He needed Parrish alive.

At least for a little while.

He rubbed his aching shoulder. He wasn't sure old Doc Brookes had done his best work with a gun held to his head. But at least he could use his arm again and the doc had given him pain pills to dull the ache. The bullet had only grazed him, so all he'd needed was stitches and disinfectant. Still, it had hurt like the devil. Parrish would pay for that. Once his friend's scheme was done, Parrish would be all his. He'd carve out his pound of flesh.

And *then* he'd kill her.

Chapter Eleven

Dillon locked the cabin door and dropped the duffel bags onto the wood floor at the end of the couch, which—aside from a coffee table—was the only piece of furniture in the small space.

Ashley turned in a slow circle, her lack of enthusiasm evident in the tightening of her mouth, the slump of her shoulders. "Is this your cabin?"

"No. It belongs to a friend. He rarely uses it and told me where the spare key is in case I ever want to use it, which I do, during hunting season."

"Are we staying here tonight?"

"That depends on Rosco P. Coltrane and whether he figures out we're here." He set the radio on the bar that separated the tiny kitchen from the main room of the cabin. "The couch does fold out into a fairly comfortable bed if we stay. And there's a bathroom with a shower behind that door over there. But that's pretty much it."

She plopped down on the couch. "What do we do now?"

"I'll unsaddle the horses and set them up on lunge lines so they can graze. After that, I figure we can put our heads together and discuss the case. I'm going to call Chris and see if he can give me more details on what Kent thinks he has against you. Sound good?"

"I suppose. Do you need help with the horses?"

"I've got it. It'll only take me a few minutes. Lock the door behind me."

ASHLEY PULLED HER feet up and sat cross-legged on the couch, staring down at the mass of paper and folders Dillon had spread out before them on the coffee table. He sat beside her, making lists, grilling her with questions.

He glanced at her legs. "You okay? Do your feet hurt? I can put more salve and fresh bandages on them."

"They don't hurt. Just shifting position."

He cocked his head and studied one of the two-columned lists he'd just finished. "From what you've told me, we should be able to prove you were in completely different states at the time three of these audits Kent told us about were performed. I'll get Chris to check out the hotel records and dates."

"That's a good thing, right? Doesn't that give me an alibi?"

He tapped his pen. "Maybe. Can you audit someone long-distance, without physically going to their company?"

"Yes, in theory. It's frowned upon, not recommended. And I've certainly never done it."

"But it can be done."

Her shoulders slumped. "Yes. It can."

"Then we still have no proof that you weren't involved in this scam." He picked up the list of companies he'd written down during his talk with Chris on the phone earlier. "It's interesting that whoever pretended to be you performed audits on a lot of companies they didn't embezzle from."

"Why is that interesting? It just shows the audits didn't yield discrepancies the fake Ashley Parrish could use to blackmail someone, right? That is, if we buy what Special Agent Kent said about what was happening."

"True." He leafed through one of the folders and frowned. He pulled another one toward him and compared some pages from each.

Ashley leaned forward. "Did you find something else?"

"More like a new avenue of questions."

She plopped back against the couch cushions. "Great. More questions. Go ahead. Ask."

He turned to face her, resting one arm on the back of the couch. "I think we're going about this all wrong. We've been focusing on proving you're innocent instead of trying to figure out who's guilty. Let's assume you're innocent and move from there."

"Gee. Thanks."

He smiled. "If this is a scheme, which we're assuming, and someone stole your identity, they're passing themselves off as a real auditor. The only red flags being raised are that after the audits are complete, money goes missing. What kind of person could fake an audit that passes muster, that no one complains about?"

Ashley blinked as the obvious conclusion dawned on her. "They have to be a real auditor, a CPA, or at least have been educated as one."

"I agree." He grabbed a notebook and pen off the table and started a new list. The first bullet said "Auditor, or trained as one."

"Our bad guy also knows your Social Security number, and enough personal information to have faked a convincing-looking website under your name. Tell me about the picture Kent said came from that website. Are you sure you've never seen it before?"

"Pretty sure. I mean, I don't live near my family anymore. It's not like I get my picture taken very often."

"Where is your family?"

"Sweetwater."

"Tennessee, just outside Chattanooga?"

"That's it."

"Far enough to keep your family from dropping in unexpectedly, but not so far you can't go home if you need to?"

"Am I that easy to figure out?"

"No." His mouth quirked sardonically. "You're just a lot like me. I did the same thing. Left home the day I graduated high school, went away to college to put some distance between me and my family. I never intended to come back."

"But you did. You were going to be a vet, right? What happened?"

His smile faded. "Life happened. Let's get back to the case. I think it's logical to assume that whoever stole your identity knows you very well—well enough to be able to take a picture of you without you thinking anything about it, someone who would have access to your personal papers so they could find your Social Security number and other personal information, someone who was trained as an auditor." He added a bullet item to his list.

"I also suspect they must not have been very successful as an auditor in their own right, or they wouldn't have tried to use your reputation and identity to get clients. As we discussed earlier, a lot of the audits this person performed didn't raise any red flags with the FBI, and weren't precursors to embezzlement. That kind of strikes me as someone who was trying to make a living as an auditor but couldn't manage to get clients off their own reputation. So they used your reputation to get a foot in the door. The embezzling came later." He wrote another entry on his list.

"To get around using your identity, this person performed audits remotely. That strikes me as a way for them to get around the whole fake-website thing."

Ashley frowned. "I don't understand."

"If they used your name and their picture, they couldn't blame you later, or frame you, really, if things went bad. To cover themselves, they used your picture. But by doing that, they forced themselves to have to do the audits long-distance, so none of their clients actually saw them."

"But what about Mrs. Dunlop? She supposedly saw the auditor, and pointed at me and said I was the one who'd worked on the audit."

He shook his head. "I'm not sure I agree with that statement. All Mrs. Dunlop said was that you were the woman who'd killed her husband. She never once said she'd actually seen you in person. Maybe Kent jumped the gun on that and gave too much credence to a grieving widow who blamed you for her husband's death. It wouldn't be the first time a witness stretched the truth when they believed the person they were identifying was really guilty."

"Well, that's kind of a scary thought."

"That's one of many reasons cops don't rely solely on eyewitness testimony. Even without a motive to lie, a witness often truly believes in their testimony, even if their testimony is dead wrong. Eyewitness accounts are notoriously inaccurate. It's human nature not to remember a face well enough to later make a positive ID, especially after seeing other pictures of that person."

He passed her the list he'd made. "Is there anyone in your life, or anyone you've ever met in the past, maybe even someone you considered to be a friend, who meets all that criteria? Someone who knows what client accounts you take so they don't end up approaching the same clients? Someone who knows where you'll be at any given time? Someone you may trust?"

A sick feeling settled in the pit of Ashley's stomach. "Oh, my God."

Dillon narrowed his eyes. "You think you have a suspect?"

She nodded and handed the legal pad back to him. "There's only one person I can think of who knows me that well. She only studied accounting in college after I started studying it. She struggled all the way through, barely passing, no matter how much I tried to help her. And later, when my company took off, she was still struggling to get her first client." She pressed her hand to her throat. "She moved away a year and a half ago, saying she needed a new start. And suddenly she calls me to tell me *her* business is taking off. She's getting clients now and finally making a good living as an auditor. I was surprised, but happy for her. And she started going on trips and cruises, things she never could have afforded in the past."

Dillon reached for her hand. "Ashley, who is she?"

She swallowed hard, and squeezed her eyes shut. "My best friend since kindergarten, the same woman who called you the night I was abducted. Lauren Wilkes."

THE THEORY THAT her best friend had perpetrated such an awful fraud against Ashley was enough to make sleep nearly impossible for her. But surprisingly, it wasn't thoughts of Lauren's possible betrayal that were keeping her awake.

It was the fact that she was sharing a bed with Dillon.

Sleeping with him should have been awkward because they'd only known each other for a couple of days. And it *was* awkward, but for an entirely different reason. It was awkward because it *should* have felt wrong, but it felt totally…*right*. And if Ashley was certain he would welcome her interest in him, she'd be in his arms right now.

She wanted him, desperately. She wanted to reach out and slide her fingers over his skin, feel his muscles bunch beneath her touch. She wanted to explore the fascinating angles of his face, experience the raspy feel of his stubble gently abrading her skin as he explored her body. And more than anything right now, she wanted to feel him inside her, loving her, and for a little while at least, making her forget all her troubles.

Her skin grew heated and her fingers ached from clenching them together to keep from reaching for him. What was wrong with her? She'd never yearned for a man's touch like this. What was it about Dillon that made her feel so…out of control? Maybe a cold shower was what she needed. Anything would be better than this torture.

She flipped back the covers and started to get up.

Dillon's strong arm immediately wrapped around her waist, trapping her, pushing her back down. The bed dipped as he rose above her, leaned over her. The moonlight filtering through the thin curtains revealed far too much of his glorious body, naked from the waist up, and had her digging her nails into her palms to stop from reaching for him.

"What's wrong? Did you hear something outside?" He turned his face toward the window, as if to listen for whatever had disturbed her.

"No," she whispered. "I didn't hear anything. I... couldn't sleep." As if of their own will, her hands reached up and feathered across the stubble on his jaw.

He sucked in a breath, but didn't pull away.

Feeling as if she'd been granted a treasure, a magical moment to satisfy her curiosity, she continued her exploration. She slid her hungry fingers down the side of his neck, lower, over the hard contours of his chest, lower still, to the tautness of his stomach muscles, which jumped beneath her touch. She hesitated, her gaze locked with his, waiting, wondering what he would do if she moved her hands...lower.

"Don't stop now," he whispered, his voice ragged, deeper than usual.

Those three words were the key that unlocked a floodgate of pent-up frustration and emotion. Ashley didn't hesitate again. She slid her hands down to the waistband of the jeans he'd worn to bed, then groaned in frustration when she couldn't get past that barrier. She plucked at the top button, but her hands were shaking so hard she couldn't get it undone.

Dillon laughed and sat back, his thighs trapping hers as he made quick work of the button and zipper. He rolled to the side and lifted his hips to shuck off his pants and underwear. Ashley followed, her eager fingers searching for their prize.

He sucked in a sharp breath when she wrapped her hands around him.

"Ashley, wait, not so fast. We have plenty of—" He arched off the bed when her mouth covered him. His hands fisted in her hair and he shuddered beneath her.

She couldn't believe how perfect he was, how hot and hard. He must have been lying awake thinking of her like she'd been thinking of him.

She couldn't seem to get enough of him—his smell, his heat, his delicious salty taste. He shuddered again and she could feel he was close. Suddenly he bent down and wrapped his arms beneath hers and pulled her off him. She cursed in frustration and reached for him again.

He gave a pained laugh and pulled her hand away, then rolled and trapped her beneath him. He grabbed her wrists in a viselike grip and pulled them up above her head.

"If you don't stop," he said, his voice hoarse, "I'm going to disgrace myself like a randy teenager. Slow. Down."

"But I want—"

"So do I. But I want to last. I want to make this good for you, too."

He reached down and pulled her shirt off over her head, then expertly removed her jeans and panties until she was naked, too. Then he covered her with his body and captured her lips with his in an open-mouthed, ravenous kiss she felt all the way to her toes.

Every stroke of his tongue against hers sent a wave of heat straight to her belly. She was so ready for him she thought she might die if he didn't take her right then. She was about to demand he do so when he slid down, his stubble against her breasts her only warning before he sucked her nipple into his mouth.

She cried out and bucked beneath him, but he was unmerciful in his assault on her senses. He lavished both her breasts with careful attention until she was aching with the pleasure-pain of it. And then he leaned up until his hot breath washed over her neck.

"My turn," he breathed.

She shivered at his dark promise, and then he slid down her body and fastened his mouth on the very core of her. Her climax was immediate, an explosion of pleasure that flared across every nerve ending in her body, bowing her spine off the bed. He continued to explore and worship her with his mouth and tongue until she begged him to stop.

He kissed her there once, twice, before pulling away. The bed creaked and bounced as he leaned over and reached for something.

"What are you doing," she whispered. "Come back to me. I want—"

"Not half as much as I want, believe me. But I have to protect you."

She lifted her head and saw he'd grabbed his wallet. The moonlight glinted off the foil packet in his hand and she dropped her head back on the pillow. Thank goodness one of them had stopped to think about protection. She'd been far too gone to care.

Before her heart had even slowed from her climax he was back, his sweat-slicked skin sliding against hers as he trapped her mouth again for another earth-shattering, wet kiss. The length of him rubbed against her thigh and she whimpered against him. She sucked his tongue and he groaned.

He reached down between them and positioned himself at her entrance, and then he pushed himself into her, slowly, stretching her, filling her, until she whimpered against him and drew her knees up, desperate to pull him all the way inside.

He withdrew again, then pushed deeper, withdrew,

then deeper still, his every movement so exquisite, so delicious it was the sweetest form of torture.

"What are you doing to me, Dillon," she gasped.

"I think…it's…the other way…around," he rasped, his breath coming in choppy pants as he thrust into her over and over. "You make me…burn."

He buried his face in her hair and his mouth did sinful things to the side of her neck. Impossibly, he brought her even higher and higher, her every nerve ending centered on where they were joined.

The first fluttering of her climax began deep in her belly. She strained against him and he clamped his mouth down on hers, ravenous, devouring her whimpers as he pumped into her so deeply she cried out and exploded around him. He thrust again, once, twice, his entire body stiffening against her as his own climax claimed him.

He collapsed on top of her, crushing her into the mattress. But she didn't mind. They could have lain there forever with their limbs entwined and she wouldn't have ever wanted to move—except that she couldn't breathe.

"Dillon, I can't catch my breath."

"Me, either. You wore me out."

"Dillon!"

He laughed and pushed himself up on his forearms. He gave her a sleepy kiss, then flopped onto his back. "That was…"

"Incredible?"

"Amazing. Hot. Mind-blowing."

"Mind-blowing? Really?"

"Really," he mumbled, sounding as if he were drugged. "Now scoot over here and let's get some sleep."

She snuggled up against him, feeling content, secure.

"I can honestly say you're the best thing that's happened to me since I came to Destiny."

He chuckled and rubbed his hand up and down her bare back. "Considering everything that's happened to you so far, I'm not sure that's a compliment."

"Oh, it is. Before you, I could count on one hand the things I liked about small towns. I grew up in one. Without much to do except explore caves in the woods or make mazes in cornfields. I detest everything about them." She shivered dramatically. "Everything except you, of course. When I go back to Nashville you're the one memory I'll treasure from my time here."

His hand stilled on her back. "What exactly do you detest about small towns?"

She drew small circles in the light matting of hair on his chest. "The way everyone knows your business. I couldn't stand the lack of privacy, and the way gossip spreads so fast. In the city, I can do whatever I want and no one cares."

"Sounds like a lonely way to live."

"I have friends. They just don't butt into my personal business, or tell my parents every time I sneeze." She yawned and closed her eyes, drifting off to sleep with a smile on her face.

DILLON LAY AWAKE long after Ashley's deep breathing turned into soft snores. For a few minutes after loving her, he'd held an idyllic picture in his head, of Ashley staying in Destiny with him and exploring the attraction between them long after this case was resolved.

For a moment he'd forgotten how fragile life was, and how long it had taken him to climb out of the dark pit he'd fallen into after his sister died. He'd barely survived her loss, and knew that it would be agony experiencing that type of loss again when his parents eventually died, or his friends. There was nothing he could do to protect himself against that kind of hurt from the people he already knew, but he'd vowed not to let anyone else close enough to him to make him even more vulnerable.

Until he'd met Ashley, he'd kept his romantic relationships casual, without any promises or hope for something deep and lasting. He preferred it that way. But then he'd held Ashley in his arms and experienced a soul-shattering closeness he'd never felt with any other lover. And suddenly he was thinking about the long-term possibilities of a life he'd never dreamed he'd want.

But that brief glimpse of forever was now a bitter taste in his mouth. He and Ashley didn't want the same things in life. That was clear. He treasured living in a small town, and she despised that type of life. What she thought of as lack of privacy, he thought of as caring and concern. Everyone in Destiny was family to him, and he couldn't imagine any other kind of life.

He sighed and feathered his hands across her satiny-smooth skin, imprinting the way she felt against him in his memory, because he knew he'd never hold her like this again.

Chapter Twelve

After using the walkie-talkie to talk to Chris early the next morning to update him on their theory about Lauren Wilkes, Dillon led Ashley out on horseback before the sun came up. He told her it was because he didn't want to stay in one place too long, in case Iceman was actively looking for her. But really, he didn't expect anyone to find them up in the foothills of the Smokies, not this far from the farm. On horseback he had an excuse not to talk to her. Because really, what else was there to say?

His plan was to head southeast toward Walland because there was plenty of tree cover that way and when that thinned out, more cornfields to hide in. Once they put enough distance between them and Destiny, he'd call in a favor and have another friend put them up somewhere. Hopefully by then Chris would have convinced Special Agent Kent that Ashley wasn't guilty, and he would have found the evidence to corroborate their theory. Even better, if they caught Iceman by then, Ashley would be safe and could do what she wanted most.

To go home, leaving Destiny, and Dillon, far behind.

He turned in the saddle to check on her. But as expected she was hot on his tail, easily keeping up. She was an expert horsewoman. Too bad she'd decided to give up that part of her life. He couldn't imagine a life without horses in it. Riding was relaxing, a way to get away from anything bothering him. And sometimes, if he rode long enough and hard enough, he could almost escape the past.

The sound of hooves clattering against stones echoed up ahead. Dillon swore and clawed for his gun, but he was too late. The silhouette of a man sitting on a horse, aiming a rifle directly at him, sat squarely in their way, fifty yards ahead.

Dillon hauled back on the reins and turned his stallion sideways to block Ashley. Her mare hop-skipped to a stop right behind him.

"Hands up where I can see them," the man up ahead called out, his face still in shadow with the sun behind him.

"What do we do now?" Ashley whispered, holding her hands up.

"I'll let you know once I figure that out." He swore again and held his hands up in the air.

"Toss the gun," the man yelled.

Dillon hesitated.

The man in shadows jerked his gun up toward the sky and the bark of the rifle filled the air.

Dillon's stallion reared up and snorted, violently tossing his head, trying to get the bit between his teeth, fighting the reins. Dillon spoke to the horse in low tones to settle him down, and glanced back at Ashley. Her mare's eyes rolled white with fear but Ashley was keeping her under control.

"Toss the gun," the man repeated.

This time Dillon didn't hesitate. He removed the clip from his pistol and ejected the loaded round before tossing it into the bushes so it wouldn't accidentally fire when he threw it down.

"All right. The gun is gone. What do you want, Kennedy?"

"I'm not Kennedy."

The man urged his horse forward and tilted the rifle so it was pointing up at the sky. As his face passed from shadow to light, Dillon let loose a string of curses his mother would have tanned his hide over. Ashley's reaction was a bit less dramatic, but her gasp of surprise was loud enough for him to hear it. But when another figure rode out of the shadows, Dillon cursed even harder.

"*Et tu, Brute?* Did he happen to give you thirty pieces of silver, too?"

"I think you're mixing metaphors," Ashley whispered.

Dillon half turned in his saddle and gave her an incredulous look.

She shrugged. "Just saying."

He turned back around as Griffin and Special Agent Kent stopped a few feet away.

Griffin reddened. "Sorry, boss. He threatened to arrest me if I didn't help him track you up into the mountains."

Dillon sighed heavily. "It's okay. Forget it. Kent, what kind of dangerous game are you playing? Firing a gun around horses is asking for trouble."

"No game. I wanted to make sure I wouldn't get shot. That's what fugitives do when they're trapped. They shoot people."

Ashley urged her mare up beside Boomerang. "We're not fugitives," she said. "Dillon's on vacation and I'm a protected witness."

Dillon grinned. "Yeah. What she said."

"Now who's playing games?" Kent demanded. "That stunt you pulled back at the station only managed to put Miss Parrish in more danger. Kennedy is still out there somewhere and he's not the type to stop until he gets what he wants. You two need to come back with me right now so we can sort all this out."

"Why, so you can arrest me? Put me in jail for something I didn't do?" Ashley demanded.

"If putting you in jail will keep you safe, then yes. That's exactly what I'll do."

"Ashley isn't guilty," Dillon insisted. "Someone stole her identity, and we believe we know who that might be."

"Let me guess. Lauren Wilkes?"

"You knew?" Dillon demanded. "The whole time?"

"No. I suspected. But my suspicions were confirmed only a couple of hours ago. I've got an entire team looking into this case back in Knoxville and they haven't let up since day one. When they got a lead late yesterday that Wilkes might be involved, they stayed on it until they got proof. They called me and I knew I needed to find you, fast, and get Miss Parrish in protective custody."

"What kind of proof are you talking about?" Ashley asked, her voice shaky.

Dillon held his left hand out and she immediately entwined her fingers with his. Kent's gaze followed that action, his brows rising, but Dillon didn't care. Ashley had been through hell these past few days, and finding out her childhood friend had betrayed her so horribly had to be tearing her apart. If holding her hand helped her, so be it.

Griffin sat on his horse slightly back from Kent, his eyes wide with confusion.

"Griffin, go back to the farm," Dillon urged him. "Everything is okay. I'll call you later, all right?"

His face relaxed in relief. "Okay, Boss." A swift kick on the side of his horse and he was trotting back toward the farm.

"What kind of proof do you have against Lauren?" Ashley repeated, her voice impatient this time.

"We followed the money—some of it, anyway. We have bank security camera footage proving she used the Ashley Parrish identity to withdraw a large amount of money. Unfortunately, most of the money is still unaccounted for. We'd very much like to talk to Miss Wilkes, but she's disappeared."

"She went on a cruise to Jamaica."

Dillon squeezed her hand. "Honey, I think we both know she didn't. She's been lying to you for a long time."

Ashley's face fell and she looked away.

"So what's it going to take?" Kent asked. "Are you two coming back with me of your own free will, John Wayne and Daisy Duke? Or do I have to get a posse together?"

Dillon laughed. "You heard about that, huh?"

"Billy the Kid isn't very good at lying. He caved quicker than Griffin did."

"You can't find good help these days."

Kent smiled. "Now that you sent my trail guide away, I'm a bit at your mercy. How do we get back to town?"

"Going back to Harmony Haven is the shortest way."

"Lead on, then. I'll follow—"

A loud bang echoed through the trees.

Kent flew off his horse as if a battering ram had hit him in the side.

Ashley screamed.

"Go, go, go!" Dillon yelled. He slapped the mare's

rump, sending her at a full gallop into the cover of trees. He kicked his stallion and galloped after her just as another rifle boom exploded through the hills.

"WE HAVE TO go back for him," Ashley yelled as she tried to pull her mare's reins out of Dillon's grip.

"He's dead. Stop fighting me. We have to get out of here." He maneuvered his horse over a fallen log, wincing when his arm felt as though it was about to come out of its socket from pulling the mare's reins behind him.

Ashley kicked her mare again, trying to pull the reins out of Dillon's hand. "You don't know that he's dead. We can't just leave him there. Oh, my God. Oh, my God."

Dillon jerked both horses to a stop. He'd finally realized there was no reasoning with Ashley right now. She was in hysterics. He couldn't blame her. She was in denial over what they'd both seen, and he wished he could somehow block the memory out, too. But it would be a long time before he forgot the sight of what that gunshot had done. No one could survive a shot like that to the head. He didn't need to turn around to confirm that.

His heart ached for the terror Ashley was feeling, but he couldn't take the time to try to soothe her. Iceman, or whoever had fired those shots, could catch up to them any second. Dillon leaned over and swept Ashley off her horse and into his arms. He settled her on his lap, draping her thighs over his, and wrapped one arm around her waist. He dropped the mare's reins, leaving her to find her own way back to the farm, and kicked the stallion into a fast canter through the woods.

IT HAD BEEN a couple of hours since Dillon had heard any sounds of pursuit, but it had also been hours since they'd seen any signs of civilization. His walkie-talkie was out of range to reach Chris, his phone had zero bars of service, and they were as deep into the mountains as he dared to go at this time of day. In a few more hours the sun would set, plunging even these foothills of the Smokies into much colder temperatures. With half their supplies gone with the mare, not to mention his gun, because Kent had made him toss it, they weren't prepared for staying the night up here. He had to get them out of the mountains and get help.

He turned his horse as close to due east as he could judge by the position of the sun and kicked him into a trot. Ashley didn't say anything. She hadn't spoken since he'd yanked her onto the saddle with him.

"Ashley," he whispered close to her ear, "I'm heading back toward town now. If I've got my bearings right, we'll end up right at my parents' farm. We can hunker down there and call for backup. We're going to be okay. Everything's going to be okay."

He waited, but when she didn't say anything, he sighed and leaned back.

She mumbled something.

He leaned back down. "What did you say?"

"We're going to your parents' house?"

"Yes. They're out of town, visiting—"

"Your brother. In Montana. I remember."

When she didn't say anything else, he straightened again. Relief swept through him that she was finally talking again, even if she wasn't saying much.

ASHLEY BLINKED AND looked down at Dillon's outstretched hands.

"Slide off the horse and I'll catch you."

Her mind was a fog and she felt as though she was waking from a horrible nightmare. Only she knew the nightmare was real. Special Agent Jason Kent had been murdered, brutally and horribly murdered, right in front of her. She shivered and looked around.

She was sitting on top of Dillon's stallion and he was standing below her, urging her to dismount. She surveyed where they were. They'd made it out of the foothills and were at the edge of another endless field of dried-up stalks of corn, ready for harvest. In the distance, the only sign of life was someone slowly driving an enormous combine in the middle of the field, perhaps two hundred yards away.

"Ashley, hurry. If Iceman's still on our trail, we're totally exposed now. We need to get out of his line of sight."

She mentally chastised herself for hesitating and putting him in danger. She immediately swung her leg over the back of the stallion. Dillon's hands came up around her waist and gently lowered her to her feet.

"I'm sorry. I know I totally checked out back there. I'm okay now."

He kissed her forehead. "Glad to have you back." He moved past her and yanked the duffel bag down from the back of the saddle. Then he loosely secured the reins around the horn and slapped the stallion's flank. The horse whinnied but didn't need further encouragement. He took off in a gallop back toward the foothills.

"Why did you let him go?"

"We're close to my parents' house now, just a hundred yards or so, at the end of the cornfield. I'm counting on Boomerang's training and homing instinct to get him back to Harmony Haven. That could buy us some time by creating another trail in the opposite direction from where we are."

He took her hand in his and tugged her into the edge

of the cornfield until the mountains fell away and all she could see was corn.

"I hope you're right, and Iceman follows the other trail."

"Me, too."

In a few minutes they emerged from the cornfield and climbed through the rails of a weathered gray wooden fence. A small gray-and-white wooden house perched fifty yards away, with graceful oaks leaning over it. A faded porch swing hung from a chain out front. An old tire moved in the breeze at the end of a rope hanging from one of the oak trees. And nestled a hundred yards behind the house was a pond with a little fountain in the middle.

"Reminds me of *my* parents' home, in Sweetwater. Minus the fountain," she said as they hurried to the front porch and paused at the door.

"Good memories?"

She hesitated, then smiled. "Yes. Good memories."

He ran his hand on top of the doorframe and pulled down a key and unlocked the door.

"I wouldn't dare keep a key there in the city," she said.

"I tell them all the time not to, but Dad's always losing his keys and Mom got tired of always calling me to come let them in. Half the windows are probably unlocked, too." He held the door open for her to enter the kitchen and locked the door behind them. "Call nine-one-one." He pointed to the phone hanging on the kitchen wall. "Tell them what happened to Special Agent Kent, and tell them to get a unit out to my parents' house. I'll check all the locks and get my father's gun."

"Wait, what's your parents' address?"

He grinned. "You don't need it. Everyone knows

where they live." He hurried through an archway into the adjacent family room.

Ashley made the call, her hands tightening around the phone as she watched him checking the sliding glass doors and windows in the next room before disappearing down a long, dark hallway.

When she hung up, she went down the hall and found a bathroom. She heard Dillon's footsteps upstairs. He was nothing if not thorough. She couldn't imagine anyone bothering to climb one of the oak trees surrounding the house to come in through one of the upstairs windows. But then again, after everything that had happened, she didn't mind him being extra careful.

She headed back into the family room, which boasted an eclectic mix of furnishings. An antique hutch filled with beautiful china sat next to a rather impressive collection of liquor bottles. She had to smile at that. A modern, dark brown leather recliner sat next to a worn couch with a faded blue floral pattern. The little decorative oak tables sprinkled around the room were covered with picture frames. But it was the mantel above the stone fireplace that held her attention. Her mother's collection of riding trophies was sparse in comparison to the awards marching across Dillon's parents' mantel.

She quickly realized there was organization to the chaos. The trophies on the left were mainly for football and all of them had the name Colton Gray on them, obviously Dillon's brother. In the middle were more football trophies and quite a few swim awards and ribbons with Dillon's name on them. That explained why he'd managed to swim through the storm-swollen river to save her on Cooper's Bluff.

When she checked out the last group of knickknacks,

she blinked in surprise. Horse-riding trophies competed with a healthy number of gymnastics awards. She read the name engraved on one of the little gold plates— Harmony Gray. So that was who the farm was named after, Dillon's sister. Ashley couldn't resist picking up a heart-shaped gold locket leaning against a plaque. She worked the delicate catch and opened it to reveal a picture of two young boys and a girl, obviously siblings, on the left side of the locket, and a picture of an older couple on the right that had to be Dillon's parents.

Dillon stepped into the room, his ever-present smile fading when he saw what she held.

Ashley had a feeling she'd just intruded into something private, but she couldn't stop herself from asking the obvious questions. "You have a sister named Harmony? You named your farm after her?"

He took the locket from her and set it back on the mantel, carefully adjusting the angle as if its exact placement mattered. When he looked back at her, there was none of the usual warmth in his expression and his eyes had turned cold. "*Had* a sister. Past tense."

He started to turn away but she put her arm on his, stopping him.

"Tell me about her."

"We don't have time."

His cold tone had her jerking her hand back.

He sighed heavily. "I'm sorry. It's just that…everyone around here knows about Harmony, so they don't ask, they never talk about her."

"I didn't mean to pry. Okay, maybe I did, a little. I was curious, but I didn't mean to open any old wounds."

He stared down at her, his expression softening. "I know. Come on. I'm going to get my dad's gun out of his safe."

They went back down the long hall into the last room on the right. A desk along the far wall held a sewing machine and an assortment of material and threads. Bolts of fabric lined racks on another wall.

"Your dad sews?" Ashley teased.

Dillon chuckled. "Not the last time I checked. Mom makes quilts and sells them to tourists at the flea market. She doesn't need the money, but since she's given nearly everyone in Destiny at least two quilts each over the years, she had to find someone else to give them to. Keeps her busy and happy."

He lowered himself to his knees on the tile floor in the middle of the room and pulled back a small rectangular rug to expose a trap door. He pulled it open to reveal a safe with a combination lock. The lock clicked and the safe opened. Dillon reached inside.

A whisper of sound had both of them turning around. Dillon threw his hands up just as Iceman swung one of the heavy trophies from the mantel at Dillon's head. Blood splattered from a gash in Dillon's scalp.

"Run, Ashley," he yelled as he warded off another crushing blow. The gun in his hand was useless, since it had a trigger lock and he hadn't had time to unlock it.

Ashley desperately looked around the room for something to use to help Dillon. But other than the sewing machine, which was too heavy to pick up, the hardest things in the room were the bolts of cloth.

Iceman swung the trophy again.

Dillon rolled out of the way just in time and Iceman fell to the ground. Dillon jumped to his feet and ran toward the other man, ready to tackle him. Iceman yanked a pistol out of his belt and pointed it up at Dillon's head, stopping him in his tracks.

The faint whine of sirens sounded in the distance.

"Looks like the cavalry is on their way." Iceman laughed. "Looks like they're too late." He steadied his gun.

Dillon lunged toward him.

The gun went off, sounding deafening in the small space.

Dillon fell to the floor, his eyes closed, blood pooling underneath his head.

Ashley screamed and dropped to her knees beside him. "Dillon, oh, my God, Dillon." She reached for him, but Iceman jerked her back. He grabbed her by her hair and dragged her out into the hall.

Ashley flailed her hands up, trying to stop the horrible burning pain in her scalp. She kicked her feet and tried to rake her nails down his arms. He stopped halfway down the hall and slapped her so hard she flew against the wall and fell to the floor.

She expected Iceman to backhand her again. When he didn't, she shoved her hair out of her eyes. The door to the antique hutch hung open, and Iceman stood in the middle of the family room pouring the contents of one of the bottles onto the area rug. The smell of alcohol hit her eyes, making them sting. What was he doing?

She braced her hands on the floor and wobbled to her feet.

A whoosh of heat and light had her flattening against the wall in shock. Oh, dear God, no. Iceman had set the rug on fire. The flames quickly moved to the couch and consumed the delicate cloth. Ashley turned and ran back down the hallway. If there was any chance Dillon was still alive, he was about to burn to death. She couldn't let that happen.

Rough hands closed around her waist and jerked her up into the air.

"No, let me go," she screamed.

Iceman ignored her struggles and ran with her down the hall, away from Dillon.

"You can't leave him here! He'll die!"

He threw her over his shoulder. When he reached the family room, he had to swerve back toward the fireplace to get around a chair that was on fire. Ashley flailed her hands out, trying to grab something to stop him, but all she managed to do was pull half the trophies off the mantel. Something small hit her hand and she grabbed it, her fingers closing around it as Iceman twisted and ran through the kitchen and outside. The back of a commercial-looking white van was a dark open maw. He pitched her like a sack of hay into the back and slammed the doors.

She cried out when her head slammed against the metal floor. She immediately pushed herself to her knees. When she saw what she'd grabbed off the mantel, she shoved it into her jeans pocket and scrambled toward the double doors at the back of the van. She jerked the handle. Nothing happened. She tried again, and again.

"Open the doors," she cried. "Please, you can't leave him in there! Dillon, Dillon!"

"It's no use. He locked it from the outside. There's no way out."

Ashley whirled around at the familiar-sounding voice just as the van took off, slamming her against the closed doors. She fell to the floor again and slammed her fist against the floor in frustration.

"I'm so sorry," the voice said again. "I never meant for this to happen. I'm so sorry, Ash."

She shoved her hair out of her face and looked into the tortured gaze of Lauren Wilkes.

Chapter Thirteen

Ashley blinked at Lauren, stunned to see her there. But when Lauren reached for her, Ashley shoved her out of the way and turned back to the doors. She put every ounce of strength she had into twisting and pulling at the handle. She fought the rocking motion of the van to keep her balance and slammed her body against the doors over and over. The doors didn't budge. The van kept barreling down the road.

And behind them, even though she couldn't see it, fire was greedily consuming the house where Dillon lay unconscious—or worse—on the floor.

A keening sound whistled between her teeth and she slid to the floor, her entire body racked with sobs.

Please, if there's any mercy in the world, let Dillon die before the fire reaches him. Please don't let him burn.

The sound of sirens rose loud in the air, closer, closer.

The van suddenly slowed, as if the driver didn't want to attract attention. Ashley didn't want the police to notice the van, either. If there was any hope of Dillon surviving, the police needed to reach the house as soon as possible.

Don't stop, don't stop. Keep going to the house!

One of her prayers was finally answered. The sirens didn't stop. Instead, they zoomed past, fading in the distance in the direction where the van had just come from.

"Ash?"

She drew great gulping breaths, then slowly straightened and leaned back against the side of the van and looked at her...friend? Enemy?

"Is it true?" she demanded. "Did you steal my identity and embezzle money?"

Lauren's gaze fell. "I...I was desperate. I couldn't pay the bills. I was about to be evicted. All I wanted was a chance to get some experience on my résumé, but my grades held me back. No one would hire me. It started out as one gig, just so I could eat. You have to understand. I didn't mean any harm."

"You didn't mean any harm? People have died! All because you were too proud to go home and ask your friends and family for help? Seriously? How many more people are going to die because of your selfishness?"

The stricken look on Lauren's face sent an automatic tug of guilt through Ashley, but she ruthlessly forced it away. Dillon didn't deserve to die because of Lauren's choices, and Lauren deserved no pity from her.

"I never... I didn't think anyone would get hurt or I never would have done it. It was so easy, and for the first time in my life I had money to buy nice clothes, go to dinner at a fancy restaurant, take trips. I know I was wrong, but it was like a snowball rolling downhill once it started. And then...I met David. We fell in love." A single tear ran down her cheek. "I was going to stop. We were going to run away together. And then they killed him." Her voice broke on a sob and she covered her face with her hands.

"David? Who's David?"

Lauren sniffled and wiped her tears. "David Dunlop. He was one of Todd Dunlop's sons. When I audited Dunlop Enterprises, I realized David was already taking money, so I...I threatened him, like I did the others, so he would give me some money. But he understood me like no one else ever has. His father was mean and cruel and made David beg for every cent even though his father was a billionaire. It was wrong how he treated David. We fell in love and made our plan, one big score and we'd get out. But his father grew suspicious and he sent Luther to investigate. Two days later, David died. The police said it was just a car crash, but Luther bragged about it to me, how he forced David off the road and he ran into a tree."

She wiped at her tears again. "Luther said I was next if I didn't give him the money David and I had taken." Her tear-bright gaze raised to Ashley's. "But I didn't have the account numbers or any way to access them. David was going to give me the account numbers, but he died before he could."

The van made another slow turn, as if the driver was making doubly sure no one would notice him or have any reason to be suspicious. It bounced and rocked on its springs, slowing even more as it made its way down what felt like a dirt road.

Lauren squeezed her hands together in her lap. "Ash, I'm so sorry. Luther threatened to kill me. You have to understand. I had to buy some time while I tried to figure a way out of this mess. I never dreamed that he would..." She squeezed her eyes shut and shook her head. "Please forgive me."

"Why do you keep apologizing to me?" The van stopped, its brakes squeaking.

A panicked look swept across Lauren's face.

"Where are we?" Ashley demanded. "What have you done?"

Lauren suddenly grabbed Ashley by the shoulders. "Listen to me. I told Luther you were in on everything with me. I told him that you had the access information for the accounts. He expects you to be able to wire the money to his account."

"What? Why? Why did you tell them that?"

Footsteps crunched outside. The mumble of low voices sounded through the door.

"You have to pretend you can access the account, Ash. You have to buy us some more time. If you can't bluff them, we're both going to die."

Ashley's stomach sank. Her mind raced, trying to absorb everything Lauren had said. What was she going to do?

A metallic noise sounded outside. The handle flipped down and the door jerked open.

Iceman stood in the opening, and he wasn't alone. Two men flanked him. All three of them wore large guns holstered on their hips. Behind the van, two more men sat in a forest-green sedan. And they were all staring at her.

"End of the road, ladies," Iceman growled. "Someone had better tell me how to get my money or you both die." He drew his gun and pointed it directly at Ashley. "I'm going to count to three, and then you either tell me what I need to know or I put a bullet in your brain."

No, no, no, what was she supposed to do?

"One."

Bile rose in her throat. She had to tell him how to get the money. But how could she do that? Only one person knew the account number and any access IDs and passwords that might be needed, and that person was dead.

She darted a glance at Lauren, but there was no help in that quarter. Lauren's eyes were closed and she was rocking back and forth, as if she'd given up and was waiting for a bullet.

"Two."

Oh, God. She had to do something. A computer. She needed a computer to buy them time, to pretend she knew how to access the accounts. But what if he had a computer with him? That would be too fast, too easy, and wouldn't buy her any time to find a way out. So what could she do?

"Three. Tell me what I want to know or I'm pulling the trigger."

"Okay, okay!" She held up her hands. "Put the gun away. Please. I'll tell you."

His eyes narrowed. "Tell me, and if I believe you, then I'll put the gun away." His finger flexed on the trigger.

"My computer," she gasped. "I need my computer."

"Use mine." He motioned to one of the other men, who headed toward the front of the van.

"No, no, that won't work. I have to have *my* computer."

He pressed the gun against her forehead. "Why?"

Why? Her mind went blank. All she could focus on was the cold feel of the barrel pressing against her skin.

"Because she has the access codes in a file," Lauren blurted out. "And they're encrypted. She has to run the file through special software on her laptop to decode them!"

Access codes? Encrypted? Decode? What was Lauren doing, trying to make it sound as though Ashley was some kind of genius corporate spy? She kept her face carefully blank, trying not to let her frustration show, hoping she could go along with Lauren's crazy lie and look convincing.

Iceman slowly lowered the gun and shoved it into the holster. "All right. Where's your computer?"

"I don't know," she whispered.

He reached for his gun.

"Wait, wait. I remember. I had it with me up in the mountains. It was in my duffel bag, the one…" She swallowed, trying to force words past the anguish tightening her throat. "It's in the bag…Dillon…tied behind the mare's saddle."

He narrowed his eyes at her. "I remember the mare. He let it go when you two raced off on the other horse." His hand relaxed away from his gun, as if her mentioning the mare had lent credibility to Lauren's made-up story. "Where's the mare now?"

She hesitated. Dillon had said the mare was trail trained, that she'd go right back home to the farm. But there were people at the farm—Griffin, the farmhands. She couldn't put them in danger by leading him there. All that would do was buy a few more minutes, or however long it would take to get to the farm. Once he realized she didn't have any special access codes, she was as good as dead anyway. She couldn't trade a few more minutes for the lives of innocent people.

"I don't know."

He whipped his gun out and pressed it against her forehead again. "Rethink that answer."

She swallowed hard. "I don't know where the mare is."

He grabbed Lauren by the hair and yanked her to the opening at the back of the van. Lauren whimpered and grabbed his hands, blinking against the rush of tears that flowed down her cheeks. Iceman pressed the gun against her temple. "Tell me where the mare is, or she dies."

"Ash, please," Lauren pleaded. "Please don't let me die."

"Hold it, wait!" she yelled, hating herself for the choice she was making, but she couldn't let him kill Lauren. She would just have to pray she could somehow do something to alert Griffin and the others before they fell prey to the Iceman. "The mare would have gone home. She should be at Dillon's horse farm by now, Harmony Haven."

He must have seen the truth in her eyes, because he shoved Lauren away and slammed the doors shut.

DILLON STARED UP at Chris, Donna and the chief and tried to make sense of why he was lying flat on his back on the grass and the three of them were on their knees, bending over him. Black smoke billowed into the blue sky above him and the acrid smell burned his nostrils and made his eyes water. Sirens sounded far off in the distance.

A violent cough racked his body and set his head to pounding as if a herd of horses were galloping around the inside of his skull. He cursed and raised his hand to cradle his head, but Chris grabbed his arm, stopping him.

"Be still, John Wayne. You're bleeding all over the place." As if to prove it, he held up what appeared to be a shirt. Dillon couldn't be sure, because it was covered in blood. Chris turned it and pressed it back against the side of Dillon's head.

Dillon sucked in a breath at the sharp pain that lanced through his skull. "What happened, Billy Bob?" he asked, his voice coming out a thick rasp.

Chris exchanged a surprised glance with the others. "It's Billy the Kid. Get it right, partner. And as for what happened, we were hoping you would tell us that."

The chief squatted down beside him. "Miss Parrish called nine-one-one. She explained that Luther Kennedy murdered Special Agent Kent and you two were holed up in your parents' house and needed backup. When we got here, half the house was on fire and the rest of it was full of smoke. Chris, fool that he is, raced inside. Lucky for you, he found you and got you out in time." He cleared his throat and looked away, as if he couldn't bring himself to say the rest.

"What?" Dillon demanded. His stomach knotted and his heart slammed in his chest as the sickening realization hit him. He didn't see Ashley anywhere. He grabbed the chief's arm. "What happened to her? Tell me!"

Chris pulled the shirt away from the side of Dillon's head as if to inspect the cut, then shook his head and pressed the shirt back. "The fire was too intense. I barely got you out before the rest of the house went up. If Miss Parrish was inside…" He shook his head. "I'm sorry, man. We got here too late."

Images slammed into him. Ashley beside him in his mother's sewing room, watching him open the floor safe. Movement out of the corner of his eye. Too late, he saw Iceman, swinging one of those damn swim trophies at him. Ashley screaming, trying once again to help him instead of running to safety like she should have. A deep, burning pain in the side of his head. Falling to the floor. Pain shooting through his head, making everything foggy. Unable to move even as he heard Ashley scream and he realized Iceman was taking her away. Then nothing, until now.

He tried to sit up, but Chris and Donna both pushed him back down.

"For God's sake, Dillon," Donna chastised him. "You've got lumps the size of Ping-Pong balls all over your head. And if I'm not mistaken, a bullet grazed your scalp. You've probably got a concussion, and if you get up you'll start bleeding again. Lie down and wait for the ambulance."

Dillon shoved Chris's hand away. "Iceman has Ashley. I remember him pulling her down the hall. He has her. I have to help her."

"What makes you think he didn't kill her and leave her in the house?" the chief asked.

"He could have killed her several times over already, but each time he didn't. He wants her alive. Whatever he wants her for, he still hasn't gotten it. He took her. He's got her. Let me up, Chris. Or I'm going to knock some teeth out."

Chris frowned but pulled his hands back.

Dillon scrambled to his feet, then wobbled as the world tilted and spun around him.

Chris swore and grabbed his arm, steadying him.

Dillon drew several deep breaths and the spinning stopped. For the first time he realized exactly where he was—the edge of the front lawn of his parents' house, or what was left of it. Flames still ate at the wooden structure, but the second floor wasn't even recognizable anymore. His chest tightened and for a moment he couldn't seem to draw a breath. All those memories, his mother's quilts, the trophies she'd treasured…all gone, including Harmony's. He dropped his head to his chest. He just couldn't watch his parents' dreams going up in smoke anymore.

And that's when he saw them.

He bent down, studying the dirt where the yard ended and the road began. "Fresh tire tracks. Wide apart. And he must have turned the wheel right here," he said, pointing. "That marks the wheelbase, longer than a car. Iceman took Ashley away in a small truck or a van of some kind. Did you pass any vehicles on the road when you came here?"

Chris shook his head. "No. This isn't exactly a high-traffic area around here. I suppose he could have gone down a side road if he heard our siren."

"Since there's not much traffic, that should make figuring out what he was driving and where it went fairly easy," Dillon said.

The sirens were much louder now. Lights flashed on an ambulance about a half mile down the road, racing toward the house. Behind it, a tanker truck turned onto the long road.

The chief stepped closer, as if to make sure he could be heard over the noise. "I bet if we make a few phone calls we'll pinpoint exactly what type of vehicle drove through here and we'll be able to track it at least until it reaches a major highway, if that's where Iceman... Luther went."

"I'm on it." Donna took out her cell phone.

Five minutes later, Dillon was sitting on a gurney in the back of the ambulance having his head sewn up. He refused to go to the hospital until Ashley was found, but he'd compromised and agreed to a quick repair while Donna worked on figuring out exactly where Iceman's vehicle—which she'd determined from eyewitnesses on the road was a white panel van—had gone.

Firemen worked to put out the blaze, even though Dillon didn't see the point anymore. The house was a total loss.

"Let's talk it out," Dillon said, not willing to put all his hopes on Donna being able to figure out where the van went. "Maybe we can figure out where Iceman would take Ashley and why. What did you find out while we were holed up in the mountains?"

"Random stuff," Chris said. "We don't have much."

"Start with the Dunlop family and their business. What do you know about them?"

"Okay. Todd Dunlop had three kids, a girl and two boys. They're all grown adults now. Patricia Dunlop, the woman who came to the station, is his third wife."

"You mean Cruella de Vil's not related to any of the children?"

"No. Why?"

"Just thinking out loud. What else, what else?" He winced when the EMT pressed gauze against his head.

"They had a prenup agreement, so if anything happened to the husband, the wife got nothing."

"What about life insurance?"

"Everything is going to charity. The wife, the kids, they don't get anything."

Dillon stared at Chris. "Nothing? He was a billionaire and he didn't provide for his family upon his death?"

"Not that we've been able to tell. The family plans to ask for an injunction while they fight in the courts. But what difference does it make? Todd Dunlop wasn't murdered."

"I know, I know. I'm trying to figure out how Iceman, Luther Kennedy, fits into all of this and why he wants Ashley alive. We know he was a thug, but that Todd Dunlop trusted him. Why would he trust a shady guy like that?"

The chief hooked his fingers into his belt loops.

"Maybe he was afraid of Luther. Maybe Luther black-mailed him into giving him a job."

Dillon glanced at Chris. "Any evidence of that?"

"No. None."

Donna ended her latest call and joined them. "I've got a call tree going like wildfire. If anyone knows anything, they'll let us know."

Dillon nodded his thanks. "We need more information on Luther. Donna, would you place a call to the Knoxville FBI office? Don't tell them about Kent yet. That will bog down the conversation and we don't have time for that right now. Tell them Kent is unavailable and we need everything they have on Luther right away."

"You got it." She pulled her phone out again.

The EMT finished bandaging the side of Dillon's head. "I highly recommend you go to the hospital, sir. You might have a concussion."

"I'll go later."

The EMT glanced at the chief.

The chief sighed and nodded. "Go on back to town. He's not going to change his mind right now."

Dillon eased himself off the gurney and out of the ambulance and stood with Chris and the chief as the ambulance headed back up the road. "Todd Dunlop essentially committed suicide by cop at Gibson and Gibson. He wanted to kill the person he felt was responsible for embezzling funds and ruining his company. Before Kent was killed, he told me he had evidence that indicated Lauren Wilkes, Ashley's best friend, was the one who stole her identity. By Ashley's own admission, her friend wasn't that good as an auditor, barely even passed her classes. That reinforces Kent's theory that Lauren teamed up with people at the companies to get them to embezzle in some kind of blackmail scheme.

What we need to know is who she teamed up with at Dunlop Enterprises."

Chris frowned. "But we already know—Luther embezzled the money."

"Are we positive?"

The chief shook his head. "It seems the most likely scenario, but no, I haven't seen any real proof yet."

"I don't think he did," Dillon said.

"Why not?" Chris asked.

"Because Luther is so determined to keep Ashley alive. He doesn't strike me as the type to go after someone that hard unless there's a benefit to him. And he's taking tons of risks—shooting at cops, killing a federal agent. If he's got millions stashed away, why not take the money and run? Why risk being killed or sent to prison?"

Chris shook his head. "Son of a... He doesn't have the money. That's the *only* reason he would take those risks."

"I agree," Dillon said. "Somehow, abducting Ashley is the key to him getting the money. We know he had it at one time, or at least access to the money. If he was partnering with Lauren Wilkes to embezzle the money, she was the only one with access to it. Somehow she has the money and he can't get to it. And he believes Ashley is his key to getting the money."

"Lauren Wilkes is the key," the chief said. "Find Lauren—"

"And we find Ashley," Dillon finished.

The chief folded his arms. "We still don't know Miss Parrish's role in this. Maybe she was colluding with her friend in the embezzlement."

Dillon gritted his teeth. "No. She wouldn't do that."

"You sure about that? Willing to bet your life on that?"

"Yes." And suddenly, he knew it was true. He trusted Ashley, with no reservations. "I'm not sure why I'm so sure, but I am."

Donna hung up her cell phone again. "You're not going to believe this." She joined their circle by the road. "Luther Kennedy wasn't just an errand boy for Todd Dunlop. Luther was Todd's illegitimate son. And that's not all. Interviews with the Dunlops' household staff indicate the marriage was on rocky ground and that Patricia Dunlop had contacted a lawyer about breaking the prenuptial agreement. She was told it was rock solid, no chance that it could be broken." Her face broke into a wide smile. "Ask me what else I found out."

"We don't have time to make guesses," Dillon said.

Her smile dimmed. "Okay, okay. With the Dunlop family being billionaires, their children's escapades tended to catch media attention. Which means a lot of their actions get caught on camera by paparazzi. And one of those camera hounds snapped pictures of one of the sons, David, with his latest girlfriend, about a month before Todd Dunlop's death. Guess who she was?"

Dillon stared at her. "Lauren Wilkes?"

"Yep. And guess who was killed in a car accident, a one-vehicle accident with no witnesses, a few days before the Gibson and Gibson shooting?"

Chris, Dillon and the chief all exchanged glances. "David Dunlop," they said in unison.

"Yep." Donna looked very pleased with herself.

"So what the heck is going on?" Dillon scrubbed the stubble on his jaw. "Did David know about the embezzlement? Do we have a love triangle here? Lauren played Luther and David against each other and tried to skip town with the money? And Luther killed David?"

"It all comes back to the money," the chief said. "But I still don't understand how it all fits together."

Donna's phone rang. She grabbed it while all eyes focused on her. "Yep, yep, right. Got it. Thanks." She hung up, her mouth flattening into a tight line. "I was able to confirm sightings of the van up to the Youngbloods' farm ten minutes west of here as the crow flies. But I haven't gotten anything after that. I'm sorry, Dillon."

Dillon gritted his teeth and gave her a crisp nod.

The chief gave him a sympathetic look. "Donna and I will go back to town. I'll get everyone looking into this case whether they're a detective or not. We'll find out everything there is to know about Luther Kennedy. We'll figure out where he went. Chris, take Dillon to the hospital to get checked out."

"I don't need to go to the hosp—"

"That's an order, Detective Gray. An order you had better follow this time." He motioned to Donna and they got in his car and headed down the road.

"Come on," Chris said. "As soon as the doctor checks you out, I'll take you back to the station so you can help with the investigation."

Without a word, Dillon swung himself up into the passenger seat of his friend's four-wheel-drive pickup. But when the truck reached the end of the road and Chris was about to turn right toward town, Dillon grabbed the steering wheel.

"Turn left," Dillon ordered.

"Left? Why?"

"Because that's the way to the Youngbloods' farm."

"No way. You heard the chief."

"Fine. I'll hitch a ride or steal a car, whatever it takes. But I'm not going back to town when I know Luther has

Ashley, and he drove west." He jerked the door handle and opened the door.

Chris grabbed his arm. "Hold it, hold it." He sighed heavily. "I guess I can always drive a tractor for a living if the chief fires me. Shut the dang door."

As soon as Dillon shut the door, Chris wheeled the truck west and floored the accelerator.

Chapter Fourteen

A short, bumpy ride later, the van jerked to a stop, its brakes squealing in protest. Lauren grabbed Ashley's hand, her terror-filled gaze latching onto hers.

It hurt Ashley even to look at the woman she'd grown up with, knowing all the death her selfishness had caused. But Ashley also knew the next few minutes might be their last. She didn't want to die with all this anger and resentment inside. She closed her fingers around Lauren's and squeezed, giving her a small smile of encouragement.

Shoes crunched on gravel, coming around both sides of the van toward the back.

"We can't outfight these men," Ashley whispered. "Our only chance is to drag this out as long as we can. Hopefully the police are looking for us. It's our job to outsmart these guys and buy the police the time they need. Or until we can figure out a way to escape. Okay?"

Before Lauren could answer, the doors jerked open. Iceman stood in the middle, flanked by his two thugs. He drew his gun and pointed it at Ashley.

"You. Out. The other one stays here."

Lauren's hand squeezed painfully tight around Ashley's, and Ashley knew exactly why. The man on

Iceman's left side had a predatory gleam in his eye as he stared at Lauren, as if he had plans for her.

"No, I can't do this alone. I need her help," Ashley stammered out.

Iceman's eyes narrowed. "You said you have the codes on your computer."

"Yes, yes, I know. But Lauren and I are a team. We each know different parts of the...encryption algorithm. We set it up that way so neither of us could take all the money ourselves. Both of us have to work together."

Greed and lack of trust were apparently things Iceman identified with. Some of his own distrust faded and he stepped back. "All right. Both of you. Get out."

The man who'd been staring at Lauren gave Iceman a sullen look.

"Later," Iceman said in a low tone as if he didn't think either of the women understood that he was promising Lauren to the other man.

A shiver ran through Lauren, transmitting to Ashley through their joined hands. They climbed out of the van, which was parked beside Dillon's big white house. Her last memories of him, lying on the floor, blood pooling around his head, had her throat closing up.

Iceman's gun shoved against her back. "Move. To the barn out back. Let's find this mare of yours and get that computer."

DILLON SHOOK THE man's hand and turned with Chris to head back to the truck parked in the man's driveway. Mr. Jones had only recently moved to Destiny and he'd been in town buying groceries until a few minutes earlier. He didn't know anything about a white van in the area. And from the way his eyes had grown big and round as he noted Dillon's bloodstained hair and shirt and Chris's soot-streaked face, Dillon was betting the man might be rethinking his decision to move here.

Chris pulled back out onto the rural two-lane highway. They'd stopped at half a dozen homes already and either the people weren't home or they hadn't noticed a van drive by. But he wasn't giving up yet. Someone had to have seen Iceman.

The cell phone holstered on Dillon's hip buzzed, letting him know he had a text.

Chris slanted him a look as he pulled the phone out. "Did the chief realize we aren't on our way into town and he's firing us both by text?"

A familiar canned message filled the screen. "It's my home security system. One of Mr. Finley's cows probably escaped again." He punched the attached picture icon. A white van filled the screen.

With Iceman at the wheel.

And behind it was another car, with two more men inside.

"Turn around, turn around. Iceman's at Harmony Haven." They'd passed his driveway ten minutes earlier.

Chris slowed and turned around in the middle of the highway. "What's he want at your house?"

"I have no idea. But he brought muscle with him. I count five guys total—three in the front of the van and two in a car following. No telling how many might be in the back of the van, though." He punched another button on his phone and put the call on speaker so Chris could hear it, too.

"Last I heard," Chief Thornton's voice came through the phone, "they don't allow people to use cell phones in the emergency room. I had better hear a nurse telling you to hang up or I'm going to be royally ticked off that you aren't where I told you to be."

"My security alarm just snapped a picture of Iceman and at least four other men heading down my driveway."

"What the heck is he going to your house for?"

Chris slowed and turned onto the long road that led to the house.

"I don't know," Dillon said. "But you need to activate the SWAT team and get them over here."

"Here? Here? Are you telling me you and Downing are at your house instead of the hospital?" The chief added a few choice swear words, not waiting for a response. "When this is over, if we all live to tell about it, I'm going to make you scrub my executive bathroom for an entire year until you learn to respect the chain of command. You got that, Gray?"

Chris laughed.

Dillon narrowed his eyes. "Yes, sir. Got it. Sir, the SWAT team—"

"Yeah, yeah. They're gearing up right now. Let me talk to Downing."

Dillon held the phone closer to Chris but left it on speaker.

"This is Downing, sir."

"The team will be there in twenty minutes. We'll bring your gear. I don't care if you have to sit on Detective Gray or handcuff him to the bumper. Do not, under any circumstances, let him go after this Iceman on his own. That's an order. If you're not both waiting for us when we get there, you can kiss your jobs goodbye. By the time I bad-mouth you all over the county, you'll be lucky if you can get a job as a door greeter at Walmart. You got that?"

Chris winced. "Yes, sir. Loud and clear. Wait for backup."

Dillon ended the call and shoved the phone back in its holster.

Chris pulled the truck to the shoulder and cut the engine. "I don't suppose there's any way to convince you to wait like Thornton ordered?"

"Not in this lifetime. And if you try to handcuff me to the bumper, I'm going to fight like hell."

"Yeah, I figured that."

"There's no need for you to get in trouble with me. Give me your gun and wait here for the team."

"Shut up and pop the glove box open."

Dillon opened the glove box and grinned. "Does this mean what I think it means?"

"I reckon I can get used to saying 'Welcome to Walmart.' Kind of has a nice ring to it."

Dillon grabbed the Glock 17 out of the glove box and they both hopped out of the truck.

ICEMAN GRABBED ASHLEY'S arm at the entrance to the barn. "If we see anyone, you'd better convince them nothing's wrong and find that computer." He shoved the gun against the side of her ribs as if to remind her it was there.

She nodded. He motioned for two of the men, the ones who'd been in the car, to accompany him and Ashley inside. The others waited outside with Lauren.

"I can have my gun out in less than a second. And there are two more gunmen behind me. Remember that." He shoved his gun in his waistband at the small of his back. "Open the door."

Ashley grabbed the handle and pulled the door back on its rails as she'd seen Dillon do the day before. She stepped inside the barn, blinking until her eyes adjusted to the darkened interior.

Griffin stood in the middle of the aisle, a scrub brush in one hand and a bucket of water in the other. His brows raised in surprise. "Miss Parrish. I figured you and the boss were still at the police station. The FBI man, he let you go?"

At his mention of Special Agent Kent, Ashley closed her eyes, horrible images flashing across the inside of her lids, images of the agent being swept off his saddle by the force of a rifleman's bullet.

Iceman nudged her. "The computer," he whispered.

She opened her eyes and saw that Griffin was frowning now, his gaze jumping from her to the man beside her, then to the others a few feet farther back. She forced her lips into what she hoped was a reassuring smile, her only goal to get Griffin to leave without becoming suspicious, so he wouldn't get hurt.

"Mr. Griffin, good to see you again. Actually, ah, Dillon is still…at the police station. He sent me—us—back for my computer. It was in the duffel bag on the back of the mare. Dillon said she'd follow the trail back to the farm. Have you seen her?"

He nodded slowly, his gaze staying on Iceman. "Yes. She's in her stall. Came back about an hour ago, along with the boss's stallion. Both of the duffel bags are in the tack room." He set the bucket and brush down beside one of the stalls. "I'll get them for you. Why don't you have your gentleman friend wait here and you can help me find it."

"Okay, thanks." She started forward, but Iceman grabbed her arm.

His gun was out in a flash and he shoved it against Ashley's side. "Hold it. We'll all get the bags together."

She winced at the feel of the cold metal shoving against her ribs. Griffin waited for them to reach him, then he slowly turned and they headed into the tack room. The two bags were sitting on top of a trunk beneath a row of harnesses.

"Stop," Iceman ordered.

Griffin looked at him in question.

"Miss Parrish will get what she needs."

Ashley hurried forward and retrieved her computer bag. Her purse was right next to it, and she knew her cell phone was inside. But there was no way to unzip the purse and get her phone without Iceman seeing. She glanced over at Griffin, then at the duffel, trying to signal him in case he could get to her purse later.

"You've got the computer now. Get over here. And you'd better not be bluffing about being able to log in and get my money out of that account."

Dread settled into the pit of her stomach like a block of ice. She hurried out of the tack room. Iceman backed up, hauling her against his side. She noticed he winced when he did so, which reminded her that she'd shot him—or at least she thought she had—in the shoulder back on Cooper's Bluff. The injury must not have been as bad as she'd thought, because he was using his arm just fine. But that little telltale wince told her it at least pained him. That was something she'd file away in case she could use it to her advantage.

"You," he said, motioning to Griffin with his gun. "How many workers are on the farm right now?"

"None. It's just me."

The deafening sound of the gun being fired filled the barn.

Griffin collapsed to the ground, holding his thigh.

Ashley gasped and started forward to help him, but Iceman jerked her back again.

"He'll live, unless he does something stupid. Like

lie to me again. I repeat. How many others are on the farm right now?"

"Four," he gasped through clenched teeth. "They're out riding the fence line, checking for breaks."

"Call them back here, now. You do anything to warn them and the next bullet goes in your brain."

Griffin kept one hand pressed against the wound on his thigh and used his other hand to pull out his cell phone. His face was pale and drawn as he punched in a number and made the first call.

A few minutes later, Griffin and the farmhands were locked in the tack room. Iceman had taken all their cell phones, ensuring they had no way to call for help. But he hadn't taken the one from Ashley's purse. She prayed Griffin or one of the others would realize that before it was too late.

One of Iceman's men kicked out some planks from a stall and used them to brace the tack room door closed, effectively sealing Griffin and his men inside.

"Stay here and keep a watch out," he instructed the three men. "If anyone approaches the house or the barn, shoot them." He led Ashley out of the barn toward the house, with Lauren and her bodyguard pulling up the rear.

DILLON AND CHRIS stayed off the road and made their way through the woods toward the house. When they reached the top of the last hill that looked down on Dillon's property, they both paused.

"Too bad we don't have any binoculars." Dillon braced his hand against the tree beside him. "I don't know if we're dealing with five men or more, or whether they're in the house or one of the outbuildings."

"Or both," Chris added.

"Yeah, or both."

"That backup is sounding really good about now." Chris looked at his watch. "The team should be here in another ten minutes."

"Ashley could be dead in ten minutes. I can't wait that long." He didn't say what they were both thinking, that she could already be dead.

"You have a plan?" Chris asked.

"Working on it." He studied his property with fresh eyes, not as the owner, but as a man who needed to sneak down the hill and into the house without being seen. There weren't any shrubs up close to the house, by design. No sheltering trees close enough to take cover behind, or to enable someone to climb into an upstairs window. Thirty head of horses grazed all over the green pastures but again, no cover. The only cover was the cornfield, but that was behind and to the right of the house, with no way to get to it without being seen, unless they went back out to the main road again and worked their way from the east side of his neighbor's property.

"I've got to hand it to you," Chris said. "You built this place like a fortress. No one's getting close to it without being seen."

"Tell me about it. Looks like we've got two choices. Either we go back out and work our way through the cornfield, which will take a good twenty minutes or more, or we take our chances, hope no one's watching, and make a run for it."

"I vote for the cornfield."

"I vote for making a run for it."

"That could be suicide," Chris said.

"We've both got vests on."

"What if they take a head shot?"

"Yeah, well, that would suck."

His cell phone vibrated again. "Maybe our backup is already here." He pulled the phone out, but it wasn't a text message this time. And he recognized the number that was calling him. He shot Chris a surprised glance and answered the call. "Ashley? Where are you?"

"It's Griffin, boss. I'm using Miss Parrish's phone. She's in trouble, sir."

The relief that had shot through him when he thought she was calling turned to a bitter taste in his mouth. "Tell me what's going on." He listened to Griffin's tale, his stomach tightening with dread. "All right. We'll get you and your men out. Hang tight." He shoved the phone back in its holder.

"What's going on?" Chris asked.

"Griffin confirmed Iceman's got Ashley with him. Iceman shot Griffin in the leg and locked him and the farmhands in the tack room in the barn. He said Iceman seems to expect Ashley to use her computer to log into an account and get his money. That's why he came here, to get her computer."

"But she's not the one who embezzled the money. Her friend did. So why isn't Iceman having Lauren log into the account?"

"I don't know. All I do know is that once Ashley isn't able to log in, she's in real trouble."

"What are we going to do?"

Dillon looked out over the fields again, a kernel of an idea popping into his head. "How much longer before SWAT gets here?"

"Five minutes, give or take."

He explained his idea.

"You're crazy. Just wait and we'll do the cornfield approach. It's the only safe way to get to the house."

"You heard what Griffin said. I've got to buy Ashley

some time. And I can't leave Griffin and his men there to die if Iceman decides to eliminate witnesses. Are you going to stand there arguing with me or are you going to help?"

He swore. "Fine. Do it. I'll intercept SWAT and tell them your idiotic plan. Dillon—" Chris put his hand on his shoulder "—don't make me have to put on a suit. I don't even dress up for church. I sure don't want to dress up for a funeral."

Dillon grinned. "You want me to be careful and don't get killed. Got it." He melted back into the trees and headed along the tree line, away from the house.

Chapter Fifteen

Dillon stopped his mad dash through the woods. He was as close to the wooden rail fence that bordered the pasture as he was going to get without stepping into the open. Hopefully, he'd have a little luck on his side. He was going to need it.

He put his fingers in his mouth and let out a shrill whistle. Moments later he heard the sound of hooves drumming against the ground, getting louder and louder. Boomerang topped the far hill and headed straight for the fence. He hop-skipped to a halt right before running into the fence and dipped his nose over the top rail in question, his nostrils flaring as he snorted a welcome.

Dillon glanced back toward the house, a hundred yards away. He didn't see anyone, but that didn't mean they couldn't see him once he left the cover of trees. He took off, sprinted to the fence, then used the bottom rail to boost himself up and onto the stallion's back.

Boomerang snorted and danced away from the fence.

"Easy, boy, easy." Dillon sat high on the withers, like a jockey getting ready for a race, and got a good handful of mane in his right hand to hold on to. He leaned as far to the left as he dared, using his legs to guide the horse and keeping his head and shoulders hidden by the long-flowing mane and the horse's thick neck. "Come on, Boomerang. Let's round up some help." He squeezed his legs and guided the stallion across the field toward a group of trail-trained horses, the kind that would docilely follow Dillon's lead.

ICEMAN SHOVED ASHLEY and Lauren into Dillon's library and paused in the doorway to speak to one of his thugs. Ashley stumbled and had to catch herself on the table in the middle of the room, the same table where Dillon and his fellow detectives had been reviewing the case notes two nights ago. A pang of sadness went through her and she glanced around the room as if she could somehow bring Dillon back just by picturing him here. Her gaze swept past the bookshelves, the bank of TV screens to the windows… Her gaze shot back to the TV screens and her mouth dropped open.

It couldn't be, could it?

There, on the bottom screen, the security camera showed a view of the northwest pasture. A group of six horses trotted through the field, and on the neck of the bay-colored stallion leading the pack clung a familiar figure—Dillon.

Ashley gasped and hurried farther into the room. She glanced back. Iceman was still in conversation with the other man in the doorway. Lauren stood beside the table, watching Ashley with a look of confusion on her face. Ashley grabbed a book from one of the nearby bookshelves and quickly dragged one of the ladder-back chairs over to the corner, praying the chair would block the TV screen from view. She plopped down and opened the book just as Iceman looked over at her.

He frowned. "Put the book down and sit at the table. Get on the computer and access that account. Now."

She got up, left the book on the seat and hurried over to the table. She sat as far away from the TVs as she could, hoping to keep Iceman from noticing the screens.

Lauren sat beside her and placed the laptop on the table. "What are you doing?" she whispered.

Ashley kept a wary eye on Iceman, who'd gone back to the doorway and was talking to the other gunman again.

"Dillon's alive," she whispered. "I saw him on that bottom screen."

"Dillon? The hot SWAT guy you told me about on the phone?" Lauren whispered back.

"Yes. I thought he was killed in the fire, back at the house where Iceman grabbed me. But he's alive."

Lauren's brows rose. "Iceman?"

"Luther Kennedy."

"Oh." She scooted closer to Ashley. "Shouldn't we power up the computer and at least pretend to access the account?"

"You're right, but we need to figure out some way to stall Iceman." She turned the laptop on and once it booted up she used her Wi-Fi hotspot software to access the internet through a cell phone network. "Now what?" she whispered. "Any ideas?"

"Why don't you access your email? If he asks questions, you can tell him you hid the codes in one of the emails in your folders."

"Good idea. I haven't checked my email since before the shooting at Gibson and Gibson. I probably have tons." She glanced up to make sure Iceman wasn't listening before opening her email.

Lauren peered over her shoulder, her face so close to Ashley's that her breath tickled the fine hairs on Ashley's neck.

"Uh, Lauren. You don't have to get quite so close."

"What? Oh, sorry. Just curious to see the kind of mail a real CPA gets every day."

The resentment in Lauren's voice sent a chill down Ashley's spine. She leaned away, wanting to put even more distance between them.

"Sorry," Lauren said, sounding contrite. "I know all of this is my fault. I was jealous of your success, and desperate. Please forgive me." Her eyes filled with tears.

Ashley gave her friend a quick hug. "Stop apologizing. Let's just make it through the next few minutes and hopefully help will arrive soon. Dillon's an amazing man. If anyone can get us out of this mess, he can. We need to be ready to move."

So far Dillon's plan was working. He'd gathered a small herd of ten horses in addition to Boomerang. And he figured since no one had shot at him yet that no one had seen him. His hope was they'd be too distracted by the group of horses to notice one man lying low against the neck of the lead horse.

He was fifty yards from the barn where Griffin and his men were being held when a man hopped over the fence by the barn. He cupped a match against the slight breeze and lit the cigarette dangling between his lips as he strode down the length of the barn. He leaned against the wood, took a deep puff from his cigarette. His brows lowered in obvious confusion as he watched the horses trotting toward him. Suddenly his gaze clashed with Dillon's, and held. He dropped the cigarette and clawed for the gun at his hip.

Dillon cursed and slapped the stallion's flank, whipping him into a gallop. The trail horses whinnied and followed his lead. The man dropped to his knees, both hands wrapped around the gun, looking for a clear shot. Dillon aimed the stallion directly at the gunman.

The man's eyes widened and he jerked around, running back toward the fence. Dillon waited until the last second, then threw his leg over the stallion's back and leaped from the horse onto the man, grabbing him around the neck and twisting as they both fell to the ground.

The flash of hooves had Dillon diving out of the way. He rolled under the fence just as the herd dodged to the side, their shrill whinnies filling the air as they whipped back toward the pasture. In their wake, the gunman's body lay broken and lifeless, facedown in the dirt.

One down, but how many more to go?

Dillon slid under the fence, pocketed the man's gun and crept toward the back of the barn.

ICEMAN FLATTENED HIS palms against the tabletop and leaned down, his fierce gaze narrowing at Ashley. "How much longer?"

Her hands froze on the keyboard and her mind raced, trying to think of another excuse, anything to buy some time.

"I think we're close," Lauren said beside her. "Give us a few more minutes."

His gaze shot to Lauren's and he abruptly nodded and went back to the doorway, where he lounged against the doorframe talking to the other gunman.

"Thanks," Ashley whispered. "My mind went blank. I didn't know what to say."

"Open that email, right there. It's from David." The excitement on Lauren's face confused Ashley even more than her words.

"What are you talking about? *Your* David? David Dunlop? Why would he send me an email?"

"Just open it already." Lauren reached over and clicked the email. A slow smile spread across her face. "This is it!" She tugged the laptop toward her. "Luther, you were right. David sent the account numbers to Ashley. We've got it!"

Bile rose in Ashley's throat as she stared in horror at Lauren.

Iceman hurried to the table and read the email over Lauren's shoulder. He smiled, and then he kissed her.

Ashley clutched her hand against her chest as Lauren's triumphant gaze locked on hers.

"Fooled you, didn't I?" she gloated. "Do you know how much I hated being in the back of that van with you, having to pretend to be your friend? But I did it. I bided my time, hoping my theory was right, that David had contacted you somehow to give you the account information. And I was right." She looked up at Luther, her obvious infatuation for him shining in her eyes. "I was right, wasn't I?"

"Yes, you certainly were."

"I don't—I don't understand," Ashley whispered.

"Not as smart as people think you are, are you, *Ash?*" Lauren laughed. "Luther and I used David as our pawn, to get to the money. But he saw Luther and me together at a stupid restaurant, of all places. We were so careful, and the one time we slipped up, David saw us. When I got home, he confronted me, told me he was going to expose me for the fraud I was and tell everyone what I'd done, starting with you."

Her eyes fairly blazed with the hatred Ashley had never known existed.

"Unfortunately, he was far more clever than I thought.

He moved the money out of the account right before Luther killed him. We didn't realize David had double-crossed us until we went to get our money and it was gone."

While she spoke, bitterness dripping from every word, Luther sat beside her and typed on the laptop.

Lauren cupped her chin in her palm. "It was my theory that David had somehow sent you the information. Luther wanted to hold you hostage and torture the information out of you. But I knew what a goody-two-shoes you are. I told him if you knew you had the information, you'd have gone to the police. So it was my idea to make you think I was a hostage, too, so I could trick you into finding the account information for us. For once," she spat out, "I was the smart one. I was more clever than you!"

"I thought we were friends," Ashley said, the words barely above a whisper as she forced them past the cold lump of fear in her throat.

"Friends?" she sneered. "How could I be friends with someone who always thought they were better than me?"

Luther finished typing and closed the laptop. He stood and motioned to the other man at the doorway.

"But I never thought—" Ashley started to say.

"Shut up. Shut up!" Lauren shoved her bangs out of her face. "You don't get to talk to me anymore. Me and Luther are going to—"

Luther grabbed Lauren's arm and pulled her up out of her chair.

"Honey, stop," she said. "You're hurting me."

He shoved her toward Ashley's side of the table and drew his gun. "Get over by her."

The other man stopped beside him and pointed his gun at them, too.

Lauren's face wrinkled with confusion. "What are you doing? We got the money. I don't need to pretend to be her friend anymore."

"Oh, Lauren," Ashley said. "Don't you see it? He used you, too, like you used me."

Lauren shook her head. "No, no! He didn't. He loves me. Luther, you love me." She stared at him, her confusion turning to dismay. "Don't you?" she whispered, sounding like a lost little girl.

He ignored her, turning to the man beside him. "The money is in my account now. Go get the others. I'll finish this."

The man nodded and hurried from the room.

Luther pointed his gun at Lauren.

"Wait, wait!" She jumped up from her chair and ran to the corner of the room. "Luther, look! I can still help you. That detective you thought you'd killed is still alive." She whipped the chair away from the monitor. Luther crossed the room to stand beside her.

How could you, Lauren? Ashley thought, even as she took advantage of their distraction and hurried across the room to the door. She paused, unable to resist a quick glance at the monitor, as well.

In the middle of the screen, right beside the barn, a body lay in the dirt. But he was too small, his hair too light to be Dillon. Relief flashed through Ashley.

Luther leaned in close to study the monitor.

Ashley dashed from the room. She raced to the end of the hallway under the stairs.

"Luther, no, don't!" Lauren's cry sounded behind her.

Ashley whirled around, expecting to see Luther pointing a gun at her, but he wasn't there.

Bam! A gunshot echoed from the library. *Oh, no, Lauren.* Grief and regret slammed into Ashley, making her double over. Luther appeared in the library doorway. He raised his gun. Ashley jerked back and ran around the corner. *Bam!* Wood exploded next to her head, raining splinters and sawdust down on her. She cried out and sprinted for the front door.

THE KNIFE SLASHED down, narrowly missing Dillon's shoulder. He slammed his fist into the other man's jaw and sent him spinning across the barn. The knife went flying and embedded itself in one of the stall doors. Dillon dove for one of his guns that the other man had made him toss when he got the drop on him. The other man saw his intent and dove, as well. They both grabbed the gun at the same time and grappled for control, rolling across the floor.

"Jack, Jack! Help!" the man yelled.

Dillon cursed. There must be another gunman close by. He twisted his body, lying half on top of the other man, but he still couldn't get control of the gun. Footsteps pounded against the dirt outside, coming closer, closer.

In desperation, Dillon lunged forward and bit the other man's wrist.

The man screamed in agony and let go of the gun.

Dillon slammed the man's head against the floor. His eyes rolled up and his body went limp. The footsteps were close, too close. Dillon twisted his body around and aimed the gun two-handed at the door just as another stranger stepped into the doorway, pointing his gun at Dillon.

The man suddenly stiffened and slowly raised his hands.

Chris stepped into the opening, his pistol pointed at the man's head. The white *SWAT* letters seemed to glow against his black flak jacket in the dimness of the barn's interior.

"The cavalry's here," he announced. He grinned as the other four SWAT team members hurried into the barn.

"It's about time." Dillon shoved himself off the floor. "Some Billy the Kid you are."

"I don't see you doing much better, John Wayne. How many more bad guys?"

"Iceman's still unaccounted for. I got one outside the barn, plus this guy. He was calling for Jack, asking for help." He waved toward the man Max was holding and Donna was currently handcuffing. "If that guy isn't Jack, there's another one close by, within earshot."

Chris pointed at two of the team members. "Check it out."

They nodded and headed out the back door again.

"That's the tack room." Dillon pointed to the door with the wood propped in front of it. "Griffin and the farmhands should be in there."

Chris kicked the boards out of the way while Dillon checked his gun's loading and grabbed another gun off the floor.

The farm hands spilled out of the room, their wide-eyed faces mirroring their relief. On the floor behind them, Griffin clutched his hurt leg but waved his other hand, letting Dillon know he was okay.

Bam! Bam! Bam!

Dillon twisted around. He looked toward the house, where the gunshots had come from.

"We've got this," Donna yelled.

Max shoved their prisoner into the tack room and squatted down beside Griffin. He motioned back to Dillon. "Go, go!"

Dillon and Chris ran out of the barn and sprinted toward the house.

"You go in the back," Dillon yelled. "I've got the front."

Chris signaled that he'd heard him and ran to the back porch. Dillon was halfway up the front steps when he heard an engine revving. He whirled around. A man stood in the rear passenger door opening of the green sedan parked behind the white van. He raised his gun. Dillon fired. The man whirled around and fell into the dirt.

The car's tires spun and it took off. Dillon caught a glimpse of Ashley's long hair in the front passenger seat just before the car topped the hill and disappeared.

He swore and leaped off the steps, landing in a crouch. He tore off back toward the barn.

The sound of someone running behind him had him twisting around, pointing his gun.

"It's me," Chris yelled, sprinting to catch up with him.

Dillon didn't stop. He doubled his efforts to reach the barn.

"What are you doing?" Chris demanded, sounding far away as he tried to catch Dillon.

Dillon fairly flew through the barn, digging his keys out as he ran past a startled-looking Donna and Max. He veered right and hopped the fence between the barn and the shed. His Jeep was fifty yards away. His long strides ate up the distance and he hopped into the front seat. He started the engine just as Chris ran out of the barn.

"Dillon! Wait!"

"Can't! Iceman has Ashley!" Dillon floored the accelerator and took off, praying he'd reach the highway before the sedan disappeared.

ICEMAN BARELY SLOWED the car for the sharp left turn at the end of the road from Dillon's farm. Tires screeched and the car banked hard, almost bottoming out before straightening and tearing off down the rural highway.

He steered with his left hand and kept his pistol pointed at her with his right.

She bit her lip, debating whether to try to grab the gun.

His gaze slid toward her. "The only reason you're alive is because Jack called and warned me the SWAT team had arrived. You're my insurance if I need a hostage. But if you give me any trouble, I can always get another hostage. You're completely expendable. Got that?"

She nodded and slid closer to the door so he wouldn't think she was going to try anything. What *could* she try, other than trying to grab his gun? She had no weapons, no phone, no way to fight him or escape. The grass beside the road went by so fast it was a blur. She could always jump. But at this speed, the fall would kill her. Was there some way to make him slow down? How slow would he have to drive for her to survive jumping from the car?

ONCE AGAIN, ICEMAN had Ashley in a car and was too far ahead for Dillon to catch up. He ground his teeth in frustration, wishing he had a faster car. The green sedan topped the next hill and disappeared.

Dillon's accelerator was already to the floor. He fished out his cell phone and called Chris. "He's heading east on County Road 224. I need air support and roadblocks."

"You're a fool, Dillon. You should have waited for me!"

"If I'd waited I wouldn't have even known what

direction he went. Call the state police and get a chopper in the air before he disappears." He hung up without waiting for Chris's response.

He topped the next hill, relieved to see he was gaining on the sedan. But he wasn't gaining on him nearly fast enough. There were a lot of turns coming up, and then the intersection with the interstate. If Iceman reached the interstate before Dillon caught up to him, and before the state police could offer air support, he could blend in with traffic or pull off an exit ramp and hijack another vehicle before anyone knew what was happening.

He slammed his fist against the steering wheel. He had to do something. Now. He had to find a way to get ahead of Iceman and stop him before he reached the interstate.

Praying he wasn't making a horrible mistake that would cost Ashley her life, he slowed the Jeep, then barreled into one of the many cornfields that bordered County Road 224.

THE CAR TOPPED the next hill. A bright red Jeep sat at the bottom of the hill, parked sideways, with a massive flat trailer full of hay bales hooked behind it, completely blocking the road from shoulder to shoulder.

Iceman swore and slammed the brakes. The car fishtailed sideways and came to a bouncing stop. Ashley shoved the door open and dove out of the car. Deafening shots echoed through the air, too many for her to count. She covered her ears and lay half under the car, curled up in a fetal position.

And then the noise stopped.

She lay there, afraid to even breathe. Her heart pounded so loudly in her ears that for a moment she thought someone was shooting again. She should run.

She knew she should run. But she couldn't get her legs to move, and she couldn't seem to force her hands down from over her ears.

Gravel crunched on the shoulder of the road. She squeezed her eyes shut.

"Ashley? Honey, it's me. Dillon. It's over. You're safe. Ashley?"

She slowly opened her eyes, afraid to hope. But there he was, crouching down beside her, his gray-blue eyes looking at her with concern. He wasn't bleeding. He wasn't dead.

Thank you, Lord. Thank you, thank you, thank you. Dillon is safe.

And suddenly, it was all too much. Horrible images flooded through her mind. Stanley Gibson, crumpling to the floor. The truck, plunging into the cold, raging river. Lauren's terrified voice crying out, moments before that first, horrifying gunshot from the library. She covered her face with her hands and started sobbing, her shoulders shaking so hard they scraped across the rough asphalt.

And just as suddenly, she was in Dillon's lap. His strong arms held her tightly against him. His hand rubbed up and down her back and he whispered soothing, nonsensical words in her ear. She put her arms around his neck and sat there in the middle of the highway, crying for all the people who'd been hurt, all the lives that had been destroyed, all because she'd been too busy, too self-absorbed, to see the pain buried deep inside the woman she'd once considered her best friend in the whole world.

Chapter Sixteen

Yesterday, after having a major meltdown on the highway in Dillon's arms, Ashley had been too exhausted and drained to give her statement to the police. Dillon had dropped her off at her rental house after making her promise to come to the station in the morning to wrap everything up.

A full night's sleep and a hot shower had worked wonders. And now Ashley was sitting in the Destiny Police Department squad room across the desk from Dillon, writing up her final statement.

A thud sounded behind Ashley, making her jump. She turned in her chair to see Patricia Dunlop standing in the open front door to the police station. The woman's eyes narrowed when she saw Ashley, and she marched toward her.

"I want that woman arrested," Mrs. Dunlop sneered.

Suddenly Dillon was standing in front of Ashley's chair, blocking the other woman from reaching her. Chris and Max hurried over from their desks and flanked him. The chief must have heard the commotion, as well, because he hurried out of his office and disappeared behind the male wall surrounding Ashley.

"Mrs. Dunlop," he said. "I already told you on the

phone that the charges against Miss Parrish have been dropped. The FBI and the Destiny Police Department are satisfied that she had no involvement with embezzlement or illegal activity of any kind."

"I don't believe that for one second," the woman insisted in a snide voice, making Ashley shudder at the hate that leached out from every word. "I want my money, and I know she knows where it is."

"Your husband's company's money was wired to an offshore account by Mr. Luther Kennedy. As I previously explained, the FBI is actively working to try to get the money returned, but it will take time. And until the court settles the dispute over your husband's will, even if we had the money we couldn't give it to you."

"This is an outrage," she complained. "How am I supposed to live? I need that money."

"Again, as I already explained on the phone," the chief said, sounding far more patient than Ashley could have been in his position, "you can petition the courts to increase your stipend. If they agree the need is there, they'll provide an increase from the estate."

"Let me talk to that woman! All I need is two minutes and I can get the account information from her."

Feet shuffled from behind the wall of protection, followed by an outraged shriek.

"Get your hands off me this instant!"

"I'm happy to talk to you and reexplain everything," the chief assured her. "But only if you quit trying to speak to Miss Parrish and come sit in my office."

"I'll do no such thing. The only person I'll be speaking to is my lawyer. I assure you, this is *not* over."

The front door banged open again, and the wall of men blocking Ashley's view visibly relaxed. Dillon went back to his seat across from her. Chris and Max both gave Ashley reassuring smiles before taking their seats at their desks in the next aisle. And the chief headed to the kitchenette and started making himself a cup of coffee.

"Well, that was…exciting." Ashley gave a nervous laugh.

"If she calls you or harasses you in any way, let me know." Dillon signed her statement and turned it around for her to sign.

When she finished, she put the pen down and blew out a relieved breath. "It feels good to be done with this. It still doesn't feel real that it's all over."

He nodded and shoved the statement into a folder. "I suppose you're going back to Nashville now. Your contract is finished and you have to get back to work."

She frowned, wondering why he was acting so formal. "Yes, my contract is finished. And I do have to get out of the rental today. My landlord already has a long-term lease with the new tenants, and they're anxious to move in."

"Sounds good. Your car's in good working order? No problems?"

"Uh, no. No problems. I drove it here."

"Good. Don't forget to change the batteries in that key fob. You're going straight to Nashville?"

She didn't answer. She waited until he finally looked at her.

"Actually, I'm going back to my hometown first, Sweetwater. The coroner released Lauren's body this morning and her parents are flying her home. I want to be there for the funeral."

He nodded, his gaze sliding away from hers.

She fisted her hands in her lap. "After that," she continued, "I guess I'm going back to Nashville." She hesitated. "Unless...I mean, well, I could come back here...if there was a reason. That is, if you...needed me to?" She waited, hoping, watching him.

He cleared his throat and tucked the folder into his top drawer before crossing his arms on top of his desk. "No. I think we've got everything we need. The FBI has cleared you of all charges, in spite of what Mrs. Dunlop said. Their investigation will continue until every little detail is covered, but as far as this office is concerned, the case is closed." His gaze finally met hers again. "There's no reason for you to come back. But thank you for offering, just the same."

His words hit her like a blow, making her spine stiffen in her chair. She blinked and looked around. Chris was one desk away, his jaw hanging open. Max had his arms crossed and was glaring at Dillon. Even the chief was staring at them, his coffee suspended midair as if he was about to take a drink and had stopped when he heard Dillon's words.

Ashley's face heated as she realized everyone in the station had witnessed Dillon's rejection of her. With as much dignity as she could manage, she pushed her chair back and stood.

"Thank you, Detective Gray. I owe you my life, many times over. I'll always be grateful for everything you and your team did to help me." She offered Chris and the others a watery smile, then slowly turned and walked out of the station.

As soon as the front door closed, Dillon raised his gaze and watched Ashley walk down the sidewalk to her car and out of his life. He ached to call her back, to tell her he wanted her to stay. But what did he have to offer her? She'd made it more than clear she hated small towns.

And he couldn't imagine living in a city. But even more than that, he didn't think he could survive if he allowed himself to love her and then lost her. No, it was better not to even go down that road.

Someone shoved him and he jerked around in his chair.

Chris planted his hands on the desk and glared at him. "You, my friend, are a complete moron and a jerk. Did you not realize she was giving you an opening, that she *wanted* you to ask her to stay?"

Dillon turned back to the papers on his desk. "Butt out. It's none of your business."

Chris swore. "You *did* know what she was asking. So why didn't you even try to talk to her? Everyone who's seen you two together knows there have been sparks flying between you since the day you met. What are you so afraid of?"

"I said, it's none of your business. Back off."

"Fine. You don't want her. Maybe she'll be interested in a guy like me. Maybe I'll head over to her house and—"

Dillon shot out of his chair and grabbed Chris by the front of his shirt. "Leave her alone."

"No. She's beautiful and smart and sexy—"

"And out of your league," Dillon growled. "And even if she would agree to date a sorry soul like you, she wouldn't hang around for long and she'd end up breaking your heart so she could go back to the city." He shook Chris. "Or worse, she'll make you fall in love with her and then she'll do something foolish like jump in front of a speeding car to save a dog or something stupid like that. She'll just up and die on you."

Chris's eyes widened. "Is that what you're afraid of? That if you love her she'll end up dying? Dillon, man, she isn't Harmony. You can't live your life afraid to love someone because you think they'll die on you."

Dillon released his shirt and shoved him out of his way. "We're done here." He grabbed his suit jacket off the back of his chair. "I'm taking the day off."

"Hold up." The chief met him halfway to the door with his cell phone in his hand. "The coroner's report on Luther Kennedy said someone stitched up his shoulder, the shoulder Miss Parrish shot on Cooper's Bluff. And I just got a call from Dr. Brookes's office manager. When she arrived at his office this morning, his car was in the parking lot but he wasn't there. And he's not answering his cell phone. Stop by there on your way home and do a wellness check."

Dillon nodded and headed out the door. He hopped into his Jeep and had just started the engine when Chris got in on the passenger side.

"Get out."

"Stuff it. I'm going with you. Deal with it."

Dillon cursed and shoved the Jeep in Reverse, then peeled out of the parking lot. Twenty minutes later he and Chris were in Dr. Brookes's living room, helping him onto the couch. Dillon worked at the duct tape still wrapped around the man's wrists while Chris held a glass of water to his dry, cracked lips.

"An ambulance is on the way. They'll be here in a few minutes," Chris said.

Dillon tossed the duct tape on the coffee table. "From what you've told us, it sounds like Luther Kennedy is the man who abducted you and made you sew up his shoulder. He's dead now. You don't have to worry about him coming back and hurting you again."

Brookes gave him a shaky smile. "Thank you, Detective, both of you. I don't know how much longer I could have lasted on that floor all taped up like that."

Sirens sounded outside, getting closer.

"You said that man is dead? Did you catch his partner?"

"Partner?" Dillon asked.

"The woman he spoke to on the phone. They were arguing about how to find some account, something about getting their money out."

"You heard her? He had her on speaker?"

"No, no. He said her name."

"Lauren?"

Brookes shook his head. "No, Trisha."

Dillon shot a look at Chris.

"Are you sure about that?"

"Positive. Why?"

Dillon took off at a run.

"Wait!" Chris called out behind him.

Dillon raced down the front steps, past two startled-looking EMTs who'd just gotten out of the ambulance. He hopped in the Jeep and wheeled it around, then slammed on his brakes.

Chris stood in the road directly in front of him with his gun drawn.

"If you try to go around me, I swear to God I'll shoot out your tires," Chris yelled.

"What are you doing? You heard the doctor. Patricia Dunlop was Luther's partner. She could be at Ashley's house right now."

"You're right, which is why we need to get over there. But you're *not* doing this alone. One of these days you're going to get killed because you're so busy trying to be the hero. You *have* to learn to trust someone else again. Trust *me*."

Frustration roiled inside Dillon. He clenched his hands on the steering wheel, sweat popping out on his forehead as he pictured Ashley facing yet another person trying to kill her. The last time she'd nearly died. If he hadn't plowed through that cornfield and gotten ahead of Luther's car, she would have died.

No, that wasn't true. Or at least, he couldn't be sure. Chris had called for the air support, and the roadblock would have been in place before Iceman reached the interstate. Dillon hadn't known that at the time, of course, but he'd learned about it later. And back at the barn, if Chris and the SWAT team hadn't showed up when they had, he might not have made it to the house in time to see Ashley being taken by Iceman.

He forced himself to ease his grip on the steering wheel. Maybe Chris was right. Maybe it *was* time he learned to trust someone else for a change.

"Get in. Hurry up."

Chris shoved his gun in his holster and ran to the passenger side. He hopped through the open plastic window into the seat without even opening the door.

"Show-off," Dillon accused.

"Being younger has its perks."

Dillon rolled his eyes and floored the accelerator. "I'm only two days older than you."

"It shows, man. It shows."

"Make yourself useful and find out Ashley's phone number. We need to call and warn her that Cruella de Vil might be stopping in for a visit."

ASHLEY LOOKED AROUND the house one last time. Since the place had come furnished, including a kitchen fully stocked with pots, pans and dishes, all she'd had to pack were her clothes and what few personal items she'd brought—which basically amounted to her laptop.

She hadn't expected to feel nostalgic about leaving, but it seemed that everything had changed since she'd come to live here four, no, almost five, weeks ago. What she'd gone through had changed her, too, and she wasn't sure yet if that was good or bad. The only thing she was sure of was that she'd miss Dillon Gray far more than he deserved after the way he'd coldly dismissed her at the station.

Forgetting him was at the top of her to-do list once she got out of Destiny, Tennessee. But that was hard to do when she had a picture of him in her palm. She looked down at the tiny gold locket she'd just discovered in her jeans pocket, the jeans she'd been wearing when she'd been at Dillon's parents' house.

When Iceman had pulled her out of the house, she'd fought with everything she had, desperate to get away and help Dillon. She remembered her hands flailing for something to hold on to and raking across the mantel. Her fingers had caught something and she'd later shoved it in her pocket and had forgotten about it. She'd grabbed the locket that contained the picture of Dillon and his family.

She'd have to give it to him, of course. Maybe it would help take the sting out of the horrible loss he and his parents would suffer after losing all those personal mementos in the fire. But she sure wasn't giving it to him in person. She'd mail it to him when she got back to Nashville.

After gently closing the locket, she slid it into her pants pocket, grabbed her purse and headed out the door. Her car was already packed, and there was nothing else to do. It was time to go.

She'd just reached her car when another car pulled down the long gravel driveway, coming toward her. She shaded her eyes against the sun, but she couldn't make out who was behind the windshield. Was the new tenant already here? Leaning against her car, she waited until the other car pulled to a stop behind hers.

Farther down the driveway, a familiar red Jeep turned down the drive. Dillon? What was he doing here? And why was he driving so fast?

A prickle of unease slid down her spine. The driver's door opened on the car behind hers and Patricia Dunlop stepped out with a gun in her hand.

Ashley pivoted to run.

"Don't move!"

She stiffened, cursing herself for not running as soon as the car turned down the driveway. The way her life had gone lately, she should have assumed the car would be carrying another person bent on killing her.

Mrs. Dunlop grabbed her and shoved Ashley in front of her like a shield as the Jeep jerked to a stop beside Dunlop's car. But it wasn't Dillon sitting in the driver's seat. It was Chris Downing.

"Don't come any closer," the woman ordered, as she shoved her gun against Ashley's spine, "or I'll kill her."

Chris slowly opened the door. "I'm just getting out of the car. I want to talk. I won't come any closer."

Dunlop turned the gun and pointed it at Chris. "I don't want to talk. I'm taking this woman with me and we're going to get my money. Close your door and get out of here right now."

"Oh, I don't think that's going to happen."

Bam!

Chris fell to the ground.

Ashley gasped in horror.

The gun fired again, but this time straight up in the air as Dillon wrenched it out of Mrs. Dunlop's hand. Somehow he'd managed to sneak up behind them. He shoved the gun in his waistband at the small of his back and quickly handcuffed Mrs. Dunlop.

Chris rolled over and slowly staggered to his feet, rubbing his chest. "Son of a... You couldn't grab her a second sooner?"

"Oh, quit whining. I got shot three times at Cooper's Bluff."

"Are you okay, Chris?" Ashley called out.

"He's wearing a vest. He's fine."

Chris rubbed his chest. "Speak for yourself. Hurts like the devil."

"Let me go," Mrs. Dunlop yelled. "I demand you let me go. My lawyers are going to—"

"Shut up," Ashley, Dillon and Chris all said at the same time.

Mrs. Dunlop snapped her mouth shut and glared at them.

"Why didn't you answer your phone?" Dillon asked Ashley. "We tried to warn you we found out she was working with Iceman."

"Dead battery."

He shook his head. "You have a problem replacing batteries, don't you?"

"Everyone has their own crosses to bear in life. What happens now?"

"We take her back to the station and book her on attempted kidnapping and a host of other charges."

"I didn't kidnap her. I didn't do anything. My lawyer—"

"Shut up," they all said again.

She glared at them and muttered something under her breath.

"Do I have to stay in town now?" Ashley asked.

Dillon looked away. "No. You can give your statement over the phone once you're home and settled in."

Chris shook his head and glared at Dillon worse than Mrs. Dunlop had. He led her to the Jeep and settled her in the back, then handcuffed her to the roll bar.

Ashley sighed and reached into her jeans pocket. She held the locket out to Dillon.

He frowned and took it. "What's this?"

"It was on the mantel at your parents' house. My hand brushed against it when Iceman was pulling me out of the house. I'd forgotten it until I was packing to leave."

She didn't wait for him to open the locket. She got into her car, started the engine, then pulled into the yard, making a wide circle around Mrs. Dunlop's car and the Jeep. When she reached the end of the gravel driveway, she couldn't resist one final look back in her rearview mirror.

Dillon stood in the middle of the driveway, a good distance away from the cars, as if he might have run after her. But as she watched and waited, he turned away and headed back toward the Jeep, in no apparent hurry. If he *had* chased her, he'd obviously changed his mind.

She made it all the way to the interstate before she burst into tears.

Chapter Seventeen

Another long day of work, another day when Ashley wanted to do anything but step out of her home office and face the rest of her empty apartment. Which was why she was once again sitting on a bar stool, nursing a bottle of beer, staring into the mirror above the bar and wondering how she'd become the pathetic woman who was on a first-name basis with the bartender.

No, she didn't really wonder. She knew the answer. Nearly two weeks ago she'd experienced the most terrifying, horrible and strangely wonderful days of her life. She'd suffered deep loss and numbing fear, and yet had somehow come out of the experience with an understanding of what really mattered, and a glimpse of a future that could have been…magical—if only Dillon hadn't been too stubborn to recognize what he had right in front of him.

She tilted her bottle to her lips, then froze. In the mirror above the bar, familiar blue-gray eyes she never thought she'd see again locked onto her. Standing right behind her, looking taller than she remembered and sexier than any man had a right to look in a white button-up shirt tucked into blue jeans, was Dillon Gray.

His gaze slid away from hers. He sat on the bar

stool beside her and ordered a bottle of beer from the bartender.

Ashley slowly set her bottle down and waited, watching him in the mirror. Her hungry gaze caressed every inch of those broad shoulders, those powerful arms that had protected her and then held her so sweetly, and the barely there stubble that made her fingers itch to touch him.

When his drink arrived, he took a long, slow pull, then set it down. He studied the polished wood surface in front of him as if it held all the secrets of the world. "Thank you for the locket. It means the world to my parents, and to me." His deep voice stroked across Ashley's nerve endings like the richest silk.

"You're welcome," she whispered, still in shock that he was even there.

His fingers idly drew tiny circles on the bar. "I suppose I could get used to a city. I could even live in a city, I suppose, if I had to. I hear they have horses in Nashville. It could work." He took another deep sip of his beer.

Ashley took a drink, too, before she trusted her voice to respond. "I suppose I could get used to a small town again. After all, I spent most of my life in one. I've even heard *some* small towns are so advanced they actually have access to the internet, which would be really handy since I work from home sometimes." She shrugged. "I could live there, I suppose, if I had to. It could work."

His lips curved in a tiny smile that quickly faded. He reached into his shirt pocket and set something on the counter.

Ashley blinked at the tiny silver disc. "What is that?"

"A battery. For your key fob. I looked up your type of car on the internet to make sure I got the right one."

Her throat tightened. "Thank you," she whispered.

He nodded. "I've been told I have trust issues. I never got it before, but I've done a lot of thinking over the past thirteen days, ten hours and—" he looked at his watch "—twenty-three minutes. I realize now that sometimes I have to let others take the lead. And that I can't really *live* if I don't let others in, if I don't share both the good and the bad with the people who matter most." His gaze collided with hers in the mirror. "You matter, Ashley. You matter very, very much."

Tears gathered in her eyes.

"Harmony was my baby sister," he said, so quietly she almost didn't hear him. "She died when I was at college. She was never a good swimmer, but she dove into a pool to save a friend instead of running to get someone else who was a better swimmer. They both drowned." He closed his eyes briefly, as if in pain, then opened them again and recaptured her gaze. "I suppose I've always blamed myself for not teaching her to be a better swimmer. And I've always been…terrified…that someone would die on my watch someday, because I allowed the person who wasn't as experienced or as good as me to jump in and take the lead. Like I said, it all comes down to trust. But I'm trying. I'm really trying."

As he watched her in the mirror, he slowly slid his hand across the bar, palm up.

Ashley met him halfway and placed her hand in his. His fingers closed over hers, his gentle touch warming her all the way to her heart.

"Tell me about Harmony," she whispered. "What was she like?"

His breath left him in a shaky rush, and for a moment she thought she'd pushed too far. But then his fingers gently squeezed hers.

"She was six years younger than me," he began, haltingly at first. But as he continued to speak and share his memories of his beloved sister, his voice grew stronger and his smile widened. And for the first time since Ashley had met him, his smile finally reached his eyes.

The future didn't worry her anymore. She didn't care if she lived in a big city or a small town, because she'd finally discovered that home wasn't about where you lived. It was about who you loved. And when she'd met Dillon Gray in a little town called Destiny, Tennessee, she'd finally found *her* destiny. How could she doubt that? After all, the man had given her what she needed most. She grinned and picked up the silver disc from the bar.

He'd given her a battery.

* * * * *

Easing back a tempting inch, she regarded him through her lashes. "I can feel the conflict in you, Eli. I know what it's like to want but know you can't or shouldn't have. I think."

"That's part of our problem, isn't it?" His eyes traveled over her face. "We're always thinking."

Her smile widened. "Not sure I'd say that, Lieutenant."

And yanking his mouth back down onto hers blasted everything that didn't have its roots in need from his head.

It might have been lightning or the glow from the taper that caused the darkness to shift.

Whatever the source, when he spotted a shadow that shouldn't be there, his body stilled...

RAVEN'S HOLLOW

BY
JENNA RYAN

Published in Great Britain 2014
by Mills & Boon, an imprint of Harlequin (UK) Limited,
Eton House, 18-24 Paradise Road, Richmond, Surrey, TW9 1SR

© 2014 Jacqueline Goff

ISBN: 978 0 263 91350 7

46-0214

Harlequin (UK) Limited's policy is to use papers that are natural, renewable and recyclable products and made from wood grown in sustainable forests. The logging and manufacturing processes conform to the legal environmental regulations of the country of origin.

Printed and bound in Spain
by Blackprint CPI, Barcelona

Jenna Ryan started making up stories before she could read or write. As she grew up, romance always had a strong appeal, but romantic suspense was the perfect fit. She tried out a number of different careers, including modeling, interior design and travel, but her one true love has always been writing. That and her longtime partner, Rod.

Inspired from book to book by her sister Kathy, she lives in a rural setting fifteen minutes from the city of Victoria, British Columbia. It's taken a lot of years, but she's finally slowed the frantic pace and adopted a West Coast mindset. Stay active, stay healthy, keep it simple. Enjoy the ride, enjoy the read. All of that works for her, but what she continues to enjoy most is writing stories she loves. She also loves reader feedback. E-mail her at jacquigoff@shaw.ca or visit Jenna Ryan on Facebook.

To my dad, Bill Goff.
It's been a long road, and there's more to go.
Please, don't forget…

Chapter One

She was being hunted.

The darkness seethed with the bloodlust of the fanatics behind her. She couldn't see them, couldn't see anything except the shadows of the hollow that twisted branches into skeletal limbs and turned everything that moved into her persecutors. The shadows hid their faces, and their bodies, but the footsteps shaking the forest floor told her they were closing in.

An ancient name swam in Sadie's head even as desperation drove her deeper into the woods. Nola Bellam. Not her, not quite, but someone who was part of her.

The knowledge did nothing to alter her flight. Fear gathered like a fiery liquid in her chest, blocking logic, preventing clear thought. The trees, misshapen and grown together, bent lower. The ground grew rougher, the bushes more tangled. Wind swooped down in bursts to claw at her black robe.

She'd run from these same pursuers many times before tonight, as herself and as her ancestor. She was fast, but they were faster, and one of them was equally desperate.

Ezekiel Blume had raped Nola Bellam, who'd been his brother's wife. Nola had taken her child and escaped, but not to safety. Nowhere was safe in Raven's Hollow. Ezekiel had been hell-bent on capturing her before his brother returned to the area. On killing her before the truth came out.

Because ignorance was the mightiest weapon of all, he'd branded her a witch and set a group of fearful townspeople on her. He'd died for that in the end. They all had. His brother, Hezekiah, had ensured it.

Words and images blurred. Ravens dived now with the wind. One of them, as large as a man, landed on the path several yards ahead.

Something about him penetrated the haze in Sadie's mind, and she slowed.

"Keep running," he ordered, but she wouldn't. It was time to make things right.

Moonbeams silvered the trees. Ezekiel's knife slashed the air while his mob of followers held their torches high, circled and salivated.

Smiling at their fervor, Sadie raised her arms and let the glittering darkness enfold her.

When Ezekiel's blade struck, pain shot through every nerve in her body. A single cry kept the man-sized raven away. Tonight, the war was hers to wage.

So let it hurt. Let her blood be spilled. This time she wouldn't try to trick death. She would accept her fate, and in doing so, she would save a man from the evil that stalked him here in the heart of the hollow.

As she lowered her arms, a knife slid from her sleeve into her palm. Resolved, she closed her fingers around it. She saw Ezekiel's face in the gloom, lit from within by the madness that consumed him.

When his blade fell yet again, she aimed and plunged her own into his chest.

His eyes widened, his hand stilled. His body froze beneath its cloak.

Ezekiel dropped to the ground at her feet, blood flowing like a river from his wound.

Sadie's breath rushed out. She'd stopped him. There was no longer a reason for the evil to be called up, no need for the poison within it to destroy an innocent soul. The man-sized raven would turn back into what he had been, what he still should be, and life would resume its normal rhythm.

Yet when she turned to watch the separation occur, her heart stuttered.

The raven stood, as solid and malevolent as ever, half bird, half man, staring at her through eyes that glowed red and vengeful.

"What is done cannot be undone, Sadie Bellam. You have your own battle to fight, and he who is me to help you conquer what comes."

What did he mean, he who was him? Frustration linked with fear even as the creature closed enormous black wings around his body and dissolved into the night.

It started slowly, a mere thread of sound beneath the raging wind. She spun back, but saw nothing. No one.

"Daughter of the witch." Laughter permeated the silky voice slithering into her head. "Do not be deceived. There is no one in the hollow who can help you. All that you see tonight, your mind has conjured…except for me!"

The voice rose to a roar as another cloaked shape reared up. This one wielded a much larger knife than Ezekiel's. She saw a gleam of insanity in the eyes that locked briefly on hers.

"Your blade struck a false mark, Sadie Bellam. Be assured, mine will not!"

As the knife pierced her skin, pain exploded in Sadie's chest. She knew then what it was to die. The taste of it was bitter copper in her throat.

The hollow faded in and out, and her mind spiraled into

a pool of black. An iron fist closed around her lungs. She saw claws reaching for her from above.

And woke as she always did—gasping for air on the floor beside her bed.

Chapter Two

"Variations on a theme."

Standing on the sidewalk outside the pharmacy in Raven's Hollow, Maine, Sadie rubbed the lingering chill from her bare arms and willed the nightmare that had spawned it away.

But the ice in her veins wasn't something her mind, or the unseasonal warm spell that had the early October temperatures hovering in the low eighties, could affect. It was simply there, so often in recent days that she was growing inured to it.

"You could exercise before you go to sleep," her cousin Molly suggested.

"Tried it. Didn't help."

"You said the dreams vary. In what way?"

Sadie considered for a moment. "The cast of characters is always the same. It's the setting that changes. But no matter where it plays out, I wind up on my bedroom floor, gasping for air and checking for blood."

"It sounds—not like fun. Especially the checking-for-blood part. Do you think you could be possessed? Or maybe channeling our ancestor?"

"You think I'm channeling a three-hundred-year-old ghost?" Even knowing Molly was serious, Sadie quirked her lips. "Okay, I doubt that. And possession's even more out there. My guess is it's a residual memory."

"Of our cousin Laura's death?"

Dropping both her sunglasses and a firm mental shield in place, Sadie regarded the cloudless blue sky over Raven's Hollow. "The anniversary of her murder's coming up in ten days."

"Yes, but, Sadie, Laura died twenty years ago."

"I know. Look, this topic's too uncomfortable for me right now. I need to move past it before I spook myself into doing something ridiculous, like consulting a hypnotist. All I wanted when I came into the drugstore was to show you a preview of tomorrow's B-Section headline." At Molly's level stare, she rolled her eyes. "Yes, fine, and buy a bottle of Tylenol."

Satisfied, her cousin lifted the ponytail from her neck. "You've bought two bottles of Tylenol in the last week, Sadie. You don't usually go through that many in a whole year." She frowned. "Meaning you have a problem either at home or at the newspaper. And since you put in three years with the *Philadelphia Inquirer* and two more with the *Washington Post,* I can't see our Mini-Me daily overstressing you. So, home it is. And seeing as you live alone..."

"Right, good, got it." Sadie waved her to a halt. "Your deductive skills are as sharp as ever—and FYI, the offer for you to come and help me run the *Chronicle* stands."

Her cousin's mouth compressed. "You know I'm not good with people."

"Molly, you're a pharmacist. You talk to people all day long."

"I'm in control—well, sort of in control behind the counter. Reporters have to wade into unfamiliar territory and be cheerful, sneaky, sly, whatever it takes to gain an interviewee's confidence."

"I said help me run the paper, not trick your friends and neighbors into telling you all their dirty little secrets."

Molly let her ponytail drop and her shoulders hunch. "I hear plenty of secrets without wading or tricking. Too many some days. Example, Ben Leamer's sister came in this morning."

"Ah." Sadie worked up a smile. "Boils or hemorrhoids?"

"Both. She went into detail for forty minutes."

"And I'm complaining about a few nightmares. Having said that, and seriously hoping you won't elaborate on the state of Dorothy Leamer's hemorrhoids, I'll ask again, what did you think of my headline?" She dangled the sample copy for her cousin to see.

Raven's Cove's Oldest Resident Breezes Into His Second Century.

"It's good." Molly pushed her hands into the pockets of her smock. "The photo of old Rooney in his cottage is perfect."

"Why do I sense a but?"

"Don't you think you're rushing things a bit? Rooney Blume's birthday is two weeks away."

"And the *Chronicle* will be running stories about his extremely colorful life until he reaches that landmark date."

"That's the point. What if he doesn't?"

"Reach the landmark? Why wouldn't he?"

"Because he's a hundred years old. He could die any day. Any minute. Writing ahead might jinx him."

Tipping her sunglasses down, Sadie stared. "Have you met the man? Rhetorical question," she said before her cousin could respond. "He smoked a pipe until he was ninety-two. I hate to think how much whiskey he knocks back in a day. He tells dirty jokes nonstop at the dockside bar that's basically his second home in the Cove, then laughs until his face turns bright red. If none of those things have gotten him, me writing a series of articles two weeks ahead isn't likely to do it."

Molly's chin came up in a rare show of defiance. "Maybe that's what your recurring dreams mean."

"What, you think they're telling me not to fly in the face of God and/or fate? They're stories, Molly. Feel-good articles that will, I hope, help stop the residents of our twin towns from going for each other's throats every time one's name is mentioned to the other. I'm sure this kind of resent-the-twin thing doesn't happen in Minneapolis or St. Paul."

"Raven's Hollow and Raven's Cove aren't twin towns. We're more like evil stepsisters. The Cove has nasty raven legends. We have a history of witches. You'll never mesh those two things. Just—never."

As if cued, a man Sadie recognized from Raven's Cove strolled past. His name was Samuel Blume. He carried a racing form and a rabbit's foot in one hand and a copy of the *Chronicle* in the other. A huge smile split his weathered face.

"Afternoon, ladies. I see you're forecasting big rain and wind tonight, Sadie. Must be your Bellam blood rearing its witchy head, because the radio and TV both say sunny and hot for at least three more days."

She shrugged. "You choose, Sam. My newspaper's going with the rain and wind."

"Good thing I brought my lucky charm. I'll be sure to get myself out of here and home safe before whatever storm you're brewing up hits."

"I rest my case," Molly said when the man moved along. "We're Bellams, he's a Blume. He assumes we're all like our ancestor. It's a battle of sarcastic wills. Hollow witches versus Cove ravens. Whose legends pack a bigger wallop?"

"Well, now you're getting weird." Sadie used the folded preview edition of the *Chronicle* to fan her face. "We're not supernatural versions of the Hatfields and McCoys, and we're definitely not Cinderella's stepsisters in town form. Besides, the Raven's Hollow police chief's a Blume, and he doesn't believe in legends at all. So pax, and thanks for the Tylenol."

Sadie turned to leave, but a tiny sound from Molly stopped her.

"Problem?" she asked, turning back.

"No. It's just—you look very nice today."

Sadie glanced down at her green-black tank top, her long, floaty skirt and high wedge sandals. "Thank you—I think."

"You seem more city than town to me."

"Okay." Her eyebrows went up. "Does that mean something?"

"I wonder how long you'll stay."

"I've been here for two years so far, plus the seven I put in as a kid."

"I've been here my whole life. You have a transient soul, Sadie. I think you'll eventually get bored with the Hollow and move on."

"Maybe." She waited a beat before asking, "Is that a bad thing?"

"For you, no. But others belong here."

It took Sadie a moment to figure out where this was going. Then she followed her cousin's gaze to the police station and heard the click.

"Ty and I were only engaged for a few months. We realized our mistake, ended the engagement and now we're friends." Her eyes sparkled. "A Bellam and a Blume, Molly. Can you imagine the repercussions if we'd challenged the natural order of things and followed through with a wedding? Although," she added, "it's been done before, and neither the Hollow nor the Cove fell into the Atlantic as a result."

"Are you teasing me?"

"Yes, and I'm sorry. Really. I know you like Ty. It's good. I like him, too, just not the way a potential life mate should."

Molly's cheeks went pink. "Everyone likes Ty. I didn't mean—I don't have a thing for him."

"No? Weird," Sadie repeated. She grinned. "Bye, Molly."

"Bye, Sadie."

With a quick—and she had to admit—somewhat guilty glance at the station house, Sadie started off again.

The fact that it took her fifteen minutes to make what should have been a two-minute walk no longer surprised her. Ten people stopped her on the sidewalk to jab fingers at the clear blue sky. Thankfully, only three of the ten inquired about the source of the *Chronicle*'s forecast.

She didn't think any of those three actually believed in witches of the warts-and-pointed-hats variety, but more than a few of them probably subscribed to the notion that Hezekiah Blume, founder and first citizen of nearby Raven's Cove, had, upon marrying Nola Bellam, in reality wed a witch.

According to Cove legend, the union had led to a fatal fallout between Hezekiah and his younger brother, Ezekiel. Ezekiel had tried to kill Nola, Hezekiah had ultimately killed Ezekiel, and the entire tragedy had ended with the gates of hell blasting open between the two towns—in the literal sense back then and still in a figurative one today.

Taking her right back, Sadie thought with a sigh, to the beginning of last night's dream.

Resisting an urge to swallow more pills, she pushed through the doors of the wood and stone building that housed the *Chronicle*.

She'd inherited the newspaper from her uncle two years ago. Next to the techno-sleek environs she'd known in Boston and D.C., it was a New England dinosaur, complete with antique wiring, fifty-year-old basement presses and fourteen employees for whom the word *change* had little or no meaning.

It had taken her the better part of a year to nudge the place past the millennium mark in terms of equipment. The employees continued to be a work in progress. But she considered it a major step forward that several of them had gone from calling her Ms. Bellam to Sadie over the past year.

She spent the remainder of the afternoon reviewing advertising layouts with her copy editor. At seven o'clock precisely, the man creaked to his feet. "My knees have been acting up all day, Sadie. Figure you could be right about that storm after all."

"The weather center in Bangor could be right," she countered. "I'm only the messenger."

"Said Tituba to her inquisitor." With a wink and a grin, he limped off down the hall.

"I give up." Rising from her desk, Sadie rocked her head from side to side. "Call me a witch. Call everyone with the same last name as me a witch. Make the nightmares I've been having go away, and I'll accept pretty much any label at this point."

She knew she'd be putting in at least another hour before packing up her laptop and heading home. With luck, a little overtime would help her sleep better. Unless the predicted storm arrived with thunder and wound up sparking another dream.

"Well, Jesus, Sadie," she laughed, and forced herself to buckle down.

She had the ad layouts sorted, two columns edited and

was endeavoring to make sense of a third when the phone rang.

With her mind still on the article—who used Tabasco sauce as an emergency replacement for molasses in oatmeal cookies?—she picked up.

"Raven's Hollow *Chronicle,* Sadie Bellam speaking."

For a moment there was nothing, then a mechanical whisper reached her. "Look at your computer, Sadie."

The darkest aspects of the nightmare rushed back in to ice her skin. Her fingers tightened on the handset. "Who is this?"

"Look at your in-box. See the card I've sent you."

Her eyes slid to the monitor. She wanted to brush it off as a bad joke. Wanted to, but couldn't. Using a breathing technique to bolster her courage, she complied.

"Do you see it?"

Her heart tripped as the image formed. The "card" showed two animated ravens. One was locked inside a cage. The other was out. The free bird used a talon to scratch a word in what looked to be blood. It said simply:

MINE!

Chapter Three

"You about done changing that tire, Elijah?" Despite the pouring rain, Rooney Blume stuck his head out the window of his great-grandson's truck. He squinted skyward as thunder rattled the ground. "Someone upstairs must be working off one big mad."

"Someone out here definitely is," Eli said, giving the lug nuts he'd just put on the tire a hard cinch to tighten them. "What were you thinking riding your bike to the Cove in this weather?"

"DMV lifted my license last year, and the sun was shining when I started out. Probably good you came along when you did, though. My balance tends to fail me in the wet."

As Eli recalled, his great-grandfather's balance wasn't a whole lot better in the dry. There'd also been a thermos of heavily spiked tea tucked in the bike's carrier, and likely close to half of what he'd started out with inside the old man by the time their paths had crossed.

Right now Rooney was pushing a metal cup through the window. Giving the last nut a tug, Eli accepted the cup, considered briefly, then tossed the contents back in a single fiery shot.

Some things, he realized, when the flames in his throat subsided, never changed. He gave the cup back to Rooney.

His great-grandfather pointed a knobby finger at a line of trees bent low by the wind. "Gonna be a bitch of a night."

Soaked to the skin, with his dark hair dripping in his eyes and rainwater running down his neck, Eli climbed back inside and started the truck's engine. "You think?" But he grinned as he spoke, and flicked a hand at the thermos. "I'm surprised that tea of yours hasn't eaten through the aluminum casing by now."

"You sound like my great-grandson."

"I am your great-grandson."

"I mean the other one. The one who's wearing a police chief's badge and sporting a big dose of attitude over in the Hollow."

"Only a town of fools would give a badge to someone who prefers carrot juice to whiskey." Eli squinted through the streaming windshield. "Self-denial that unswerving upsets the balance of the universe."

"Spoken like a cop after my own heart. And while we're on the subject of badges and balances, did you know your carrot-loving cousin's not gonna be putting a wedding ring on Sadie Bellam's finger?"

"Heard about it." Eli kept his tone casual and swept his gaze across the mud-slick road. "I also heard it was Sadie who ended the engagement."

Rooney's expression grew canny. "You got awful good hearing for a man who spends most of his time hunting down killers in New York City."

"It's not so far from there to here. As the raven flies."

The old man chortled and offered him another cup of "tea." "I won't say you're a jackass, Elijah, only that among other more valuable things—and for 'things,' read 'Sadie'—the badge on Ty's chest could've been yours if you'd wanted it."

"And an executive position at the *New York Times* could've been Sadie's if she'd wanted it. We do what we do, Rooney, and live with the consequences."

His great-grandfather made a rude sound. "You're as stubborn as twenty mules, the pair of you. You knew each other as kids, connection was already there. Life'll take you down different paths because that's how it goes sometimes. But it goes in circles other times, and you and Sadie came to the end of a doozy when you met up last April in Boston."

"Rooney—" Eli began.

"I was there, Eli. I saw you. And let me tell you, there wasn't a soul at that wedding reception who even noticed the bride and groom with the fireworks you two set off. Suddenly, next thing I know, Sadie's back at the *Chronicle*, and you're tracking a serial killer through the underbelly of Manhattan. Me, the universe and pretty much everyone at the reception are still scratching our heads over *that* turn of events."

Eli sighed. "You, the universe and pretty much everyone at the reception read too much into a time-and-place chemical reaction. Sadie was engaged in April."

"Only until she got back from Boston. Two days later, your cousin Ty was drowning his sorrows in goat milk and a double dose of wheat germ."

"Sadie's not ready to be married, and my life's good the way it is. Cops and relationships don't mix."

Rooney snorted. "If you expect me to buy that load of bull, you're no kind of cop. And no kin of mine."

"In that case, happy hundred and first in advance, and I'll be heading back to New York right after I drop you off at Joe's bar."

"I need a favor before you go."

"Yeah?" Eli raised a mildly amused brow. "I could

say I don't do favors for people who claim to have disowned me."

"But that would make you unworthy of any badge, and we both know that's as far from the truth as it gets."

The vague humor lingered despite the fact that Eli could no longer see either the road or the dense woods next to it that stretched from the Cove to the Hollow and beyond. The rain fell in blinding sheets now. "What do you need?"

"Ty's on duty tonight. I want you to go by his office in the Hollow. He's got a bulldog there named Chopper. Family in town's heading south and can't take him, so I said I'd think about it."

"You want a dog?"

"Don't give me that look, Eli. If I die before Chopper does, I'll leave him to you."

"Still a cop here. I can't have pets."

"No pets, no women. You're not a cop, you're a monk."

"Who said anything about no women?"

"No women of consequence, then. Now, you take my last serious relationship versus the last woman I had sex with."

"Jesus, Rooney."

The old man drank from his thermos before offering back a mostly toothless smile. "You think because I'm old I don't have sex?"

"Yes—no. Dammit, I don't think about it one way or the other." Ever.

"Why not? I'm human."

"You're also my great-grandfather, and I do my level best to keep thoughts of sex, parents and grandparents out of my head."

"You're a prude, Elijah. Doesn't bother me to picture you with a woman."

The first bolt of lightning shot down deep in the hollow. "Are we actually having this conversation?"

"I am." Rooney peered into his thermos. "Seems to me you're doing more avoiding than conversing."

Eli swerved around a barely visible pothole. "What I'm doing is trying to figure out how anybody's sex life, mine included, relates to me checking out a bulldog."

"So you'll do it?"

"What, have sex or check out the dog?"

"In a perfect world, both, but I'll settle for the dog and enjoy thinking about you and Ty firing daggers at each other while you picture, but deliberately don't talk about, the lovely Sadie Bellam."

"You have a wide streak of mean in you, old man." But a slow grin removed the sting of Eli's remark. In any case, glaring down his resentful cousin would be hell-and-gone preferable to visualizing Rooney naked with a woman.

As the wind picked up, and the truck began to buck, even his garrulous great-grandfather stopped talking. The road, such as it was, became a river, complete with currents, broken branches and sinkholes that could rip out the undercarriage should Eli happen to hit one. That he didn't was more of a miracle in his opinion than a testament to his driving skills.

Twenty minutes later, he pulled up outside his second cousin's shabby dockside bar, Two Toes Joe's. He saw Rooney safely through the door, turned down a mug of coppery green beer—old Joe really should have his lines changed—and jogged back to his still-running truck.

The dashboard clock read 9:30, which surprised him since it seemed to have been dark for hours. If he'd believed in omens, as at least three-quarters of his relatives in the area did, he'd check out the dog—couldn't not do that—then say screw an early arrival for Rooney's birthday and return to New York. Return to sanity, and more important, the safety of a no-Sadie zone.

What had flared between them last April had been unexpected and intense. Sadie had been a kid the last time he'd seen her. Seven years old and shocked speechless over the murder of her cousin Laura, who'd also happened to be his stepsister.

Although the residents of both Raven's Cove and Raven's Hollow had been horrified, few had been as badly shaken as he and Sadie. How could anyone who'd never had the misfortune to do so possibly understand what it felt like to discover the body of someone you loved? And not merely discover, but, in Sadie's case, literally stumble over.

Her family had left Raven's Hollow six months later. His had stuck it out for another six years, searching for a closure they'd never received.

To this day, Laura's killer remained at large. A handful of suspects and numerous persons of interest had been questioned and released. Over time—two decades at this point—what had started as a countywide manhunt had been reduced to a dusty homicide report in the back of the sheriff's filing cabinet. Clues gathered at the scene had resulted in nothing, and, as they so often did in situations like these, the case had gone cold.

For Eli, the memory of Laura's murder had dimmed but never disappeared. Not completely. Every similar crime he worked to solve these days took him back to her death. When that happened, the raw pain and guilt would slam through him as hard as it had done the evening he and Sadie had met in the hollow.

On a less grisly note, Eli couldn't deny that, even at seven years of age, Sadie Bellam had been a beauty. Fast-forward twenty years, slide her into a clingy silver dress, and she'd quite literally stripped the breath from his lungs.

He'd prowled around the edges of that Boston reception hall, watching but not approaching her for thirty wary minutes, until one of her aunts had swept in and sealed the deal by insisting they dance.

The idea of taking the memory deeper tempted, but unfortunately, a gust of wind upward of forty miles an hour had other ideas. It grabbed his four-by-four and sent it sliding toward a deep gully. Eli rode the wave, felt the kick of wind abate and urged the truck back onto the road.

It had been a sunny seventy-eight degrees when he'd left New York City. The clear skies had held to Bangor. Then, less than ten miles from the Cove, a mass of boiling black clouds had rolled in and let go.

He glanced left as thunder rumbled up and out of the hollow. Jagged forks of lightning split the sky overhead. His truck, three years old and heavy as hell, shuddered through another blast of wind.

Only a seriously disturbed person would stay out in this. Would *be* out in this. The dog could have waited while he went head-to-head with a glass of Joe's toxic beer.

Without warning, twin beams of light appeared directly ahead. They slashed through the murk, momentarily blinding him. Swearing, Eli jerked the steering wheel hard, felt the truck's back end fishtail and had to compensate to keep the entire vehicle from tumbling into the ravine.

He might have won the battle if something—tree, car or possibly both—hadn't become a sudden and solid road-block in front of him.

Using his forward momentum, together with muscle and brakes, he went for a one-eighty turn. But the mass was too close and the road too slick for him to gain the traction necessary to execute it.

The collision sent his head and shoulder into the side window. A clap of thunder underscored the hit, but the sound was nothing more than a murmur in Eli's mind. By the time the truck stopped moving, the storm, the night and the hollow had faded to black around him.

Chapter Four

"Eli, can you hear me?"

A woman's voice reached him. Possibly Sadie's, possibly not. She was far away but definitely calling his name. Did that mean he was alive? Because if not, he'd gone someplace dark, wet and incredibly uncomfortable.

"Eli, damn it, open the door!"

Someplace where the angels—at worst, he hoped, angels—shouted orders, and every thought was coated in a bloodred haze.

The haze pulsed for several seconds before subsiding to a repetitive and annoying thud.

He cracked his eyes open to a different kind of darkness. This one was loud and it moved. Both sound and motion jabbed at him like dull knives. He was tempted to sink back under until it stopped.

"Wake up, Eli, and open the door."

Sadie's voice—he was sure of it now—sounded impatient, yet held the barest hint of a tremor. He let the memory of her face draw him to the surface and most of the way through it to consciousness.

Levering himself upright, he swore. And kept swearing because it helped him clear out the last of the haze. Once it was gone, he located and hit the lock release.

The door shot open. It very nearly flew off its hinges

judging from the screech of metal and the ferocious howl of the wind that grabbed it. Eli managed to clamp a hand on to Sadie's arm before the unexpected backward motion sent her into the ravine.

He'd forgotten she had the balance of a mountain goat. Without missing a beat, she bunched his wet T-shirt and gave him a hard shake. "Are you hurt?"

He almost smiled. "Been better. Need a minute for my brain to settle."

"In that case, Lieutenant, shift your excellent butt to the passenger side, and let me in."

Not quite a storybook angel, but close enough. He grinned. "Helluva time to decide you want to do what we managed not to do in Boston."

With a glance into the hollow, she pushed on his shoulder. "If we do now what we didn't do, this really thin rock ledge that your rear tires are barely sitting on is going to crumble apart and send us straight to hell. Or into Raven's Bog. Jury's still out on which name's more appropriate."

Either place was jarring enough for him to snap his head around.

"Bet that hurt—" she began, then gasped when he lifted her inside and deposited her on the passenger seat. "What are you doing?"

"Don't move." He reached for the ignition key.

Swinging her legs around and down, she snagged his wrist. "The engine's running, Eli. You just can't hear it over the Tarzan roar of testosterone in your brain."

"Pretty sure I spun out trying to avoid a head-on with your vehicle, Sadie."

Keeping an eye on the rearview mirror, and using a spectacular bolt of lightning to aid his vision, Eli shoved the truck in gear. After several seconds of maneuvering, he crawled it away from the edge.

Sadie let out a relieved breath. "I'd be impressed if I didn't know for a fact that I could have done the same thing a full minute sooner."

"We're not on a deadline, sweetheart." He fingered a cut on his forehead, and wasn't surprised when he spied a smear of blood. "Are you hurt, and did we hit?"

"No, I'm not, and yes, we did. But not each other." In the process of wringing out her long red-brown hair, she nodded at the windshield. "It's difficult to see right now, but that big black thing in front of us is a pine tree. It started to fall, I hit the brakes. At the risk of fueling your already massive ego, you must have done one wicked spinout to avoid being flattened by something that could have pancaked an eighteen-wheeler."

"Speaking of." Eli sized up the tilt of his truck's back end. "Unless one of my tires is sitting in a hole, I've got a flat."

She waved a hand in front of his face. "Did I mention the tree was huge, with the potential to destroy both you and your vehicle?" A frustrated sound emerged. "Why are you even on this road, Eli? Why are you in Maine at all for that matter?"

"Did you think I wouldn't come for Rooney's hundred and first?"

"No, I figured you'd come, just not until the last minute."

"I'd be offended if I wasn't sure about that flat and apparently in need of a lift."

She stabbed at the windshield, repeated very clearly, "Big tree, tremendous crushing power."

His lips curved. "Yeah, I get the luck part. What I haven't got is a second spare."

He told her, in bullet points, about Rooney, the bicycle that was currently strapped to his roof rack and Joe's bar.

Laughing, she dropped her head back onto the seat. "If I said any of that surprised me, I'd be lying." She slanted him a speculative look. "Still a little shocked to see you, though. On this road. At this time of night."

"Right back at you. And don't tell me you didn't know there was a storm rolling in."

"I knew," she agreed, far too softly for his liking.

He studied her profile in the next flash of lightning. "Something's wrong."

"Nothing I can't handle."

With his brain back on track, he reached out and wrapped his fingers around her neck. "You were driving from the Hollow to the Cove, Sadie, in weather no sane person would take on without extremely strong incentive. As I recall, you're stubborn, but relatively sane."

She started to speak, then broke off and grabbed his chin as lightning snaked through the clouds. "You're bleeding!"

"A little. It's not…" He hissed when she poked at the gash. "Well, it *was* going numb."

"Sorry." She lightened her touch and her tone. "Eli, you were barely conscious when I found you. You could have a concussion."

"I could also be halfway back to New York. Might have been except for a damn bulldog. Don't ask. Just trust me when I tell you I've been hit on the head more times than I can count."

She formed her lips into a smile. "To which I'll simply say, no comment—and you can let go of me now."

"I will, just as soon as you tell me why you were heading to the Cove in a storm that scared Rooney spitless for close to twenty minutes."

"I—seriously?"

"Talk to me, Sadie."

She blew out a breath. "Fine, I got an email. It was—unusual. I don't know how or why, but it also seemed familiar. Like a memory buried deep in my head. So deep I can't visualize it."

"You got a familiar feeling from an email?"

"Well, I say feeling. It was more like a punch of pure creepy. And a strong sense that the sender was watching me."

"Was he?"

"I don't see how. I was in my office at the *Chronicle*. The guy on the phone couldn't have…" She halted there, bit her lip. "I, uh, didn't mention him, did I?"

"Not unless my brain's shorting, and I doubt that." Because his fingers were still curled around her neck, she couldn't draw away. That she made no effort to do so told him a great deal—most of it not good. She was scared. "What did the guy on the phone want?"

"If I knew that, I wouldn't have been going to the Cove in a storm that scared your great-grandfather spitless." Her eyes, as gray and stormy as the night, slid past him to the trails of mud that slithered down the driver's window. "The ravens must be significant."

Eli's grip tightened. "You wanna back that up for me?"

"The card was animated. One of the ravens was inside a cage, the other was out. The outside one scratched the word MINE in blood with his talon. I freaked at first, but after a while I convinced myself it was no big deal."

"How long's a while?"

"Not sure, maybe fifteen minutes. Afterward, I decided to proofread a column I'd imported for the weekend edition about fanatics and the rising numbers of them who've begun to act on their so-called beliefs. And there I was, right back to freaked. Seeing as he knows everything raven-related, I figured the best thing to do would be talk to Rooney, who, in case you're unaware, never answers his phone."

"I am aware of that, actually." But Eli's response was preoccupied as he searched his mind for—something. "A raven in a cage," he repeated. "Why can I almost picture that?"

"No idea, but please tell me there isn't a legend in the Cove about this kind of thing."

"Not that I know of, and it's the card part that's ringing a really distant bell."

"That bell could be your head still ringing from the whack it took when you almost wound up in the bog."

"There is that," he agreed.

When thunder caused the ground to tremble, she stared straight into his eyes. "You know where we are, don't you."

It wasn't a question, Eli reflected. "Yeah, I know. This is where you and I met the night we discovered Laura's body."

"Met, argued, walked and found."

"It's been two decades, Sadie."

"I have a long, and vivid, memory."

"Ditto, but right now I have a more immediate problem."

The breath she released ended on a laugh. "You really don't, you know. You've got a flat and no spare, which means your vehicle's stranded. Mine, on the other hand, has all four tires intact. Seeing as it's on the other side of the pine, the Hollow as a destination wins by default." A light danced up into her eyes. "Looks like you get to check out that bulldog after all, Lieutenant."

"Yeah, well." He moved too quickly for her to react. One moment, his gaze was sliding across her mouth. The next, his own was covering it.

The last thought Eli had before his brain shut down was that kissing Sadie Bellam would be either the best thing he'd ever do or the worst mistake he'd ever make.

Chapter Five

For a suspended moment, Sadie's mind and senses blanked. Then everything inside began to sizzle and snap.

She hadn't kissed him in Boston. Oh, she'd wanted to, too many times to count, but whenever she'd thought about it, the ring on her finger had become a lead weight reminding her that she was engaged to another man.

There was no ring on her finger now, Sadie's overheated senses pointed out. But that still didn't make kissing him a good idea.

Unfortunately, the sound that emerged from her throat more closely resembled a purr than a protest. She also suspected the fingers she'd curled into his hair were holding his mouth on hers rather than trying to push him away.

Fascination wove a greedy path through the sparks. Eli was seducing her with his lips and tongue, with his whole mouth, in fact. Although it was difficult to form a thought, Sadie wondered if she'd ever been kissed quite this thoroughly before. If she had—and she doubted it—the memory eluded her.

A crackle of lightning preceded another ground-shaking peal of thunder. The storm sounds matched the heat currently shooting through her veins. With her fisted hands, she tugged him closer. She wanted to climb over the console and onto his lap, to let herself slide from fantasy into reality. She wanted to return the demands of his mouth, then simply sink in and not think at all.

The fingers on her neck slid up into her damp hair, and his thumb grazed the side of her jaw. Her skin tingled everywhere, and her breathing—well, maybe she'd stopped breathing, because her head was alive with sensations she couldn't hope to untangle.

The next thunderbolt vibrated the body of Eli's truck and shot straight up into her bones. Prying her mouth free, Sadie raised uncertain eyes. "Why do I feel like someone just reached down and gave us a really hard shake?"

"I thought it was my brain trying to shake some time-and-place sense into us."

Or sense in general, Sadie reflected. A sigh escaped as she forced her spinning emotions to disengage.

Did it surprise her that his kiss would be off the scale? Hardly. After one dance in Boston, she'd expected that scale to blow eventually.

It was an effort to separate herself from him and keep her voice steady. "This shouldn't have happened, Eli. We shouldn't have let it happen."

Skimming his knuckles over her cheekbone, he held her gaze. "I won't argue with you, but only because I know what I can and can't give a woman. More than sex is more than I've got inside me right now."

She laughed out a breath. "When I unscramble that remark, I'll probably agree. In the meantime..." She leaned forward just far enough to whisper a teasing "Your kisses rock, Lieutenant, with or without the drama of a full-blown storm beneath them."

Sadie knew he was considering tossing caution aside and diving in again, but he went with the wiser, if somewhat disappointing, alternative and reached behind them for his backpack. "It's time we put some distance between us and these trees. Where's your—" he raised a humorous brow "—car?"

"Cars are neither bad words nor bad vehicles. I spent half my teenage life wanting to own a Maserati."

"You own a Maserati?"

"No, I own a Land Rover, because I'm not in my teens, and I knew when I came back to the Hollow that the roads, in a pothole-to-pavement ratio, strongly favor the potholes. My mother had a man friend once who leased a Maserati, but I was thirteen when she left him, so I waved goodbye to that wish and switched to boys instead."

"I didn't know your parents had broken up, Sadie. I'm sorry."

She twitched away any residual sadness. "They were barely together when we lived in the Hollow. Molly says it's the Bellam curse."

"What is?"

"The inability of Nola Bellam's female descendants—my mother in this case—to commit to people, places and/or things. An inability she believes is supplemented by the fact that those female descendants insist on passing the Bellam surname on to their own female children."

"Would this be your cousin Molly who only left Raven's Hollow long enough to go to college?"

"That's the one."

"Making her the notable exception commitment-wise."

"So it would seem."

With a smile grazing his lips, Eli indicated the outside storm. "You ready?"

"Would saying no change the situation?"

His smile deepened. "Between lightning bolts, then."

He would be gorgeous, Sadie thought with a sigh. A hot, gorgeous cop. A loner, with a reputation for getting the job done—however distasteful that job might be.

As homicides went, Eli did it all. He'd go undercover for weeks, often months at a time, if going under meant bringing down a New York crime lord. During his tenure on the force, he'd worked countless night shifts while investigating gang-related murders. He'd hunted down serial killers, sunk his teeth into a dozen or more cold cases and, in at least one instance that she knew of, apprehended a man who made Hannibal Lecter appear well adjusted.

Of course, it also didn't hurt that he wore his dark hair long, always looked a little dangerous and somehow kept his truly superior six-foot-two-inch body totally cut.

"There's less than five seconds between thunderbolts," he said now. "We'll need to move fast and stay low."

"My way's better." Dragging her eyes from his profile, she regarded the storm-tossed trees. "Don't count, don't think, just do."

"Which is why, as a kid, you stepped in groundhog holes and sprained your ankles on a monthly basis."

"Two groundhog holes, two twisted ankles." And one dead hand, she recalled with a chill that she couldn't quite battle back. "On three?"

"Your count."

They exited the truck simultaneously. With her skirt tied into a thigh-baring knot, Sadie led the way to the narrowest part of the fallen tree's trunk. Before she could boost herself up and over, Eli scooped her off the ground.

"Wait, don't! Are you..." He deposited her without ceremony in a puddle on the far side. "...crazy?" she finished through her teeth.

Joining her, he shouldered his pack and grabbed her hand. "Come on."

Because arguing was pointless, Sadie ran with him to her Land Rover. They fell inside on the heels of a triple fork of lightning that illuminated the woodland hollow as far as she could see.

"Road's a single lane here." Raindrops flew from the ends of Eli's hair as he looked in several directions at once. "You're the DD, sweetheart. How are you at maneuvering in reverse?"

She summoned a tight smile. "Guess we'll find out."

Fortunately, she knew the twists and dips well enough to feel her way back through them. Eli's flashlight helped. So did the sky-wide slashes of lightning. Still, her nerves didn't stop jumping until they reached a point where the vehicle could be safely turned around.

"I'd say that was worthy of a Maserati should the opportunity for you to own one ever arise."

"Highly unlikely in this lifetime. And please don't say I could've had a fleet of them if I'd gone to New York, because everyone except my uncle—who looks on the *Chronicle* as a father might a beloved only child—has already pointed that out."

She felt more than saw his stare. "I get family loyalty, Sadie. You love your uncle, so you wanted to keep his dream alive. What I don't get is why he asked you to do it rather than someone who already lived in the Hollow."

"Back to Molly again, huh?"

"Rooney says she's smart, and given her history, I don't see her leaving town any time soon."

"She's an introvert, Eli."

"She worked at the *Chronicle* part-time through high school."

"As a proofreader. Look, I'm sure my uncle talked to her before approaching me. If Molly had wanted to run the newspaper, she'd be doing it." But she angled him an impressed look. "You've kept up, haven't you?"

"It's a hard loop to escape. There are six Blumes within

a six-block radius of my apartment. One of them lives across the street from me and drops by twice a week to make sure there's food in my fridge."

Sadie regarded the scattering of blackened houses as they approached Raven's Hollow. "Power's out. All I see are glimmers of light in a few… Stop it, Eli."

He hid most of a grin. "Stop what?"

"You're giving me a Molly smile. Those flickers are candles, not the spirits of Bellams past."

Now he chuckled. "I don't know, Sadie. Word has it Raven's Hollow was recently named one of three most haunted towns in New England."

"It was not." But she lowered suspicious lashes. "Who told you that?"

"Rooney."

"Well, in that case, consider the source. The man's propagating a myth to encourage tourism in the area."

"Always possible. One of my more ambitious cousins lived with him for a few years. He might have planted the thought. Does it bother you?"

Her lips curved into a deceptively sweet smile. "Do witches ride broomsticks?"

"I'll take the Fifth at this point. Something tells me you're only marginally tolerant when it comes to people who believe in the local lore."

"That's because I'm part of the local lore. Unfortunately."

She eased the Land Rover along a narrow, densely wooded road that wound up and up to a rocky promontory. The jagged point of land speared into a small bay where the waves, even on a calm day, broke white against the base of the cliff.

Built entirely of faded gray stone, Bellam Manor could at best be called forbidding. Although, Sadie mused, foreboding might be a more appropriate description. Either way, two large towers stood at opposite ends of a structure made up of multiple juts and protrusions, and would forever make her think of the wicked queen's castle from Sleeping Beauty.

The mansion had taken fifteen years to construct. Storytellers swore that the evil secreted within the walls of Blume House in Raven's Cove had nothing on this place. But of course, Blume House had never been home to a family of witches.

When she'd returned to the Hollow, Sadie had promised herself she would do so with an open mind. The manor, as remote as it was, and for all the tales that had been spun around it, was simply a place to live. Or a small portion of it was.

She had an apartment in one of the two habitable wings. Molly occupied the second. It didn't take a structural engineer to determine that the central core and several of the outbuildings were in desperate need of restoration. Unfortunately, a full fix would take more money than she and her cousin would earn in fifty years.

When a slash of lightning delineated the manor from tower to imposing peak, she glanced over. "I'm waiting, Lieutenant."

"Working on absorbing here, Sadie. I feel like we've been swept off to the Black Forest by a freak tornado."

"That's how I felt when I saw the place again two years ago. It was more of a fairy-tale castle when I was young, but then I only came out here twice that I can remember." She made a circular gesture. "My apartment backs onto the ocean. Molly's overlooks the woods. It's an interesting trek from my door to hers. Still no comment?"

"Still absorbing."

"Mmm, well, when you're done, I'll tell you that I'm not

eager to make the drive back down to town tonight, so I'm going to be generous and let you borrow my Land Rover."

Eli grinned. "Some would call that avoidance."

"My mistakes often have that result. For the most part, I circle around Ty the way Cocoa circles Molly's long-haired Chihuahua."

"Who's Cocoa?"

A dangerous smile appeared. "My cat. She's black. I've heard her referred to as my familiar. Ready?"

They waited through another flash of lightning, then made a dash for the porch. In the shelter of a wide overhang, Sadie shoved the dripping hair from her face. "I could sit on a rock at the base of Bellam Point and not be this wet. Cocoa's going to think she scored a giant rat if she sees…me." When her eyes picked out an odd shadow, she bent forward to point. "Uh, Eli, can you shine your flashlight on that—whatever it is on my doorstep?"

He followed her gaze, frowned and, handing her the light, moved in for a closer look.

She clicked the switch. And immediately jerked back in disgust. "Oh, yuck. Dead bird. That's…" An ominous creak of hinges had her raising the beam slowly to the door. "…definitely not right."

Eli rose from his crouch. "Meaning you locked up this morning?"

"City girl. It's a habit." Her eyes traced the outline of the dark wooden frame. She honestly didn't know which was worse—the open door or the unfortunate creature lying outside it. Fighting a swell of fear that had already slicked her skin with ice, she said evenly, "What kind of sick person would put a dead raven on my welcome mat?"

"More to the point," Eli countered, "is that sick person waiting inside?"

Sadie's heart threatened to slam right out of her chest. "This is hell-and-gone creepier than my nightmares."

Already checking out the darkened entryway, Eli offered an absent "You have nightmares?"

She prodded his shoulder. "Later. There's a puddle of blood around the raven's head."

"Better its than yours. Stay behind me."

"Then keep moving. Dead animals are gross."

"Getting shot's grosser."

"Shot?" Astonishment halted her on the threshold. "Who'd want to shoot me?"

"You'd know that better than I would."

"It was a rhetorical question, Lieutenant. I'm not…"

A flurry of unexpected motion cut her off as someone leaped from the foyer shadows. Whoever it was knocked her into the doorframe, swung a lamp at Eli's head, then tossed it and bolted.

Trapping her arms, Eli stared into Sadie's slightly starry eyes. "Are you all right? Sadie, did he hurt you?"

"Yes—no." She willed the dizziness away. "I'm fine, I'm good. Go."

Cold metal brushed her wrist as he pulled a gun from the back of his jeans and vanished into the night.

Before she could turn, something swished across her calf. Swallowing a scream, she grabbed the discarded lamp and raised it like a bat.

A tiny meow floated upward from the floor.

"Cocoa…" Her breath rushed out in relief. "God."

She closed her eyes for a long moment, then, rubbing her head with the heel of her hand, retrieved the flashlight she'd dropped and pushed the door closed. When she touched the switch, a powerful beam of light bounced off the hall mirror and straight into her eyes.

"Oh, that was smart."

She needed another moment, she decided, to slow her spinning mind and regroup.

Three feathers on a door foreshadowed death in Raven's Cove. That was a matter of legend. She couldn't recall any mention of dead ravens on doorsteps in Raven's Hollow.

There had to be a crazy person on the loose.

But this didn't feel crazy, or not entirely. This was twisted and cruel and, when added to the email she'd received earlier, personal. It was...

The thought dissolved as she spied a slash of red on the wall opposite the mirror. The wall on which she was leaning!

Pushing off, she whirled in a half circle. And took three unbelieving steps back.

A single slashed word covered the plaster from end to end. It appeared to have been written by a giant claw. And said simply:

FOREVER!

Chapter Six

"Slow down. Let me get this straight." Sadie's former fiancé, Tyler Blume, gave her a light shake and sent Eli, several feet behind her, a fulminating look. "Someone broke into Bellam Manor, placed a dead raven on your doorstep and wrote a message in red on the wall. This person, who was still inside when you arrived, then proceeded to knock you down and fled the scene on foot with Eli in pursuit."

Sadie eased free of his increasingly tight grip. "Something like that, yes."

Ty's ice-blue eyes met the shadowed green of his cousin's. "I gather you lost him."

Eli's expression gave nothing away. "Unfortunately."

"So he was faster than you."

"Apparently."

"And smarter."

"If by that you mean he had a head start and a vehicle hidden in the woods, then yes, he was smarter."

"Were you able to obtain the license plate number of this hidden vehicle?"

"No."

"So all in all, your presence at the manor wasn't overly helpful."

Sadie drew her iPhone from her shoulder bag. "I didn't

come into town so you and your cousin could have a pissing contest, Ty."

"You shouldn't have come into town at all," he fired
back. "Why didn't you call me from the manor?"

She wagged her phone. "I did, three times. There was
no signal, and by the time I got one, we were in the Hollow." She made a frustrated gesture. "I heard the vehicle
Eli mentioned roar off."

"Direction?"

"East," Eli told him. "Toward Raven's Hollow."

A four-year stint in the army had taught Ty how to control his facial muscles, if not his entire expression.

"I'll need to inspect the site, gather more facts. You took
pictures of the bird and the wall. Kudos for that. But Eli
can't provide me with a license plate number, and neither
of you can describe the intruder, leaving me with nothing
except a dead raven, an eastbound vehicle and a single
painted word to go on."

"It was a truck." Eli kept his tone conversational.

Ty's dark blond eyebrows came together. "What was?"

"The eastbound vehicle. I'd guess a Dodge Ram,
twenty, maybe thirty years old. I'd also go with stolen
since the guy was smart enough to send the raven-card
email Sadie told you about from a toss-away phone." He
shrugged at his cousin's glare. "Police computer. I linked
to Sadie's office line. There's no owner registered on her
last incoming. Sender's got a plan, and it doesn't involve
being identified."

She'd known that, Sadie thought, of course she had.
She'd been a journalist far too long to delude herself. "I
don't suppose you have any idea, beyond terrifying me,
what that plan might entail?"

She felt Eli's gaze on her face. "Working on it."

Across the cramped room, Ty drummed a pen on his

blotter. "Tell me, cousin, how do you determine twenty or thirty years old in a truck?"

"Three back-breaking summers spent on my grandfather's farm in Idaho. Why are you wet?"

Ty frowned down at his soaked shirt and pants. "I—was hungry, stepped out. Figured the diner might be serving on emergency power."

"It's after eleven," Sadie remarked. "Johnny's closes at ten."

"The time thing didn't occur until I was halfway there. I was heading back when I spotted a couple kids outside Dorothy Leamer's antique store and made a detour."

Eli grinned. "Does she still keep her cash float in a cigar box under the counter?"

"It's her lucky box. She's been robbed a dozen or more times, but she always gets the money and the box back. Neither thing made it out of the store tonight. Unfortunately, the kids ran off before I could identify them."

"Making you and Eli even in the 'oops' department." Sadie indicated the curb outside. "The lamp the intruder used is in my Land Rover. I picked it up after he took off, but you could still check it for fingerprints."

A muscle in Ty's jaw ticked. "You figure there'll be any to find?" he asked Eli.

"Doubt it. You might get a clue from the bird. It was shot through the head."

"Did he use blood or paint for the wall message?"

"Paint. There wouldn't have been enough blood in a single raven to write a message that large."

"I assume you secured the scene."

"Do I really need to answer that?"

The tick in Ty's jaw deepened. "I think you should stay in town tonight, Sadie."

"And leave Molly alone out on the point? Answer's no."

"Fine." He yanked out his smartphone. "Is she at the manor?"

"Not when we were there. Save your battery, Ty. I've left five unanswered messages. All I can think of is that she went somewhere after work, turned her phone off and hasn't turned it back on yet."

"Right, then I'll just drive you home myself and spend the night.... Crap!" He scowled at his beeping cell, then breathed out and punched Talk. "Raven's Hollow Police Station. Chief Blume."

Leaving him to the call, Sadie joined Eli at the rain-streaked station window and studied his face. "Even in shadow, I can see the wheels turning. Talk to me, Lieutenant. Why would someone want to torment me with words that read like threats, and a raven with a bullet in its head?"

"*Mine forever.* Says it all, don't you think?"

She did, actually, or would have if she'd been willing to take it that far.

Ty's voice cut in. "Stay calm, Liz. I'll be right there." Frustration etched itself into his handsome features. "A six-year-old girl ran off in pursuit of her new puppy after it wiggled through a window. Now puppy and child are both lost. Mother's hysterical. Are you sure you secured the scene?" he demanded of Eli.

"I didn't ditch my badge and training at the state line. Everything you need to see will be there in the morning."

His cousin's response came in the form of a snarl. "See that it is." Giving Sadie's arm an awkward pat, he said, "Watch your back." Then he shot an accusing look in Eli's direction. "Unless you want a knife in it."

As soon as he was out the door, Sadie plastered a serene smile on her lips. "Well, that was horrible."

"Can I say I told you so?"

"Only if you want to walk to wherever it is you plan to sleep tonight."

"I was originally thinking Rooney's cottage."

"In that case, you're facing a long and treacherous hike."

He chuckled. "I haven't checked out the bulldog yet, Sadie. You know how Rooney gets stuck on a point."

"So…Ty's sofa it is. Good luck with that."

"Uh-huh." When she turned away, he tugged on her hair and swung her gently back around. "You know where I'll be sleeping tonight, and there won't be any old men, dogs or hostile sofas involved. Your front door lock's been compromised, Sadie."

Reaching behind her, Sadie extricated his hand from her hair. "You're trying to frighten me into letting you sleep at my place. Not only is that an unworthy tactic, it's also an unnecessary one, because while I don't appreciate your high-handed I'm-a-cop-and-you're-not attitude, I do in fact recognize that I've been threatened, and there was both a bullet and blood involved. So let's slide past the sleeping arrangements and the mind games, drive back to Bellam Manor and make sure Molly and Cocoa are safe."

The hand that had been in her hair moved to trap her chin. Eli's green eyes stared straight into hers. "This guy doesn't want Molly or Cocoa, Sadie. That's not what it's about."

She held his gaze. "What aren't you saying? I'm totally terrified to ask. In my experience, crazy people will steamroll anyone who gets in their way. Or so the theory generally goes."

"Generally," Eli agreed. "Except this isn't general, it's specific. And in terms of the email card you received, it's a virtual carbon copy of what happened to Laura a week before she was murdered."

TELLING SADIE WHAT had suddenly clicked in his mind did more than shock her into silence. It catapulted Eli back to the night his stepsister—Sadie's seventeen-year-old cousin, Laura—had died.

Sadie's aunt had married Eli's widowed father when Eli was ten. The melding of their families had been a seamless affair. But no doubt about it, Bellams and Blumes living under the same roof in Raven's Cove had been like Christmas on the local grapevine.

Eli and two friends from school had gone to a movie in the Cove the night of the murder. Laura had been babysitting Sadie, but she'd driven to the Hollow in her mother's cherry-red '69 Mustang with a promise to pick them up as soon as her aunt and uncle returned home.

He could have told her not to bother, Eli thought now. Less of a hassle to walk or let someone closer come and get them, but there'd been intermittent hailstorms all day, and face it, what adolescent boy would turn down a ride in the coolest car in town?

So he and his friends had wandered over to the arcade to wait. They'd slain dragons, bludgeoned knights and smashed castle walls, until, finally, the manager had come in and told them he was shutting down.

Eli had felt the first prickle of fear at that moment. He hadn't known why, not exactly. It hadn't been until later that he'd remembered hearing Laura on the phone three days earlier, pleading with someone to stop pestering her.

Drama queen, he'd figured at the time. People called Laura a diva, and, what the hell, she'd stuck her tongue out at the handset after slamming it down, so how serious could the call have been?

He'd gotten his answer that weekend when, feeling sick and guilty, he'd trudged into the hollow to search for her. Everyone had been looking by then, yet oddly enough, the only person he'd bumped into in the dense woods was Sadie.

He'd known something was terribly wrong, because he'd snuck into Laura's room and discovered a card with two ravens on it in the wastepaper basket under her desk. She'd torn it up, but the pieces had been easily reassembled, and once whole, had made even a fourteen-year-old boy's blood run cold.

The scrawl inside had read MY LOVE in bold red letters. There'd been no signature, and of course, nothing on or in it could be traced. Not to the boyfriend Laura had recently broken up with or to anyone in the Cove or the Hollow.

But someone had written those words. Someone who'd either sent the card or slipped it to her before she'd died. Someone, Eli reflected darkly, who'd sent Sadie an eerily similar message—two full decades later.

SADIE LET HIM drive her Land Rover up the treacherous road to Bellam Manor. They didn't talk much, which was normal enough for Eli and perfectly fine with her. Staving off terror took concentration and strong mental locks.

Two ravens, though, on two separate cards, two decades apart. One imprisoned, one free. And no signature in either case.

Determined not to think about where this was leading, she attempted to contact Molly again. But her cousin's voice mail picked up, and as it did, frustration slipped past the knot of fear in her throat. She turned in her seat. "Why didn't I hear about Laura's card before tonight, Eli? Or the phone call you say she got?"

He kept his eyes on the road and his tone mild. "You were seven years old. You found her body in Raven's Bog. Literally tripped on her hand and went down. The doctors in both the Hollow and the Cove agreed you must be in shock. And I repeat—only seven."

"A resilient seven." She tapped an impatient thumbnail on her phone. "The only call I've gotten came in conjunction with the email that was sent to me today at the *Chronicle*."

"Still a call."

She thought back. "The voice was computer altered. I didn't recognize it."

"Male?"

"Inasmuch as a synthesized voice can have a gender, yes. In any case, the intruder at the manor was male. And don't you dare suggest an accomplice. This is twisted enough already. Whoever hit Laura with a tire iron left her and her car in what used to be the heart of the hollow. But twenty years ago, the road we were on tonight—which is the only drivable road from end to end—was nothing more than a goat path. So, obvious next question. How did her car wind up in the bog?"

"The consensus was that Laura let the killer get into the car. Once inside, he forced her to drive to Raven's Bog. They exited the car, he struck her, then left her body, the Mustang and the murder weapon at the scene."

"Do you know where the tire iron came from?"

"An auto scrap yard in Bangor."

"So, summing up, there were no fingerprints on the murder weapon, there was no blood in the car and nothing but… God, why am I doing this?" Unbelieving, Sadie drilled her index fingers into her temples. "It's insane, like Laura's murderer—who's apparently been in the area all along. Whoever he is, this guy's a volcanic time bomb on a really slow tick. And he seems to have it in for Bellam females." When Eli didn't respond, she lowered her hands.

"A little reassurance would be nice here, Lieutenant—before I totally freak out!"

He made the final turn to the manor. "Would it help if I said we could be dealing with a copycat?"

"Which would be better—how exactly?"

"Different perpetrator, potentially different...motive."

She pounced. "You hesitated before you said 'motive.'"

"I hesitated because something just blew off one of the manor's towers and across my line of vision."

"You were going to say 'outcome,' weren't you? Potentially different outcome. As in he might shoot me instead of using a tire iron."

"Sadie..."

"I know." She went back to pushing on her temples. "Freaking myself out again. I need to refocus, and lucky me, I see a light in Molly's window. I can distract myself by reading her the riot act for turning off her phone."

"Isn't shouting at Molly a bit like kicking a puppy?"

"I said read, not shout. All I really want to do is make sure she's safe. Because I don't believe, and neither do you, that there's a copycat at work here. It's twenty years later, Eli, and somebody's doing to me almost exactly what he did to Laura. But who's to say that after such a long hiatus, this person doesn't have a different plan in mind? How do we know I'm the only Bellam he intends to threaten? Or kill?"

HE SAT IN the dark, with the storm shrieking around him, and he breathed. In and out, in and out.

It was all about making the right moves at the right time. He wanted Sadie. He needed Sadie to know he wanted her. But he also needed her to know she'd hurt him.

Love and fear and anger fought a bitter, three-way battle in his head these days. Twenty years ago, he'd discovered that a sleeping monster lived deep inside him. What if the monster woke up and consumed him? He might kill Sadie the way he'd killed Laura.

Would he, though? Could he? He loved Sadie so very, very much. He saw himself spending the rest of his life with her. Was it possible this newer, deeper love might stop the monster from clawing its way out?

Possibly, but one thing he'd learned tonight was that accidents could happen when you carried a gun.

The raven should have been a symbol of his love. He hadn't meant to kill it, but at least the bullet hadn't wound up in Sadie's head. He could take comfort in that.

When he started to shake, he dropped his face into his hands. He was tired, so damnably tired. Should he try to sleep? Did he dare? Or would the monster know and seize the opportunity to go on a rampage?

To go on a witch-hunt?

Chapter Seven

"The battery in her cell phone died."

Twenty minutes after they walked through her cousin's front door. Sadie returned to the thickly shadowed room Molly called a parlor.

"She stayed in town to have dinner with a friend who's afraid of thunderstorms. Neat, tidy, logical. Mystery solved, Lieutenant."

"One mystery, anyway." Eli held up and examined a double-edged dagger. "Any reason she collects and displays lethal weapons?"

"Witch's tools," Sadie corrected. "That dagger you're holding is an athame. Its white-handled counterpart is a boline." She swept a hand along the sideboard. "Chalice, ritual candles, tarot cards, protective crystals—dog."

Eli regarded the tiny, ratlike creature at the far end. Its pointy ears quivered as the animal stared back.

"His name's Solomon." Sadie bit back most of a smile. "He and Cocoa don't get along. Seeing as Molly's coming with us to my place, it should be a lively gathering."

"Especially if Cocoa's in the mood for a midnight snack."

"I'll make sure she's well fed. By the way, you might want to put that dagger down before Molly sees you. She's proprietorial about family heirlooms."

"Seriously? These things belonged to your ancestor?"

"Most of them did. Molly's a buff. She's searched the manor from subcellar to tower peak. If you look closely, you'll see Nola Bellam's initials inscribed on the larger items."

"So Hezekiah Blume really did marry a witch."

"Depends on how you look at it. Nola possessed the implements of a witch, but then Molly currently possesses those same implements, and no one's ever accused her of witchcraft."

"I'll let that one pass."

"And I'll light a metaphorical fire under my cousin." But Sadie paused in the doorway. "Do you have any ideas, theories, even vague thoughts on tonight's intruder?"

"Having seen this house, I'd say he doesn't believe in curses."

"Oh, well, if that's true, you can take almost every male in both towns out of the running."

"There you go. Should be an easy solve."

"Five minutes." Giving the molding a double tap, she left Eli alone with the lash of rain and wind outside and a tangle of thoughts in his head.

He was a cop, he reminded himself. Solid facts and cold, hard evidence were his life. What was screwing it all up for him at the moment was his inability to slam a mental door on the welter of Sadie-related emotions he didn't want to feel.

She'd been a beautiful child, with her wild mass of red-brown hair and her amazing storm-gray eyes. Fortunately, back then—kid. Unfortunately, now—woman.

His own eyes shifted as wind whipped through cracks in the ceiling and rattled the window glass.

"No one's going to rob you, Molly." Sadie returned a

few minutes later with her cousin in tow. "And the more people under one roof tonight, the better."

Yes, no, maybe. Eli managed not to grind his teeth as he watched Sadie bend to pick up her black trench coat. "Could you bring Solomon?" Her expression solemn, Molly dragged her Bellam red hair into a ponytail. "He doesn't bite."

Did he even have teeth? But Eli tucked the dog under his arm and followed the women into the storm.

Confusion reigned from the moment they entered Sadie's plant-filled home. As predicted, Cocoa chased the Chihuahua under a tall cabinet. The lights flared and died three times, and in spite of the fact that he'd draped a sheet over the sinister message, on one of his trips through the foyer, he found Molly easing a corner up for a look.

"Morbid curiosity?" he inquired from the shadows.

She jumped back a full foot before finding him in the dark. "I was just—I wanted to see. It's not that I don't believe what Sadie said, I'm only surprised anyone would come into Bellam Manor to do it. A lot of people are afraid of this place."

"But not you."

"No. I mean—why would I be?" She touched her ponytail. "The house wouldn't turn on one of its own."

Okay, that was weird. But, as he recalled, so was Molly. Or had been back when he'd lived in the Cove.

With a small smile, she and her flickering candle more or less melted into the darkness. Unsure what to make of her, Eli checked the writing behind the sheet, listened to the storm for another moment, then made his way to the kitchen.

He saw Cocoa sitting calmly on the windowsill while Sadie rummaged in a high cupboard. "No offense," he said genially, "but your cousin hasn't gotten any less strange with time."

"I've heard that before. Yet people keep coming into the pharmacy to have their prescriptions filled. Not to worry, her plan for the rest of the night is to lock herself in my guest room with her tarot cards, her laptop and, I'm pretty sure, since it appears to be missing, my grandmother's carving knife."

Eli straddled a hard chair while she continued to rummage. "Am I responsible for that, or does Molly generally sleep with knives?"

"I think you unsettle her."

"Makes us even."

Sadie laughed, and the sound of it was a punch of pure lust in his gut. "You are not afraid of my cousin, Eli."

"No? I heard a story in my junior year. A girl who humiliated her wound up with a bad case of warts."

"Where do you get this stuff? Never mind." She held up a hand. "Rooney. Ah, good, found them." She set a taper and three pillar candles on the table. "Your great-grandfather is leaning as heavily on our witchy legend as he is on the Raven's Tale in order to entice tourists to visit *your* town."

Warily fascinated, Eli tracked her movements. "Nola Bellam married Hezekiah Blume, Sadie. That's a fact. The legends are intertwined and fair game for anyone wanting to use them as an enticement."

She aimed the taper at him. "This is why my great-grandfather went to live in the north woods."

Sadie had a hypnotic way of moving, Eli noted. By the glow of a single taper, she appeared to float around the kitchen. Her still-damp tank top and skirt clung to her in a way that made his lower body burn and brought him right to the edge of begging.

Common sense and a hard slap of memory would keep those reactions in check, but it would still take every scrap of restraint he possessed not to jump her.

When he realized she was watching him, he shrugged off her last remark. "You want to talk fear factor, your great-grandfather's got it all over Rooney. What is he now, ninety-five?"

"Ninety-nine." Sweeping around behind him, she ran a teasing finger over his hair. "Hot on Rooney's colorful heels."

With a silent curse, Eli caught her hand. Coming smoothly to his feet, he murmured, "This sleepover thing actually might not be such a good idea. We're standing here talking about weird cousins and Hezekiah, a man people think is a ghost, and what I'm really wondering is why the hell we're talking at all."

She resisted ever so slightly as he drew her toward him. "We agreed back at your truck not to do this."

"I remember the conversation." He held her gaze. "And you can stop me any time. We both know there's nowhere for it to go. Cops and relationships don't work. Trust me, I've been there and back again."

With his thumb and fingers, he captured her chin, tipping her head up until he saw the glimmer in her eyes. He recognized the challenge in them, but right then he didn't care. He wanted his mouth on hers, and screw the consequences. The moment for any last chance objections came and went as he brought her lips slowly up to meet his.

He'd keep it brief, he promised himself, hot and fast, a flash of desire satisfied.

It would have worked if she'd been another woman. Any woman other than the one he'd met and danced with in Boston.

Her fingers curled into his hair, and she moved against

him in a kind of sinuous samba. He let his hands roam over her ribs, then around them so his palms cupped her breasts. He breathed in the scent of her while his tongue explored her mouth. She smelled like wild roses. She tasted like sin. She felt like the answer to a prayer.

If there were answers.

If he'd had prayers.

Easing back a tempting inch, she regarded him through her lashes. "I can feel the conflict in you, Eli. I know what it's like to want but know you can't or shouldn't have. I think."

"That's part of our problem, isn't it?" His eyes traveled over her face. "We're always thinking."

Her smile widened. "Not sure I'd say that, Lieutenant." And yanking his mouth back down onto hers, she blasted everything that didn't have its roots in need from his head.

It might have been lightning or the glow from the taper that caused the darkness to shift. Whatever the source, when he spotted a shadow that shouldn't be there, his body stilled.

Sensing the change, Sadie drew back. "What is it?"

"Not sure." He scanned the spread of black rocks that led to the edge of the cliff. "No, don't look." He held her in place when she started to turn. "Pretend we're talking."

"We are talking." But she gave the ends of his hair a playful flick with one hand, and skimmed the fingers of her other across his cheek. "What do you see?"

He kissed her forehead. "Unless Molly's taking a late night stroll, someone's out there."

"Wonderful. Can you tell if 'someone's' carrying a gun?"

"I'll need more than a glimpse for that. The light's pretty much nonexistent."

"I am so getting a generator."

Ten seconds ticked by. "There it is." He drew his own gun from the back of his jeans. "Considering its remote location, Bellam Manor's a busy place tonight. Is there a side door?"

"Through the pantry. Eli, are you sure...?"

"Dead raven," he reminded her, and she held up her hands in surrender.

A feeble streak of lightning flashed as the storm limped grudgingly out to sea. With his gun pointed skyward, and his eyes alert, Eli inched the pantry door open, waited a beat, then stepped out into the gusting rain.

"Come on," he muttered to the shadowy caller. "Give me a target."

He got one ten seconds later in the form of a barely there movement that indicated the caller was creeping along the back of the house.

Whoever it was wore a long coat and had one hand pressed to the outer wall. The other hand—he couldn't tell. Might be carrying a weapon, might be holding something else. Like another dead bird?

Able to just make out the flat rocks ahead, he jammed the gun in his waistband and went for a takedown. When the shadow lost its balance on the slippery ground, Eli knew it was over.

One solid tackle was all it took. Surprised by the ease of the capture, rather than plant a knee, he flipped his quarry over. And found himself face-to-face with a writhing, swearing female.

Even fully pinned, she bucked, thrashed and squirmed, twisting her head from side to side. At length, she settled for spitting at him.

"Stop fighting me," he shouted above the wind. "I don't want to hurt you."

She either didn't hear him or didn't care, and spat again.

Cursing now, Eli released her left hand. It flew straight up toward his face, but he blocked the blow with his elbow and snatched her hood back.

Bared teeth and furious eyes greeted him. In that same split second, she succeeded in freeing a knee and immediately aimed at his groin.

"Not tonight, lady." He knocked it off to the side. "Who the hell are you?"

She tried to heave him up and off. "None of your business. Get—off—me!"

They shot wildcats in Maine, didn't they? "Calm down," he said again. "I'm a cop."

"Screw that, pal. I know Ty Blume and his deputies. You're not one of them."

Firming his hold on her wrists, he focused on her face. "You know Ty?"

It didn't surprise him when Sadie dropped down beside him and squeezed his arm. "She knows Ty, Eli. And I know her. You can let her go, but do it carefully. She has a spiteful temper."

The female snorted. "Pot, kettle, Sadie."

"We mostly tolerate each other," Sadie continued in an unruffled tone. "You remember my cousin, Orley, Eli. She's a veterinary assistant by day and, I'll assume, Ty's watchdog by night." Nudging his shoulder, she added an amused "Good thing you know your job, Lieutenant, because Orley here is also a former state champion in mixed martial arts."

Chapter Eight

"We've been over this, Sadie," her cousin maintained the following morning. "Yes, Ty sent me. But the word 'spy' never came up."

"Implied's as good as stated."

Arms folded, Orley slumped down in the passenger seat. "The guy was worried about you. He couldn't leave the station house, and he couldn't get through to Deadbeat Molly, so he called and asked me to spend the night at the manor. Easy breezy."

"There's no easy in Ty's world." Sadie shoved her four-by-four into a lower gear for the descent to Ben Leamer's farm. "He didn't want me to be alone with Eli, and he had no idea if and or when Molly might show. Solution? Recruit a stand-in."

Orley thrust up her bruised forearms. "You're bitching, but I'm the one who got mowed down and pinned by Officer Sexy."

"Lieutenant Sexy," Sadie shot back, then made a growling sound. "If you think Eli's so hot, why aren't you with him instead of me? A tow truck was waiting with a new tire when we dropped him off at the fallen pine."

Her cousin snorted. "News bulletin, sunshine. The über-hot Lieutenant Blume only has eyes for you. He also only didn't insist on going with you to Ben's farm because he needs his truck back, and I'd already agreed to ride shot-gun. He might have liked it better if Molly had done the honors, but her being totally anal and all, that wasn't going to happen. The pharmacy must be unlocked precisely at eight a.m. She has OCD, you know. Undiagnosed, but even you can't deny she's peculiar, and getting worse every day."

Amusement rose as Sadie spied the farm. "I can deny a lot of things, actually. It's the curse—or the gift, your choice—of a vivid imagination."

"Do not use the word 'curse' in any conversation that involves Molly. If it pertains to the Cove or the Hollow, it's under an evil spell as far as she's concerned. Now, using that as our segue, talk to me about the messages you've received."

Sadie pulled into the driveway and, with the park brake set, regarded the sky. Angry black clouds threatened an-other deluge, but so far so dry. "I know you love ghoulish details, Orley, but I've given you all there are, so bury your curiosity and back off. I have pictures to take of what I'm told is a truly spooky corn maze."

Her cousin made a dubious face at the high field of corn that spread out forever from the side of a secondary barn. "The maze is an okay deal, but the rest of Leamer's farm creeps me out. Animals die, you cremate or bury them. You do not set up a side business to stuff them for people who are as icky-minded as you are."

"I'm not here to watch Ben preserve someone's dead pet. Getting lost in a cornfield has snowballed into a pop-ular October event. Kids love it."

"Kids are easy marks."

Sadie grinned. "You weren't."

"Neither were you. Face it, kid, we're Bellams. Nobody expects us to be normal."

"Then why do you have a problem with Molly?"

Hopping out, Orley zipped her coat. "Partly because she and I are both a few years shy of forty, and while I can see her not being married, I haven't figured out why it's never happened for me. I'm not an anal fusspot that people avoid because they're afraid they'll wake up with a face full of warts." She blew at her long red bangs. "That sounds small-minded and mean, doesn't it?"

"A little."

"Do you understand why?"

"Because Molly was a straight-A student, and you weren't?"

"Well, hold the phone, cousin—neither were you."

Sadie regarded her over the Land Rover's roof. "How did this get to be about me?"

"It didn't. It isn't. I just can't figure Molly, and I hate it when people compare me to her. She's a freak, even by Bellam standards."

"She's an introvert, Orley, but before we bite each other's heads off over this, let's change the subject. Otherwise, you'll challenge me to a kickboxing match where I'm sure to wind up on my butt, in what I hope, but seriously doubt, is mud."

"Awkward sentence, excellent call."

After tugging a short red jacket over her T-shirt and jeans, Sadie crawled into the backseat to hunt through her camera bag. When her cousin didn't speak, she rolled her eyes. "I can feel your curiosity from here." Crawling back out, she looked around. "Come on, Ben, I haven't got all day.… And no, Orley, we didn't have sex."

Her cousin strolled closer, smirking. "Does that mean he's a lousy kisser?"

Sadie sent her a guileless smile. "If you mean Ben Leamer, I wouldn't know. If you mean Eli, it's none of your business."

"Why not? You're a public figure, he's a public figure."

"Eli defends the public, he's not a figure of it."

"Public's public. Also please note, I said kiss, not sex."

"You're working up to sex. And what makes you think I've kissed him—as if I can't guess?"

"You have a big kitchen window. No blinds, easy pickup."

"Yeah, for anyone creeping around the manor." Sadie made a shooing motion with her fingers. "Creep over to the maze entrance, will you? I need a point of reference."

Orley's shoulders hunched. "I don't like having my picture taken. And I wasn't creeping. I didn't get an answer at the front door, so I went around to the back, and there you both were, getting hot and bothered in the kitchen. Being a considerate sort, I opted to retrace my steps to the front. You saw how it went from there. FYI, your sexy lieutenant's very strong."

"Know it." Sadie crouched for a better angle. "Move left."

"I'm freezing. Where did the stupid heat go?"

"South. Stop fidgeting."

Her cousin snarled out a breath. "Any chance we'll be done by noon? Brady and I are supposed to do a dental on a Doberman—assuming the road to the Cove gets cleared and he makes it to the clinic with the anesthetic we have almost none of. While we're on the topic, have you thought about…?"

"Adding a veterinary procedure of the month column to the *Chronicle*? You've asked me that twenty times already."

"Animals are cute, Sadie."

"Animals are adorable. Procedures aren't. Will you please stand still?"

"I'm cold. I'm also trying to normal things up around

here. People are talking, and not just about Rooney Blume's birthday."

A chill that had nothing to do with the dipping temperature skated along Sadie's spine. "I don't want to talk about Laura."

"Neither do I. I was referring to the Hezekiah Blume, Nola Bellam story."

"Legend." Sadie snapped three quick shots. "Based on historical fact."

"Fictionalized fact."

"Only certain aspects. A record of the marriage between Hezekiah Blume and Nola Bellam exists. We also know, via the family Bible, that the union pissed off Hezekiah's brother, Ezekiel, to the point that Ezekiel got drunk and raped Nola while Hezekiah was out of town."

"What a sweetheart," Orley muttered.

"Yeah, really sweet. To cover his butt, little brother branded Nola a witch—not a difficult thing to do given the strange nature of her family and the grim state of the Hollow in those days—whereupon, he and several fearful residents of Raven's Cove proceeded to hunt her down in the woods. He thought he killed her, but, oops, he missed." Sadie adjusted her camera lens. "When he returned to the Cove, Hezekiah, also believing Nola was dead, went on a rampage and murdered not only Ezekiel but every one of the townspeople who'd been involved in the hunt."

"After which—enter fiction." Orley wiggled her fingers. "Hezekiah recanted the evil spirit he'd taken into himself, and was ultimately transformed into a raven. The whole witch thing might have faded into folklore if Nola hadn't popped up again or, as the locals saw it, returned from the dead."

"That was just her outsmarting Ezekiel and his nasty compatriots."

"Ezekiel loved Nola, Sadie. He was willing to take her daughter as his own. And don't forget he met her before she and Hezekiah ever laid eyes on each other."

"Meaning what? First come, first served? Nola was in love with Hezekiah and vice versa. The order of meeting is irrelevant."

"Little bro was head over heels. From his perspective, big bro screwed him around. Guy went a little crazy is all."

"Right, because witch-hunts are only a *little* crazy." Sadie's gaze touched on a pair of rusted-out tractors and a wooden plow from the early twentieth century. "Doesn't look like Ben's going to show, does it?"

"Nope, ergo he must have had one whopping big emergency, because he was strutting around the Hollow yesterday, pleased as punch, telling anyone who'd listen that his corn maze would be getting a full page spread in next Sunday's edition." Blowing on her balled hands, Orley moved away from the entrance. "You know, Sadie, with all this talk about Hezekiah, Ezekiel and Nola, it occurs to me that you and Eli and Ty have a kind of parallel story happening here. Except you don't have a daughter, and Nola did."

"And Ezekiel was insane, and Ty isn't. Not to mention that Eli wouldn't turn to the dark side and wind up damned no matter what the inducement. Otherwise, though, absolutely, parallel story."

"It was an idle observation, cous. Tell me we're ditching this spook farm, and I'll zip it."

"We'll leave." Sadie grinned at her. "Right after I try out the maze."

"Damn, I knew you were going to say that."

"You can play with my iPad in the Rover. It shouldn't take me more than twenty minutes to work my way through."

"Okay, but word of caution. Ben's got jumping things

in there. Scarecrows and ravens, and pitchforks and supersized spiders that drop from webs."

"Consider me warned."

She'd have done this in any case, Sadie thought, but with Orley determined to explore in detail a legend that had haunted her sleeping mind for more than a week, the idea of getting lost in a cornfield took on added appeal.

They hadn't been close as children. Orley, Molly and Laura had all been a full decade older than her. And with her parents' marriage being about as crappy as it got, family gatherings had been few and far between.

The child she'd been hadn't thought much about the lack of contact with her relatives—until her aunt Cordelia had married Eli's father. Then she'd paid attention. Because little girls developed big crushes. And she'd tumbled hard for dark-haired, green-eyed Eli Blume.

Had it ever worn off? she wondered, as she pushed through the rustling stalks. Difficult to say, but her dreams had certainly taken on a different flavor with Eli at the manor last night. The tension inside her had been less bloodcurdling and more sensual. Which might mean that her heart was in as much danger as her life.

As Nola's had been when she'd chosen Hezekiah over Ezekiel?

Don't go there, Sadie, a voice in her head ordered. Far less terrifying to think about Eli's kisses than the dead bird on her doorstep. And better not to do either thing since navigating the maze required more than a little concentration.

She dead-ended twice and had to backtrack to forks that arrowed off in multiple directions. Ravens circling overhead emitted rough, taunting caws. The wind whistled eerily through the stalks. And, as Orley had predicted, all manner of things jumped out at her.

She made it past the swinging brooms easily enough, but gritted her teeth when a spider the size of a dinner plate dropped down five inches from her face. Half a step later, its eight-legged mate shot down to join it.

Okay, arachnids were definitely worth a pause.

With the tarantulas on steroids still bobbing in the breeze, Sadie glanced back down the path. It wasn't fair to blame Ben Leamer for the raw state of her nerves, but even setting that aside, she thought this portion of the maze might be a little too realistic for kids under ten. Not being under ten herself, however, she told the spiders to smile and snapped a close-up shot.

Did she only imagine the tarantulas were leering at her through the lens?

"Get a grip, Sadie," she muttered, and pushed past the pair of them.

She chose her next path at random. A scarecrow holding a wooden ax leaped out as she rounded a corner. She handled that one, but when a much nastier version burst out ten steps later, a laughing scream escaped.

Score one for Ben, she decided, and proceeded with greater care. So what if fat drops of rain were beginning to plop on the stalks? Unless it flooded the maze, a little water wouldn't hurt her.

Neither would a human-sized raven wearing a black cloak, but having one swoop into sight while she was glancing skyward sent her heart into her throat and stopped her in her tracks.

"Okay." She said it slowly, then took a moment to gather her wits. "Hezekiah Blume, I presume." Red eyes shone from the folds of a bulky hood. "Did not see you coming at all." Releasing a cautious breath, she lowered her gaze.

And spied an envelope fastened to the front of his cloak. Everything inside her turned to liquid. But that was an automatic first response. Her second was to spin in a stationary circle. "You are not going to frighten me." She kept her voice even and her senses alert. "I won't let you." Then a twig snapped directly behind her and her muscles went rigid. She whirled, blew out a breath. "Jesus— Orley."

"Yes, Orley. Who did you think?" Clearly out of sorts, her cousin brushed at her coat and short hair. "I felt like a coward sitting in your Jeep, plus Ben's hired hand showed up, and I did not want to hear about his six and a half kids, so I sucked it up and followed you. All was well until a damn bat attacked me in one of the…" When her eyes locked on the envelope, her voice trailed off. "What's that? No, sorry, obvious answer. But—" she ticked a finger "—don't think I'm liking the white thing with your name on it."

"Tell me about it."

Although she would have preferred to burn the envelope, Sadie yanked it free and ran her thumbnail along the sealed flap.

Inside she discovered a card with a jagged red heart just beginning to crack. "Hell," she whispered. And bracing for the worst, opened it.

While I love, the monster sleeps.

Orley offered a breathy "Holy crap" while Sadie reread the fractured scrawl.

When several wet drops of rain landed on her head, she shot a dangerous look at the clouds. "Stop raining!"

Orley stabbed a finger. "That is a gonna-get-you threat, Sadie."

"I know what it is."

She also knew—though she wasn't sure how she heard it over the roar of blood in her head—that her phone was ringing.

With the card and envelope in one hand, she slid the fingers of her other into her jeans pocket.

Orley read the screen over her shoulder. "Bob's Cleaning Service?"

Eyes still fixed on the effigy, Sadie hit Speaker. "What is it, Bobby?"

"So sorry, my love, but I borrowed your janitor's phone."

The computer voice hit her like a physical blow—until she pictured the gray-haired cleaning man who'd given her gumdrops as a child. "Where's Bobby?" she demanded, ignoring Orley's attempts to mime a message. "What have you done to him?"

"I don't hurt old men, Sadie. I simply borrowed—well, stole—his phone." A long pause preceded a raspy "I know you got my message."

Sadie executed a warier circle this time. "Which one?"

"The card with the heart."

He was here, she realized. He was watching.

A sudden horrible thought occurred. "Where's Ben Leamer?"

"Sleeping. Soundly."

"You knew I'd go into the maze when he didn't show."

"Hoped," the caller replied. "Saw. Used the opportunity."

"How long have you been following me?"

"Long enough to know you're not...alone."

Orley's fingernails bit into her arm. "We need to get out of here."

Still searching the stalks, Sadie managed a steady "What do you want me to do?"

Even disguised, the unexpected pain came through. "I want you not to break my heart. I want you to care. I want you to please, please not wake the monster!"

Chapter Nine

By Eli's estimation, less than a quarter of his attention was focused on the task at hand. Not the ideal scenario for someone using a chain saw to cut up a fallen tree.

His cousin Brady, who operated the Raven's Hollow Veterinary Clinic, had come and gone three times in the past two hours. Each time he reappeared, he had a more powerful saw in the back of his battered Ford truck.

"This could be the best cutter in the county." Hopping up into the box, he shifted the tool so Eli could view the massive blade. "Problem is, Paul Bunyan's not here to operate it, and I've never used anything this big before."

The tow truck driver, a beefy man with nervous eyes, slapped his gloves on his thigh. "Might be two could lift the thing. Eli?"

"Pass. I'm not eager to hack off a foot. Midsized version works for me."

Brady hunkered down. "What we need is a plow horse."

"What we need is an ox." With all four of his wheels intact, Eli tossed a chain around a freshly cut section of pine and fastened it to his winch. "All we have to do until the road crew arrives is make an opening wide enough for an emergency vehicle to get through."

The driver from Cove Towing made an anxious sweep of the woods. "Not sure I wanna picture emergency vehicles when I'm standing in the middle of the hollow. Lots of folks hereabouts swear this is a haunted place, and near the bog most of all."

Eli tugged on the chain to secure it. "You're letting Rooney's wild stories get to you, Brick."

"Nothing wild about your stepsister's death. A believer would say there's possession involved. The guy she dumped two weeks before had Blume blood."

Brady glanced at Eli. "The guy she dumped also had an alibi for the time of the murder."

"Yeah, but who gave him that alibi? His own ma, that's who."

Rain began to spit from a nasty-looking sky. Eli figured they'd be soaked in a minute whether he pursued this or not. "Her ex's name was Cal Kilgore, Brick." He turned to his cousin. "Is Cal still in the Cove?"

"More out than in," Brady told him. "He built a cabin in the north woods and got himself a forge. Last I heard, he was making specialized metal products and selling them to a wholesale outfit in Bangor."

"How often do you see him?"

"Three times in the last fifteen years. And not much more than that before he left town. He was older than Laura by about five years, so that'd put him around forty-two these days."

Interesting, Eli reflected. Not necessarily relevant, but worth a back-check.

He heard a squawk from the tow truck, which signified an incoming call, and noted the instant expression of relief on Brick's face. "Looks like we're about to lose some of our muscle."

Dragging on a rumpled jacket, Brady grinned. "Happens a lot in this spot." He nodded at the tree. "You can tell me to mind my own, but seeing as your truck was stuck on the Cove side, how is it you wound up spending the night in the Hollow?"

Eli drew off his work gloves. "It's a long story. Short version, I hitched a ride with Sadie."

His cousin's brown eyes registered surprise. "Sadie was out on this spit-slick road in last night's storm? Why?"

"She got a crank call at the newspaper. It pissed her off."

"That'd make sense if Ty's office wasn't in exactly the opposite direction from the one she must have been taking."

"Think it through, Brady."

"Just did. Clever avoidance of an ex." He sighed when Brick waved an arm out his window and roared off. "As predicted, there goes a third of our muscle. Do you hear a siren?"

"Yep."

Brady tucked his wire-rimmed reading glasses inside the jacket and murmured a semi-amused "Let the fireworks begin."

With his more ornery cousin still a good distance away, Eli returned to his truck and used its mechanical muscle to drag a large branch off the road.

The prospect of a second confrontation with Ty didn't bother him. But spending the better part of the morning with his mind caught between a threat and a kiss? That just plain sucked. It also irritated him that not one but both things scared the hell out of him.

He'd tried for a relationship once, with an entertainment journalist...and where in hell had that disaster of a memory crawled in from? She'd messed up; then he'd messed up, and they'd both paid the price for it. End of nightmare.

Eli squeezed his truck through the new opening and was prepping the chain again when Ty squealed to a halt.

Surly and spoiling, he strode over to plant his booted feet less than eighteen inches from where his cousin crouched.

"Problem?" Eli asked, not looking up.

"You didn't leave the damn bird."

"Yeah? Where was I supposed to leave the damn bird, Ty? On your desk in an unlocked police station?"

"Raven's Hollow isn't the back of beyond. We have an evidence room with an automatic lock."

"Right." Now he looked up. "Did you expect me to shoot out the lock to gain access to the room? You left before us, Chief, and street-entrance dead bolts only work with keys—which I didn't have. Next accusation?"

Ty widened his stance. "Do you want it in the face or the stomach?"

Perfect, Eli thought, and stood. "You want to fight me? Here? Now?"

"What he wants," Brady put in from a wise distance, "is a free shot. My advice? Take it in the stomach. He's got a tricky uppercut."

Rain had begun to dribble past the collar of Eli's jacket. That, combined with a petulant wind and his deteriorating mood, made the prospect of a good fistfight more appealing than it might otherwise have been.

Still, he was a cop, and trained to defuse volatile situations rather than encourage them. "Do you really think physical's the way to go here, Ty?"

"What I think," his cousin snapped, "is that you've messed with Sadie's head the same way you did with Lisa Johnson's."

"Who's Lisa Johnson?"

"Twelfth grade biology. You dissected a frog together."

"Well, Jesus." But his cousin was dead serious and slammed the heel of his hand into the side of Eli's truck.

"I was engaged to Sadie until you came along."

Brady stepped between them. "Don't you think this is a bit counterproductive? Also, if we're keeping score, I'm the one who took Lisa Johnson to the prom. Spiked the punch, too."

One of Eli's eyebrows winged up. "That was you?"

"It was watered-down vodka—which is neither here nor there. Lisa Johnson's not the point. Sadie is."

"The point," Ty retorted thin-lipped, "is that someone threatened Sadie's life yesterday. Yet here you are, Eli, on the Hollow Road—and where the hell is she? I'll tell you where. She's out at the farm of a man who's a taxidermist and who also has a corn maze big enough to swallow Rhode Island."

Eli controlled his expression and his temper. "You know all that, and yet here you are, as well, accusing me, among other things, of being a crappy cop."

"Sadie's—"

"Got a mind of her own." Despite the assertion, guilt began to slither in his stomach. "She's also not alone. Orley's with her. And Leamer's expecting her."

"I guess that's just one of the many difference between us, cousin. I wouldn't have delegated the responsibility."

"You see Sadie as a responsibility? Not sure she'll appreciate that."

"I'm sure," Brady murmured.

"You're deflecting the blame," Ty ground out.

"No, I'm being reasonable. You're suggesting I should glue myself to her side whether she wants me there or not, to which I repeat, she's got a mind of her own."

"You always have an answer, don't you, a way to twist what you don't want to hear?"

"It's a Blume trait. Sadie's her own woman, Ty, Orley's a former kickboxing champion and Ben Leamer's a staple in the community."

"So, nothing to worry about."

The guilt tangled into slippery knots. Eli kept the curses inside and his features neutral, but dammit, his cousin wasn't wrong. And both the cop in him and the man who'd allowed Sadie to become a fever in his brain had managed to miss it.

"Doing things by the book never suited you, did it?" Ty set his jaw. "You just rewrite it to suit your purpose."

"I don't see how—" Brady began.

"Shut up. I'm talking to Eli—who showed up oh so conveniently on the heels of the first threat Sadie received. How do I know it wasn't you who killed the stupid bird and issued those threats?"

"If you believe I'm deranged, you don't. Not sure how a roll in the mud'll change anything, but I'm game." Holding his hands out to the side, Eli fixed his gaze on his cousin's face. "Go for it."

He knew Ty would have accepted the invitation in a heartbeat if an approaching vehicle hadn't diverted everyone's attention.

"Sadie?" Like a switch flipped in his head, Eli's focus shifted. "What the hell did she do with Orley?"

"She looks pissed," Brady noted. "If she's also got contusions, I'd say you probably shouldn't have left them alone together."

Eli heard him, but he'd already covered half the distance to the Land Rover. When she shoved the door open and hopped out, she did look angry. But what made his blood run cold was that she looked even more agitated.

He caught her arms before she took two steps. And only vaguely questioned the wisdom of doing so when her eyes flashed a warning.

"I need to move," she said through her teeth. "Nothing

personal, Eli, but if I don't walk this off, I'm liable to kick something. Or someone."

He studied her face for a moment, then stepped back, hands raised. "Talk to me," he told her. "Straight, no side trips, or I'm liable to go all cop on you."

A half smile appeared. "You'll do that anyway." She sent the black clouds a smoldering look. "I said—stop raining! Here." She shoved a white envelope at him. "My sick wall writer left this for me in Ben Leamer's corn maze. And I say 'left,' but I really mean 'planted.' He was in the maze with me, Eli. With us. With Orley and me. Orley stayed at the Leamer Farm because the guy who gave me the card also drugged old Ben. Between Orley and me and his hired hand, we managed to get two cups of coffee into Ben's system. He's fuzzy but otherwise okay."

Calling himself every foul name he could think of, Eli handed the card to Ty and concentrated on Sadie. "How do you know the guy was in the maze?"

A tremor rippled through her. "He phoned me. He said he'd hoped I'd go in. He attached the envelope to an effigy of Hezekiah Blume as a raven."

Ty scowled. "Did you or Orley see anything suspicious?"

"Only the ghosts our minds invented." Calmer now, Sadie breathed out. "I think we panicked a little."

Eli cycled through the possibilities. "Are you sure the caller was actually in the maze when he contacted you, though?"

"I'm…not sure, no." Her anger faded as her curiosity grew. "Is that significant?"

"Hardly." Ty examined the card from several angles.

"Possibly," Eli said.

"Why?" Brady offered an apologetic shrug. "Sorry, Eli, but if I'm following this, I have to wonder why it would matter whether or not some guy who gave Sadie a strange card and an equally strange phone call was watching her while they talked."

Eli saw Sadie's eyes flick from him to Ty and back. Yeah, she felt it, he thought, the charge in the air that was more electric than last night's storm.

"It's a detail," he said. "Maybe important, maybe not, but a piece of the puzzle one way or the other."

Watchful herself now, Sadie motioned at the squad car. "Ty, your two-way just went off."

"What?" He surfaced as if from a deep fog.

"Two-way?" She pointed. "Someone needs you."

"Right." He blinked. "Right. Damn. Okay, my jurisdiction here, people. Card stays with me while I deal with whatever problem's on the other end of my radio. Much as I hate to say it, Eli, you and Brady need to head out to the Leamer Farm. Sadie?"

She retracted her finger. "Sorry, but I need to go back to Ben's place."

"Right," he said again.

"I've covered stories like this before, Ty. The solution's always in the details." Walking over, she placed her hands on his shoulders and kissed his cheek. "If Eli's right, what's happening to me goes back twenty years to my cousin Laura's death.

"And if he's wrong?"

She stepped back, as much from the envelope as her former fiancé, Eli suspected.

"A monster's a monster. If that's what we're dealing with, it might be a good idea to remember that nothing and no one sleeps forever."

BEN LEAMER WAS still groggy when they reached the farm. The doctor hadn't arrived yet, but with the infusion of a little fear of God from a still-rattled Orley, he was happy enough to let Brady examine him.

While Brady obliged, Sadie led Eli through the corn maze. Hezekiah, minus envelope, put in an encore appearance. Eli noted the time of the call she'd received, asked her and Orley a thousand questions and was doing something on his iPhone when Brady emerged from the house.

"Regular doctor should give Ben a once-over, but he's a tough old guy. He was chloroformed. You'd have smelled it right off," he said to Eli. "Orley didn't, but then she was pretty freaked, and, bottom line, there's no real reason for her or Sadie to have recognized it."

Pressing on the tension knots in her neck, Sadie wandered around the farmyard. "All I smelled was his sister-in-law's sauerkraut."

"Why didn't you call Eli from the house?" Brady asked her.

"I tried, but Ben's line is down."

"And the bog's a notorious dead zone for cell phones." Eli leaned against the Land Rover. "Two-ways work, but that's it."

"Be glad anything works on the Hollow Road." Shouldering his instrument bag, Brady glanced at Orley, who was marching toward them, grim faced and hugging her arms across her chest. "Hard to believe it's only eleven o'clock. That being said, I have three pointy teeth to extract and a batch of anesthetic to pick up. Take care, Sadie. Watch for stray uppercuts, Eli."

"I am not doing favors for anyone ever again," Orley muttered in passing. "Later, people."

Sadie willed the stabbing pain in her skull down to a manageable level before dropping her hands. "At the risk of sounding like a whiny child, Eli, why are we still here? Shouldn't you and Ty be punching each other out or something?"

He gave the screen of his iPhone a final tap and looked up. "I should have come here with you."

The beginnings of a smile touched her lips. "Did Ty say that?"

"Yeah, but the thought had already occurred."

"In that case, Lieutenant, listen up and pass this on. I am not a maiden in distress, and I don't want or need you or Ty or even Orley dogging me everywhere I go."

"Sadie, Laura—"

"Didn't realize her life was in danger. At best, she was probably thinking pest. Believe me, I'm thinking something very different."

Pushing off from the Land Rover, Eli advanced on her. "Did you tell that to the guy who called you in the maze?"

"No, but I didn't go, 'Eek,' and faint, either. I took a self-defense course while I was in D.C. Don't," she warned, and drilled a finger into his chest when his advance brought him to within a foot of where she stood. "I'm not in the mood to fend off all the sexual vibes that bombard me whenever I make the mistake of touching you. I have work to do at the *Chronicle*. Stuff to approve, printing presses to swear at...."

"I get the picture, Sadie. I also still owe Rooney a canine favor."

His eyes glinted just enough to have hers narrowing in suspicion. "Why are you being so agreeable all of a sudden?"

"Maybe I'm just giving you credit for being able to handle yourself in any situation."

And maybe Rooney would breeze through another full century of life, but Sadie doubted it.

Keeping her finger on his chest, she nudged him back a

step. "Let's do it this way. You can follow me to the Hollow in your truck. We part company and maybe, maybe," she emphasized, "meet up again at Rooney's favorite dockside haunt around dinnertime."

"It's one plan," Eli acknowledged. "But if you're up for it, I have an alternative."

"Does it involve you playing watchdog as part of some clever plot to circumvent me?"

"No, it involves you and me making what will undoubtedly be a messy trip into the north woods."

Her laugh was mostly disbelief. "You want to visit my great-grandfather? Now? In the middle of hell week?"

"I was thinking more along the lines of us having a chat with Cal Kilgore."

"Ah, right. Laura's former boyfriend." Her gaze traveled northward. "Directions to the cabin would be an easy get. Not sure how happy he'll be to see us. Howard Hughes was a party animal compared to Cal after Laura died." Mistrust crept back in. "At the risk of sounding contrary, why do you want me to go with you? Or is this part of that clever plot I mentioned before?"

In spite of the finger still pushing into his chest, Eli caught and raised her chin. "What this is, Sadie, is me being impressed."

"By what?"

"You. Back on the Hollow Road, you told the rain to stop falling." A smile appeared as he kissed the tip of her nose. "A few seconds later, it did."

Chapter Ten

"I hope you realize, even my formidable strength of will won't hold the rain back indefinitely."

"Just do your best for as long as you can, and I'm good."

No, he wasn't, Sadie thought with a flicker of amusement. But then she wouldn't be, either, if it was her vehicle taking a beating instead of his.

There'd been details to deal with before they headed north. First and foremost, she'd wanted to check on her cleaning man, Bobby. He'd lost his cell phone but was otherwise unharmed. Next, she'd contacted Molly and asked her to feed Cocoa in the event that she and Eli didn't make it home as planned. She'd attempted to call her great-grandfather on his SAT phone, but the thickening cloud cover made satellite communication impossible. Last, because she'd ventured into the north woods enough times to know, she'd loaded a canvas pack with personal items and emergency supplies, and stowed it in Eli's truck.

From the passenger seat, she watched a line of evergreens, as tall as the towers of Bellam Manor, sway like happy drunks.

"If memory serves," she mused, "Cal gave me the willies when I was a kid. His eyes moved independently of each other, causing many of the Hollow residents to avoid him like the plague. It goes without saying that everyone who knew Laura seriously questioned her taste in males."

Eli braked at an odd-shaped fork. "Go for it."

She ticked a considering finger. "Left."

"Are you sure?"

"Eli, of the two of us in this truck, who's holding back the rain?"

Lips twitching, he took the left fork. "Tell me, how strongly does Molly believe in your witchy heritage?"

"Hard to say. She's superstitious on one hand and completely practical on the other."

"She told me Bellam Manor wouldn't turn on one of its own."

"That's a relief. Now if we could get it to tell us who broke in last night, we'd be set." She let a few seconds pass before sliding her gaze sideways. "Eli, what's the deal with you and Ty?"

"No deal, other than if I'm smart, I won't walk in front of him after sunset."

"There's a cheerful prospect."

"Guy's in love with you, Sadie."

She smiled a little. "He's really not, you know. He might still love me, but not the way you're interpreting it."

"He wanted to trade punches on the Hollow Road."

"What he wanted was to show you that he's as good a cop as you are."

"Ty knows he's a good cop. As much as it pains me to say this, he'd have been a decent husband, too."

Now her smile blossomed. "Every part of you just clenched up. But you can relax. Bellam females, from Nola to now, have had a notorious lack of success where relationships are concerned. Ask either of my parents which one of them screwed their marriage up worse, and they'll both tell you it was my mother." Leaning forward, she regarded the bruised sky. "Aw, see what you've done? It's starting to rain again. You rattled my concentration with that 'decent husband' remark. Now my mind's stuck in the bedroom."

"Pretty sure we were talking about you and Ty, Sadie."

"Yes, but I'm in your truck, post-Boston, and I have all these sexual vibes jittering around inside me."

His lips curved, but the gleam in his eyes smacked of danger. "Is that how you see us? As opposing masses of barely controlled vibes?"

"I used the word *jitter,* Eli, specifically because jitters are in fact controllable. By women, anyway."

"Is that your opinion of all men, or just me?"

"Oh, I have a much higher opinion of you than I do of most men." Her smile teased him now. "You charmed me in Boston, Eli. The bigger miracle is that you also charmed my aunt, who's as practical as Molly and wouldn't know a jitter if it bit her. She thought you were hot, and I was insane not to jump you."

"Yeah, well, that same aunt told me that you were her favorite niece, and if I so much as made you frown, she'd turn me into a jackass."

Sadie waved off the remark. "She uses that threat on men all the time. It's a private joke. In her opinion, there isn't a male alive who needs a hit of magic to become a jackass. It's a natural condition."

He grinned. "I could refute that, or shut up and drive. I'll go with the easier option."

"Making you the smartest jackass in the class. Turn right," she said without looking. "Follow the so-called road as far as you can, and I'll do what *I* can, sans spell book, to keep the ground underneath us as navigable as possible."

"Appreciate that, sweetheart. While you're at it—" he

nodded through the windshield "—you might want to tell that moose thirty feet in front of us to move along."

HE'D EXPECTED HER to jolt. Instead, the smile that lit every one of her features had his brain blurring with lust.

"She's gorgeous." Clearly captivated, Sadie scooted forward in her seat. "The size of them never fails to amaze me. This one's bigger than most males."

Noting a movement, Eli gestured. "This one has a calf."

"Really? Where? Oh, it's gorgeous, too."

He reached into his waistband. "Don't know about baby, but Mama moose is a hell of a lot more than gorgeous."

"The word you're looking for is dangerous. But only if she sees us as a threat." She made an uncertain motion. "Then again, it's mating season, so that could be a problem if there's a horny male in the vicinity. Present company excluded."

"Funny." But when he started to open the door, she caught his arm.

"Eli, you are not going to shoot that magnificent creature."

He half smiled. "I thought we agreed I wasn't the biggest jackass on the planet. I only want to move mother and child along before a hormonal bull shows up and sees my truck as a worthy opponent."

"What makes you think...? Oh, never mind. Just do it."

Four harmless shots later, Mama moose, having carefully considered her options, nudged her calf along and clomped into the woods behind it.

"Huh." Sadie sat back. "Bear would have been more fun."

"Proof that you've never ventured into the high Rockies. No encounter with a grizzly could ever be called fun."

She waited until he slammed the door, then reaching

over the console, grabbed a handful of his hair and yanked his mouth onto hers. When she drew away, her gray eyes glittered. "I love a man who can transition from back alleys to the backwoods without missing a beat."

He'd figure out what she'd said, Eli reflected, when the flames at the back of his throat subsided and his heart—which had missed several beats—kick-started again.

A blast of wet wind bore down on the truck. Releasing his hair, Sadie dropped back into her seat. "Looks like my focus is shot, Lieutenant. Good thing we brought our rain gear."

Rain gear, right. Eli struggled to think past the need currently blasting through his bloodstream. The road they were on ended two miles from Kilgore's cabin—as the raven flew.

Given that Sadie had long since mastered the art of a guileless expression, he could only speculate as to what was running through her mind right now. Probably nothing his male pride wanted to hear. Happy enough to let it ride, he flicked on the wipers and upped the volume of Whitesnake on his iPod.

By the time they ran out of drivable track, the shadows between the trees made gloomy afternoon feel like weird twilight.

"Rooney says the north woods are even more haunted than the hollow." Sadie zipped herself into a bright yellow raincoat. "I'm curious to know what that means."

"It means he's got a friend with a still in the area."

She pulled on a pair of rubber boots. "Eli, Rooney doesn't need to come all the way out here for his whiskey. Ben Leamer—" she caught his level look and ramped up her smile "—has a refreshment stand in one of his barns. Kids get a free bottle of fruit juice with the price of admission."

"Uh-huh. Does Ty know about this stand?"

"No need." She scooped her hair into a ponytail, popped a ball cap on her head and pulled up her hood. "He doesn't have any kids. Ready?"

He'd leave it alone, Eli decided. Rooney had survived without his help for more than a century. If they didn't stop the person threatening her, Sadie might not make next Friday.

Over his dead body, of course, but his darker sense didn't think that would be much of an issue in her stalker's mind.

Rain continued to fall in miserable wind-driven sheets. When the ground gave way and almost sent Sadie into a rocky chasm, Eli barely managed to catch her.

Rebalanced, she exhaled. "Imagine how bad this would be if my mind wasn't holding back the worst of it."

"Given the strength of those gusts, we'd probably be landing in Oz about now. Keep to the right," Eli told her. "The path's higher there."

Not that it made much difference since calling the ground a quagmire would have been a generous description.

"We should have hired a helicopter to drop us onto Cal's roof." Sadie began the tricky descent into a wide gully. "Between last night's storm and this one, if he's home and dry, I say Laura's ex isn't the person who threatened me."

But still worth the trip in Eli's estimation. As far as he could tell from the information on file, both Cal Kilgore's mother and his grandmother had alibied him for the night of Laura's murder. Although similar, their stories hadn't quite jibed in terms of where he'd been on the property and what they'd believed he was doing.

The points were small, but interesting when added to the fact that Cal had personally delivered three shipments of hardware to Bangor this fall. In other words, a guy who seldom surfaced had passed through Raven's Hollow as many times in one month as Brady had seen him in the last fifteen years.

"Do you remember what Kilgore looked like?" he asked Sadie from behind.

She shoved through a tangle of branches. "I remember him as tall, with long, stringy brown hair that he wore in a ponytail."

"What about his features?"

"Sorry, all fuzzy. Guess the guy didn't do it for me when I was seven. The story I heard is that Cal's mother left the Hollow when she was found to be in possession of a stolen cameo pendant. She used to clean houses part-time. She claimed she accidently dusted the cameo into the pocket of her apron. The owner didn't press charges, and a few weeks later, Mrs. K just sort of faded from sight."

"What about Grandma K?"

"Molly said she died in her sleep while watching the Shopping Channel."

"Wouldn't anyone?"

Sadie hopped over a deep crevice. "Molly also said that Grandma Kilgore and Rooney used to share a corner table at Two Toes Joe's Bar on Saturday nights."

An image he did not want to see slid through Eli's head. "Okay, you need to stop right there."

"Sundays at Joe's were reserved for Rooney and Ben Leamer's sister."

"Any time you wanna stop."

"Rooney and Ben's sister used to hold hands between drinks. Oh, and there was also—"

"Sadie." Snagging her collar, Eli brought her to a smooth halt. "Shut up." To make sure she did, he tipped her head back and set his mouth on hers.

Bad idea, he realized instantly. The taste of her simply blanked his mind. Fortunately, it also set off about a thousand warning bells. With the last of them clanging loudly, he reeled in an urge to take her on the forest floor, and while he could still form a rational thought, he murmured a quiet "Got to stop doing that."

He nudged her ahead of him on the path, where they carried on in silence for several minutes. He figured she was channeling her mental energy upward rather than cursing him, because with every step they took, the wind gusts grew more fitful and the rain slowed from a downpour to a steady drizzle. He sensed he should be grateful.

"You're welcome," she called over her shoulder. Boosting herself onto a fallen tree, she swung her legs over and hopped onto a weedy slope. "Cal's cabin's dead ahead. I don't see any chimney smoke, but there might be a light—"

It was as far as she got. Metal glinted in one of the windows. Eli heard the sound of glass breaking and glimpsed a long barrel through the scrub. He shoved Sadie to the ground a split second before a hailstorm of bullets erupted.

SADIE COULDN'T SEE or think or feel. She could only breathe in shallow gasps. It was better than being shot, she supposed, but barely.

The initial barrage of bullets stopped at twelve. Although half of them came from Eli's Police Special, he kept her firmly beneath him during the entire exchange. When the last echo subsided, the weight on her rib cage lifted, allowing her to draw her first desperate breath.

"Are you hit?" Eli yanked her zipper down and pulled her top up. "Talk to me, Sadie. Where's the wound?"

With black spots still swimming, she sucked in more air. "I'm not…" The word *hurt* dissolved when she saw the blood on her raincoat. "Eli, stop. It's not me, it's you. You're the one who was shot."

He frowned, glanced down—then shoved her under him again as five more bullets zinged through the low leaves.

She wriggled out far enough to shout, "Cal, stop shooting. It's Sadie Bellam and Eli Blume. We're not here to—whatever you're thinking. We need to talk to you!"

"Get off my land," a man's voice bellowed back. "I protect what's mine."

"You must have known the guy, Eli." She wriggled out farther. "Say something buddylike. Then roll over so I can look at your shoulder."

"It'll keep." He stilled her busy hands. "You sound friendlier than I do. Identify yourself again, and mention Laura."

She raised her voice. "Cal, I'm Laura's cousin Sadie, from the Hollow."

"I don't care if you're General Lee come back from the dead. I want you and your pal to haul your trespassing butts off my land, or else I'll shoot 'em off."

"O-kay," Eli said in a tone that fell somewhere between enlightenment and anticipation.

"We're trapped, and you're bleeding." Sadie yanked his T-shirt down. "It's just a graze, but there's nothing okay about any of this."

"His accent's wrong."

"I—" she thought for a moment "—didn't notice that," she realized, and replayed the shooter's warning. "Mississippi?"

"Or Louisiana."

"So, not Cal, and not friendly. But in Cal's cabin with a gun."

"Rifle."

"Aimed at our trespassing butts."

"And where's Cal?" Eli wondered aloud. "Alive, dead or somewhere in between?"

"I see two grazes, Eli, one on your shoulder, another on your upper arm."

His eyes remained on the cabin. "They're scratches, Sadie. I've had worse." He shifted his weight. "I need to get down there without him seeing me. Can you keep him talking?"

She could argue, Sadie supposed, or accept and deal as he was apparently doing. Gnashing her teeth, she glanced one last time at his injuries before switching her attention to the cabin. "Not sure how long he'll want to chat."

"Do what you can." Reaching into the top of his boot, he drew a second gun. "You've got fifteen shots. Brace when you squeeze the trigger. This thing has a wicked kick."

"That's so reassuring."

"Have you ever fired a gun before?"

"Only in my dreams at an unpleasant boss. Better for all concerned if talking works."

Pressing a hand to her neck, Eli cautioned her to keep low, then vanished into the underbrush. And people called her a witch?

"We're not here to hurt you," she shouted downward. "We just want to talk to Cal."

A bullet clipped the trunk of an elder behind her and sent bits of bark flying.

"I don't give a damn who, what or why, lady. Ain't no one in this foxhole but me and Old Faithful, and we'd as soon kill you as look at you."

"Like I haven't figured that out," she muttered. Double-handing the gun, she braced her arms on a rock and tried again. "Look, you're in Cal's Kilgore's cabin. How were we supposed to know he'd moved?"

"Well, you know now, so beat it and let me be."

He released three more shots, one of them so close to her cheek she felt the air move as it whizzed past.

Fighting to keep her voice even, she countered, "If we leave, do we have your word you won't shoot us in the back?"

She swore she heard him snicker. "Yeah, sure, you got my word. You want me to give it in your language, too?"

Sadie opened her mouth, closed it again. Her language?

She glimpsed a movement through the foliage. A second later, three rapid-fire shots exploded. Glass shattered, wood splintered and someone—not Eli, she prayed—gave a short, sharp cry.

Her arms ached from holding them over a rock. Lowering her forehead to her wrists, she counted to five, heard nothing except the wind in the trees. She had to believe Eli had made it inside. But had he done so safely?

Raising her head, she started to call out. She actually had Eli's name on her lips when the underbrush rustled behind her. Rolling sideways, she snapped the gun up. But had no time to fire as a large black mass leaped at her.

Chapter Eleven

Eli distracted the shooter by tossing a stone through one of the side windows. He fired as he ran along the porch, then kicked at the latch of a rickety-looking door.

Inside, the man with the rifle spun, ready on the trigger. Anticipating him, Eli used a branch he'd snagged in the woods, knocked the barrel away, then grabbed the tip and yanked.

When the rifle clattered, the shooter stumbled backward, smashing a table and landing on the floor, where he thrashed his arms like an addict in the throes.

A fist plowed into Eli's bad shoulder, but once he had the guy on his stomach, it was over.

"Kill me!" his prisoner ordered. "You kill me now, I don't care how. I ain't gonna rot in one of your stinking prisons."

"Wanna bet?" Holding him down with a knee in the small of his back, and his gun pressed to a grimy nape, Eli batted aside an erratic arm and found a lamp cord. The struggle that followed had him longing for a pair of handcuffs and uniformed backup. However, despite his throbbing shoulder, the guy, who had a good thirty years on him, was trussed and turned inside a minute.

"Kill me," the man demanded while Eli wound a second cord around his feet. "I got a right to die with dignity."

The words registered as much as the ravings of a junkie ever did. It wasn't until his gaze landed on the big, round table near the kitchen that those white-noise ravings gave way to a sharp click.

There were two bowls. Two bowls, two mugs, two plates.

Like a solid blow to the midsection, the truth stripped the air from his lungs and turned everything inside him to ice.

The shooter wasn't alone.

Cursing his lack of forethought, Eli grabbed his gun and, shoving in a fresh ammo clip, ran back to where he'd left Sadie.

THE BLACK MASS would have landed on her if the ground hadn't been sloped and relatively free of obstructions. Sadie reacted quickly, but he still managed to pin her hips.

She heard snarls like those of an enraged bull. That he wasn't actually a bull only made its way into a side pocket of her brain. The rest was more concerned with gaining her freedom and, barring that, figuring out how to shoot him before he tore her apart.

With Eli's gun still tightly clutched, she used her other hand to scoop up a handful of mud and pebbles and fling it in his eyes—wherever they were.

A floppy hood covered his head and obscured his features. Her mind immediately conjured Ezekiel's face, but that was her nightmare. The man on top of her wasn't Ezekiel Blume, and waking up wouldn't save her from whatever horror was in his mind.

When he stretched out for the gun, she managed to buck him sideways and get an elbow up into his jaw. The impact knocked him back far enough for her to free a foot. Unable to kick him in the crotch, she brought her heel down on his calf and at the same time sank her teeth into his wrist.

Swearing, he snatched his arm away and squared up for a punch. His knuckles clipped her cheekbone, but when he groped for the gun again, she worked her knee loose and shoved it between his legs.

That he didn't crumple had ripples of fresh fear racing along her nerve ends. She didn't know if she tasted blood or only imagined it. Whatever the case, the gun remained in her possession, and that was key.

She used her heel again, but this time he slammed a forearm across her windpipe and pressed until her vision went spotty. She was endeavoring to bite his hand when suddenly his weight and the spots were gone, and she was skidding downhill.

"What the…?" Startled, with her lungs screaming for air, she dug in and scrambled to her knees. By the time she whipped the gun into position, however, all she saw was her captor and Eli disappearing into the underbrush below.

Pushing the hair from her face, Sadie tracked their movements. It was easy enough to do. Fists slammed repeatedly into bone and flesh, and the growls were growing feral.

She could help, she thought, and found a rock. Curling her fingers around it, she slid awkwardly down the slope.

Maybe Eli could take the guy—probably could, in fact—but his opponent was big, strong and likely hadn't been grazed by two bullets. So…

Using her senses, she pushed through the bushes. When she spotted them, she didn't aim—no time for that— merely trusted her instincts and brought the rock down hard on the man's neck. A second later, Eli kicked him up against a tree. Sadie saw part of a beard, heard a whoosh of breath and watched the man slide bonelessly into the mud.

Regaining his feet, Eli took a single unsteady step. He wiped at a trickle of blood on his mouth as he angled his gun down. "Twitch a muscle, and you'll be leaving these woods in a box. Did he hurt you?" he asked Sadie in the same breath.

"No more than I hurt him." Curious, she eased forward and gave the black hood a tug.

Stringy gray-brown hair, no longer confined, lay in rats' tails across a pair of sallow cheeks. His eyes remained shut while his mouth opened and closed like a woozy codfish's.

She straightened with a sigh. "Cal Kilgore, two decades later. Now I remember the face."

"Who are you?" he slurred from the ground. "And what're you doing on my land?"

She would have answered, but it seemed he wasn't as woozy as he looked. A leg snaked out in Eli's direction.

"I've met smarter," she murmured, and wisely backed off.

A few seconds later, with Cal spread-eagled in a mound of lichens, his eyes wheeling from a punch to the face, she smiled at Eli, who stood shaking out a fist. "Impressive, Lieutenant. However, if you and Laura's former stud are done here, we should probably think about heading down to the cabin. It's getting awfully close to dinnertime."

Stashing his gun, Eli bent to one knee and hauled his prisoner to a sitting position. "I've been inside that cabin, sweetheart. Pretty sure you won't want to eat there."

"That wasn't quite what I meant." She helped him lever Cal to his feet. "Unless I'm hallucinating, that black thing heading down the hill from the trees is a very large, probably very hungry bear."

"YOU'RE WAY OUT of your jurisdiction, Eli," Cal accused thirty minutes later. "You also didn't identify yourself as a cop. Not to me or to my uncle. You press charges, we'll press charges."

"Then I'll press charges," Sadie added. "And we'll turn the courtroom into a three-ring circus."

She spoke from the far side of the room where she sat cross-legged on the floor, observing Cal's uncle while he snored, jerked and shuddered in his—she supposed you could call it sleep. Judging from the empty prescription bottle on the kitchen counter, he'd taken more than a few tranquilizers that afternoon.

She indicated the older man's military tattoos. "Post-traumatic stress syndrome?"

"Used to be called shell shock." Cal fixed his left eye on her. "He spent four years in Nam and every year after that paying for the pleasure." His other eye glared at Eli. "You've got no business showing up here unannounced."

"We announced ourselves loud and clear to your uncle." Eli flexed the shoulder Sadie had done her best to clean and bandage. "His response was to open fire on us."

"Shell shock," Cal repeated.

Sadie regarded the grizzled man who looked like a hermit and snored like a buzz saw. "He needs more help than you can give him, Cal."

"Don't we all, Sadie Bellam? Me, I could use a double shot of the whiskey my uncle polished off two days ago, but life's always been a kick in the crotch that way. Oh, no, wait. That was you who kicked me."

"After you jumped me," she reminded. "Come on, Cal, you and Eli are distantly related. Help us out just a bit here."

"Why should I?"

Eli stared him down. "Because odds are that whiskey your uncle polished off came from a storehouse I noticed that's sitting on your land. And helping us is a good start toward helping me forget that once we're back in the Hollow."

Cal started to boil up, but reconsidered when he looked

at his sleeping uncle. "Aw, hell, go on, then, fire away, Sadie."

"Were you upset when Laura ended your relationship?"

"Not upset enough to do her."

"You didn't come to the funeral."

He showed his teeth in a nonsmile. "Ex-boyfriend. Think that one's been established."

"It has, yes. A month after Laura was buried, someone left a bouquet of wildflowers on her grave."

"Good for someone."

"On the anniversary of your first date with her." She sent Eli a blithe smile. "I went into the *Chronicle*'s archives on my computer last night after the break-in at the manor and found an article. One of the reporters interviewed your grandmother, Cal. And please don't tell me the flowers were a coincidence, because somebody's doing to me what he did to Laura, and it's freaking me out."

"It's pissing me off." Moving to an unbroken window, Eli made a thorough scan of the clearing.

"If you're looking for Mr. Bear, Eli, he only comes around when the urge strikes. I let him raid my trash cans, he lets me pass when we accidentally bump. I gave the police everything I had way back when, Sadie. Nothing more I can tell you now."

But she sensed from the way neither of his eyes met hers that there was in fact something more. Something he hadn't told the police, or possibly anyone.

She studied his body language. Irritable with traces of resentment around the edges.

"If it makes a difference, Cal, I don't think you're involved in Laura's death or in any of the threats I've received."

"Haven't heard the lieutenant say that yet."

"Storehouse," Eli reminded him from the window.

Cal paced in stiff strides around the room. "I saw my

life going differently back then. Figured Laura and me'd get married, but I guess the bad-boy thing wore thin. I said some stuff after she broke it off. Not that I wanted to kill her, but that I thought maybe she was seeing another guy. She said she wasn't and wouldn't be for a long time, because she was going off to college, then down to Ecuador. She wanted to be a nurse and work where there was a need."

"Was that the last time you talked to her?" Sadie asked.

"Last time I called her, yeah. I went into a funk for a few weeks afterward. Didn't work or wash, just watched TV and drank beer." One eye rolled, the other remained on her face. "She phoned me two nights before she died, mad as a hornet. She wanted to know if I had put a big, folded piece of paper in her gym bag, because what was on it was sick and low, and it wasn't going to change anything between us."

Sadie's stomach muscles tightened. "Do you know what the paper said?"

"All she told me was that it was sick and like something she figured I might do if I was drunk and feeling ornery. Fact is, I *was* drunk, but truth is, I didn't know what the hell she was talking about. That's when she got all pissy and said I might as well have signed my name to it."

Sadie ran the thought through her head. "That's—really interesting, actually."

"Not to mention incriminating," Eli put in. "Keep talking, Cal. What did you say back to her?"

A shoulder jerked. "Stuff she didn't like, nothing that came out like a threat. It wasn't until right before she slammed the phone down that she finally told me what she meant." He raised and wiggled all ten fingers. "I'm what you call ambidextrous. Means I can write with either hand. But the writing looks different, depending on what hand I use. That's why she thought I'd given her the paper. Because partway through the message, the writing changed. Those were the last words she spoke to me, and every one came out clear as a bell. She said, 'The writing changed.'"

LATE AFTERNOON BLED far too quickly into early evening. They had to leave because no way did Sadie want to be on foot in the north woods after dark. Lions and tigers and bears, she could handle, but not a crazed killer who shot ravens and, twenty years after the fact, saw her as his next victim.

They made it to Eli's truck less than ten minutes before the last shimmer of daylight faded to black.

While the headlights provided a measure of comfort, they also turned the drizzle into thin white needles and revealed vague movements that gave the shadows life and fed the fearful chill that had been making Sadie's teeth want to chatter since Cal had talked about his final conversation with her cousin.

Not for the first time, she wished she could push her fingers directly into her brain. Anything to blot out the monstrous images that played and replayed like a carousel of horror.

"I've got this Jekyll and Hyde film clip running through my head," she confessed as they drove. "Except in my case, Jekyll's as dangerous as Hyde. And just as mad. Apparently."

A smile ghosted around Eli's lips. "With Ezekiel Blume in the starring dual role?"

"It would have to be Ezekiel, wouldn't it? He wanted his brother's wife dead. It turned out Nola was able to cheat death, but initially, everyone involved believed she'd gone to hell where she belonged. Laura wasn't a witch, though, Eli, and all teasing aside, neither am I."

"I don't think this is a witch-hunt, Sadie."

"What, then? Obsession?"

"Mine forever," he repeated.

She sighed. "I guess in a weird sort of way, death could be construed as forever. Someone wanted Laura. Couldn't have her. Killed her. It's straightforward enough from a psychological standpoint in that obsessed people frequently turn on the person after whom they lust. But when you factor in what Cal told us about the writing changing, straightforward becomes a wobbly line to nowhere."

"Unless Cal's the murderer and, as Laura believed, he simply changed hands while writing a message that only she saw."

"Obsessed with Laura, I get. Obsessed with me, not at all. Except for our red hair, Laura and I look—looked—nothing alike. Also, the last time Cal and I met face-to-face before today, I was a kid. I really think you can scratch him from the suspect list."

"Move him farther down anyway. Another possibility is that we're dealing with a split personality. It would account for the fact that the writing changed and obsession ultimately descended into death. Not to mention this morning's reference to an inner monster."

Sadie swore her brain was going to explode. "That's not much of a comfort, is it? Go left at the next fork. The road improves, and my great-grandfather's place is only a mile farther on."

Eli glanced at her, then gave her hair a light tug. "Ninety-nine years old, huh? And living alone in the middle of haunted nowhere."

His deliberately humorous tone eased a portion of her tension. "I know what you're thinking. Major neglect on our part. But there's a twelve-member family who make canoes and live in a collection of cabins half a mile west of Great-grandfather's place. One or another of them checks on him faithfully morning, noon and night. He wasn't happy in the Hollow, Eli. He's very happy here." She smiled. "He also loves to play chess."

"How do you know I…ah, right. Rooney."

"Man's a font." She relaxed more as the road leveled off. "I only wish he was clairvoyant. Or I was."

"Are you completely convinced that Molly isn't?"

"Yes, but you can decide for yourself. Before we left the Hollow today, she told me not to make any plans for Monday night."

"Do I want to know why?"

"Probably not. She's arranging a séance."

Chapter Twelve

"You played a game of chess with that old buzzard?"

An outraged Rooney brought his cane down on the front desk of the Raven's Hollow Police Station and made the deputy jump. Eli merely raised an eyebrow.

"That old buzzard beat the crap out of me in under three hours without a drop of alcohol in his system."

"Probably smokes funny cigarettes instead." Rapping his cane on the floor now, Rooney raised his voice. "Where's the damn dog, Ty? My former grandson here says he's a winner. He's gonna get Brady to give him a once-over. Then he's going to fetch Sadie from the *Chronicle*. I want her down at Joe's bar to cover the fights."

Ty came in with a brown and white bulldog on a leash. "I hope we're talking televised fights."

"Nope, live action. Cove versus Hollow. And no, I'm not naming names, because you always take it upon your chiefly self to lecture the participants until their morale is lower than Chopper's jowls." Rooney pushed the leash into Eli's hands. "Take the dog to Brady, stranger, while I remind your spoilsport cousin who in this room is sixty-seven years older than whom."

"Sixty-five." Ty grimaced. "I wasn't a model grade school student."

The old man cackled. "I thought the pair of you would

be forty before you graduated." When Eli's eyes narrowed, he waved his cane. "I meant Ty and Brady. You just trot Chopper over to the v-e-t for that exam while I lay a little guilt trip on your cousin."

"It's Sunday," Eli reminded him. "Brady's day o-f-f."

"Then go up to his apartment and n-a-g him into doing an old man a favor."

More than done with the spelling bee, Eli headed for the door. He turned up his collar against a whippy north wind and jogged with the bulldog down Main Street to the edge of the square.

Bad weather notwithstanding, it was good to be out-doors. He'd spent the better part of the day on his com-puter, studying Sadie's Facebook and Twitter pages and poring over all the files he could access about the inves-tigation into Laura's death. He'd talked to several people at the *Chronicle* and others who'd known both Laura and Sadie since they were children. Although he'd come up empty in the clue department, he'd enjoyed looking at the vacation pictures Sadie had posted online.

It surprised him to see Orley through the clinic win-dow, counting bags of dog food. Farther in, Brady tapped away on his laptop.

"No more favors," Orley warned when the door swung shut behind him.

"This one's on Brady." Eli unzipped his jacket. "Why's it so hot in here?"

"Molly brought Solomon in an hour ago. Emergency ingrown claw. The dog freaked, we sedated, then had to up the temperature to the high side of unbearable be-cause Molly and Solomon want what they want and Molly doesn't go away until they get it. I woke up with a scream-ing headache, and listening to Cousin McStrange bitch wasn't something I wanted to add to an already poopy

Sunday. We're doing inventory," she said heavily, and made another tick with her marker. "A little help would be nice."

"Sorry. I'm picking Sadie up at the *Chronicle* after Brady checks out Chopper. She's determined to talk to Ben Leamer, and I gather Ben's equally determined to talk to her."

"Meaning you're gonna tag."

"You got it."

Brady came out, took the leash. "We'll make this quick, in that case. Exam would go faster if you'd take Chopper's temperature for me."

"What, did hell freeze over and no one told me?"

"Coward." Orley snickered over her shoulder. Then she made a sound of disgust as she stared out the window. "Seriously? Break bottles on your own sidewalk, Molly, not ours."

"Perfect." Brady appealed to his cousin. "If you won't help with the dog, at least keep Orley from scratching Molly's eyes out for whatever disaster just occurred."

He'd do it, Eli reflected, if only to escape the cloying heat.

Outside, Orley scowled at the sidewalk. "I am not getting down on my hands and knees to clean up a mess you made because you decided to wobble around on six-inch heels so Ty would notice your legs."

Molly shrank into herself. "It's only ink. It can be eradicated."

"Oh, now, there's a word. What do you think, Eli? Can indelible ink be eradicated?"

He didn't know or care. And he didn't listen to the rest of the barbed exchange. What he did do was look at Molly's unrevealing face. Then down at the bright red ink that seeped like blood across the sidewalk.

"GIVE ME FORTY minutes, Ben." Sadie glanced at the clock on the typesetter's desk. "Maybe an hour. We'll get it done today, I promise. I'm glad you're feeling better." Disconnecting, she raised her voice to her assistant. "Make sure those photos of Rooney's first wedding don't blur when they're enlarged. And don't remove the red from the eyes of the background ravens. It's a cool effect."

"Done and done. You sure you don't mind if I leave early?"

"If I did, you'd feel the negative ions."

"Like I did the time I failed to notice that the camera shop's 'Shot in the Dark' ad layout ran with an *i* in place of the *o?*"

"Exactly like that. I'm off tomorrow, so bright and early, okay?"

"No problem."

The door creaked open and closed, leaving Sadie alone with the cleaning crew and a welter of troubled thoughts.

She knew it was her own fault that she felt unsettled. While Eli and her great-grandfather had played chess last night, she'd foolishly gone over one of the many accounts he'd collected detailing their family's sordid history.

She'd skipped the chapters that dealt with their persecution in Europe and zeroed in on Nola Bellam's life in New England.

An unwed eighteenth century mother, Nola had never named the father of her daughter. Some speculated it was Hezekiah, and that the two of them had had sex after a Halloween-style party at Blume House without Hezekiah ever knowing the name of the young woman he'd bedded. Others claimed the child was Ezekiel's, and he'd known exactly who Nola was.

Sadie didn't buy either story. Her feeling was that Nola had simply fallen under the spell of a handsome stranger who'd been passing through the Hollow en route to parts unknown, and she'd wound up pregnant as a result.

Whatever the case, Nola had come to Hezekiah with a seven-year-old child.

Sadie had fallen asleep with the book in her hands while her great-grandfather and Eli continued their chess match. Of course the dream had snuck in and played out as usual. Until the end.

In this new, altered version, the cloaked shape that appeared after Ezekiel's death missed the mark with its enormous knife. There was no pain in Sadie's chest, no cry of triumph from inside the voluminous hood, and for the first time in memory, she hadn't woken up gasping on the bedroom floor.

In her still-sleeping mind, astonishment had quickly given way to hope.

She'd unpinned her cloak and, twirling it outward, trapped the figure's knife and arm with the hem. The figure had fought to free itself. As it did, the wind swirled up, filling the huge hood with air.

Though she'd never been able to in the past, this time she'd glimpsed a man's face within the folds. Hezekiah's perhaps, or Ezekiel's. The features had been unclear, as if they'd been distorting before her eyes. Or maybe they'd been transforming. Into what or who, she couldn't say.

As suddenly as it had swirled up, the wind died, the hood deflated and only darkness and death remained.

Alone in the silent woods, Sadie had heard the voice again. As the moonlight faded away, it had seemed to whisper directly into her ear.

"You are no longer mine alone, Sadie Bellam. The monster is awake...."

"YOU SHOULD HAVE told me about your dream, Sadie." Still parked in Ben Leamer's farmyard, Eli stowed her camera bag. "Yes, I'm a cop, but I'm also a Blume. I was raised on similar stories. With Rooney, legend trumps history every time."

"For me, legend crowned dream. Or maybe it was the other way around." Mission finally accomplished in terms of Ben's corn maze, Sadie leaned against the side of Eli's truck while he opened the passenger door. "In any case, I had a much better second dream."

Setting his hands on her waist, Eli boosted her onto the truck's running board. "Any reason you didn't mention that before now?"

"I thought about it." She leaned into him. "The thing is, my great-grandfather's not as sexually liberated as yours. Having been at the wrong end of a shotgun wedding himself, he'd have no qualms about threatening you with the same fate in the not-unlikely event that our jittering vibes, in combination with my überhot dream, had gotten the better of our personal resolves and sent us stumbling out to the backseat of your truck."

"Your great-grandfather had a shotgun wedding?"

Laughing, she pushed an elbow into his ribs. "That wasn't the point, Eli."

"I got the point, Sadie. Hot dreams plus hot vibes create explosive situations."

"Then again…" Seated now, she bent forward to brush her lips over his cheek. "As a cop, you'd be accustomed to excessive heat."

"Then again."

Her eyes sparkled as she slid a finger over his jaw. "Is that your subtle way of suggesting we abandon our personal resolves and fumble around in the backseat before we head over to Joe's bar? Because, I promise you, one swig of his green beer, and hot sex will be the last thing on your mind."

He kissed her fingers before closing the door between them. "Is that why Ty doesn't drink?"

"No, he doesn't drink because he likes to be in control of his faculties at all times. He's quite particular about that."

With a look at the darkening sky, Eli climbed into the truck. "Tell me, Sadie, how did it happen that you very nearly married a fussy old lady?"

"He's not…" she began, then remembered that Eli and Ty were cousins and gave his leg a gentle swat. "Ty's a good man, and I wanted, or thought I wanted, Andy Griffith. You know—Mayberry, the fishing hole, Sunday dinners, that kind of thing."

"You wanted to marry Andy of Mayberry?"

"No, I wanted the front porch swing—and you're laughing at me." Her next swat wasn't quite so gentle. "I'm baring my soul here, Eli. Haven't you ever wanted normal?"

His lips twitched. "Okay, first of all, no TV family was ever normal. Second, you don't strike me as a porch swing kind of woman. And third, where you're seeing white picket fences in Mayberry, I'm seeing you waking up one morning and suddenly realizing you're in Stepford."

She sent him an exasperated look. "When I said Ty liked to be in control, I didn't mean he wanted to turn me into a robotic zombie with a perma-smile and no will of my own."

A shrewd brow rose. "You don't think he'd have tried?"

"No." But after a quick search of her feelings, she shrugged. "Maybe. To some degree. He's a little old-fashioned."

"He's the apple that fell from the tree, Sadie. You've met his parents, right?"

"Not since I've been back. His father's asthmatic. They moved to Santa Fe a year after Ty graduated from college."

"Daddy's choice, not Mommy's."

"Asthma is a medical condition, Lieutenant, not a choice. Where are you going with this, anyway, because you and I both know Ty's not stupid enough to believe he could have run roughshod over me, no matter how close the apple fell or where the parental tree currently lives?"

"You said it yourself, he still loves you."

"I also said he's not in love with me."

"It's a small step from one to the other."

"It's a huge step from love to obsession, which I realize now is what you've been hinting at since this conversation began. Ty's a straight guy. He doesn't drink, he doesn't obsess and he would never threaten someone he cared about."

Eli sent her a fathomless look. "Anyone can have a monster lurking inside, sweetheart. I was part of a team that brought down a serial killer three years ago. The killer ran a family supermarket in Yonkers. He did the baking himself every morning. He had a wife and three kids, and he came to Manhattan four times a year for conventions and ball games. Every time he left, there'd be at least two less women alive and working the streets."

She sighed. "Look, I can understand, even appreciate your mistrust. I just can't believe I'd have missed seeing it if Ty had a side to him as evil as the spirit that possessed your ancestor. How old was Ty when Laura died? Sixteen, right?"

"Just."

"But you were fourteen. Funny, when I was young, I thought you and Ty and Brady were the same age."

"Nope. I squeaked through grade school at the usual pace. Ty and Brady had a hate-hate relationship with a couple of our teachers and took a bit longer."

Amusement stirred. "Would one of those teachers be Mr. Hart?"

"Heard about him, huh?"

"Heard about and met." She widened meaningful eyes. "Your Mr. Hart is Orley's father."

ELI HAD TO look twice to be sure she was serious. "Orley's father? How the hell did I miss that?"

"Raccoon on the road," Sadie warned. "Eyes forward, Lieutenant, and I'll give you the easy answer. All girl babies born to Bellam females are given the Bellam surname. It's tradition. My dad's is a Winter, Molly's is a Prewitt and Orley's is a Hart. Orley claims he was nicer at home than at work, but my family's situation being what it was, we didn't interact a lot. Plus, I was ten years younger than her. Your situation being what *it* was, however, I'm surprised you were never forced to endure weekend dinners. Maybe your dad and hers didn't get along. Does your father hunt?"

"No."

"There you go, then."

Elbow propped, Eli ran a finger under his bottom lip. "I'm trying really hard here to picture no-Hart with a kid. Does he still live in the area?"

"Nope. North Dakota. Could be that's why Ty and Brady felt it was safe to take jobs here."

Eli geared down when the moon slipped behind a cloud and the wind booted up to kick the side of his truck. "Is it ever not blustery in this hollow?"

"Weather's a crapshoot once summer's done." She regarded the endless stretch of darkness ahead. "Molly's in love with Ty."

He allowed himself a brief smile. "Yeah, got that one from Orley. Six-inch heels. Ink spill on the sidewalk."

"Molly uses red ink and a raven's quill to do the place cards for her séances. She thinks it's more authentic."

"It's bizarre."

"Molly's a deep person, Eli, unlike—look out!"

He spied the glint of metal as she did and swung the truck into a wide arc. Not in time to avoid the obstruction, he realized instantly. The entire vehicle shuddered, then began to lurch. He glimpsed a five-foot boulder and heard a screech as the back end scraped across the rock face and sent them stuttering toward the edge of the ravine.

He didn't think, just grabbed Sadie's hand and helped her climb over the stick shift. "With me."

They jumped together from the still-rolling truck. Eli made sure she landed on top of him, then lost his grip and half slid, half tumbled over mud and weeds and slime. He flew through an air pocket and finally came to rest in a patch of cattails.

Between the wind in the trees and the thrum of blood in his ears, he needed a moment to get his mind and body back in sync. He took half of that moment and rolled onto his stomach. "Sadie?"

"Are we dead?"

Her voice came from the right. Working himself to his knees, Eli fought to steady his thoughts. Through the hair that dripped in his eyes, he caught a movement. When he pushed upright, however, the entire mud hole tilted. "Where are you?"

"I never want to do that again." The movement he'd noted became a squelch of wet weeds. "I can hear you, Eli, but all I see is mud and black."

On his feet now—not quite sure how he pulled it off with his muscles reduced to rubber—he made his way over to her, then lowered himself to a crouch and inspected her face. "Anything broken?"

"Other than my skull and tailbone, no. Or—I might have twisted my knee." She used both hands to swipe the hair from her eyes. "What in living hell did we hit back there?"

He glanced up. "It looked like a spike strip. Blew all four tires simultaneously."

"Spikes. In the middle of the road. Why?"

"Someone wanted to impede us, I imagine."

"Impede or impale. I thought…" She halted, swiveled her head. "Damn. Damn! We're in the bog, aren't we? Those spikes were only a few feet past the place where the pine tree came down. This is where we found Laura's body!"

Wrapping the fingers of one hand around the back of her neck, Eli stared into her eyes. "You're not going to get hysterical on me, are you?"

"Not sure. Maybe."

"Better if it could wait until we're out of here."

Little shivers ran through her, but she held his gaze in the faint wash of moonlight. "Where's your truck?"

"Probably ass up in the bog."

"Okay, well, you had to figure. At least we know the way out on foot. Or we did twenty years ago."

"Let's hope nothing's changed." He scoped the shadows that appeared to be multiplying around them. "Fog's rolling in."

"That's not possible." She plucked leaves from her hair. "There can't be fog when there's…" Pausing, she raised her eyes. "Where did the wind go?"

"Good question. Can you stand?"

"Stand, no problem. Walk, we'll see. Eli, wait." She tapped a fingernail lightly to his wrist. "We're being watched."

"Felt it. But watched isn't the problem."

"Of course not. That would be too simple." She was bending to examine her knee when a lethal-looking shaft whizzed over her head. "Uh…"

"Stay down, Sadie." Placing himself in front of her, Eli reached for his gun. "That was a crossbow arrow."

"Someone's using a crossbow at night?"

"Yeah." Eli held his gun barrel up. "Looks like the monster wants to hunt."

Chapter Thirteen

Every shadow became a monster to Sadie. Fighting through her fear, she sketched a quick mental map of Raven's Bog. Trouble was, with the exception of her recurring nightmares, she hadn't ventured deep into these woods since she was seven. And back then, no one had been shooting arrows at her with frightening skill and accuracy.

Eli pulled her to the ground several times as they ran. With good reason, she realized, as arrows began to embed themselves chest high in the tree trunks.

"Avoid the direct moonlight," he said from behind. "And don't trip."

A hiss formed. Of all the things he could have said, that was the least helpful. How could she not trip on a path bulging with roots from a bunch of gnarly old trees that reminded her of the faceless mob from her nightmare?

"Stop." Catching her shoulders, Eli halted her so abruptly her feet almost shot out from under her. "Behind the stump."

Sadie landed on her sore knee but didn't cry out. Instead, she strained to separate shadow from substance behind them.

Ground fog slunk through the rocks, slithered out of crevices and crawled up over the marsh vines. A few leaves rustled in the high branches, but otherwise the woods had gone silent. Unless she counted the drumbeat that was her heart, hammering against her ribs. Because that sound could drown out a rock band.

"Give me something," Eli invited their pursuer. "Put one damn foot wrong."

The moon disappeared behind thin fingers of cloud. Far in the distance, a frog croaked. Then another. And a third.

"Any chance you could shut them up?" Eli asked her.

"Is it possible they're communicating because the danger's gone?"

"Only in cartoons, Sadie. Someone who lays down a spike strip and follows up with a crossbow isn't likely to go away. Did you see anything before the first arrow flew past?"

She shook her head, and would have preferred not to think beyond that, except… "Military troops use crossbows to detonate land mines, right? Eli, Ty was in the military."

"Means nothing. Brady and I were competitive marksmen in high school archery."

"And many of the local residents are hunters, or come from hunting backgrounds."

Eli made a slow visual circle. "Don't discount the spike strip that landed us here, either."

"Who'd own…? Ah, Cal Kilgore."

"Man forges metal products." He nodded through the trees. "There. Someone moved. Looks like he's keeping his distance and circling."

Sadie's throat muscles tightened. "In that case, shouldn't we be leaving?"

"Ten seconds."

She tried not to grind her teeth. "If we head west, there's a cave that climbs up to the road. My great-grandfather took me through it when I was six."

"Knee okay to stand?"

"As I will, so mote it be." She worked up a humorless smile. "Means I'll take pain over death."

It also meant staying low and not disturbing the ground cover.

With only the occasional moonbeam to guide them, Sadie would have missed the cave if she hadn't spotted the haunted tree. The old oak was massive and had probably died before she'd been born. Yet it continued to stand, a home for ravens and, many believed, Hezekiah in his transformed state.

Like a wizard casting his spells, two large branches stretched upward, leaving the smaller limbs at the top to spread and curl like claws. There was even a black oval where a face might have been.

They had to backtrack twenty yards to locate the overgrown cave entrance.

"I'd sacrifice a year's pay for a flashlight," Sadie whispered once they'd wedged themselves inside. "Even a jarful of fireflies would help."

"In that case, you'll be pleased to hear I smoked until last summer."

"You have a lighter?"

"Yeah. Not sure how much juice it has left, though. Feel around the ground for a dry branch, the thinner the better."

"Lovely," she said, but took a bolstering breath, shoved up her sleeves and explored the ground with him.

"I should have grabbed an arrow," she muttered. "Except they're made of metal, not wood, aren't they? Taking us right back to Cal."

"He's reclimbing the list."

"Wouldn't he also be signing his name?"

"Some criminals think the most likely suspect becomes the least likely suspect in the eyes of the police," Eli said.

"Why?"

"No idea. Most likely's most likely. Investigators don't play games."

"Good to know. But staying in the criminal mind-set, who's the least likely suspect? Other than Rooney, who doesn't count because—well, duh."

"I thought you'd figure Ty for least likely."

"And I figured Ty was a given from your perspective.... Oh, wait. I found something."

She handed him a two-foot-long twig. "Six of one," she murmured. "Either we stumble along in the dark and risk breaking a leg, or we risk having whoever's after us see the flame."

Thankfully, no arrows flew out of the dark, and Sadie prayed all the crunching footsteps she heard belonged to them. Then she turned a corner, walked into a spiderweb and spent the next minute trying to keep the scream that leaped into her throat from escaping.

It frustrated her that she also had to battle a strong urge to grab Eli's gun and start firing into the shadows behind them.

"Don't think so hard, Sadie," Eli advised. "You'll only mess up your mind more than it already is. You need to focus on putting one foot in front of the other until we're out of here."

She trudged another fifty yards up the sloping ground before deciding to hell with it and declaring over her shoulder, "I want to have sex with you, Eli."

Snagging the belt of her trench coat, he drew her to a halt and lowered his mouth to her ear. "Say that again, sweetheart, this time without the underlying threat of you turning me into a lizard if my answer isn't to your liking."

Pushing the burning twig he held to one side, she turned to face his glittering eyes. "I want to have sex with you, Eli,

when we're out of this cave, out of the hollow and somewhere, anywhere, warm and safe and dry." Even knowing
her timing was way off, she pressed her hips to the front of
his jeans. "I don't want to die, but even more than that, I
don't want to die and never know what it would have been
like to make love with you."

She saw the glitter deepen. "I'd want to make love to
you even with the threat of life as a lizard hanging over
my head." His gaze dropped to her mouth, then rose. "No
matter what my form, though, Sadie, I won't let anyone
hurt you." Capturing her chin, he grazed her lips with his
and added a soft "Especially not me."

"Kissing me, then going all enigmatic cop isn't going to
get you out of explaining what you meant." Sadie ducked
under a rough protrusion and immediately had her face
slapped by an embedded weed. "You'll also never convince
me that you're a threat to my life, so—oh, good, there's
the opening—if you're not into sex, just say so and we'll
leave it at that."

"Find a foothold" was all he said, and gave her a boost
from behind. "When you reach the exit, move aside and
let me go first."

He had the gun, he was the cop—it made sense. But
Sadie was irked enough to say nothing while he pushed
through the underbrush and took a long look around.

"We're about a mile south of the bog," he revealed when
he returned. "Maybe a hundred yards from the road."

Using an elastic band from the pocket of her trench, she
secured her hair. "That would put us midway between the
Cove and the Hollow. Do we flip a coin?"

"Anyone we want to talk to should be down at Two
Toes Joe's Bar."

"The Cove it is. Eli." She caught his arm. "Once we're

on the road, we're exposed. The wind blew most of the clouds away, and the fog's not thick enough to obscure the moon."

"Which is why you'll be carrying my backup and trying to reach Ty on your cell phone."

She took the gun and pulled her iPhone from her pocket. A rueful smile appeared when the screen lit up. "Second duh of the night. We could have used this as a light source in the cave."

"Fire worked well enough. If we'd killed your battery, there'd have been no way for us to call for help later."

"You didn't think of it, either, huh?"

He sent her a distant grin. "Other things on my mind, sweetheart."

It felt as if the night wanted to close in around them. Sadie slammed a firm lid on the more insidious aspects of her dream. No point making everything worse. If anything could be worse.

"Tell me what you're thinking," she said as they approached the narrow strip of road. "I can hear your mind clicking, but I can't read it."

"Oh, I imagine you could if you tried."

"You kissed me to shut me up."

"Skip ahead, Sadie."

"Any of those dozen or so arrows we avoided in the bog could have hit you as easily as me. More easily, in fact, because you were shielding me."

"Which I'll do every time, so lose the accusing tone and stay on track."

She tapped the phone screen with her thumb, glanced behind them. "Obsessed person transforms into monster. Monster's pissed at me for—what? Not understanding his message?"

"Go with that."

"He's also pissed at you for coming to the Hollow and getting in his way. So he's decided to eliminate both of us for his—host?"

"Good a description as any."

"Once we're gone, the monster retreats, the host mourns and soon enough, life resumes its normal rhythm." She ran the idea a few times. "Going back to Laura, and assuming Cal's not the killer, that could explain why he's not dead. He and Laura broke up. He ceased to be a problem. The monster set his sights on Laura alone. Am I babbling?"

"A little. It's better than freaking."

Following his lead, she glanced into the darkness behind them. "Why do we keep looking over our shoulders?"

"Someone's back there."

Her fingers tightened on her phone. "I was really hoping that was my imagination."

"Keep calling, Sadie."

"I can walk, talk and check an i-screen at the same time. It's a dead zone until we begin the descent into the—whoa—Cove!" With no forewarning, she found herself airborne as Eli tackled her into a ditch. "What now?" she demanded, climbing off him.

"Gleam of metal. Keep quiet."

She obliged and listened. And, dammit, heard footsteps. Stealthy footsteps, squishing on the shoulder.

"How far back does this ditch run?" Eli asked.

"Maybe fifty yards. Wait." She gripped his wrist. "He's stopped."

"Noticed." Pivoting, he took hold of her arms. "I need you to stay right here."

"While you walk into an arrow? Because you know that's what he wants...." She trailed off, raised her head. "I hear a car. No, a truck. It's coming from the Cove."

To her relief—and, she suspected, Eli's annoyance—the

engine grew louder. When the fog lamps came into view, he hoisted himself from the ditch and flagged the driver down with his badge.

The man who stopped was a farmer named Ray. Their weapons didn't faze him, but one look at her, covered in mud and sludge, with leaves and bark clinging to her hair, had his thick eyebrows winging up and laughter gurgling in his throat. Until she gave him the short version of their story. Then he reached behind him for a rifle.

"You and me could take a walk," he said around her to Eli.

"Do you have a night-vision scope?"

"Three of 'em." He scratched his throat. "Sorry to say, they're at home."

"Would it matter if they weren't?" Sadie turned to Eli. "The guy was behind us. He'll know we got a ride. He also knows the area, because I didn't hear him behind us in the cave. Every witchy sense I possess tells me that he and his crossbow have vanished into the night. We can drive slowly, keep an eye open for anything suspicious, but you know it's done for now. We're safe, and he's gone. We should be grateful for small—well, okay, big—favors."

Eli scanned the road. "Big and small are relative terms, Sadie. Small picture, we're safe for the moment. Big one, the killer's still out there. And we have no idea who he is or where he'll surface again. The only thing we can be sure of is that his homicidal alter ego won't stop until it does what it came out of hibernation to do."

HE WOKE UP facedown on the bathroom floor, with the shower running and the spray gone icy. Every part of his body ached, but his head most of all. Crawling to the tub, he prayed the cold water would shock some clarity into his brain.

Even with the haze dispersing, he couldn't remember the night. He knew he'd opened a can of beans for dinner, thought he'd eaten most of them, plus coffee and a few stale cookies. But that's where it ended. His mind went blank after the first bite of gingersnap.

Okay, back up. He'd been tired. He'd drifted off. Then what? What grim horror had unfolded while he slept?

His palms felt damp. The skin on his neck prickled. It wasn't morning yet, not quite. First light was coming, but slowly, like the panic that was starting to pitch and roll inside him.

"What did I do?" he whispered to the walls. "What did we do?"

The bathroom held no answers, so he shut off the water and grabbed a towel when he left.

There was no sign of blood. Maybe it wasn't too terrible. Swallowing the grit in his throat, he moistened his lips. He should contact Sadie. Yes, he needed to stay calm and ascertain her status.

Ascertain her status? Whose thought was that? And why couldn't he remember?

Feeling like a man after a weekend drunk, he walked with his face buried in the towel. When he walked into a table, he lowered his hands and forced his bleary eyes to travel from point to point in the room. Chair to window. Window to floor. Floor to door.

When they stopped, so did his heart, for several long seconds. Then it started to gallop.

He stared, sweat dribbling, at the entryway, at the shoes he wore for special occasions. And the layers of green-brown mud that coated them.

Chapter Fourteen

"Word has it the fights at Joe's bar got out of hand last night." Molly picked up and shook the bottle of Tylenol on Sadie's kitchen counter. "When all was said and done—long after midnight, I'm told—Rooney called Ty, who never showed, and reamed him out. Ty called Brady, also a no-show, and on down a twisty, turny path, until sometime around 2:00 a.m., our great-grandfather called me from the north woods. Among other things, he wants you to listen to your landline and cell phone messages more often. Same memo to Eli…. Er, where was I?"

"You lost me after 'the fights at Joe's bar got out of hand.'" At the table, Sadie raised her forehead from her arms. Molly had invaded her kitchen at 6:00 a.m., on her one and only day off after a night of pure hell that had not resulted in her and Eli having hot sex or even a reasonable facsimile thereof. "Why are you telling me this?"

"Because Rooney's upset that you weren't there wearing your journalist's hat. Your only saving grace is that he's miffed at several of us for doing other life things when he believes we should have been drinking Joe's gross beer and throwing up in the bathroom between bouts. Do you want coffee?"

Sadie propped her chin in her palms. "Do ravens have feathers? My guess is Joe's was packed to the rafters, and everyone in attendance snapped a dozen or more photos with his or her phone. My assistant—" she emphasized the word "—will have plenty to choose from when she opens her morning emails."

"I noticed you didn't get home until close to midnight." Molly measured out the ground beans. "Would that be Eli's doing?"

How much should she reveal? Sadie wondered. "Eli and I had an incident on the Hollow Road. By the time we got to the Cove, we were wet and muddy and not very happy. We spent close to an hour trying to locate Ty, only to be told he was still in Raven's Hollow. So, back we went. At a snail's pace, though, because Eli wanted to see if he could locate his truck."

Molly stopped her measuring spoon halfway to the machine. "Eli lost his truck?"

"Long story. Short answer? Yes. With it went my camera bag and all the pictures I'd taken of Ben Leamer's corn maze—which I flatly refuse to walk through again after discovering a wolf spider the size of Solomon on my coat sleeve yesterday afternoon."

"I have shots of the maze," Molly told her. "Lots of them. In a way, you could say I helped design it."

Sadie slid her eyes sideways and up. "Say what?"

"More accurately, I helped Brady, who helped Ben design it." She returned to her task. "Think, Sadie. Brady's a vet. He takes care of Ben Leamer's livestock and pets. He spends a lot of time at the farm. Ben asked for help, Brady made suggestions and when we—Brady and I—drove into Bangor together for medical supplies, I did a little tweaking for him." Her mouth tipped up into a rare smile. "I remember Orley smoldering over that trip, because it left her alone at the clinic. According to her, hell broke loose that afternoon, and being a complete putz at channeling her emotions, she blamed me for taking Brady away. Put another X in the 'I hate Molly' column. Did Eli find his truck?"

"What? No. It's in the bog somewhere, though, has to be."

She glanced up to find Molly gaping at her. "Why is Eli's truck in the bog?"

"Have you ever heard of a spike strip?"

"No."

"Picture spikes on a chain meeting tires on a road. Going back to Ben's maze for a minute—who designed the layout of the paths?"

"I imagine Ben did. Ty warned him to keep things on the low side of terrifying, but I think Ben added a few more figures after he—Ty—did his walk-through."

"Ty did a walk-through?"

"You sound like a broken record, Sadie."

"I know. Why didn't Ben tell me any of this?"

Molly's eyebrows came together. "Because it wasn't important?"

"Right." Sadie regarded the hissing coffeemaker. "Right. It wasn't—isn't." Was it? "I need to wake up more." And sift and sort and process. She opted to change the subject. "Do you need help with the séance?"

"Not on the inside. You know what they say about too many cooks. But you should probably know Ty will be there. Ty—Eli." She made a spacing motion with her hands. "I'll seat them far apart. I was going to invite Cal Kilgore, too, but I don't know how to reach him, do you?"

"Not without dodging bullets." Sadie grinned. "Rooney might know."

"Why would Rooney know how to contact a metal maker from the north woods?"

"Because being so tied up with his maze, one or two

of Ben Leamer's other ventures have been shunted to the back burner lately."

"Are you being cryptic on purpose?"

"At six in the morning, absolutely not. Talk to Rooney." Pushing away from the table, Sadie headed for the now-spitting machine. "Why do you want Cal at the séance, Molly?" It struck her as she reached for the pot. "Oh, damn. Tell me you're not going to do what I suddenly have a horrible feeling you're going to do."

Her cousin linked and twisted her fingers. "I have to do it, don't I? I saw the writing on your entry wall. I also heard you and Eli talking. I know what you're thinking. What's happening to you is a lot like what happened to Laura." She worked up a smile. "Think of it this way. We're making a phone call. A very long distance phone call."

It ONLY TOOK from predawn until noon to get his truck out of the hellhole that was Raven's Bog. Cursing and snarling by turns, Eli inspected the scraped and dented body. But when he saw the shredded tires, it hit him what he could have lost if even one small part of last night's horror show had gone down differently.

"I have to say, this is much worse than the tree." Brady circled while Eli crouched to inspect the rear axle. "Is Ty looking into what happened, or are you taking it on yourself?"

"What, you think he'll stay out of it if I ask nicely?"

"I think I don't want to wind up in the middle of things."

"In that case—" Ty slid down the gentlest portion of the embankment "—you should consider removing yourself right now. Arrows, Eli? Someone shot arrows at Sadie last night?"

Eli regarded him from the ground. "That was act two, Ty. The first was even more fun."

"Right, the spike line." He made a show of searching the ground. "Funny, I don't see one lying around anywhere, but your tires are screwed, I'll give you that."

Shaking his head in mild amusement, Brady leaned on the banged-up box. "Don't mind me. I'll just stand here and try to figure out what I'm going to tell Rooney when he blasts me again for not showing up at the fights last night."

In spite of everything, Eli could still chuckle. "Consider yourself lucky. I got my encore blast before I was fully awake."

Ty's eyes shot hot spikes. "And just where were you, cousin, when this encore blasting occurred?"

"Where you probably think," Eli returned. "Or close to it."

"What the hell does that mean?"

"Oh, come on, Ty," Brady called out. "You're not dense. He was at Bellam Manor, but not in Sadie's bed. At least not when he talked to Rooney."

Eli wiped his hands on an old rag. "You're enjoying this, aren't you?"

Brady shrugged. "Fair's fair. I had to euthanize a sixteen-year-old Lab late yesterday afternoon. I need some enjoyment. Having said that, I'll do what I can to make Brick's tow truck work for me. Just remember, hauling's not my strong suit."

Ty's scowl became a sneer. "Couldn't get either one of the Majerki brothers to help you, huh?"

Eli tossed the rag. "Is that the burning question, or would you rather have the details on my night at Bellam Manor?"

Ty's neck went red. "I don't see a tail and long ears, so neither of the resident witches turned you into a donkey. Sadie'd say anything else was between you and her. Speaking of, is she someplace safe?"

"She's at the manor with Molly."

"Who's not exactly a ninja. Do you ever think of anyone but yourself?"

"About as much as you do. It's covered," he said before his cousin could protest further. "She's safe."

"Guess I'll have to take that on faith."

"Guess you will."

Ty showed his teeth. "Where's the spike chain?"

"Long gone, unless whoever planted it is a complete fool. Not very likely."

"Sloppy's been known to happen in cases like this."

"Yeah? How many cases like this have you known?"

His cousin moved a shoulder. "I poked into Laura's death some after I came to the office."

"And?"

Ty's grin fell just short of feral. "If I told you that, you'd have nothing to challenge your slick investigative skills, would you?"

"Sounds like he turned up a big fat zero to me." Brady used the heavy lift chain to get Eli's vehicle airborne. "Is a spike line what it sounds like?"

"Pretty much." Eli's stomach clenched when the hoist bobbled and almost dropped his truck back into the bog. "Know anybody who has one?"

"No, but Ben Leamer's got a long, spiky, rake-like thing out at his farm."

Ty snorted. "Why would old Ben want to wreck Eli's truck?"

"Just answering the question." Brady disengaged the safety chain. "Ben's whatever-it-is is the only object I can think of that's got the potential for a wicked bite."

"Unless you count Rooney's signature tea." Eli hopped onto the flatbed. "Let's get this done, okay?"

Leaving Brady to secure the front of the vehicle, he

worked on the back while Ty strode around and did his best to be a complete ass.

Would he be an ass if their situations were reversed? Eli wondered. And he had to admit that, yeah, he might.

"Is this Sadie's?" Fighting the door open, his cousin reached for a mud-encrusted black leather bag. "Unless I'm wrong and it's yours, I hope there was nothing important inside." He unzipped it to rummage through the contents. "Camera, lenses, iPad, shorthand notes—all dry and unbroken." His smile could have cut glass. "Lucky her." He kicked the dented door as closed as it would go. "Not so lucky you. Go long, Lieutenant."

Eli nabbed the bag halfway to the slimy water. "Nice of you to zip it back up."

"Nice isn't what I'm feeling at the moment. In fact, what I'm feeling is in the mood to participate in one of those borderline legal fights Rooney is forever arranging behind my back. Problem is, we're nowhere near Two Toes Joe's bar."

Eli glanced into the camera bag. "Mud works for me." He rezipped as he spoke and only looked down again when the teeth snagged. The corner of a folded paper stuck out, but it wasn't until he drew the pull tab back and spied the red lettering that his blood ran cold.

Ty's voice faded to an irritating buzz. Freeing the caught corner, Eli removed a sheet of paper that ran a full two feet in length. The words slashed across it were like acid in his system.

While the man's away
The monster can play.

"WHY DOES THIS monster hate me so much? Or at all? Because it can't control the side of itself that's got a weird obsession with me?" Sadie dipped under a low branch in the woods near Bellam Manor. "We need to find haw-thorn leaves."

"Let me know when we do." Eli held the branch up. "Jealousy's not uncommon with a split personality, Sadie. One side often wants what the other side has."

"Yes, but that's not the case here, is it? The nonmonster doesn't actually have. He only wants."

"And the monster doesn't want the nonmonster to get. Simple solution? Eliminate the prize."

Sadie studied Molly's wish list for the séance. Bendable willow branches, wild lavender, fennel, thyme and rose-mary from the old garden. "The writing didn't change, Eli. The paper was long and folded, like the one Laura found in her gym bag, but the writing in my message was con-sistent. Creepy, but consistent. Theory?"

"Cal's trying to throw us off track."

Stepping into an overgrown herb garden outside the original Bellam graveyard, she snipped some thyme, sniffed the leaves and dropped them into a paper bag. "Then why did Cal tell us he was ambidextrous? He didn't have to. Obviously, the police missed that fact during their investigation into Laura's death."

"Obviously, the police were out of their depth and re-ceived very little peripheral help when it came to Laura's case."

She tilted her head. "Hate to point this out, Lieutenant, but you're not receiving any peripheral help, either. Or looking to bring any in as far as I can tell."

The gleam in his eyes made her breath hitch in a ridic-ulously exciting way.

"One click of a computer key, and I have a wealth of information at my fingertips. The trick is to sort through the clutter until you hit pay dirt. The coroner's report on

Laura's homicide said she was struck from behind by a left-handed person."

"Meaning she felt comfortable enough to turn her back on the killer?"

"Or she was forced to turn it. Left-handed's the gold, Sadie."

"Yes, I got that." She sighed. "And now you're going to ask me how many of the men I've interacted with between the Hollow and the Cove are left-handed. My answer is, not Ty."

"Not Brady, either."

She laughed. "Well, hell, Eli, I can hardly read what Brady writes with his right hand." She paused midsnip. "Wait a second. Rewind. You think Brady could have a monster living inside him?"

"Brady, Two Toes Joe, Brick from the tow yard, his brother, one of Ty's deputies."

She cut a sprig of lavender, but instead of bagging it, she stood, twirled the stem in her fingers and strolled slowly toward him. "That's quite the voice you have there, Lieutenant Blume. Of experience, I mean." Touching her tongue to her upper lip, she dropped her gaze for a meaningful second. "It's very—sexy."

His eyes caught and held hers. "You had to know my last relationship didn't work out well on either side."

She hooked a finger in his waistband. "Gathered that."

"I almost hurt someone I cared about."

And tugged. "Almost being the operative word."

"I'm not going to do the same thing to you."

"I'm not going to let you do the same thing to me—whatever it is or was." Reaching for his oh-so-tempting mouth, she asked, "Any more pointless objections?"

"Yeah, but to hell with them," he muttered, and pulled

her so hard against him that she could feel every muscle in his body, from sleek biceps to tantalizing arousal.

It felt good, she thought, as pleasure hummed through her veins, not to be balanced on the high wire of her nerves. If only for a few minutes, she wanted to let the heat build and the fever, which was a wicked blend of need and desire, take hold.

The second Eli's mouth captured hers, his tongue plunged inside to feast.

He tasted like the night, like darkness and danger. The restless hunger that had been part of him for as long as Sadie could remember flowed out of him and into her. It made her blood pump and her skin tingle.

She breathed in, then blissfully out. This was how she'd felt when they'd danced that first night in Boston. In that single heady moment she'd known with absolute certainty she wouldn't be marrying Ty.

Cupping her face in his hands, Eli deepened the kiss, then ran his fingers lightly over her shoulders and arms until they found her breasts. She moaned, and the moan became a low purr as his thumbs grazed the nipples under her T-shirt and bra. His lips moved from her mouth to her jaw and along the column of her throat.

"Gonna melt in a minute," she warned, but didn't know if she spoke the words or merely thought them.

"Already have," he murmured against her neck.

Letting her head bow back, Sadie savored the sensations sweeping through her. Desire mixed with the heat that spiraled upward from her belly. Breathless, she took a moment to revel in the kind of liquid need she'd never expected to feel. Wasn't entirely sure she'd wanted to feel.

She dug her fingers into his upper arms, felt lean muscle and hard bone and knew, *knew* she should push herself away. Should never have started this in the first place, because...

When he took her mouth again, the thought simply turned to dust and scattered.

He awakened every one of her sleeping senses. Wanting him even closer, she slid her hands upward, until her fingers were impossibly tangled in his hair. Rough bark scraped her back, and the first drops of rain hit her cheeks. She could feel him hard and pulsing against her. All she had to do was jump up, wrap her legs around his hips and let gravity and hunger take them down into the remains of the flower bed. The setting was perfect, and the thunder that rumbled over the hollow merely layered anticipation over desire.

She spied it before she sank all the way into him. A misty shadow that wasn't a shadow but a solid figure. Like the zealots from her nightmare, it wore a black cloak and held something in its hand.

Dragging her mouth free, Sadie managed a breathless "Gun!"

Eli reacted so swiftly she barely noticed the move. Shoving her to the ground, he pulled his Police Special and spun into a kneeling crouch.

The figure's first bullet struck the tree behind them. The second—no idea. The third blew one of the herb bags apart.

Crawling to him, Sadie felt for Eli's backup and tugged it free. There was a fence, a crooked line of pickets between him and the now-secreted shooter. Not much of a shield in her opinion.

Flat on the ground, her breath held to the point of discomfort, she squeezed the trigger. The gun kicked pain up to her elbows, but she continued to squeeze off shots.

She might have heard some thrashing at that point, and

maybe she glimpsed receding black, but if she was honest, the whole thing had become a jumble of sight and sound. So she continued to pump out shots until she heard nothing but empty clicks.

Before the last echo died, Eli was up and gone. Sadie dropped her face onto her extended arms and breathed. She heard the double tone from her phone but ignored it until her senses rebooted. When they did, she raised her head and scoured the nearby woods.

There was nothing. No sound, no movement, no clue as to where Eli had gone.

"Just once," she muttered in frustration, "I'd like an easy answer."

She was debating her limited options when her phone beeped again. Preoccupied, she dug it from her jacket pocket.

More raindrops plopped onto her head, and the thunder that shook the flower bed and grave markers was creeping closer. High in the trees, ravens cawed. One of them swooped in for a landing on a tippy picket.

"Give me all the evil looks you want, pal." She went to her message app. "After what I've gone through lately, I'm immune."

The bird cawed noisily, but Sadie didn't hear it, or anything. The text message that appeared on the screen stopped her breath and sent a shaft of pure terror into her heart.

I WASN'T SHOOTING AT YOU!

Chapter Fifteen

"People don't vanish," Ty maintained an hour later. "Outsmart other people, yes, but even on Bellam land, they can't twitch up a broomstick and fly off into the ether."

"I was thinking more along the lines of jumping into a rabbit hole. Or a cave, like the one Sadie and I used to climb out of the bog." Eli flicked through files in his cousin's private office. "Don't you have any maps that predate the nineteen fifties?"

"The *Chronicle* might." Sadie glanced up from her iPhone. "There are a lot of boxes in the basement. I can look tomorrow. We really should be leaving for the manor soon, if we want…" Pausing, she peered around Ty's arm at the veterinary clinic across the street. "Orley's pulling in," she told them. "Back in a sec."

"Bad mood happening here, Sadie." A scowling Orley climbed from her car. "Brady and I just chased down a deer with an arrow in its hind leg. We had to use a tranquilizer dart on it. The tranq worked, but naturally the deer toppled into a pile of dung and had to be worked on where it lay."

"Is it all right?"

"It will be. Gorgeous animal. A buck."

"In that case, and given that you like animals a thousand times better than humans, how could saving a deer put you in a bad mood?"

Orley bared her teeth. "I'm wearing my Gucci suede boots. I swear, if I find out who launched that arrow, I'm going to shoot him in the leg and leave him to bleed in the woods." Her grimace morphed into a weary expulsion of breath when a truck creaked to a halt behind her. "Dr. Dolittle in the flesh."

Climbing from his truck, Brady shouldered his medical bag and picked up a crossbow arrow.

"I hate hunters," Orley muttered. "My dad hunts, so opposite sides of the fence there, but at least he knows you can't kill an animal by aiming for the ass end. Any poacher worth his salt should know that, too."

"You can't be sure it was a poacher, Orley." Brady followed Sadie's narrowed stare to the arrow. "What? I'm not the nitwit who pulled the trigger."

"Sorry, knee-jerk. Where was the deer?"

Orley picked at one of her ruined boots. "In the hollow."

"Near Raven's Bog?"

"Within spitting distance. Why?"

"Can't write an article without all the facts."

Brady arched a surprised brow. "An arrow in the haunch of a deer's newsworthy?"

"It is today." She wiggled her fingers. "Can I see the arrow?"

"You must be having one very slow news day." But Brady relinquished the metal shaft. "And here they come—the never-gonna-be Bobbsey Twins."

Sadie heard Ty's snort of disgust at the same time Eli's arm dropped across her shoulders.

"Might want to keep that arrow away from your ex, sweetheart," he murmured, "or it could wind up in an innocent back."

Ty sneered. "Now, why would I want to impale the town vet? Hand it, Sadie."

At a small nod from Eli, she complied.

"Ah, right, got it." Brady's face cleared. "You think this is one of the arrows that was shot at you and Eli on Sunday night. Instead of hitting its intended target, it hit a deer."

"Always possible," Eli agreed.

"I want to talk to Cal." Ty twirled the arrow. "Are you sure you didn't get a disclaimer after the attack in the bog, Sadie?"

Still out of sorts, Orley raised her gaze from her ruined boots. "Since when do would-be murderers put out disclaimers?"

Sadie shrugged. "Someone in a black cloak and hood put one out earlier today. He was shooting at Eli and me near the graveyard at Bellam Manor. Shooter rabbited. A few minutes later, I got a text. He said the bullets weren't meant for me."

Orley snorted. "Sounds like someone's head is seriously messed up. No offense, cous."

"None taken."

Brady ran a hand over his face. "What about the attack in the bog?"

Eli watched Ty play with the arrow. "I think whoever was behind that wanted both of us dead."

"You're not in the guy's head, though, are you?" Ty looked up with a level expression. "You're also not on your own turf, so maybe you're reading the whole thing wrong, or at least coming at it from the wrong direction. I know the Hollow and the Cove. I know how the people here think, and what they think and why."

"Ty, Eli grew up here, too… Uh, right." Palms out, Brady backed off. "You two hash it out. Triangles aren't my…"

"Eli, that's Cal in the truck at the corner!" Sadie grabbed the wrist still draped over her shoulder. "What's he doing here? No, wait, don't spook… Why do I even talk?" she wondered, as first Eli, then Ty, then Cal bolted. "It's like being in a *Rambo* movie. Séance starts at seven, Orley," she called back as she ran for her Land Rover.

Eli was already inside. "Forget it," he said, and started to slam the lock down.

But Sadie got the door open a split second faster and climbed in. "My vehicle, my decision. Go, or you'll be fighting Ty for road space."

He slanted her a dark look but didn't argue further. Couldn't because Ty fishtailed his cruiser around the corner and set off after Cal with a screech of tires and a series of short bursts on the siren.

Sadie gripped the dash with one hand and the side of Eli's seat with the other. "Any chance you two could work together on this?"

"Any way you know of to transmit that request to Ty?"

"He has a cell...."

"Any way that'll work?"

He had her there. She kept Cal's gray truck in sight. "If we assume he's heading back to the woods, you could take the Post Road and cut him off at the junction before the hollow. Then if Ty squeezes him from behind..." She made a dubious motion. "It could work."

But it didn't. Instead of cornering their quarry, Eli wound up in a near collision with Ty's cruiser, leaving Cal to bump through the junction and roar away on a rocky path few mountain goats would attempt.

Recognizing the expression on Eli's face, Sadie covered the gearshift with her hand. "Please don't. I can't afford a new vehicle, and I'm not insured for extreme off-road adventures. Cal knows these woods better than we do. Plus, we have his home address."

When the light in his eyes didn't diminish, she did the

only thing she could think of. She reached over the console, took his face in her hands and set her mouth on his.

Because she only meant to distract him, the sudden burst of heat surprised her. It also caused every thought in her head to wink out.

A dazzled "Wow" was the best she could manage when she eased herself away. "I didn't expect...hmm."

His lips curved. "Serious understatement. But as long as we're here."

He had her over the console and straddling him before her brain restarted.

The hunger bottled inside her shot need and adrenaline into her veins. Bunching his jacket, she let her eyes sparkle into his. "As first times go, this wouldn't be my setting of choice, but it's better than—oh, damn, Ty!"

The memory of the near collision had her whipping her head around. "He's—gone," she realized in relief. Then frowned. "Why is he gone?"

Eli rested his forehead against her hair. "He didn't go after Cal, if that's what you're thinking."

"Oh, I'm not up to thinking quite yet. My head's still buzzing, and I'm in kind of a nice place physically." She shimmied her butt on his lap. "However..."

Employing every scrap of self-restraint she possessed, Sadie climbed off and dropped back into her seat. "Bet he saw us."

"If he didn't, he should be declared legally blind." Moving carefully, Eli grinned. "Message received. No wild rides."

"Only where my Land Rover's concerned. Anything else is fair game." When her gaze drifted to the dash clock, her eyes widened. "Is that the time? We need to go. Molly sets a strict schedule."

"For a séance? Sorry, sweetheart, I have to say again, your cousin's very strange."

"Strange is the middle name of every Bellam and Blume descendant I know. Molly schedules bathroom breaks, Eli. She'll follow through whether we're there or not. And if the monster who wants me, you, or me and you dead shows up—very likely—the last thing I want to do is not be there and have him decide to vent his rage on people I care about."

Eli regarded the brooding sky. "Okay, we'll go through with it. But I want to check out Molly's apartment top to bottom before we start."

"It'll be Nola's apartment." Sadie flicked the ends of her hair. "In order to achieve the proper atmosphere, Molly does her summoning in what our family believes was Nola Bellam's inner sanctum."

"Great. Anything else I don't want to know?"

"You decide. At her last séance, two years ago, after Molly commanded the spirit in question to signal her presence by knocking three times, we heard three consecutive taps at the window."

"Signals can be rigged, Sadie."

"Not done yet. Nola's room is on the third floor of the manor. When we opened the shutters, we found a raven sitting on the sill."

"Which is unusual because?"

"He had a locket at his feet, which belonged to the dead woman. A locket no one had supposedly seen since before the spirit being summoned passed on."

"Uh-huh." Now his lips twitched. "Can I assume this locket belonged to your ancestor?"

"Ten points to you, Lieutenant."

"What was inside? A miniature painting of Hezekiah?"

Unable to resist, Sadie leaned over the console and used

her index finger to trace the line of his jaw. "Not quite. There were two locks of hair inside, one red, one black. And beneath them was a tiny piece of paper that read:

Whosoever shall open my locket

Will find no peace.

In this life or the next."

Eli curled his fingers around her neck. "Gotta be more to it than that. Who opened the locket?"

She touched her mouth to his in the lightest of kisses. "You already know the answer. I did."

SADIE DIDN'T BELIEVE in portents or omens, never had. However, a séance in her ancestral home in the throes of the chaos that was unfolding around her, had her wishing she'd taken that job at the *New York Times* after all.

She opted to wear traditional black—an ankle-skimming dress with a deep V, long pointy sleeves and just cling enough to bolster her slightly battered confidence.

She got a major boost when she opened the front door of the manor. Eli's eyes glinted dangerously even as Rooney hobbled in to wedge himself between them.

Beaming with delight, the old man wrapped his bony fingers around her upper arms. "Nola won't be putting in an appearance with one of her progeny looking as drop-dead beautiful as you do tonight, Sadie Bellam." He inhaled deeply. "Smell like a dream, too. Hope your cousin's got a standby spirit up her witchy sleeve."

"It wouldn't surprise me." She looked at Eli, then past him into the teaming rain before escorting Rooney slowly up the stairs to the third floor.

"No need to fuss," he assured her as she seated him. "You just make sure the tea's hot and the whiskey that makes it drinkable isn't of the soda pop variety. On the off chance my heart stops from fright, I'll be needing something stronger than chamomile to jump-start it."

Sadie set a hip on the round table, crossed her arms and regarded him with a semihumorous expression. "I thought you were a firm believer in all the local lore, not merely your own."

"Oh, I believe, young Sadie, but I also know shinola when I see it. Molly's got the trappings down pat. Hanging plants, rocks and crystals scattered, participants seated where she chooses, mood music for effect, candles for light. It all looks, sounds and smells perfect, but is it real or just a show for the tourists?" He tapped his nose. "One way or another, with a hundred-plus years under my belt, I'll sniff out the truth. Now, let's get down to basics." His cane hit the floor between his knees. "Firstly, are you or my great-grandson gonna tell your favorite centenarian why I got a half-crazed phone call from Brick Majerki late this afternoon? And secondly, does a man's heart actually need to stop before he can get a mug of tea in this house?"

On cue, Orley slammed a tray holding four pots and several mugs onto the table, growled out a hello and marched off.

"Green pot's yours," Sadie stage-whispered to Rooney. "Hey, Jerk," she said to the man just entering the room. "Rooney here was asking about your brother. Seeing as Brick's so fearful of all things Bellam, I never expected to see either of you at the manor."

The big man scratched his cheek. "Well, I'm not Brick, now, am I, Sadie? The story of *Hansel and Gretel* sent little bro under the bed for a week. Me, I only cared about sinking my teeth into a big chunk of that gingerbread house."

Sadie had known Jerk and Brick for two years. When they weren't hauling or tearing apart dead vehicles, they liked to tinker with old machines. They'd been tinkering with the printing presses at the *Chronicle* since before her uncle retired.

Rooney winked at her. "Maybe Molly's crystal ball's on the fritz and she called Jerk here to fix it. Even she knows you'd never get the Brickman within a mile of this place on a night like this, not for all the whiskey in Ben Leamer's—"

"Corn," Sadie inserted smoothly. Her eyes found Eli in the doorway. "Not for all the corn in Ben Leamer's maze, Rooney. Is Molly's crystal ball on the fritz, Jerk?"

Brick's brother grinned. "Can't say as I know why she asked me to come."

"I didn't ask you to come," Molly said from behind him. "You asked me if there was an empty seat."

"And then you asked him to come," Sadie put in. "Which is why he's here, undoubtedly against his brother's wishes, but hey, you have to go your own way, right, Jerk?"

The big man poured himself and Rooney a mug of tea. "I've seen that gleam in your eyes before, Sadie. You wanna punch someone in the balls, Eli's made the rounds and he's heading this way right now."

Rooney clinked his mug to Jerk's. "If I were you, Sadie, I'd leave the ball punching to Ty. He looks hissy as a snake, don't you think?"

"Oh, this night's going to be so much fun," she predicted, then twirled in a half circle. "What about you, Lieutenant Blume? Are you up for a little fun?"

"Only if the word *fun* has suddenly become a synonym for debacle." He snagged a mouthful of Rooney's tea before propelling her into a corner crammed with dusty, sheet-covered furniture. "This gathering is a ticking time bomb. You should be as far away from it as possible."

She sent him a guileless look. "Your suggestion might have worked out better if you'd mentioned it earlier. That way, instead of being here, Jerk could be playing pool with Brick, who's completely freaked at the thought of his brother participating in a Bellam séance." She pushed a meaningful fist into his stomach. "How long has Jerk been guard-dogging me?"

Catching her balled fingers, Eli brought them to his lips. "Since you and Orley went into Ben Leamer's corn maze and you came out with the news that a monster had been added to the mix."

Part of her softened, couldn't help it. Another part resented his need-to-know attitude. "I thought we'd established that all murderers have monsters living inside them."

"They do, but I sense a growing separation of entities with this guy."

"We've established that, too, Eli. Monster wants me dead, stalker wants you dead."

Tipping her chin up with his knuckle, Eli stared into her eyes. "Which creates the very intriguing question, Sadie. Who is it that wants both of us dead?"

THE QUESTION HAUNTED her throughout the séance.

As if an order had been placed for the occasion, the thunder that had been rumbling over the north woods crept closer. Rain lashed the windows and pummeled the old roof. The raft of candles Molly had lit fluttered atmospherically in a dozen different drafts. Even with Sadie knowing that not a single aspect of this was real, her fingers felt like ice when they joined with those of her tablemates.

Rooney sat in apparent thrall, his eyes closed, his features thrown into skeletal relief by the center candle. Orley seemed annoyed, but surprisingly offered no snotty comments. Brady wore an expression that suggested his mind was elsewhere. Ty looked tense and a little uneasy. Molly might or might not have been in a trance. Jerk jiggled a leg in his chair—out of boredom, Sadie suspected, more than nerves. As for Eli, he watched the entire gathering without appearing to, and occasionally let a small smile cross his lips when her eyes slid to his profile.

Keeping her own eyes firmly closed, Molly attempted to invoke her chosen spirit. "We call to the one who left our world too soon. We seek the knowledge she possesses. We seek truth. We seek—"

The last word was swallowed up by a peal of thunder that made the lids of the teapots rattle.

"You, who were threatened long ago, are dead in body. None among us can say why. But there is one in our realm who knows the truth. One who seeks to repeat his heinous act, who would commit to the afterlife another of your blood. If you can hear me, sister spirit, if you can help us, let your presence and your knowledge be apparent to all. Speak in whatever manner you choose. Send to us a sign that you are among us."

The candles flickered wildly as lightning split the blackness beyond the window. The table bumped. A second later, the door flew open, a blast of cold air rushed in and the candles blew out as one.

It couldn't have been more than two seconds before Eli's flashlight flared. Yet in those seconds, chairs were shoved in all directions and feet clattered. A body—no idea whose—slammed into Sadie, who stumbled into Eli. The flashlight fell and rolled. Ty barked out an order while Jerk—she thought Jerk—grunted.

Eli caught Sadie before she wound up on the floor. "Are you all right?"

"What? Yes. I'm just… Where are we going?"

"We need light."

It took them several seconds to access the wall switch.

By the time the chandelier flared, everyone except Rooney was on his or her feet and scattered.

"Okay." Halfway across the room, Orley raised both hands. "That's it, folks. That was one creepy interlude. I'm not a believer, but I swear, something cold and wet brushed across my face."

"Don't be ridiculous," Ty scoffed. "It was the wind. A shutter blew open in the other room. That blew the door in, and the wind did the rest. Tell her, Eli. Someone's playing a sick prank is all."

"I'd take it a step further and say someone wanted to scare the crap out of us. One of us more than the others, I imagine." En route to the covered furniture, Eli crouched beside his great-grandfather's chair. "You still with us?"

"Didn't spill a drop," the old man replied with a toothless smile. He lifted his mug at Sadie. "Pure shinola."

"Sadie?" Molly ventured tremulously.

Willing her heart out of her throat and a calm expression onto her face, Sadie exhaled. "It's fine, Molly. I'm fine. I think Eli and Ty are right. Shutter, door, wet-wind effect, mass palpitations. And yeah, the crap pretty much scared out of us." She regarded Rooney. "It was really good shinola."

Molly's features remained ghost white in the dim overhead light. "I think we can agree that's an ending. Someone or something did not like what we were doing."

"Oh, I wouldn't say that." Sadie glanced at Eli and made a subtle gesture for him to look down. "Someone or something was nice enough to leave me a gift. Not in quite the same condition as the last time I saw it, but I imagine that's the point." Raising her hand, she let Nola's locket dangle on its chain for everyone in the room to see.

The once oval-shaped locket had been smashed so badly out of shape it was barely recognizable. And what she

could see that the others couldn't were the two chilling
words that had been scored into the old gold backing.
  DIE WITCH!

Chapter Sixteen

Yes, she was rattled, but no way would she let it show.

The sight of Nola's locket, which, as far as Sadie knew, had been placed in a safe-deposit box at the local bank two years ago, wouldn't have shocked her or anyone quite so much if it hadn't been hammered flat.

So, not merely struck once or twice with intent to cause damage, but rather bashed to within an inch of its life. Or metaphorically, she supposed, hers.

It took the better part of two hours to search Nola's rooms, clear out the guests and ensure that Rooney was transported safely home. On the way back to the manor, with rain bouncing off the roof of her Land Rover and thunder still rumbling, Sadie turned the ruined locket over in her palm.

"I know this is the monster's handiwork, but why does everything suddenly feel so tragic to me?"

Eli glanced over. "Is that how it feels? I was thinking repressed violence myself. Teetering on the edge of insanity and building for an enraged final act."

"Huh." She regarded the scored words in the next flash of lightning. "You got a lot more out of this particular message than I did. Or maybe than I wanted to. Now, on top of everything else, the killer—monster—whatever—has branded me a witch." She couldn't control the shudder that started in her belly and rose. "Does this mean I'm facing the prospect of eighteenth-century torture tactics, or is it just an incredibly effective way to terrify the living hell out of me?"

"I'd go with the second thing. The witch label's the killer messing with your head."

"In that case, his gamesmanship's bang-on, because I feel totally messed right now."

Eli's next glance held an undercurrent of steel. "Dead's not an option, Sadie, unless your twisted gift giver's playing the part of the corpse."

"He rigged that shutter to blow open and the door after it, didn't he?"

They'd reached a fork in the woods. Braking, Eli reached over and turned her head until their eyes met. "Don't let him do this to you. This is a killer acting out what he can't physically achieve. It's words, and him planting seeds of fear, then hoping they'll take root so you'll do something stupid."

"Like go to a séance in a house full of shadows and draped furniture and really bad lighting. The killer could have shoved a knife in my back as easily as he gave me this locket."

"No." Eli kissed her lightly on the lips. "He really couldn't."

"Trying very hard to believe you here, Lieutenant." She waited through a lightning strike before asking, "Why?"

"Your dress has pockets, right?"

"Yes."

"And you discovered the locket inside one of those pockets."

"Again, yes."

"Did you find it because you felt it being slipped to you?"

"No. I found it when I was helping you look for the light switch, and I bumped into a chair. I felt it—ah, right—on my hip. Got it." The smallest of smiles touched her mouth. "The locket could have been placed in my pocket any time, even before the séance started."

"I'd put my money on before. Were you ever alone in the room?"

"Not really. Molly and I were there together for a while."

"Doing what?"

"Arranging plants and crystals, lighting candles, creating scent zones."

"Did you do a test run with the chandelier off and only the candles lit?

Amusement stirred. "You've met Molly, right? Of course we tested it, several times."

"Were you and Molly alone at that point?"

"By light-testing time? No. Orley, Brady and Ty arrived in a clump. And she paid a couple of delivery guys from the supermarket to bring party trays for after the séance. They came, gawked, placed their trays and left."

"So there were people milling, however briefly. Lights on, lights off, furniture covered, shadows everywhere and you wearing your signature perfume."

"You noticed it?" A smile blossomed. "That's...nice, actually."

His eyes slid down, then up. "There's not much I don't notice about you, Sadie."

Because teasing was easy and fun, she fluttered her lashes at him. "Does this mean we're going to have spectacular sex after all? And before you ask, yes, I've been accused of having a one-track mind before, many times."

"Ditto, but we need to ride out the first track before we switch over. No matter how it was delivered, Nola's locket was intended for you."

"Meaning my monster's target-specific—with lockets, bullets and likely crossbow arrows, as well. Big sigh of relief for anyone who's not me. Or you. Well, sometimes you. I'm confused."

"Actually, you're right on top of it. The killer's not after Rooney or Orley or Jerk."

"Lovely. Again, though, only if you're not me. Or us. Are we done with this conversation, because my brain's about ready to implode?"

"Done enough." He skimmed his thumb over her lips. "For the moment."

Completely off-kilter, Sadie sat back to regard the turbulent night sky while Eli completed the tricky climb to the manor. "You're thinking Cal could have snuck in at the prep stage and given me the locket, aren't you?"

"Ty figures Cal hid under a sheet or behind a piece of furniture while the participants filed in. Séance started, stuff happened, the room went dark and Cal snuck out, nice and tidy."

"Is that what you think?"

"No."

"Gonna tell me why?"

"Are you up for a crash course in police logic?"

"Another 'no' would have done there, Eli." She indicated the far side of the manor. "Park in the carport. If the wind picks up and decides to topple a tree, I don't want it falling on my Land Rover, which still has six months of lease payments left on it."

"You bought this vehicle on a lease?"

Her eyes fired a dangerous warning. "Don't start with me. I know exactly what I gave up to come here and run the *Chronicle. New York Times,* buckets of money, Manhattan condo and monsters who, for the most part, wear business suits." She waited through a long peal of thunder before angling her head at him. "Are you ever going to tell me who it is you almost hurt?"

He parked the Land Rover under the shelter, cut the engine, but left his iPod running. Nirvana might not have been the most romantic of bands, but a driving beat coupled with the screw-you lyrics added an edge to his suddenly closed features.

When he didn't immediately respond, she took a chance and added a gentle "I get that you don't want to talk about it, or her. But if something that happened in your past is preventing us from having amazing sex in the present, can't I at least know part of the reason why?"

Sadie couldn't begin to read his expression when he finally did look at her.

Troubled, angry, brooding, distant. What she could see was his mind sliding back to whatever time had generated those particular emotions.

"Her name was Eve," he revealed at length. "And I came so close to shooting her—killing her—that I blew out a window right behind her."

Whatever horror she'd been anticipating, it wasn't that. Sadie started to speak, reconsidered and sighed. "I don't know what to say, Eli, what I should say. 'I'm glad you didn't shoot her' seems awkward and obvious. But I also know there must have been a reason for that to have happened, and it doesn't involve you falling off some shaky psychological ledge. So let me sidetrack and ask you this. If it was only for one night, and we both knew that, understood and accepted it, could you get around what's been and give yourself permission to enjoy what could be? What is, right now, at this moment?"

Staring out at the night, he gave a small laugh. "You mean can I live, however briefly, in the present rather than the past?"

"Well, yes, but my way sounded much more profound. There's a person out there, Eli, an Ezekiel Blume who wants me dead. If you're Hezekiah and I'm Nola, it makes sense that this modern-day Ezekiel wants you dead, too, before the legend kicks in all the way and you get desperate enough to bring in an evil spirit—and for evil spirit, read backup—to help you trap him."

Traces of that vague humor lingered on his face. "Those recent dreams of yours have really done a number on your head, haven't they?"

"Dreams, bullets, phone calls, text messages, a dead raven, a decimated locket and the knowledge that there are very few places in or out of the Hollow where I actually feel safe."

"I won't—"

"I know. You won't let him hurt me. Kill me. But what if you die trying to save me? Or you die because the monster half of my stalker wants it? I can't think of you dead, Eli. I'm not sure I could live knowing you were gone, whatever the reason." Threads of tension began to creep up her neck and into her skull. "Would leaving Raven's Hollow help either of us at this point?"

"Sadie…"

"Didn't think so. And even if it would, Laura's murderer would still be out there. He'd continue to go unpunished for a crime he committed twenty years ago…. And I have absolutely no idea how we got here from where this conversation started."

"We were talking about me setting aside my emotional baggage long enough for us to make love."

"Interesting how a side trip through hell can put such a huge crimp in such a simple—or I thought simple—question. Forget I asked it, okay?"

"So you don't want to have sex?"

When her temples began to throb, she used her fingers to push back the pain. "I thought I did, but honestly, at this moment? All I want is about six aspirins and a whack on the head to induce sleep. Just walk me inside so I can feed Cocoa, fall into bed and pretend no part of tonight ever happened. You and Ty are clever cops. Join forces and you might actually have this nightmare dealt with before you and or I wind up facedown in Raven's Bog."

She didn't wait for him to open her door, but slid out and set her sights on the entrance.

Painkillers, hot drink, hot bath, bed. It wasn't what she'd thought she wanted, but it would do.

Thankfully, there was no dead raven on the welcome mat, and her front door was locked and bolted. Small favors, major relief. As long as the entry wall was still draped and taped, she'd be fine.

If Eli didn't want to be with her, that was fine, too. No sex, no problem. He wasn't the only person at the manor who had issues. Bellam women sucked when it came to building and maintaining relationships. And she compounded that with a constant need for change. She'd moved from city to city to town so many times over the past seven years that there was very little point in unpacking anymore.

Fortunately, those city stints had taught her how to walk quickly in high heels. She had the door unlocked and opened before Eli made the stoop.

Or thought she did.

One of his hands planted itself on the frame while the other grabbed her arm and spun her around. "Was that your idea of a dramatic exit line?"

He was angry, she realized, and wanted her to feel the same way. No problem. She moved her lips into a sugary smile. "Sorry to disappoint you, Lieutenant, but there was no drama intended. I changed my mind about us, simple as that. Go with the cliché of it being a woman's prerogative. You're not interested, and I'm not willing. Anymore."

She started to turn back, but he held her in place with his body. "You were willing enough a minute ago."

"Well, that's the thing about women in general and Bellam women in particular. We're changeable creatures. One minute we want chocolate, the next it's ice cream. The trick is to catch us before we switch."

His eyes slid down to where he pressed her against the door. "You seem caught from where I'm standing."

"Physically, yes. Unfortunately, I'm not in the mood for chocolate anymore, so back off, Lieutenant, before I call on my ancestor to turn you into that lizard you mentioned once."

His eyes glittered in the next bolt of lightning. "A raven would be more appropriate."

Both her temper and her blood heated up. "Already been done. I'm going for something new. Step back, Eli. Now."

"When we're done here, sweetheart. It's not about me being interested."

It took a second for Sadie to recall her earlier accusation. "If being interested's not part of it, you and I have very different ideas about why people have sex."

"I'm married to my work, Sadie. I have been for the past twelve years."

"Congratulations." She shot him another come-and-go smile. "I hope you make yourself very happy." Exasperation took root. "I said sex, Eli, not a lifetime commitment. I already told you, Bellam women are terrible at forever, so no worries there."

Bracing his other hand on the door, he lowered his head. They were so close now that when the lightning flashed, she saw flecks of gold in his green eyes. "I don't want sex with you, Sadie. I want to make love to you."

"It's the same…." But it wasn't, and her heart recognized the difference instantly. Her mind was another matter. Reining in her annoyance, she sighed. "If that's true, why are we fighting?"

"Probably because I don't want to fall in love with you."

"What? Fall…?" Who said anything about falling in love? Panic scuttled in. "Eli, I'm not… I can't… Did you hear anything I just said? Have been saying all along? Love, marriage, relationships, Bellam women. We're the 'd-y-s' in dysfunctional." She planted her palms flat on his chest. "Most of us never make it to the altar, and those who do make everyone involved wish they hadn't. Ty might not know it, but he's a very lucky man."

"Yeah? So what am I?"

She fisted the T-shirt under his jacket. "About two seconds away from turning ice cream back into chocolate. Eli, understand, this is insanity."

If it was possible, his eyes grew darker. "I'm a direct descendant of Hezekiah Blume, Sadie, remember? Insanity works for me."

Before she could utter another word, he took her mouth with his.

Chapter Seventeen

A dozen objections sprang to mind. Shoving all of them aside, Sadie let her heart—no, not her heart—desire. She let desire take the lead.

Heat scrambled in her veins. Her skin burned. Eli's kiss tortured her senses. And the feel of his body pressed against hers created a ball of lust that gathered in her stomach and then surged upward and out.

Her fingers found his face and held on while he gave and took and ignited. Freeing a hand, she fumbled behind her for the latch—and almost pitched into the manor backward when Eli got to it first.

He caught her easily and swung her around so her spine was plastered to the tall window next to the door.

Every movement spawned a new and exciting sensation. Every touch sparked another flame. Her bones turned to liquid, her thoughts to smoke, her common sense to smoldering ash.

Skimming her curves with fingers and palms, Eli explored her ribs and waist, her hips. Every inch of skin pulsed where he touched. Hunger flared with need trembling close behind it.

She'd wanted this, wanted them to be for so long now it almost seemed surreal. Desperate to taste, she pushed him to the limit, then let him push her back, to the edge and over.

Sadie swore she heard the last threads of protest snap. She'd warned him, and he hadn't listened.

Then again, neither had she.

Playful seduction was one thing. This blind plunge to a place she'd never expected to go stunned her senseless. A small part of her also knew it could and would come back to haunt her.

With the last of her willpower gone, she let the cravings of her body take over. Her head bowed back as she reveled in the shivers that chased themselves over her skin. It was, all of it, magic, a spell whipped up by a mad witch whose mind had been distorted by elemental need.

The air in the manor came alive. Sadie felt the storm swirling around her, into her, through her. She wanted to be closer, to move against him, but her muscles seemed to have deserted her. So she wrapped her arms around his neck and hung on as his mouth returned to feed on hers.

Eli's hands were their own kind of magic. They lit fires everywhere they roamed, and those fires made her energy level swell. As her body grew accustomed to her mind's out-of-control spin, she found herself eager to play catch-up.

Her fingers went in search of his jeans, latched on to button and zipper.

"You want to do this on the entry floor, Sadie?" She heard the faint amusement that lurked below restraint. "Afraid you'll change your mind if we take the time to move?"

She kissed him hard and deep, several times. "Afraid we both will," she said between breaths. "I want this, Eli, more than I've ever wanted anything. It's like—" Her fingers arced through black air. "I'd say it's like flying, except it's more like sinking, and really not caring if you surface or die a happy death and come up smiling when it's over. And since that makes absolutely no sense, why don't we just...?" She finished the question by giving his mouth a nip and bringing the glitter she loved so much to his eyes.

"Yeah, why don't we?" He took the kiss much deeper than she had done. "But not on the floor."

In a finger snap of time, the front hall miraculously transformed into the second-floor landing. She laughed. Crystal night-lights gave off just enough of a glow to guide him along the winding corridor to her bedroom.

Tightening her arms, Sadie caught his earlobe between her teeth and whispered, "Much better than a broomstick, Lieutenant. I never felt my feet leave the floor."

"Glad to hear your mind's not on your feet."

Thunder rumbled through the woods as he set her down in the bedroom. The night-lights dimmed but didn't go out. With need and desire humming, Sadie let him topple her onto the bed. Then her strength returned, and her hunger for him ramped up to critical.

Lightning streaked through the sky. As it did, she wrapped her legs around his hips, tightened and rolled him to a sitting position. "You undid me in the foyer, Lieutenant Blume." Eyes gleaming, she reached for his leather jacket, yanked it off and let it fly. "Now it's my turn."

Holding his arms out to the side, he grinned. "Take your best shot, sweetheart."

"Well, actually—" she got rid of his T-shirt with a quick upward tug "—the shot part's on you. Think of me—" she gave him a push that ended with him on his back "—as your enabler."

She left him his jeans, then sliding from the bed, switched the focus to her. The long slither of black might have been created especially for a striptease. Sadie took full advantage of the design, easing the sleeves along her arms, before running her fingers over her body and up into her hair. Holding it there, she gave her hips a little shimmy until the dress formed a sexy pool of black at her feet.

Stepping out of the fabric, she strolled to where he lay, propped up on his elbows, watching. If her eyes were any judge, he was more than ready to take that shot.

Raising her arms all the way, she allowed her hair to fall and her lips to curve in a deliberate seduction. "Coming to get you, Eli Blume." She crawled onto the bed. "In case you don't know this, a Bellam woman always gets what she wants."

With one very big exception, her heart whispered.

She stopped the whisper before it became a thought and set her mind on the man whose hands were already gliding over her, who flipped her onto her back and under him in a move so smooth she barely noticed it.

Then his mouth came down to plunder, to take everything she could pour into him. The sounds that collected in her throat emerged in a long, low purr. The lightning showed her that his jeans were gone and the only barriers left were her barely there bikinis and a bra that was little more than a whisper of black lace.

When he raised his head, his eyes shone in the slivers of crystal color. A short lightning bolt later, the lace was gone as well, leaving her naked and dazed with the thrill of exposure shooting hungry tremors to all her pulse points.

He had protection and, because of it, her distant but sincere gratitude. A pregnancy, planned or otherwise, was not on the agenda at this point in her life.

Locking his eyes on hers, he bracketed her wrists and drew her arms above her head. She raised her hips to rub against him, a quick tease. He held her there for an endless moment, then uncurled his fingers and ran them lightly down her arms.

His body shifted and lowered. A quick jolt raced through her when his mouth found her breast. He teased the nipple with his teeth and blurred her mind.

Everything around them swirled together in her head. The spears of lightning, white on black, the laser-thin beams of colors, the heat that built so high it threatened to burst through her skin....

She whipped up and over the peak yet still managed to understand that much more waited for her. There'd be another, larger comet tail to grab and ride if she could find the strength to reach for it.

"Now, Eli." Her breath hitched. "Please, now."

She saw him smile. And with thunder shaking both the floor and her bed, he plunged inside her, deep and hard and hot.

Sadie knew she cried his name. Eli simply filled her up. He took her to a place that was both foreign and exquisite. A sensory plane where nothing and everything felt real.

She hovered there for a delicious stretch of time before the ride slowly began to wind down. If the rise had been beyond words, the free fall back was only a little less stunning. A lovely numbness swirled around the edges of her mind and made her want to drift for as long as she could.

Eli was still rock hard inside her, but a deadweight on top. She'd have mentioned it if her tongue had been working. Or her vocal cords. In the end, a hazy "Mmm" was the best she could manage.

"If that was you wanting me to move, not sure I can." Eli spoke the words into her hair. "Not even sure I'm breathing."

"Know the feeling." She set her fingers experimentally on her chest. "Don't think I care." She managed a sleepy smile. "Excellent shot, Lieutenant. I may never walk again."

"I'd say I always aim to please, but you'd probably hit me, and it wouldn't be strictly true anyway."

Keeping her eyes closed, Sadie rode on the ripples of pleasure flowing through her bloodstream. "Spoil my swoony mood, and you're a dead man."

"Not much of a threat all in all. Died about the time I hit peak."

She laughed. "So this really was a one-shot—no pun intended—deal."

"Depends on how good you are at CPR."

The lazy tone of his voice got her juices flowing again, just enough that she wriggled beneath him. "Any chance of a revival happening down there, Lieutenant?"

She heard his smile. "Could be. A little." He raised his head to kiss her. "You said one night, right?"

It took a moment for her thoughts to untangle. "One night of what?"

"Us, Sadie. You said if we only had one night, and we knew it, could we enjoy it without repercussions?"

Unsure whether to be amused or offended, she settled for middle ground and stroked a considering fingernail along his back. "I have to say, you've got a much better postorgasmic memory than I do."

Rising on his elbows, he brushed the hair from her face. "I'm a cop. It's my job."

Offense gained ground. "You do your job in bed?"

His eyes glinted. "I do it everywhere but there, Sadie."

"O…kay." She drew the word out. "That was a fairly decent save. As usual, however, we're sliding off topic. And yes, to the one-night question—though I'm still wondering, in a not entirely nice way, why you asked it."

The glint deepened. "Guess I didn't do my not-cop-related job as well as I thought."

"That being what? To make me forget the who, when and where of tonight's séance?"

He slid his knuckles across her cheek. "For a few hours, anyway."

"In that case…" Her strength restored, she grabbed the duvet and rolled them off the bed. "Storm's still circling the hollow, the night's relatively young and I'm not done with you yet. We did it your way the first time. Now it's my turn." Locking her knees around his hips, she bent forward to whisper, "Wanna bet I can make you forget who, when and what you are?"

"That's a sucker bet, Sadie, but I'm game. Twenty bucks and dinner says not a chance."

She smiled. "Oh, you are so on, Lieutenant." Reaching between them, she stroked him lightly. "Bellam women might not make the best life mates, but we're always up for a challenge." Drawing out a slow kiss, she altered her grip and smiled at his instant response. "I was right about one thing earlier." She kissed him again around his hissed breath of reaction. "This night's gonna be so much fun."

ELI THOUGHT HE'D trained his mind to circumvent any and all nightmares. But with thunderbolts crashing, rain streaming and his senses riding a sexual buzz that made him wonder if someone had slipped him some new and highly illegal street drug, the worst of them returned with a vengeance.

He was in Manhattan, dead tired at the end of a killer double shift. Coupled with the undercover operation he'd completed two days ago, he'd been lucky to remember his own address.

He didn't expect Eve to be there waiting for him, truthfully didn't want her to be. He'd done battle with a lot of demons lately. Junked-up for the most part, but demons all the same. Throwing his own into the mix would simply feed the anger simmering inside him.

Five unrelieved weeks of living in a violent criminal world had scraped his nerves raw. He'd only agreed to the double shift afterward so his partner could be present for the birth of his first child.

Thunder trailed him up a set of dark, endless stairs. His captain said he needed to go under for a while. Threats from the crime boss whose right-hand man Eli had helped expose were the real deal. Anyone, anywhere could have a gun aimed at his back.

Good to know, he thought as he climbed. He was fast and accurate with his own weapons, but if the captain was right and he wanted to live on, he'd need to get faster and even more accurate.

Did he want to live on? he wondered grimly. Or had Eve and her lover sucked his emotions dry?

He'd cared about her, and believed she'd understood. Police officers did not lead normal lives. Her father had been a sergeant in Vice. Between them, hadn't he and Daddy made that simple truth clear? Or had the entertainment magazine she worked for given her a false set of ideals? Yeah, sure, anything was possible—in Hollywood.

He'd gone to her place one night without calling ahead. His mistake, according to her. He'd discovered Eve and her male model lover in bed. Her bed, not his, Eli recalled, which had helped, but hadn't stopped the anger from pushing him into accepting an undercover assignment he hadn't really wanted....

The upper landing of his apartment building took shape at last. Lightning slashed across the East River. He slid his key into the lock, then the dead bolts. Three clicks later, he was inside. Could have hit the light switch, but why bother? He didn't need light to find his bed.

His boots echoed on the worn floorboards. A woman's face flirted on the edges of his mind. Beautiful face, stunning features, incredible smoke-gray eyes....

"Gonna make you forget all the bad stuff, Lieutenant," she crooned. "If Eve had loved you, really loved you, there wouldn't have been another man in her bed...."

Thunder shook the entire building. The foundation bucked and almost threw him into a wall. Okay, got it, totally exhausted.

Then he heard a sound that wasn't thunder, or his boots on the floor, or a sexy female voice turning him on in his head.

Deep inside the shadows, someone moved. So did Eli, simultaneously. He saw a flash of motion, aimed for the torso and only jerked the barrel away at the last second because he spied blond hair.

It was too late to call the bullet back. He swore when the glass shattered, and for a horrible moment thought the shot had gone through flesh before taking out the window.

The woman in the shadow didn't scream. That felt wrong to him. Didn't she always scream in the nightmare? Didn't she scream and run, then stop when shock changed to fury and start throwing things at him?

None of that happened here. Because it didn't, the fear that formed a spiky ball in his belly turned to ice.

He couldn't remember the blond woman's name all of a sudden. Instead, he pictured red-brown hair and features striking enough to make even his great-grandfather's jaw drop.

He froze on that point. Why was Rooney in his head? Why red-brown hair?

The icy ball tightened, shot up into his throat. He saw

her clearly now. Not the woman who should be here, but Sadie. She stood in front of the shattered window, staring at him through eyes as dark as the storm. A figure in a black cloak slunk through the shadows behind her.

Blood gleamed on her left shoulder. Low on her left shoulder. The figure behind her stopped when he saw that, and started to laugh. It tossed the knife it held from its right hand to its left, caught it by the blade.

"Thank you, Lieutenant," it said with a chuckle. "You've made my task extremely easy."

Muscles bunching, Eli lunged. But in the next lightning strike, Sadie was gone. Only her blood remained and the sick, sinking knowledge that he'd killed the only woman he would ever love.

The eerie chuckle seemed to be everywhere. "So sad, but that's how it goes for men like us. We who have monsters inside us are what we are. If it will ease the pain of your loss, however, I give you this balm."

Rearing back, he flung the knife into the center of Eli's chest.

"Life in hell is deserved, Eli Blume." The voice took on a weird cadence. "You've forgotten the conjoined legend. Nola didn't die that night in Raven's Hollow. It only appeared she did. Switch to the present. In this reality, I, who am Ezekiel, have killed you. You, who are Hezekiah, will leave this earth before the evil can possess you, while she, who is Nola—that would be Sadie in case you're getting lost—will be mine. As it always should have been, Elijah Blume. Sadie will be mine!"

Chapter Eighteen

Eli woke on the bedroom floor, swearing in the unrelieved darkness.

"What?" Sadie rushed in from the hall. Her feet were bare, and she wore a pair of red pajama pants with a white tank. She held a bottle of wine in her hand like a club. "Why did you shout? What's going on?" Her eyes scanned the room. "There's no one here, Eli. Why is no one here if you're shouting? Unless..." She used the base of the bottle to point while he dragged on his jeans. "You had a nightmare, didn't you? The kind that makes you want to turn on every light in the house because it was so damn real."

Crossing to her, he pushed the bottle aside and settled the queasy aftereffects of the dream by kissing her long and deep.

"It was real once," he told her simply, then rested his forehead against hers and breathed in her scent. "I came home under threat after a brutal shift, saw a shadow and pulled my gun on it."

"Except the shadow turned out to be Eve."

"At first, yeah. In my dream it became you, and instead of blasting the window apart, the shot I fired went through your heart. Or seemed to."

She planted the wine bottle in the middle of his chest. "Some people would call that transference, coupled with post-traumatic guilt, bound together with an unabiding sense of frustration. Then and there meets here and now."

"With Ezekiel on a rampage thrown in for good measure." The horror continued to swim in his belly and his brain. "I thought I'd locked the worst of those memories away."

"The subconscious mind's a bitch, isn't it? I do constant battle with mine. Unlike yours, however, mine usually wins, which is why I get headaches, and am not overly fond of going to bed." She kissed the corners of his mouth. "With one stellar exception, plus two on the floor and still plenty of night left as it's only a little after two a.m." Lifting a hand to his face, she softened her tone. "You didn't kill me, Eli, and you and I both know you're not going to. Though I do appreciate the worry."

"The word's panic, Sadie." He motioned at the bottle in her free hand. "Are there glasses to go with that?"

"I dropped them in the hall when you freaked."

"Killed you," he reminded her. "And at worst it was a shout."

"You weren't halfway up the stairs, pal. Cocoa shot past me like she'd been launched from a cannon, and trust me, there's nothing—or very little—that can drag her away from fresh food. However—" she poked his ribs "—if you want to reestablish your manhood, you could light the fireplace for me. I keep it laid and ready. Unfortunately, the chimneys in this house don't draw like they did back in Nola's day."

"You want details, don't you?" Going down on one knee, Eli checked the flue. "It's not a particularly original story."

"Neither was my engagement to Ty. But it was personal, so that makes it important. I'll get the glasses and corkscrew while you ponder and light."

He did ponder, and relive as he stared into the spreading flames. By the time Sadie returned, he had the short version mapped out.

Then tossed it and told her everything, from an interested first meeting through the final night when Eve had thrown a cast-iron skillet at his head.

Afterward, with the fire crackling beneath the sound of heavy rain, Sadie refilled their wineglasses. "I'll give her marks for weaponry, but not for the tawdry affair. Ten bucks says her male model stud was really a wannabe Broadway actor who figured she could use her magazine connections to help him get onstage."

Eli smiled into the excellent burgundy. "I already owe you twenty plus dinner."

"I like Italian, by the way."

"Do what I can."

His eyes strayed from her navel to the swell of her breasts. He knew she was fully aware of his thoughts when she set her glass down and stretched like the cat she'd just fed downstairs. Maybe she was a witch at that. How else could he be rock hard in the time it took to swallow a mouthful of wine?

On her feet and mesmerizing him with every sinuous movement, she reached out to him with both hands. "Don't sweat the—well, I'd say the small stuff, but that's so not true in your case. Leave the past in the past, Eli. This is now." She tugged. "This is us." He stood. "This is hot."

She took the last step between them. Then brought him with her into the fire.

MAYBE THE RAIN would never end. Maybe the thunder would keep him awake. Maybe the monster would develop a conscience and go away. Stay away. Forever.

But he doubted it.

So he was down to pills. Amphetamines. Because he didn't dare fall asleep feeling the way he did.

Sadie didn't want him, would never love him. He understood that now, and the knowledge burned like acid. Not merely in his heart, but in his stomach, in his brain. In the fists he could no longer keep unclenched.

Why did she want Eli, love Eli? Why couldn't she see what was right in front of her eyes?

Because she wasn't looking, that's why. No one ever did, although that was probably for the best. If no one looked, no one saw, and no one would guess the ugly truth.

Anger and jealousy might be the only things saving him from exposure at this point. People bought in to the obvious, shook their heads and felt for the poor rejected soul. Ah, well, they clucked, he'd get over it. Meanwhile, on with life....

He swallowed another pair of pills, rubbed his eyes and tried not to feel bitter. Bitterness was a hot prod in the monster's side.

Why, though, why couldn't he make his fists unclench? Or his teeth? He breathed through them and told himself to let it go. To let her go.

To, please, please, not kill her.

The sound of the rain grew louder. His heart beat faster, his knuckles turned white.

Then, just when he thought his head might explode, someone knocked on the door....

SADIE FIGURED SHE squeezed in two hours of sleep, tops. But she could live with that, because awake, she'd squeezed in, and just plain squeezed, much better things than her sleeping mind could have offered.

Eli was RoboCop, with a cool and sexy twist. He didn't

short out in the shower. They'd gotten wet, had two more bouts of wild sex, then suddenly—morning.

With it had come a grim reality check. What had really happened during last night's séance? Who'd brought the shinola?

Eli wanted answers and after a quick cup of coffee, he rushed her out the door.

Sadie appreciated that he cared so strongly about keeping her alive, but a second cup of coffee and something more substantial than a cereal bar would have been nice. On the upside, the early rush got her to the Hollow just as Molly was stepping out of the pharmacy.

"Eight oh three and all's well. Apparently." She aimed a warning eye at Eli. "Do not destroy my Land Rover."

"Nag, nag, nag." He kissed her twice, then a third time. "Got it. Six months left on the lease. A few more bets like the half dozen you won last night, and it'll be my money covering those payments."

"Never gamble more than you can afford to lose, Lieutenant. Jerk's coming by to stick more duct tape on the printing presses this morning."

"Know it."

"Know you know it. And while we could go back and forth with that one all day, I want to talk to Molly before the eight-fifteen downpour. Vehicle in pristine condition, Eli, or you might find yourself climbing the walls tonight. Literally."

Molly waited for her on the sidewalk. "How can you possibly look so happy after that séance, Sadie? It was horrible."

"I'm picturing a lizard in a black leather jacket—and that séance was staged."

Molly straightened quickly from her slouch. "I didn't set it up. I'm not... Is that what Eli thinks? And Ty?"

"About you, no. About the staging, yes. Eli does anyway. I haven't talked to Ty."

"He came over to my apartment for a few minutes afterward. He was very upset."

"I think we all were."

"All except the person who wants you dead."

"Monster," she corrected. "And I imagine he's beyond upset at this point."

"Ty says it was never actually proven that Cal didn't murder Laura. It was more that the authorities couldn't find sufficient evidence to arrest him."

"I've done the reading, and gone over it with Eli. I know Cal's still a question mark in many people's minds, but why would he want me alive or dead? I'm not sure I even met him as a kid, and as an adult—well, suffice to say, our one and only face-to-face wasn't exactly amiable."

Molly stuffed her hands into the pockets of her smock. "If he's crazy, does it matter why he wants you? For all you know, he might see you as Laura."

"How? There's no physical resemblance between us. Get right down to it, you look more like Laura than I do."

"You're outgoing like she was. You—what's the expression—shoot from the hip."

"Oh, well, now you're talking Orley. She's the straightest shot in the Hollow."

"Maybe Cal's taste in women has changed."

Sadie glanced at the threatening sky. "I really think you're wrong about Cal, but I'm not…"

"He conveniently came into town yesterday, to pick up a prescription for a relative."

"His uncle?"

"If his uncle's Phineas Kilgore, yes."

"So why did he take off when he saw me—us?"

"Sadie, your new beau wears a badge and carries a big gun."

"So does—did Ty."

"You broke off your engagement to Ty. That might have given Cal hope."

"I broke up with Ty in April. It's October now. Cal's had six months to make his move—and don't say he could be a slow mover. Ben Leamer's shown more interest in me since I broke up with Ty than Cal Kilgore has."

"Then Cal has that you know of." Molly emphasized the last four words. "You're perceptive in a lot of ways, Sadie, but not necessarily in the ones that matter, at least not the ones that might make you feel uncomfortable."

The answer stung enough to kindle Sadie's temper, but it was also valid enough that she didn't lose it. Ignoring the first drops of rain, she narrowed her eyes. "What do you mean uncomfortable?"

"You were never going to marry Ty, but you said yes to him anyway. You didn't really love him. Deep inside you knew that, but it took meeting Eli in Boston to pound the truth home."

Guilt coiled in her stomach. "I never meant to hurt Ty."

"I know that, and so does he. It doesn't change the fact that you weren't self-aware enough to know what you wanted or tuned in enough to see that he was totally gone on you."

What Sadie wanted right then was to tell Molly she was wrong, and walk away believing that. But the guilt had a slimy quality to it now, and some of it crawled up into her heart.

She stole another glance at the clouds, then relented. "I'm not saying you're right about all of that, but I did talk to Eli about my—well, choices. Problem is, I didn't go past the words and think about how Ty must have felt when I told him we shouldn't get married."

Molly relaxed her rigid stance. "If it helps, Ty might have been under the same delusion as you. He loved you, and when he thought the future was sealed, he built a fantasy of your life together in his head."

"Then I came back from Boston and blew that fantasy to hell." Which had hurt and disappointed him, Sadie realized, but hadn't resulted in any overt displays of anger until Eli had appeared in the Hollow.

"You look confused." Molly's tone was shrewd, her expression assessing. "I've done my morning prescription check. I came in earlier than usual after no sleep last night. If you want to talk, we can have breakfast at the café."

Because it was unlike Molly to do anything disruptive to her routine, Sadie accepted the offer without thinking.

Maybe she'd been making excuses all her life, she reflected, buying in to a convenient lie. Maybe it wasn't so much that Nola's descendants couldn't commit, but rather that those who chose not to, or failed to do so for the long term, used their heritage as an excuse to walk away. To take the easy and ready-made out rather than deal with life's more difficult problems. And wasn't that an unpleasant conclusion to come to first thing in the morning?

"Sadie?" Molly's voice broke in. "Are you all right?"

"What? Yes…no. I don't know. What time is it?"

"Eight-twelve."

"Okay. We've got three minutes to get to the café, and forty-five after that for you to tell me everything you've noticed about everyone you can think of since Eli came to town. Before that, as well, if it applies."

"I don't know anything about what's happening to you. Or any more than I've already said."

Sadie pulled her down the street toward the café. "We'll talk about Laura, then. You and Orley hung out with her."

"Orley hung out with her." Molly's shoulders hunched. "I was jealous of her." Her eyes rose. "Like I was of you."

"Me? Why?" Frowning, Sadie searched her mind. "When?"

"Well, recently, obviously."

With an absent wave for the counterman, Sadie nudged her cousin out of the incoming flow. "Okay, jealous of me because of Ty, I get. But why jealous of Laura?"

Molly's mouth moved into a tight little smile. "Everyone thinks she was so sweet, but really, Laura was worse than you."

"Me again?"

"Worse than you relationship-wise," Molly clarified.

Completely baffled now, Sadie backed off, hands raised. "All right, I give up. What are you talking about?"

Molly regarded the downpour that had people on the sidewalks running for cover. "Laura wasn't as decent as you were. She didn't break up with Cal until after she found someone else."

"How do you know Laura found someone else?"

"I saw them. Together. In her mother's car. They were making out."

Intrigued, Sadie nudged her farther into the corner. "Did you tell the police?"

"No."

Uh-oh. "Who was she making out with, Molly?"

Her cousin looked her straight in the eye. "You know the answer. You know *because* I didn't say anything." Her lower lip trembled slightly before she firmed it up. "It was Ty."

Chapter Nineteen

Eli had a list of cross-checks in his head and five files open on his cousin's computer when Ty strode into the cramped rear office of the Raven's Hollow Police Station.

"Make yourself at home, Lieutenant."

Absorbed, he switched files. "You okayed this last night, remember?"

"Yes, but I thought you'd at least wait until I came on duty to invade my workspace."

"You were busy with a thing on the other side of…" Eli indicated the monitor. "How secure are the safe-deposit boxes at the bank?"

"Not as secure as they should be if we're talking about Nola Bellam's locket. Molly has the only key. Yes, I asked her where it was, and big surprise, she can't find it."

More comfortable standing than sitting in Ty's office chair, Eli bent over the back of it to open a new folder. "There's a prescription waiting for Cal's uncle at the Raven's Hollow Pharmacy. Order was phoned in yesterday morning."

"Giving him a handy excuse to show up in town yesterday afternoon."

"Handy excuse or legitimate reason."

Ty shrugged out of his rain gear. "My money's on the first thing."

"Why?" Changing folders, Eli looked up. "Come on, Ty, why would Kilgore be stalking Sadie?"

"He forges metal products. Spike strips are metal products."

"He's never sold one to any of the outlets he deals with in Bangor."

"So naturally, never having sold one means he's never made one."

"What it means, if you'd bother to look through his outbuildings, is that Cal makes far more money making moonshine than he does forging metal."

"Which translates to the guy's not a stalker? Sorry, I'm missing the connection."

So was he, Eli reflected and that, together with his cousin's attitude, was starting to piss him off. "One of us should go out to his place."

Ty regarded his cell. "Not sorry to say, Lieutenant, it'll have to be you. Looks like there's some dumb-ass jerk playing chicken with drivers out on the Post Road." For a moment, his scowl appeared to be directed elsewhere. "We all know Kilgore did it. Chief at the time said he'd bet his badge on it. The guy had motive, opportunity and complete crap for an alibi."

"Yeah, I read the report. Mother and grandmother— marginally different stories. The discrepancy wasn't enough to get him arrested."

Pausing in the doorway Ty allowed himself a sneer. "You want the complicated answer, don't you? The one that shows just how good a cop you are."

Eli met his glare. "What I want is the right answer. The one that means Sadie's stalker has been apprehended."

Ty wiggled the fingers of his left hand. "So, no heroics."

Irritation tiptoed through anticipation as Eli pushed

off from the desk. "This isn't about me, Ty, not the way you're thinking."

The fingers of Ty's other hand tightened on the door-frame, but he kept his response level. "If you believe that load of bull, it's more than probable we'll be celebrating two happy events next week. Old Rooney's birthday." He showed his teeth. "And your death."

SADIE'S BRAIN BUZZED for a full hour after she reached the *Chronicle*. In forty-five short minutes, Molly had filled it with more hearsay than she'd have found in a year's worth of newspapers. Most of it had no bearing on her stalker-monster, but the information about Laura could prove useful. All she had to do was separate the things that might connect them in the killer's eyes from those that were merely family ties.

Ty was an obvious connection. However, at different times in their lives, she and Laura had both worked with Brady, organizing large events. In Laura's case, a pair of Cove-Hollow Halloween high school parties. In hers, two charity costume balls.

According to Molly, Laura had also two-timed—or was it three-timed?—Cal with one of the Majerki brothers. Her cousin hadn't been clear as to which brother it was, and possibly it made no difference since Sadie had weekly contact with both men.

Okay, so—candidates for suspicion in place. What next?

After five hair-pulling hours behind her desk, she opted to leave any further business decisions to her PA and headed down to the basement. The ancient presses whirred and clanked and gave new meaning to the term *unholy racket*.

"I could work on these relics for the better part of a year, and they'd still, jam, spit and rattle every time you started them up." Jerk gave the oldest machine a clunk with his oversized wrench. "You should upgrade to newer models."

She patted the press he'd struck. "If I did that, you and Brick would lose your lucrative second income."

"Good point. Are we square about the me-keeping-an-eye-on-you thing?"

"Square enough." She moved toward the archive room. "I'll be breathing in dust until break time, Jerk. Do your best to keep my uncle's babies up and running."

He adjusted his sweat-stained headband. "Your uncle's ancestors, more like. No sneaking out, right, or I could find myself on the wrong end of a witch-hunt."

"A Bellam never sneaks." She grinned. "But you should worry if a raven with red hair flies past you."

The door to the archive room gave an ominous creak as she entered. With its lack of windows, stacks of boxes and general airless atmosphere, it wasn't her favorite place. But this was where the old files and newspapers were stored, and she'd promised Eli to try and dig up a map of the manor grounds.

She started with the back issues that predated Laura's murder by six months. Because the newspapers had been thinner in those days, she was able to go through them, front to back, in a matter of minutes.

Not surprisingly, there was nothing of import prior to her cousin's death. Afterward was another matter—and a more difficult task than she'd anticipated.

Laura had been pretty and smart and fun, and Sadie had loved her. If Molly was to be believed, however, she'd also been busier than most people realized in the dating department. Assuming you could call making out with Ty in the backseat of her mother's car dating.

But so what? So Laura had liked guys. They'd all been hormonal teenagers once, even Molly.

She read the write-ups on the actual murder two times apiece. Nothing unusual jumped out at her. Cal Kilgore remained the number-one suspect in the eyes of most Cove and Hollow dwellers, but the people in charge of the investigation had apparently disagreed. Although he'd been questioned, in the end he'd walked. Out of the spotlight and into the haunted north woods.

While she mulled that over, she unearthed three maps, and one in particular riddled with hidden caves and tunnels that might work for Eli. Speaking of, and given that she'd only caught herself thinking about him twenty or thirty times since entering the room, Sadie felt she was holding her own very well in terms of concentration.

Four months after the fact, the stories surrounding Laura's death began to wane. Other local occurrences took precedence. Some were important and relevant. Many were merely fill.

For instance, in her senior year, Molly had been written up as the girl most likely to become a psychic and open a tearoom in the Hollow. Instead, she'd set her sights on medicine and returned to the Hollow immediately after receiving her degree.

Not to be outdone, Orley had been slated to move to Africa and become the next Jane Goodall. She'd been offered a scholarship to the University of New England, but in the end had chosen to work at the Hollow Veterinary Clinic for three years before heading off to Michigan State.

According to the Blume news feed—that being her uncle's assistant at the time—neither Ty nor Brady had earned anything approaching a scholarship. Brady had fought his way to and eventually through veterinary college, while Ty had hitched a ride to Portland. After eighteen months of bouncing from job to job, he'd finally decided to enlist in the army.

Brick and Jerk had never set foot outside the sister towns—nor been tempted to as far as Sadie could tell.

In Eli's case, the future had been a toss-up. He'd become either a New York state senator or the ultimate pinball wizard. Only Rooney and her uncle's assistant had seen him as a cop, and they'd thought Los Angeles would be his destination of choice.

With her eyes starting to blur, Sadie reboxed the old editions. She hesitated briefly when she spied a headline about a young girl named Lisa Johnson who'd driven her daddy's 1942 pickup through the barrier on Ridge Road in Raven's Cove and been killed on the rocks below. Evidently Laura wasn't the only person in these parts who'd died far too young.

She was hefting the last box onto a high shelf when her cell phone rang. The lack of a name on the screen had her running a palm along the leg of her pants. It took three yoga breaths before she could muster up sufficient courage to answer, "Sadie Bellam."

"Hello, Sadie." The computer-altered voice set her teeth on edge. "You're a very brave woman to go to work under threat of death. Do you have a gun nearby?"

Sidestepping to the door, she looked out. All she could see was the top of Jerk's head, but the sight of him reassured her.

"If you're calling to tell me I'm a dead woman, your threats are getting a little old."

"Don't push me, witch!"

Anger punched through icy fear. "Why? You're pushing me."

"I've also shot at you, with bullets and arrows. It's only Bellam luck that's keeping you alive, and it won't last forever." The rasp dropped to a creepy caress. "I'm an excellent shot."

Sadie scrambled through her memories. Who did she know that was an excellent shot? With guns? Far too many people. With arrows? Eli, Brady, possibly Ty—and every hunter in the area, including, she strongly suspected, Cal Kilgore.

Slipping into the main area, she said, "You made a mistake coming to the séance last night. You've narrowed the field of suspects considerably."

"Only if I let myself be seen. Do you think I did, Sadie? Or is it possible I'm more clever than that?"

When Jerk's head dropped out of sight, Sadie's heart plummeted. But she kept her voice steady and made her way carefully through the presses. "I'll give you clever," she agreed. "But I'm still alive, and that's what counts in the end."

She heard a sudden loud bang above the din, and ducking, raised her eyes to the shadowed rafters.

A low chuckle reached her. "My, you live in a noisy world, Sadie Bellam. But only for a short while longer. Only until you and your cop lover are dead. Then, finally, I'll have what should have been mine from the start."

Still in her crouch, Sadie frowned. "What should have been yours—?"

She had no chance to finish as a deafening explosion rocked the presses and made the floor beneath her tremble.

A second later, the basement went dark.

OUT ON RIDGE Road, Eli finished clamping Rooney's bicycle to the Land Rover's rear rack.

"You know it's five miles to Two Toes Joe's, right? With off-and-on rain and the probability of more thunder and lightning."

The old man made a dismissing motion. "Off-and-on rain's fine, and the *Chronicle* said fog, not another thunderstorm. Weather Channel's only right half the time, grandson. Sadie's closer to ninety percent."

Eli climbed back into the driver's seat. "Still five miles to the Cove," he reminded him. When his phone rang, he read the name and immediately picked up. "Tell me this is a let's-do-coffee call, Sadie."

"If coffee's all you want from me, you must be on speaker with company."

His great-grandfather cackled. "The girl's a regular Miss Marple."

"You think I'm a nosy old woman? That's some compliment, Rooney. In terms of the call, Lieutenant, sharpen your mental pencil. I had another chat with my stalker's nasty side."

Swearing inwardly, Eli looked toward the Hollow. "More of the same, or something new?"

"A little of both, actually." She related the conversation and ended with a sound of frustration. "I'm sure he was going to say more, but one of the presses surged. The motor blew, the electrical panel overloaded and Jerk's eyebrows got singed."

He swore again. "Are you all right? Is he?"

"I'm fine, and you know Jerk. He's already torn the bottom half of the press apart. He says no frigging fossil of a machine's going to get the better of him. Now, before you to do a major burnout in my not-paid-for vehicle, let me add that Brick's already here helping his brother, and I promised Ben Leamer I'd cover a grade-school tour of his corn maze. Personal favor," she added before he could object. "Otherwise, I'd get one of my reporters to do it."

An eager Rooney leaned forward. "Tell Ben I need…" Then he clamped his mouth shut and let a smile lift the corners. "Never mind. Stay safe, young Sadie."

"That shouldn't be difficult in a crowd of more than

sixty." Amusement marked her tone. "Kids love cops, Eli—if you find yourself getting bored in, oh, say, fifteen or twenty minutes."

"I can think of better ways to deflect boredom than by herding a bunch of kids through a maze."

"You were a child once yourself, Lieutenant Blume. That being said, I need to prep for a major headache."

"So basically, you just called to scare the crap out of me."

She laughed. "You said to let you know if anything unusual happened. I think my afternoon qualifies. Oh, and, Rooney? It's as dangerous to ride a bike in the fog as it is during a thunderstorm."

"How can you possibly—?" A sharp burst of static stopped Eli midquestion.

"Hollow Road's not the only place phones tend to pack it in." Rooney shrugged. "She's right, of course, but I like my bike, it's mostly downhill and someone or other's usually driving by if I find myself getting winded." He pointed east. "You heard the lady. Cove's that way, and as you can clearly see, fog's rolling in."

Fine. Great. Sadie had a knack for weather forecasts and a soft spot for Ben Leamer. Eli knew he could live with that. But how much longer would Sadie live if he didn't identify the monster who wanted her dead and bring the bastard down?

"You know," Rooney philosophized, "it'd be better all around if you and Ty worked on this investigation together."

"Still believe in miracles, huh?" Eli glanced in the rearview mirror. "Listen, how'd you like to have dinner with Brady instead of going into the Cove to Two Toes Joe's?"

"I could probably be persuaded—long as he's not neutering something or trying to make me drink that disgusting green liquid he calls tea." Rooney wrinkled his nose. "Gets it from Molly. Supposed to clear the mind, but all it did was put me to sleep. A stiff shot of Ben's..." He glanced sideways. "Let's just say my special tonic does the job much better." He thumped his cane. "Now, talk to me, grandson, about this man who's haranguing our Sadie."

"He's not haranguing her." Eli squinted at a truck several hundred yards ahead. "He's trying to kill her. Or half of him is."

"That'll be the Ezekiel half."

A wry smile formed. "You don't miss much, do you?"

"Sure didn't miss the expression on your face when you talked to Sadie."

"Would that be the expression of abject fear or ball-crushing fury?"

"Some of both, I expect, mixed with what I'm betting was a night of mutual satisfaction and multiple org—"

Eli cut him off with a look. "Finish that thought, and I'll strap you to the rack with your bike."

His great-grandfather made a scoffing sound. "Does Sadie know you're a prude when it comes to discussing sexual relations?"

"She's a woman, Rooney. No conversation's taboo. You're welcome to have this one with her and leave me with the simpler task of keeping her alive." He spaced out the last three words for effect and at the same time managed to get a clear enough look at the truck ahead that his adrenaline began to pump. "Oh, yeah. Time you and I had another chat, pal."

Rooney snorted. "Chats with prudes bore me."

"Not you and me." Eli nodded forward. "Me and him. That's Cal Kilgore's truck."

"Well, hell, in that case, put the pedal down, and we'll head him off at the pass."

"What pass?"

"Hang a left at the crippled oak, and I'll show you." He flapped a blue-veined hand. "Left, left."

With curses rolling off his tongue, Eli made the turn. At Rooney's urging, he bumped along a rough path, down a hill, through a river of mud and into a stand of trees that came within an inch of scraping the paint off both sides of Sadie's vehicle.

"There, you see?" his great-grandfather crowed. "Road."

But not before dip, crevice, pothole, pothole, pothole. Eli had a quick vision of himself as a lizard, then miraculously the pathway opened up and he was back on the main road. He saw Cal's truck barreling toward them, swung into a hard one-eighty and, slamming on the brakes, successfully blocked both lanes.

There was no mistaking the blind panic on Cal's face as he executed a squealing quarter turn. The maneuver put the two men door to door with less than eighteen inches of misty air between them. While Eli squeezed out, gun drawn, Cal scrambled across the passenger seat and into the gully.

There was nothing Eli relished more than a chase, and Kilgore was agile enough to give him a good one. If he had a weapon, he didn't use it. Or he'd left it behind.

The minute he skidded into the hollow, Cal ditched the path and started to weave—through the trees, around a murky pond and over a pair of questionable bridges. With Eli gaining, he splashed through puddles, used logs as launching pads, and finally made the mistake of trying to cross Raven's Creek on a scattering of crooked stones.

Tucking his gun, Eli bypassed the stones, took aim at his ankles and went for a low tackle.

A muffled "Oomph" preceded a sharp back kick and

a twist that almost allowed Cal to kick him in the face. Eli just managed to get a forearm up to deflect the blow.

"Bastard," Cal spat.

"Took the words," Eli muttered, then rolled sideways as his quarry's scrabbling fingers got hold of a stubby branch.

He swung it hard, but another roll took Eli out of range and probably sent pain singing up Cal's arm when he struck a tree.

Eyes watchful, Eli redrew his gun. He didn't aim, merely held it up and off to the side while he gauged Cal's labored body language. His wet clothes appeared to be weighing him down to the point of exhaustion.

"Are we done?" he shouted.

On his hands and knees, Cal brought his head up. A snarl formed. He pounded the water with his fists.

"We'll call that a no."

When the other man flew toward him, Eli bounced to the right, used his elbow, his foot and his fist, in that order.

The guy had a granite jaw, but a poor stance in the stony creek bed. The punch he attempted to land resulted in a yelp as he lost his balance and flopped onto his stomach in the water.

"That works." Stuffing his gun in his waistband, Eli planted a knee in Cal's lower back, grabbed a handful of his hair and gave it a deliberate yank. "Talk," he ordered, "or I'll turn you over and make a eunuch out of you."

Cal locked his good eye on Eli's face. "You're too well trained to hurt a prisoner."

"Don't count on it. I'm in a pisser of a mood right now."

A long glare preceded a hiss of breath. "I'd say bull, except there's a woman involved, so you might just follow through. If this was about a guy..."

"It is about a guy." Eli wrenched him none too gently

onto his back and set a warning knee on his thigh. "It's about a stalker with a homicidal id."

Cal's other eye circled wildly. "You're not a shrink and I'm not a murderer. We went through all this when you showed up on my property unannounced."

"We went through some of it," Eli agreed. "Things have happened since. Why did you take off yesterday when Sadie noticed your truck?"

"You can't guess?"

"You hate cops."

"Damn straight. Every one I've known has tried to pin Laura's death on me."

"And you think running's going to change that?"

"I didn't run until you and your tight-ass cousin came after me."

Shifting his knee, Eli pressed a little harder on Cal's thigh. "People who run usually have something to hide. What're you hiding, Kilgore?"

"Not a secret yen for your lady, if that's what you're thinking." He sucked air through his teeth when Eli shifted his knee again. "You hurt me, Blume, and I'll sue. I've got rights."

"What you've got," Eli corrected, "is about five seconds to start talking."

"You're out of your jurisdiction."

"Two seconds."

Cal uttered a single rude word. "All right, you win, upper hand. I came to get some pills for my uncle."

"Figured that much. Why take off yesterday?"

Cal swung his good eye to the side, gave a mirthless laugh and closed both. "You won't believe me."

"Stalling's not your best bet here."

"I'm not stalling. The brown truck gave me heebies."

"Brown truck," Eli repeated. "Brady's truck?"

"I saw him get into it maybe an hour before Sadie spotted me in town. Only this wasn't your average man in the woods. This guy was wearing a long black cloak with a big, floppy hood. So floppy you couldn't see his face."

"Go on," Eli said when he paused.

"He was moving fast. He opened the door of the truck, tossed a mother of a gun inside and took off. I didn't know if he'd seen me or not, so I stayed put until I was sure he was gone."

"Where were you, Cal? Exactly."

"Partway up the hill that leads to Bellam Manor."

"Yeah? Why is that?"

"I was waiting for someone. Look, d'you want this or not?"

Did he? Slick knots twisted in Eli's stomach, but he loosened his grip and sat back. "Go on, finish it."

"From the look on your face, I don't have to." Cal regarded him half-lidded. "My eyes only act wonky, Lieutenant. They see fine. The guy pushed his hood back when he drove off. Then he turned his head just far enough that I got a real good look at his face."

Something like dread slithered into Eli's chest, but his gaze didn't falter. "I said finish it."

"It was your cousin in that truck. Your cousin, wearing a big black cloak and carrying a badass gun. That's why I ran. He was standing next to that brown truck when I stopped at the intersection in town. He looked up when he saw me, looked right straight at me, and I'm telling you, my guts turned to water. I'll tell you something else, too. Thinking back like I have been since that happened, I realize yesterday's not the first time I've looked at his eyes and felt that way."

Because no part of him wanted to hear this, Eli snagged another handful of Cal's jacket and yanked him up. "Are you telling me my cousin Brady shot at Sadie and me in the woods near Bellam Manor?"

Cal's eyeball swam in its loose socket. "I'm saying I saw a guy in a cloak get into a brown truck. But yeah, it could be I'm saying he used that gun on you, because I heard shots a few minutes before he came crashing out of the old tunnel."

The last two words only registered on the fringe of Eli's mind. Right then, all he could see was Sadie's face. And behind it, like an evil black cloud, his cousin Brady's.

Brady, who'd taken the time to text her as he drove away. Brady, who'd told her he hadn't been shooting at her. Because Brady was only obsessed with her.

It was the monster that wanted her dead.

Chapter Twenty

Sadie planned to leave the newspaper immediately after talking to Eli. Unfortunately, as she was pulling on her leather coat, another printing press decided to go down—and take two-thirds of the *Chronicle*'s power with it.

When she reached the basement, Jerk muttered something about never having eyebrows again. Then he bared his teeth, stripped off his shirt and dived headfirst into the wires.

It was closing in on six when she finally jogged across the parking lot to the ancient Bronco her copy editor had—maybe kindly, maybe not—offered to lend her.

She called Ben as she went, half hoping he'd tell her not to come, but it seemed the school buses hadn't arrived on time, either, so everyone was running late.

The Bronco was so old and worn she couldn't even use her rusty standard-shift driving skills as an excuse to cancel. The engine ground a bit but slid obligingly from gear to gear whether she engaged the clutch properly or not.

So—plenty of time to think about Eli, the night they'd spent together and how the hell she was going to deal with the fact that her heart did a tap dance whenever his face popped into her head—which was every other minute at this point.

The big question had been rearing its head all day. Did

she love him? To her dismay, the big answer scared her as much as it thrilled her.

How could a relationship between them work? Did he even want a relationship? Did she?

Love, she reminded herself, was supposed to make overcoming obstacles not only possible but also enjoyable. Of course, in their case she had to factor in a strong fear of commitment on both sides, a near tragedy on Eli's and a massive failure on hers. All in all, their obstacles read more like mountains, and that was before she compounded them with the grisly fact that someone who had two distinct personalities appeared to want both of them dead.

It might be a formidable weapon, but even love couldn't deflect bullets or arrows. Meaning, for the moment at least, she needed to set her feelings aside and focus on staying alive to pursue them.

She eased up on the gas as she drove past the police station. Maybe she should have told Jerk she was leaving. If nothing else, she'd have had peace of mind knowing he was tailing her.

But the presses had to be repaired, and no one except Jerk would be stubborn enough to make that happen.

As she drove past the police station, she noticed that Ty's cruiser was gone, and both the veterinary clinic and the pharmacy had closed an hour ago.

No lights burned either in Brady's apartment or in Orley's. Or none that she could see through the layers of fog that were thickening as she drove.

Would Eli really attempt to track a monster in this stuff? Was it possible that he and Ty had joined forces?

Well, yeah, about as possible as the prospect of her stalker packing up and moving to Florida.

Pressing on a temple that had been threatening to throb all day, Sadie concentrated on the road. More correctly, she concentrated on the two feet of road she could see with her eyes and not her memory.

The passing minutes stretched into forever. Even with Van Halen and David Lee rocking it out, her hands were damp on the steering wheel. It wasn't until she realized that her fingers were strangling it that exasperation took over and had her growling, "Enough!"

One resolved breath in and out relaxed her shoulder muscles. For a moment. Then the tension knots doubled as something—no, someone—took shape directly ahead.

Clenching her teeth, Sadie braked hard and stared at the haloed person for three disbelieving seconds. Then her trance broke, the jagged edges of fear gave way to spikes of temper and she kicked the Bronco's slightly dented door open.

"Are you insane?" she demanded, striding forward. "I could've killed you."

Her cousin Orley scooped the fingers of both hands through her hair. "Start with me, Sadie, and that's exactly what I'll do to you. I picked up a nail—left rear tire. It's the third puncture I've had in six months on this ridiculous excuse for a road."

Still steaming, Sadie went toe-to-toe with her. "Why, unless you're suicidal, are you standing in the middle of this ridiculous excuse for a road?"

"In a word? Favor. In a name? Ben Leamer." She rapped the sides of her head. "You'd think I'd learn, wouldn't you?"

"What? Not to do favors, or not to stand on foggy roads?"

"Both, apparently. And to carry a spare tire that doesn't have a frigging hole in it." When Sadie's lips quirked, a warning finger came up. "Laugh and I'll toss you into the hollow, take your—whatever that thing is you're driving—and leave you stranded." She gestured from herself to Sadie. "Black belt, no belt."

"Been a lot of years since you earned that black belt, Orley." Tipping her head from side to side, Sadie said, "If you want a ride, you'll have to follow through and come to the farm with me. I don't think my copy editor's spare will work on your Jeep."

"As we appear to be the only live humans on this god-forsaken road, offer accepted. Here, take my flashlight. I'll get the rest of my..." Trailing off, she peered past Sadie into the swirling fog. "Do you hear something?"

"Other than the receding sound of my heartbeat, no." But she turned to listen.

"I know that engine. Do I know that engine?" Brow knit, Orley strained to see. "Whoever it is, he's coming fast."

Sadie gave her a nudge, then a push. "He's coming fast, and he's not slowing down."

"That's Brady's truck, I'm sure of it."

"Then Brady must be drunk."

Sadie tried to gauge his wild approach so they wouldn't actually have to jump into the ditch to avoid him. She was on the verge of diving in when he screeched to a halt ten feet ahead.

After several noisy attempts, the driver's door crashed opened and Brady tumbled out. He leaned heavily against the side. "Don't die! Please, don't die!"

"Wasn't planning to," she murmured, then raised her voice. "Why are you here, Brady?"

"Monster." His head snapped up. "Gonna kill you."

Sadie swore. "Move," she said to Orley.

"What? Where? Wait a minute, what am I saying? It's Brady."

"Who just said the monster's going to kill me." She

dug out her phone. "Why do I know this thing's not going to work?"

Bracing his hands on his thighs, Brady shouted, "Get away. You have to get away!"

"It must be drugs," Orley whispered. "Mixed prescriptions maybe. He looks really zonked."

Eyes widening, Sadie snapped the phone from her ear. "He's got a gun!"

The hand holding it shook as Brady straightened. "Run, Sadie." He looked straight at her. "Run from the monster!"

Orley eased behind her. "Please say your phone has a signal."

Sadie shook her head, watched Brady's trembling right hand. "We need to go. Now."

"But there's only the hollow. Nowhere else, only there."

Weapon arm raised, Brady took aim.

"Run!" Sadie shoved her cousin toward the ravine. "Climb down or slide, it doesn't matter which."

Brady's mouth stretched into a horrible grimace. "Gonna kill you, Sadie. Get away!"

Luckily, he caught his foot and stumbled sideways. The gun went off. Into the air, Sadie hoped as she followed Orley over the edge of the road and onto the treacherous slope that dropped more than a hundred feet into the hollow.

Stopping on a ledge halfway down, Orley muttered, "This is not happening."

Sadie gestured with the flashlight. "Go right. It's less of an obstacle course." But she ran into two rocks and wound up skidding on her butt even so.

Didn't matter. Brady was right behind them. She could hear him breaking small branches and dislodging stones as he mimicked their descent.

Momentum would have flung her into a tree at the

bottom if she hadn't slammed feet-first into a huge exposed root.

A short distance away, Orley groaned. "Are you alive? Am I?"

"I'm here." Unwilling to use her flashlight, Sadie found her more by feel than sight. "We need to keep moving."

Nodding, Orley climbed to her feet.

The fog in the hollow varied from thick and swirling to layers of gauze. In an odd moment of clarity, Sadie saw the moon raining thin beams of silver through the mist.

It wasn't her nightmare, not exactly, but it felt close. Something evil chased her through the woods. Instead of a knife, however, all she had was her cell phone—and no signal!

"I'm not the monster!" Brady's echoing shout reached them from several yards back.

"He's sounding fuzzier by the minute," Orley gasped from behind. "We could ambush him. Not hurt him, but—you know—quick bop on the head, send him under."

Halting, Sadie drew in much-needed air. "Incapacitate Brady, incapacitate the monster."

Orley cast an uncertain look around. "Right. How do we make that happen?"

"I'll get his attention." She steeled herself. "You'll have to hit him." As the thrashing came closer, she shone Orley's flashlight on the ground. "We need a branch."

They found one stuck in the mud and yanked it free.

"Ready?" Her cousin took up a stance, arms over her head and poised to strike.

Sadie had no chance to reply as Brady burst out of the fog.

He slowed when he saw her. His face crumpled. "I'm not the monster," he promised. "I don't think I ever—"

Darting into a wash of moonlight, Orley brought the branch down on his head.

Brady went rigid. He staggered a step, let the gun slip from his fingers. Then, just as Ezekiel had done in her nightmare, his eyes rolled back and he dropped to the ground at Sadie's feet.

FOR THE FIRST time in his life, Eli knew what it would be like to live in slow motion. Every second was an agony. Only his mind raced, and the thoughts it spawned shot through so fast he couldn't catch most of them.

He hauled Cal back to the Land Rover—no idea how or what kind of time that took—then headed for the Hollow, another underwater slog. More terrifying than anything, however, was the fact that he couldn't get hold of Sadie, either at the *Chronicle* or on her cell phone. What he did discover was that Jerk hadn't gone with her.

It felt as if hours passed before the lights of Main Street appeared. Reaching over, Eli braced Rooney for a squealing stop outside the police station. He only glanced briefly at Cal, who sat in mutinous silence in the backseat, cuffed to the door.

"Get Ty or one of the deputies," he told his great-grandfather. "I'm going up to Brady's apartment."

His cousin's truck was gone, he noted as he ran. No lights burned upstairs, the clinic was dark—and Sadie was driving to Ben Leamer's farm in the fog. Alone.

He climbed the stairs two at a time and didn't bother to knock, just booted the door open and led with his gun. Using his elbow on the light switch, he let his mind spin through the possibilities as his eyes searched the room.

Cal insisted he'd seen Brady coming out of the woods yesterday afternoon. But was that a true account provided by a witness or a desperate lie concocted by a murderer?

Eli crossed the floor with caution, because he knew, somehow knew, Cal hadn't been lying.

A teapot sat on the dining table. A hard-backed chair lay on the floor. He spotted a single black mug, three-quarters full. The contents were warm but not hot.

Rescanning the room, he speed-dialed Sadie's cell. And ground his teeth when the call failed. He tried Brady with the same result.

He was checking out the teapot when his phone vibrated. "Brady's the stalker," he said to Ty on the other end. "Sadie's on her way to Ben Leamer's farm. I called Ben and told him to send his hired hand to meet her on the Hollow Road."

A confused "What?" was the best Ty could manage. "What?"

"I'm in Brady's apartment. There's powder residue on the lid of the teapot. Could be PCP."

"What?" Ty demanded again. "You think Brady's doing drugs? And that he wants Sadie dead?"

"You need to meet me on the Hollow Road."

"I can't. Not quickly. I'm miles from there, all the way out on Spirit Point. There was a call. Three-car collision. Except..."

"There was no collision."

There was something, though. Eli could feel it. Some not-quite-right detail that held him in Brady's apartment when he should have been breaknecking it for the hollow. Some twisted truth that needed to be unearthed.

A photo album covered with cartoon animals lay on the floor under the table. With Sadie's face flashing in his head, he crouched to flip it open.

Some not-quite-right detail.... Something he needed to know before he went after Brady....

The pictures glared up at him. Hell, they all but sprouted

fingers and grabbed him by the throat. Shot after shot, page after page, year after year, in a sick and steady progression that chronicled the life of Brady Blume.

And the monster who wanted Sadie dead.

"Don't get too close to him, Orley." On her knees, Sadie searched the ground for Brady's gun.

"It's here. I've got it." Orley squatted near his head. "Don't worry, he won't be waking up any time soon. Between the whack I gave him and the cat tranqs, he'll sleep for at least four or five hours."

"Four or five...?" Something in her cousin's tone sent a wintery chill through Sadie's bloodstream. She flattened her palms on the ground and without looking up forced a calm "What cat tranqs, Orley?"

"I put them in his tea. I always put them in his tea or coffee when I need him to be good and sleep for me."

Sadie's heart began to thud. "Sleep," she repeated carefully. "For you."

The gun came into view first, followed by the hazy oval that was Orley's face as she smiled over Brady's prone body.

"Surprise." She spoke softly and with no small amount of malice. "Aw... you thought Brady came here tonight so the monster inside him could do its nasty worst, didn't you? Well, take heart, cousin, I daresay he thought the same thing. Although—hard to say, maybe not. Oh, there's a monster, but it doesn't live in Brady. It lives, Sadie dearest, in me." Her smile widened. "It's green and it's mean and it's sick to death of not getting what—or rather who—it wants. Who it's wanted since before it made Laura a corpse and left her in the slime pool we call Raven's Bog."

Astonishment simply robbed Sadie of thought. "You're not serious," she managed. Yet even through a curtain of shock, Orley's gleaming eyes told her she was. Serious and deadly. She'd murdered their cousin Laura twenty years ago.

And would, without qualm or hesitation, murder another of her cousins tonight.

Chapter Twenty-One

Waving the gun like a pennant, Orley forced Sadie to stand. "I can't say I'm impressed. You're supposed to be a crack journalist, someone who sees what others miss. How did you miss what's inside me?"

It amazed Sadie that her temper would rise with her fear. "You weren't a story to be dissected and probed. You were just my cousin with an attitude."

"And a gun."

Wisdom elbowed temper aside. "And that." Although she couldn't see it succeeding, she went with a rational approach. "Oh, come on, Orley, why would I think you had a monster inside you? We're family. I've always seen you as one of the most stable people I know. I think of us as friendly rivals."

"Excellent. Shot to the heart. Applause, applause. Won't work, of course, but marks for effort. See, here's the thing. While I do in fact like you much better than Laura, I don't like you enough to let the man I've wanted—since I was five years old—" she enunciated the last six words "—destroy his life and my dreams, which I swear are going to come true as soon as you're gone. Brady thinks he has an alter ego. He believes that alter ego is murderous. But like most of us, he doesn't relish the prospect of spending the rest of his life behind bars. So—self-preservation mode."

Sadie heard her through an ever-increasing shriek of denial. Orley had killed Laura two decades ago when they were seventeen. Killed her because Brady had wanted her. Really? Seriously?

"This is sick, Orley. This is totally sick."

"This is necessary."

An incredulous laugh emerged. "You think making Brady believe he has a monster inside him is necessary? You think that's love?"

"Don't psychoanalyze me, Sadie. Brady's the one who decided he had a slice of Hezekiah Blume in his soul, not me. I just went with it."

"Why? Because it worked for you?"

"Yes. And the only thing I'll say in my defense is that it's not what I had in mind the first time I drugged him."

She adjusted her grip on the gun she held—in her left hand! The irony of that observation struck a note of absurd humor and had Sadie closing her eyes for a moment.

"Ah, there. You see it now, don't you? But give yourself a break, cousin. You weren't looking for a left-handed woman. Surprise again." Orley's smile stretched wider. "I worried about the chop to Laura's skull after I'd done it. Then it occurred to me. Given the phone calls she'd surely have mentioned to someone, and the obsessive notes that would undoubtedly turn up at some point, no one would be thinking 'female killer.' Plus, there was Cal. So I relaxed, played the sorrow game and kept a close eye on Brady."

Impossible images swam in Sadie's head. "You found out that Brady wanted Laura, so you murdered her. Simple as that."

"Murdered her after she broke up with Cal." Crouching, Orley set her fingers on the pulse point in Brady's neck. "Until then, she was unattainable. I could deal with that. Dumping Cal was her fatal mistake. Brady started thinking he could have her, and—well, that wasn't going to happen. So—desperate-measures time."

"You worked at the veterinary clinic in high school." Sadie forced herself not to look at the gun, not to appear to be looking at anything while her mind raced. "You had access to sedatives and anesthetic."

"The doc at the time didn't keep accurate supply records. Neither did his assistant. All brilliant me had to do was read and learn and come up with a dosage that would work on humans."

"A dosage of what?"

"Ketamine. Street name, cat tranqs. It causes all sorts of nasty problems—hallucinations, confusion, agitation and, of course, unconsciousness. I slipped it to Brady from time to time, hoping I could scare Laura into leaving town. I tacked on a threat to a larger-than-life love note Brady gave her. Just intercepted it before she was aware and turned Brady's love note into a monster's portent of doom."

"That's why the writing changed," Sadie murmured.

"That's why. Didn't have the desired effect, of course. Laura's senior year loomed, and she had a brand-new family that she liked. All I had left was death."

"Right. Death. With no second thoughts. No remorse. Nothing."

Orley leaned in to stage-whisper, "We weren't friends, Sadie, only unfortunate relations. I never liked her, or Molly—or people in general for that matter. In your case, all was well enough while you were engaged to Ty. Oh, Brady saw and Brady wanted, but lucky you, Ty got there first. A long courtship blossomed into an engagement. Then, uh-oh, wedding in Boston. Chance meeting with Eli. Next thing I knew, Ty was unengaged, and Brady's hopes were soaring. Damn. Time to start plotting again. Here's the kicker, though, cousin. Who should appear on the very day that Brady worked up the nerve to make an anonymous phone call to your office but Eli Blume?"

Sadie struggled to keep up. "Are you saying Brady sent me that animated e-card?"

"Yep. It was his way of testing the water. Far as I can tell, the dead raven on the doorstep was more of a gift gone wrong. He meant to leave a live raven in a gilded cage. But the raven got loose and flew up into the porch rafters. Brady tried to flush it out with a gunshot—and, well, I guess the bird wasn't where he thought, and it plopped down dead at his feet."

"Why did he leave it there?"

"I imagine killing it rattled him. Plus, he still had a message to write. So in he went, home you came and uh-oh, gotta run. If my deductions are correct, and I'm sure they are, he 'borrowed' one of Ben Leamer's old trucks for the occasion. You know Ben. He's got a barn full of the things. Talk about your perfect setup. FYI, the call Brady made to you that day was his last. I used the same freaky computer voice to do the rest."

Sadie stared. "How do you know all this?"

"I get him to talk. After I drug him and before he goes under, I grill him. Sometimes he slips away before I get everything, but mostly I can eke out the details. I'm a very clever Bellam, Sadie. And Brady's mind has always been wonderfully malleable."

"Is that what you call it?"

"You think he's unbalanced, don't you?"

"I don't know what I think at this point. Maybe unbalanced. Or maybe confused—because he thinks he's got a homicidal maniac living inside him!"

"Don't take that tone with me," Orley warned. "Remember who's holding the gun here. Any imbalance in Brady's personality is a result of him being totally repressed. Fortunately, I haven't got a repressed bone in my body."

"Okay, wait." Hands raised, Sadie took a step back, both physically and mentally. "Backtracking here. You're telling me that, being repressed, Brady had to resort to weird tricks to get my attention, whereas you, who aren't the slightest bit repressed, have no problem approaching anyone."

"I'm way ahead of you, Sadie. You're wondering why I didn't just let Brady know I wanted him instead of going all extreme killer."

Anger seeped through terror. "It would have been a saner option. Not to mention kinder, and—brass tacks here—less of a risk to your own—" she almost said "stupid" but swallowed that and left it at "—life."

Closing the gap between them, her cousin tapped Brady's gun to Sadie's chest. "You see, now, that's why I like you so much better than Laura. You're mere seconds away from death, and here you stand, totally pissed off at me for not telling Brady how I felt about him."

"Thereby avoiding the 'seconds away from death' part," Sadie said through her teeth.

Orley's features hardened, and this time when the gun struck Sadie's collarbone it stayed put. "I did tell him, in every way I could think of. I even lowered my career goals so I could be his assistant. I tried to seduce him at high school dances, went for it again at college and twice more after we came back to the Hollow. Every damn time I came on to him, he got awkward and flustered and insisted we were friends. Best friends but—and this part was strictly between the lines—friends without benefits."

He hadn't wanted her. A very small part of Sadie actually felt sorry for her.

Orley shook back her hair. "Didn't matter what he said, what he felt then or what he thinks he feels now. He'll be mine after tonight, I'll make sure of it. Just know this. He wanted you more than he wanted Laura, and I still did everything I could not to kill you. For some reason, he refused to be deterred by Eli. Guess he got tired of backing down. He wanted you to be his and Eli to be gone."

"Are you saying it was Brady who tried to kill Eli?"

"Hell, yes. And while my intention at first was simply to be rid of you, that plan changed when I realized what Brady was prepared to do to get you. I knew he'd bungle the whole thing and wind up in prison, so I decided to do it all. I'd kill Eli for him and you for me. Problem solved—at long, long last."

"Who shot the crossbow arrows at us?"

"Oh, come on. My father's a hunter. I'll admit I hate that about him, but he insisted on teaching me how to handle a crossbow. I told you, my original goal was to frighten you into leaving the Hollow. Eli, too, if possible. The love thing was obvious, so I figured if you left together, the monster could go back into hiding."

"When did it all become real for you?"

"When Brady went after Eli near Bellam Manor. The bullets he shot were meant to kill. I used the concerned citizen call about the injured deer to cover for him, when in fact I dealt with the problem all by my lonesome."

Sadie stared. "Is this really happening?"

"Talking here, Sadie," Orley warned. "Brady didn't show up until I was almost finished. And I didn't know what he'd done on the manor grounds until I spotted the cloak and gun in his truck. I talked to you a little while later, but it wasn't much of a leap from the cloak and gun alone, given his rattled condition and my intuitive nature. I gave him the crossbow from the deer—call it a prop—

got him to help me clean up the mess and off we went in our separate vehicles, back to the Hollow."

"You make it sound like an average day at work."

"Hardly average. I still had a séance to rig, and a locket to steal and decimate. The last two things were easy enough, but my fingers were crossed big-time during the séance. Storm helped, and we all know how old the manor's window latches are. To be honest, I wasn't sure every last candle would blow out when the window burst open, but what do you know, they did. I took it as a sign that I was meant to succeed."

"Yes, you're a lucky monster, aren't you? Still, you know as well as I do that nothing, not even luck, lasts forever."

"Shut up, Sadie. This conversation is over. I'm going to kill you and Eli and give Brady an airtight alibi for the time of the murder. Ty's off on a phony emergency call, and sooner or later, Eli will come looking for you. He'll see your body, rush in and whack, whack, end of problem."

Keep her talking, Sadie's instincts whispered. She took a cautious step back. "What about your car?"

"It's well hidden. Unfortunately, Brady's truck isn't, so—time we moved this party along."

Panic spurted through Sadie's veins. "It won't work, Orley. You got lucky with Laura. This is far more complicated." At Orley's fierce look, she gestured behind her. "You can't carry Brady out of here."

"I'll hide him and his truck. Convince him to let me handle everything once it's over."

"And let him go right on thinking he's a monster."

"It'll keep him in line and indebted to me. One lovely side effect of ketamine is that when a person wakes up after ingesting it, he or she has no recollection of what transpired. Brady invented the monster, Sadie, not me.

Remember that. And stop backing away. One step more or less won't make you a smaller target."

Sadie edged sideways instead. The ground was growing increasingly slippery as it began its descent to the murky water of the bog.

"They'll trace the gun, Orley."

"Well, duh." One of her cousin's feet slipped, but she seemed not to notice and wagged the barrel instead. "This is a .45, if you don't know weapons. It belongs to Ben Leamer. I lifted it the day we met Hezekiah's effigy in the corn maze. Let me tell you, that message you got about not waking the monster came as quite a shock to me."

Sadie fought to hold her balance in the mud. "I'm sure I'll sound obvious, but if you really loved Brady, you wouldn't be doing this."

"If I did nothing, I'd be Molly." She raised the gun. "Time to die, cou—"

As Sadie had hoped, the slippery ground took Orley's feet out from under her. She landed on her hip and lost her grip on the gun.

The instant she fell, Sadie bolted. Away from the bog and into the heart of the fog-shrouded woods.

She didn't know if Orley was behind her or not. She only knew this was very much her nightmare. A deadly pursuit through the hollow by a person whose sanity had deserted her.

She should have called Eli, asked him to come to Ben's farm with her. Or let Jerk follow her as he'd been instructed to do. Instead, she'd driven straight into a trap. Yes, she was fit, and she could run. But Orley was hell-bent on killing her, and of the two of them, her cousin knew the hollow best.

Because of that, Sadie had no choice. As much as she hated the thought, she circled back toward the bog, where the ground was slick and balance an ongoing issue. If she could reach the cave she and Eli had used, she might make it back to the road. Road, Bronco, escape.

A sketchy map formed in her mind. So did a picture of Eli's face. But he wasn't here. This was between her and Orley…. And where was the stupid cave entrance?

She wove a haphazard path through the hollow. Were those Orley's footsteps behind her? Was she shouting at her through the fog? Sadie thought she glimpsed a light, but she couldn't be sure and didn't dare slow down to look.

The ground beneath her oozed and almost sent her sliding into the weeds. Determined not to die, she hung on and kept going.

Unlike the shouts, there was no mistaking the thwack of three bullets as they struck a tree directly ahead of her.

Orley would want her to stay visible. Fine. As long as she avoided any direct moonbeams, she'd still present a difficult target.

She hoped.

Sadie's heart hammered louder in her chest. Two more bullets zinged past. Did they come from the same direction as before? Her instincts said no. She had a split second to glimpse the movement, but no time to react as Orley flew out of the darkness and tackled her to the ground.

"Black belt," her cousin grunted, and attempted to work Sadie onto her stomach.

"D.C.," Sadie panted back, and swung the flashlight she still held hard into Orley's ear.

Orley howled and grabbed a handful of Sadie's hair. Ignoring the pain in her skull, Sadie took aim at her cousin's face, then used her fingernails to rake her cheek. When Orley jerked upright, she punched her in the throat and kicked free.

Unfortunately, by the time she scrambled to her feet, Orley was on her knees with the .45 aimed at her head.

"You, Cousin Sadie, are so dead."

A single shot rang out. Freezing, Sadie squeezed her eyes shut and waited for the rush of blackness. To her astonishment, it didn't come. Although her pounding heart drowned out almost every other sound, she thought she heard someone calling her name.

Inching her eyes open, she spotted Orley on the ground. Her left arm was outstretched, and she lay facedown in the mud.

Then suddenly, Eli was spinning her into his arms. Before Sadie could utter a sound, he crushed his mouth to hers and for a blissful moment made all her fears disappear.

If the kiss had never ended, she might have been able to erase everything that had come before. Unfortunately, as she'd told Orley, nothing lasted forever. When Eli raised his head to search her face, the horror flooded back in.

She breathed out slowly. "I don't want her to be dead."

"I know. I'm sorry, sweetheart, I have to..." Framing her face with his fingers, Eli kissed her again, long and deep. "You don't have to look."

"Yes, I do."

He wasn't rough, but Sadie suspected he wanted to be. He knew, and so did she, that Orley would have shot her in a heartbeat if Eli's bullet hadn't struck first.

The groan that emerged from her cousin's throat told Sadie she was alive. The blood on her jacket suggested she might not remain that way for long. With her emotions reeling, Sadie walked around to kneel beside her.

"I aimed for her left shoulder," Eli said. "If she's tough, she'll make it."

Sadie thought of Orley's confession and worked up a

faint smile. "Trust me, Lieutenant, she's tough. She's also determined." As her eyes came to rest on her cousin's face, she sighed. "And very, very sick."

Chapter Twenty-Two

Being a journalist, Sadie knew she'd put all the bits and pieces in order at some point—but she doubted it would happen any time soon.

Ty showed up within ten minutes. Using his two-way, he relayed a message through Ben Leamer's hired hand to the Raven's Cove paramedics. It took a great deal of time and effort, but eventually, Brady and Orley were admitted to the Raven's Cove Hospital and placed under county guard.

By midnight, everyone at Two Toes Joe's Bar had heard some version of the story. By morning, Sadie figured, very little of the factual account would remain. How could it in an area so steeped in lore and legend?

As the tale began to build, Rooney plunked himself between her and Eli and looked grimly from one to the other. "If I'm kin to a murderer, I need to hear the details."

Sadie shook her heard. "You're a Blume, Rooney. Orley and I are Bellams. You're not kin to a murderer. I am."

"Think intent," Eli told her. "He's talking about being related to Brady. It's a fine line between actual and attempted murder."

She sent him a grudging smile. "You're just trying to make me feel better."

"Is it working?"

"Not really." She made herself go back. "In the bog, Orley

talked about the night Laura died. Apparently, while Laura was braiding my hair—babysitting me—right outside the window, Brady was watching her do it. Talk about creepy."

"It's contemptible," Rooney spat. "My great-grandson was a Peeping Tom in high school."

Sadie patted his arm. "He was a lot of things, Rooney, in school and out, but not a murderer. Not even a wannabe twenty years ago. The night Laura died, he was watching her and drinking the coffee that Orley drugged after she 'accidentally' bumped into him at the café. In went just enough ketamine to put him under. Orley hid, waited through a few sips outside my parents' house, then moved in and guided him to an empty lot. A few more sips, and he was out for the night. Knowing that Laura would head back to the Cove as soon as my parents came home, she went to the road that led out of town and waited again."

Rooney gripped his cane a little tighter. "So it was Orley who got Laura to stop, then made her go into the hollow."

"It wouldn't have been an easy drive," Eli remarked. "But at the point of a gun—Orley's father's gun, we'll assume—the difficult became much more possible."

"That's the backstory, Rooney." As she leaned over to kiss his wrinkled cheek, Sadie whispered, "I'll leave the telling of the present-day version in your capable hands."

"Let's call that our cue to leave." Before his great-grandfather could object, Eli stood and drew Sadie to her feet. "Unless you want to stay and help him rearrange the facts to suit."

To grin and mean it felt wonderful—until she saw Ty swaying in his chair across the room while Molly nudged a boilermaker toward him.

"What the...?"

"Let it go, Sadie." Eli set an arm over her shoulders to keep her moving.

"But Ty doesn't drink. Molly knows he doesn't drink."

"Molly's not Orley, and Ty's a big boy."

"I know, but—"

"With a badge."

Shaking it off, Sadie gave his stomach a poke. "Speaking of, Lieutenant, how is it you managed to find me in the hollow?"

He dropped a hard kiss on her lips. "I knew she had you. I called the *Chronicle* and your assistant told me you'd taken your copy editor's Bronco to Ben Leamer's farm."

"Which explains how you located my vehicle, but not how you found me."

"If I say I used my instincts, are you going to go all Raven's Tale on me and suggest I might have been channeling Hezekiah?"

"I would," she teased, "except that Hezekiah wouldn't be tuned in to me so much as my Bellam blood, which would mean I'd have to have been channeling Nola—and I really don't want to go there."

His lips quirked. "In that case, I used criminal logic. Orley murdered Laura in Raven's Bog and got away with it. It stood to reason she'd use the same location again."

"I was looking for the cave when you showed up and shot her."

"I accessed the hollow through the cave."

"Spooky, isn't it?" She caught the hand that dangled over her shoulder and linked their fingers. "As tragic as all of this is, what say we ditch this town, go back to Bellam Manor and make love until Rooney's birthday?"

For an answer, he motioned her ahead of him through the crowd. Sadie took a last bemused look at Molly and Ty, then gave up and stepped outside.

On the dock, she turned to regard Eli. "Brady said he wasn't the monster right before Orley knocked him out.

I know you sort of talked to him at the hospital. Did he give you any details?"

"He only drank a small amount of the tea she brewed for him tonight. There were traces of the tranq she used on the lid of the teapot, and an album filled with computer-altered photographs on the floor. Brady suspected she'd been doping him, so he let her think he was going to settle in for the night with the tea. As soon as she left, he went across the hall and searched her apartment."

"And, lucky for me, found what he was looking for."

"He claimed he was horrified. But under Orley's eagle eye he'd already consumed enough of the tea that he was also disoriented and starting to slide under."

Letting her head fall back, Sadie breathed in the ocean air. "Instead of submitting, he fought the drug's effect, took the Hollow Road and tried to stop her from killing me." She shuddered. "Before the paramedics arrived, Orley told me she murdered a girl named Lisa Johnson right after Brady's senior year."

"Heard that. Brady took Lisa to our senior prom."

"Worse and worse. Orley also swiped a pair of Brady's shoes and muddied them up the night she shot at us with a crossbow. Her father's weapon again. Brady must have thought he was going crazy—or, well, crazier." Bringing her head up, she met Eli's eyes. "Is that why he tried to kill you in the woods near the manor?"

"In for a penny, in for a pound. I don't imagine he thought he had much to lose at that point."

"So how will Rooney spin it in terms of our conjoined legends? Obviously Brady was Ezekiel, and you were Hezekiah."

"And you were Nola. Not sure how he'll work Orley in. As an even darker version of Ezekiel maybe."

Sadie summoned a half smile. "Orley's not a Blume,

Eli. She's my cousin. I honestly can't believe I'm talking about her like this. My own cousin tried to kill me. Legendwise, she'd have to be Sarah."

"There's a Sarah Bellam?"

"In history, yes. In the family archives, not so much. Sarah was Nola's sister. Pretty sure sanity wasn't her strong suit. Oh, and as long as we're tidying this up, Orley also told me that in the process of searching for various chain saws to use on the fallen pine, Brady snuck into the maze and pinned the envelope I found to Hezekiah's cloak. As soon as he saw me go in, he loaded up the chain saw he'd come to borrow and left. He made the call that scared the living hell out of me while he was driving away. That was the same day Orley stole Ben's gun. As for the spike strip, she made that herself, because, well, hey, who hasn't watched cop shows on TV? We both know the rest of the story. And what we don't know really doesn't matter since we're standing here together—with no idea where our lives are headed, but still—standing."

Catching her arm, Eli swung her around and trapped her between the outer wall of Joe's Bar and his body. "We can work on the where, when and how, Sadie. But the with who's not open for debate."

"No?" Hooking her arms around his neck, she stared into his eyes. "Then I guess it's a good thing I love you, Lieutenant Blume. Be warned, however, I'm still a Bellam female. Very high-risk as relationships go."

"Still a cop on this side, Sadie. That's an even higher risk."

She ran a teasing finger over his cheek. "Leaving us with the rather intriguing where, when and how."

Lowering his head, he covered her mouth briefly with his. "Raven's Cove hasn't had a police chief of its own for quite some time. Could be an interesting change of career."

"Okay…" Sadie drew the word out while she played with the ends of his hair. "In that case, and while we're on the subject of interesting, why don't we see what kind of magic we can conjure between us? Think ravens, Eli, and you and me soaring through an autumn night sky. Picture the fog being sucked down into the hollow where it belongs. Then imagine us above it all at Bellam Manor, making love under a gorgeous harvest moon."

He grinned. "I don't have to imagine, Sadie. We're halfway there, and I haven't even formed a thought yet."

"Which in noncryptic language means?"

Only his eyes moved, first to the soft orange moon overhead, then toward the Hollow Road, currently shrouded in layers of filmy white.

"What do you know?" Sadie laughed. "You said I had a knack for predicting the weather. Guess you were right." Smiling, she reached for his mouth. "Might want to brace yourself, Lieutenant." She gave his bottom lip a bite. "The mood I'm in, you never know what else I might have a knack for."

* * * * *

A sneaky peek at next month…

INTRIGUE...

BREATHTAKING ROMANTIC SUSPENSE

My wish list for next month's titles…

In stores from 21st February 2014:

❑ The Girl Next Door – Cynthia Eden

❧ Rocky Mountain Rescue – Cindi Myers

❑ Snowed In – Cassie Miles

❧ The Secret of Cherokee Cove – Paula Graves

❑ Bridal Jeopardy – Rebecca York

❧ The Prosecutor – Adrienne Giordano

Romantic Suspense

❑ Deadly Hunter – Rachel Lee

Available at WHSmith, Tesco, Asda, Eason, Amazon and Apple

Just can't wait?

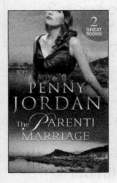

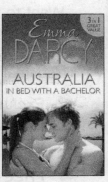

Join the Mills & Boon Book Club

Want to read more **Intrigue** books?
We're offering you **2 more** absolutely **FREE!**

We'll also treat you to these fabulous extras:

- **Exclusive offers and much more!**

- **FREE home delivery**

- **FREE books and gifts with our special rewards scheme**

Get your free books now!

visit www.millsandboon.co.uk/bookclub
or call Customer Relations on 020 8288 2888

Discover more romance at

www.millsandboon.co.uk

- ❤ WIN great prizes in our exclusive competitions
- ❤ BUY new titles before they hit the shops
- ❤ BROWSE new books and REVIEW your favourites
- ❤ SAVE on new books with the Mills & Boon® Bookclub™
- ❤ DISCOVER new authors

PLUS, to chat about your favourite reads, get the latest news and find special offers:

- 📘 Find us on facebook.com/millsandboon
- 🐦 Follow us on twitter.com/millsandboonuk
- ❤ Sign up to our newsletter at millsandboon.co.uk

The World of Mills & Boon®

There's a Mills & Boon® series that's perfect for you. We publish ten series and, with new titles every month, you never have to wait long for your favourite to come along.

By Request
Relive the romance with the best of the best
12 stories every month

Cherish™
Experience the ultimate rush of falling in love
12 new stories every month

Desire™
Passionate and dramatic love stories
6 new stories every month

nocturne™
An exhilarating underworld of dark desires
Up to 3 new stories every month